Enid Blyton's

THE TWINS
AT ST CLARE'S

The Enid Blyton Newsletter

Would you like to receive The Enid Blyton Newsletter?
It has lots of news about Enid Blyton books, videos, plays, etc.
There are also puzzles and a page for your letters. It is published
three times a year and is free for children who live in the
United Kingdom and Ireland.

If you would like to receive it for a year, please write to:
The Enid Blyton Newsletter, PO Box 357, London WC2E 9HQ
sending your name and address. (UK and Ireland only.)

THE ENID BLYTON TRUST
FOR CHILDREN

We hope you will enjoy this book. Please think for a
moment about those children who are too ill to do
the exciting things you and your friends do.

Help them by sending a donation, large or small, to
THE ENID BLYTON TRUST FOR CHILDREN.
The Trust will use all your gifts to help children who
are sick or handicapped and need to be made happy
and comfortable.

Please send your postal order or cheque to:
The Enid Blyton Trust for Children,
Bedford House,
3 Bedford Street,
London WC2E 9HD

Thank you very much for your help.

Enid Blyton's
THE TWINS
AT ST CLARE'S

containing
The Twins at St Clare's
The O'Sullivan Twins
Summer Term at St Clare's

complete and unabridged

Illustrated by Jenny Chapple

DEAN
in association with
Methuen Children's Books

The Twins at St Clare's first published 1941
The O'Sullivan Twins first published 1942
Summer Term at St Clare's first published 1943

This edition published 1991 by Dean
an imprint of Reed Consumer Books Limited
Michelin House, 81 Fulham Road, London SW3 6RB
and Auckland, Melbourne, Singapore and Toronto
Reprinted 1992, 1993

ISBN 0 603 55063 0

Enid Blyton is a registered trademark of Darrell Waters Limited

A CIP catalogue record for this book is available from
the British Library

Printed in Great Britain by The Bath Press

THE TWINS
AT ST CLARE'S

CONTENTS

I THE TWINS MAKE UP THEIR MINDS

One sunny summer afternoon four girls sat on the grass by a tennis-court, drinking lemonade. Their rackets lay beside them, and the six white balls were scattered over the court.

Two of the girls were twins. Isabel and Patricia O'Sullivan were so alike that only a few people could tell which was Pat and which was Isabel. Both girls had dark brown wavy hair, deep blue eyes and a merry smile, and the Irish lilt in their voices was very pleasant to hear.

The twins were staying for two weeks with friends of theirs, Mary and Frances Waters. The four girls were talking, and Pat was frowning as she spoke. She took up her racket and banged it hard on the grass.

"It's just too bad that Mummy won't let us go to the same school as you, now that we have all left Redroofs School together. We've been friends so long – and now we've got to go to a different school, and we shan't see each other for ages."

"It's a pity that Redroofs only takes girls up to fourteen," said Isabel. "We could have stayed on together and it would have been fun. I loved being head-girl with Pat the last year – and it was fun being tennis-captain, and Pat being hockey-captain. Now we've got to go to another school that doesn't sound a bit nice – and begin at the bottom! We'll be the young ones of the school instead of head-girls."

"I do wish you were coming to Ringmere School with us!" said Frances. "It's such a nice *exclusive* school, our mother says. *You* know – only girls of rich parents, very well-bred, go there, and you make such nice friends.

7

We have a bedroom to ourselves and our own study, and we have to wear evening dress at night, and they say the food is wonderful!"

"And we are going to St. Clare's, where anybody can go, and the dormitories take six or eight girls and aren't nearly as nicely furnished as the maids' bedrooms are at home!" said Pat in a disgusted voice.

"I can't imagine why Mummy made up her mind to send us there instead of to Ringmere," said Isabel. "I wonder if she has *quite* decided. We're going home to-morrow and we'll both do our very very best to make her say we can go to Ringmere, Mary and Frances! We'll ring you up in the evening and tell you."

"We'll jump for joy if you have good news," said Mary. "After all, when you've been head-girls at a marvellous school like Redroofs, and had your own lovely bedroom and the best study with the best view, and a hundred girls looking up to you, it's awful to have to start again in a school you don't want to go to a bit!"

"Well, do your best to make your parents change their minds," said Frances. "Come on – let's have another set before tea!"

They all jumped up and tossed for partners. Isabel was a splendid player, and had won the tennis championship at Redroofs. She was really rather proud of her game. Pat was nearly as good, but much preferred hockey.

"They don't play hockey at St. Clare's, they play lacrosse," said Pat, dismally. "Silly game, lacrosse – playing with nets on sticks, and catching a ball all the time instead of hitting it! That's another thing I'll tell Mummy – that I don't want to play lacrosse after being hockey-captain."

The twins thought hard of all the reasons they would put before their parents when they got home the next day. They talked about it as they went home in the train.

"I'll say this, and you say that," said Pat. "After all, *we* ought to know the kind of school that would be best for us – and St. Clare's does sound too fierce for words!"

So the next evening the girls began to air their thoughts about schools. Pat began, and, as was her way, she attacked at once.

"Mummy and Daddy!" she said. "Isabel and I have been thinking a lot about what school we're to go to next, and, please, we don't want to go to St. Clare's. Every one says it's an awful school."

Their mother laughed, and their father put down his paper in surprise.

"Don't be silly, Pat," said Mrs. O'Sullivan. "It's a splendid school."

"Have you quite decided about it?" asked Isabel.

"Not absolutely," said her mother. "But Daddy and I both think it will be the best school for you now. We do think that Redroofs spoilt you a bit, you know – it's a very expensive and luxurious school, and nowadays we have to learn to live much more simply. St. Clare's is really a very sensible sort of school, and I know the Head and like her."

Pat groaned. "A sensible school! How I do hate sensible things – they're always horrid and ugly and stupid and uncomfortable! Oh, Mummy – do let us go to Ringmere School with Mary and Frances."

"Certainly not!" said Mrs. O'Sullivan at once. "It's a very snobbish school, and I'm not going to have you two girls coming home and turning up your noses at everything and everybody."

"We wouldn't," said Isabel, frowning at Pat to make her stop arguing for a while. Pat lost her temper very easily, and that didn't do when their father was there. "Mummy dear – be a pet – just let's try at Ringmere for a term or two, and then, if you think we're turning into snobs, you can take us away. But you might let us try.

They play hockey there, and we do so like that. We'd hate to have to learn a new game, just when we've got so good at hockey."

Mr. O'Sullivan rapped with his pipe on the table. "My dear Isabel, it will be good for you to start at the beginning again, and learn something new! I've thought the last year that both you girls have become very conceited, and thought far too much of yourselves. If you have to learn new things, and find you're not so wonderful as you thought you were, it will be very good for you both!"

The twins went red. They were angry and hurt and almost ready to cry. Mrs. O'Sullivan felt sorry for them.

"Daddy doesn't mean to be unkind," she said. "But he is quite right, my dears. You've had a wonderful time at Redroofs, had things all your own way, been head-girls and captains, and really lived in luxury. Now you must show us what kind of stuff you are made of when you have to start as youngsters of fourteen and a half in a school where the top classes are eighteen years old!"

Pat looked sulky. Isabel's chin shook as she answered.

"We shan't be happy, and we shan't try to be!" she said.

"Very well. Be *un*happy!" said their father, sternly. "If that's the sort of silly attitude you've learnt at Redroofs, I'm sorry we let you stay there so long. I wanted to take you away two years ago, but you begged so hard to stay, that I didn't. Now say no more about it. I shall write to St. Clare's myself tonight and enter you for next term. If you want to make me proud of you, you will cheer up and make up your minds to be good and hard-working and happy at your next school."

Their father lighted his pipe and began to read his paper again. Their mother took up her sewing. There was no more to be said. The twins left the room together and went into the garden. They found their own secret place behind the thick old yew-hedge and flung themselves down on the ground. The evening sun threw its slanting golden rays around them, and they blinked in its brightness. Tears shone in Isabel's eyes.

"I never thought Mummy and Daddy would be so hard," she said. "Never!"

"After all, *we* ought to have some say in the matter," said Pat, furiously. She took a stick and dug it hard into the ground. "I wish we could run away!"

"Don't be silly," said Isabel. "You know we can't. Anyway, it's cowardly to run away. We'll have to go to St. Clare's. But how I shall hate it."

"We'll both hate it," said Pat. "And what's more, I'm jolly well going to turn up my nose at everything there! *I'm* not going to let them think we're babies of fourteen, just come from some silly prep school. I'll soon let them know that we were head-girls, and tennis- and hockey-captains. How horrid of Daddy to say we are conceited! We're not a bit. We can't help knowing that we're good at nearly everything, besides being pretty and quite amusing."

"It *does* sound a bit conceited when you talk like that," said Isabel. "We'd better not say too much when we get to St. Clare's."

"I'm going to say all I like, and you must back me up," said Pat. "People are going to know who we are, and what we can do! All the mistresses are going to sit up and take notice of us too. The O'Sullivan twins are going to be SOMEBODIES! And don't you forget it, Isabel."

Isabel nodded her dark head with its black waves of hair. "I won't forget it," she said. "I'll back you up. My word, St. Clare's will get a few surprises next term!"

2   THE TWINS ARRIVE AT
         ST CLARE'S

The time soon came when the twins had to leave for the winter term at St. Clare's. Their mother had had a list of things they were to take with them, and the twins examined it carefully.

"It's not nearly such a long list as we had for Redroofs," said Pat. "And golly – how few dresses we are allowed! Mary and Frances said that they were allowed to take as many frocks as they liked to Ringmere – and they had both got long evening dresses like their mother! Won't they show off to us when they see us again!"

"And look – lacrosse-sticks instead of hockey-sticks!" said Isabel in disgust. "They might at least play hockey as *well* as lacrosse! I didn't even bother to *look* at the lacrosse sticks Mummy bought for us, did you? And look – we are even told what to bring in our tuck boxes! We could take what we liked to Redroofs."

"Just wait till we get to St. Clare's. We'll show that we can do as we like," said Pat. "What time is the train tomorrow?"

"Ten o'clock from Paddington," said Isabel. "Well – we shall get our first glimpse of the St. Clare girls there. I bet they'll be a queer-looking crowd!"

Mrs. O'Sullivan took the twins to London. They taxied to Paddington Station, and looked for the St. Clare train. There it was, drawn up at the platform, labelled St. Clare. On the platform were scores of girls, talking excitedly to one another, saying good-bye to their parents, hailing mistresses, and buying bars of chocolate from the tea-wagons.

A simply-dressed mistress came up to the twins. She knew that they were St. Clare girls because they had on the grey coats that were the uniform of the school. She smiled at Mrs. O'Sullivan, and looked at the list in her hand.

"These are new girls," she said, "and I am sure they must be Patricia and Isabel O'Sullivan, because they are so exactly alike. I'm your form-mistress, Miss Roberts, and I'm very pleased to see you."

This was a nice welcome and the twins liked the look of Miss Roberts. She was young and good-looking, tall and smiling – but she had a firm mouth and both Pat and Isabel felt sure that she wouldn't stand much nonsense from her form!

"Your carriage is over here, with the rest of your form," said Miss Roberts. "Say good-bye now, and get in. The train will be going in two minutes."

She went off to talk to some one else and the twins hugged their mother. "Good-bye," said Mrs. O'Sullivan. "Do your best this term, and I do hope you'll be happy at your new school. Write to me soon."

The twins got into a carriage where three or four other girls were already sitting and chattering. They said nothing, but looked with interest at the scores of girls passing by their compartment to their places farther up the train.

At their last school the twins had been the oldest and biggest there – but now they were among the youngest! At Redroofs all the girls had looked at Pat and Isabel with awe and admiration – the two wonderful head-girls – but now the twins were looking at others in the same way! Tall, dignified girls from the top form walked by, talking. Merry-voiced girls from other forms ran to get their places, calling out to one another. Younger ones scrambled into the carriages as the guard went along to warn one that the train was about to go.

The journey was quite fun. Every one had packets of sandwiches to eat at half-past twelve, and the train steward brought bottles of ginger-beer and lemonade, and cups of tea. At half-past two the train drew in at a little platform. A big notice said "Alight here for St. Clare's School".

There were big school-coaches waiting outside and the girls piled themselves in them, chattering and laughing. One of them turned to Pat and Isabel.

"There's the school, look! Up on that hill there!"

The twins looked. They saw a pleasant white building, built of large white stones, with two towers, one at each end. It looked down into the valley, over big playing-fields and gardens.

"Not nearly so nice as Redroofs," said Pat to Isabel. "Do you remember how sweet our old school used to look in the evening sun?" Its red roof was glowing, and it looked warm and welcoming – not cold and white like St. Clare's."

For a few minutes both girls were homesick for their old school and their old friends. They knew nobody at St. Clare's at all. They couldn't call out "Hallo, there!" to every one as they had done each term before. They didn't like the look of any of the girls, who seemed much more noisy and boisterous than the ones at Redroofs. It was all horrid.

"Anyway, we are lucky to have got each other," said Isabel to Pat. "I would have hated to come here all alone. Nobody seems to talk to us at all."

It was the twins' own fault, if they had but known it. They both looked "stuck-up" as one girl whispered to another. Nobody felt much inclined to talk to them or make friends.

There was the same rush of unpacking and settling in as there is at all boarding-schools. The big dormitories were full of girls putting away their things, hanging up their dresses and putting photographs out on their little dressing-tables.

There were a good many dormitories at St. Clare's. Pat and Isabel were in number 7, where there were eight white beds, all exactly alike. Each was in its own cubicle surrounded by curtains that could be drawn open or closed, just as the girls pleased. Pat's bed was next to Isabel's, much to their joy.

When the girls had unpacked a tall girl came into the dormitory calling out, "Any new girls here?"

Pat and Isabel nodded their heads. "We are new," said Pat.

"Hallo, twins!" said the tall girl, smiling, as she looked at the two sisters so exactly alike, "Are you Patricia and Isabel O'Sullivan? Matron wants to see you."

Pat and Isabel went with the girl to where the school matron sat in her comfortable room, surrounded by cupboards, chests and shelves. She was a fat, jolly-looking person, but her eyes were very sharp indeed.

"You can't deceive Matron over anything," whispered their guide. "Keep in her good books if you can."

Matron checked over sheets, towels and clothes with them. "You will be responsible for mending all your own belongings," she said.

"Good gracious!" said Pat. "There were sewing maids at our other school to do that."

"Shocking!" said Matron, briskly. "Well, there are no sewing-maids here. So be careful of your things, and remember that they cost your parents money."

"Our parents don't need to worry about torn clothes," began Pat. "Why, once at Redroofs I got caught in some barbed wire, and everything I had on was torn to bits. They were so torn that the sewing-maid said she couldn't mend a thing, and . . ."

"Well, I would have made you mend every hole, every rent, every tear," said Matron, her eyes beginning to sparkle. "There's one thing I can't bear, and that's carelessness and waste. Now mind you ... What is it, Millicent?"

Another girl had come into the room with a pile of towels, and the twins were very glad that Matron's attention was no longer given to them. They slipped out of the room quietly.

"I don't like Matron," said Pat. "And I've a jolly good mind to tear something so badly that it can't be mended, and that would give her something to think about!"

"Let's go and see what the school is like," said Isabel, slipping her arm into Pat's. "It seems much barer and colder somehow than dear old Redroofs."

The twins began to explore. The classrooms seemed much the same as any classrooms, and the view from the windows was magnificent. The twins peeped into the studies. At their old school they had shared a fine study between them, but here there were no studies except for the top form girls and the fifth form. The younger girls shared a big common room, where there was a wireless, a gramophone and a big library of books. Shelves ran round the common room and each girl shared part of a shelf, putting her belongings there, and keeping them tidy.

There were small music rooms for practising, a fine art room, an enormous gym, which was also used for assembly and concerts, and a good laboratory. The mistresses had two common rooms and their own bedrooms, and the Head lived in a small wing by herself, having her own bedroom in one of the towers, and a beautiful drawing-room below.

"It's not so bad," said Pat, after they had explored everywhere. "And the playing-fields are fine. There are many more tennis courts here than Redroofs – but of course it's a much bigger school."

"I don't like big schools," said Isabel. "I like smaller

schools, where you are somebody, not just a little no-body tucked away among heaps of others!"

They went into the common room. The wireless was on and a dance-band was playing cheerful music, which was almost drowned by the chatter of the girls. Some of them looked up as Pat and Isabel came in.

"Hallo, twins!" said a cheeky-looking girl with curly golden hair. "Which is which?"

"I'm Patricia O'Sullivan and my twin sister is Isabel," said Pat.

"Well, welcome to St. Clare's," said the girl. "I'm Hilary Wentworth, and you're in the same dormitory as I am. Have you been to boarding-school before?"

"Of course," said Pat. "We went to Redroofs."

"The school for snobs!" said a dark-haired girl, look-ing up. "My cousin went there – and didn't she fancy herself when she came home! Expected to be waited on hand and foot, and couldn't even bear to sew a button on a shoe!"

"Shut up," said Hilary, seeing that Pat went red. "You always talk too much, Janet. Well, Patricia and Isabel, this isn't the same kind of school as Redroofs – we work hard and play hard here, and we're jolly well taught to be independent and responsible!"

"We didn't want to come here," said Pat. "We wanted to go to Ringmere School, where our friends were going. Nobody thought much of St. Clare's at Redroofs."

"Dear, dear, dear, is that so?" said Janet, raising her eyebrows till they were almost lost in the dark hair on her forehead. "Well, the point is, my dear twins – not what you think of St. Clare's – but what St. Clare's thinks of *you*! Quite a different thing. Personally, I think it's a pity that you didn't go somewhere else. I've a feeling you won't fit in here."

"Janet, do be quiet," said Hilary. "It's not fair to say things like that to new girls. Let them settle in. Come on, Patricia – come on, Isabel – I'll show you the way to the Head's room. You'll have to go and say how-do-you-do to her before supper."

Pat and Isabel were almost boiling over with rage at what dark-haired Janet had said. Hilary pushed the twins out of the room. "Don't take too much notice of Janet," she said. "She always says exactly what she thinks, which is very nice when she thinks complimentary things about people, but not so good when she doesn't. You'll get used to her."

"I hope we shan't," said Pat stiffly. "I like good manners, something that was taught at our school anyway, even if it's not known here!"

"Oh, don't be stuffy," said Hilary. "Look, that's the Head's room. Knock on the door first – and try some of your good manners on Miss Theobald!"

The twins knocked on the door. A pleasant, rather deep voice called "Come in!" Pat opened the door and the twins went in.

The Head Mistress was sitting at her desk, writing. She looked up and smiled at the girls.

"I needn't ask who you are," she said. "You are so alike that you must be the O'Sullivan twins!"

"Yes," said the girls, looking at their new Head Mistress. She was grey-haired, with a dignified, serious face that broke into a lovely smile at times. She shook hands with each twin.

"I am very glad to welcome you to St. Clare's," she said. "I hope that one day we shall be proud of you. Do your best for us and St. Clare's will be able to do its best for you!"

"We'll try," said Isabel, and then was quite surprised at herself to find that she had said that. She didn't mean to try at all! She looked at Pat. Pat said nothing but stared straight in front of her.

"I know your mother quite well," said Miss Theobald.

"I was glad when she decided to send you here. You must tell her that when you write to her, and give her my kind regards."

"Yes, Miss Theobald," said Pat. The Head Mistress nodded at them with a smile, and turned to her desk again.

"What funny children!" she thought to herself. "Anyone might think they hated to be here! Perhaps they are just shy or homesick."

But they were neither shy nor homesick. They were just two obstinate girls determined to make the worst of things because they hadn't been sent to the school of their choice!

3   A BAD BEGINNING

The twins soon found that St. Clare's was quite different from their old school. Even the beds were not nearly so comfortable! And instead of being allowed to have their own pretty bedspreads and eiderdowns to match, every girl had to have the same.

"I hate being the same as everyone else!" said Pat. "Goodness – if only we were allowed to have what we liked, wouldn't we make everyone stare!"

"What I hate most is being one of the young ones," said Isabel, dismally. "I hate being spoken to as if I were about six, when the top form or fifth-form girls say anything to me. It's 'Here, you – get out of my way! Hi, you! Fetch me a book from the library!' It's just too bad."

The standard of work was higher at St. Clare's than at most schools, and although the twins had good brains, they found that they were rather behind their form in many ways, and this, too, annoyed them very much. They had so hoped that they would impress the others in so many ways – and it seemed as if they were even less than nobodies!

They soon got to know the girls in their form. Hilary Wentworth was one and the sharp-tongued Janet Robins. Then there was a quiet, straight-haired girl called Vera Johns and a rather haughty-looking girl called Sheila Naylor, whose manners were very arrogant. The twins didn't like her at all.

"I don't know what she's got to be so haughty about!" said Pat to Isabel. "It's true she's got a lovely home because I've seen a photo of it on her dressing-table – but my goodness, she sometimes talks like our parlourmaid at home. Then she seems to remember she mustn't talk like that and goes all haughty and silly."

Then there was Kathleen Gregory, a frightened looking girl of fifteen, who was the only one who really tried to make friends with the twins the first week. Most of the other girls left them alone, except for being polite, and telling them the ways of the school. They all thought that Pat and Isabel were very "stuck-up".

"Kathleen is funny," said Isabel. "She seems so eager to make friends with us, and lend us books and shares her sweets. She's been at St. Clare's for a year, and she doesn't seem to have any friends at all. She keeps asking me to walk with her when we go out, and I keep saying I can't because I've got you."

"I feel rather sorry for her somehow," said Pat. "She reminds me of a lost dog trying to find a new master!"

Isabel laughed. "Yes, that's just it! I think of all the girls that I like Hilary the best in our form. She's so natural and jolly – a real sport."

The twins were very much in awe of the older girls, who seemed very grown-up to them. The top form especially seemed almost as old and even more dignified than the mistresses! The head-girl, Winifred James, spoke a few words to the twins the first week. She was a tall, clever-looking girl with pale blue eyes and pretty soft hair. St. Clare's was proud of her, for she had passed many difficult exams with flying colours.

"You are the new girls, aren't you?" she said. "Settle in and do your best. Come to me if you are in any difficulty. I'm the head-girl and I should like to help you if ever I can."

"Oh, thank you," said the twins, feeling quite overcome at being addressed by the head-girl. Winifred went off with her friends, and the twins stared after her.

"She's rather nice," said Isabel. "In fact, I think most of the top form girls are nice, though they're awfully serious and proper."

They liked their form-mistress, Miss Roberts, too, though she would stand no nonsense at all. Sometimes Pat would try to argue about something, and say, "Well, that's what I was taught at my old school!"

Then Miss Roberts would say, "Really? Well, do it that way if you like – but you won't get very far up your form! Do remember that what suits one school won't work in another. Still, if you like to be obstinate, that's your own look-out!"

Then Pat would stick out her lower lip, and Isabel would go red, and the rest of the form would smile to itself. Those "stuck-up" girls were having to learn a lesson!

The art-mistress, Miss Walker, was a merry soul, young and jolly, and very good at her work. She was pleased to find that both twins could draw and paint well. Pat and Isabel loved Miss Walker's classes. They were very go-as-you-please, much more like their old school. The girls were allowed to chatter and laugh as they worked, and it was often a very noisy class indeed.

Mam'zelle was not so easy-going. She was very strict, elderly, conscientious and fierce. She wore pince-nez glasses on her nose, and these were always slipping off when she was cross, which was fairly often. She had enormous feet, and a rather harsh voice that the twins hated at first. But Mam'zelle had also a great sense of fun, and if anything tickled her she would go off into enormous roars of laughter that set the whole class laughing too.

Pat and Isabel came up against Mam'zelle very much at first, for although they could speak and understand French quite well, they had never bothered very much about French grammar and rules. And Mam'zelle bothered a great deal about those!

"You girls, Patricia and Isabel!" she cried. "It is not enough to speak my language! You write it abominably! See this essay – it is abominable, abominable!"

"Abominable" was Mam'zelle's favourite adjective. She used it for everything – the weather, a broken pencil, the girls, and her own eye-glasses when they slipped off her big nose! Pat and Isabel called her "Mam'zelle Abominable" between themselves, and were secretly more than a little afraid of the loud-voiced, good-hearted big French-woman.

History was taken throughout the school by Miss Kennedy, and her classes were a riot. Poor Miss Kennedy was a frump, and could not manage any class of girls for more than five minutes. She was nervous and serious, always tremendously polite, listened to every question that was put to her no matter how silly, and explained every difficulty at great length. She never seemed to see that half the time the girls were pulling her leg.

"Before Miss Kennedy came we had her friend Miss Lewis," said Hilary to the twins. "She was marvellous. Then she fell ill in the middle of last term, and asked the Head to have her friend, Miss Kennedy, until she was well enough to come back. Old Kenny has got umpteen degrees, and is supposed to be even cleverer than the Head – but my word, she's a goose!"

Bit by bit the twins sorted out the various girls and

mistresses, grew to know the classes and the customs of the school, and settled in. But even when two weeks had gone by they had not got used to being "nobodies instead of somebodies" as Pat complained.

One thing they found most annoying. It was the custom at St. Clare's for the younger girls to wait on the two top forms. The fifth- and sixth-form girls shared studies, two friends having a study between them.

They were allowed to furnish these studies themselves, very simply, and, in cold weather, to have their own fire there, and to have tea by themselves instead of in the hall with the others.

One day a girl came into the common room where the twins were reading and called to Janet, "Hi, Janet – Kay Longden wants you. You're to light her fire and make some toast for her."

Janet got up without a word and went out. Pat and Isabel stared after her in surprise.

"Golly! What cheek of Kay Longden to send a message to Janet like that! I'm jolly sure I wouldn't go and light anybody's fire!" said Pat.

"And neither would I!" said Isabel. "Let one of the maids light it – or Kay herself."

Hilary Wentworth looked up from her embroidery. "It will be your turn next!" she said. "Look out next week for sudden messages, twins. If the fifth or sixth want anything doing, they expect us to do it. It's the custom of the school – and anyway, it doesn't hurt us. We can have our turn at sending messages and ordering the lower forms about when we're top-formers ourselves!"

"I never heard of such a thing!" cried Pat, furiously. "I jolly well won't go and do a thing for any one. Our parents didn't send us here to wait on lazy top-formers. Let them light their own fires and make their own toast! Isabel and I won't do a thing! And they can't make us either!"

"Hoity-toity!" said Hilary. "I never knew such a hot temper. Get further away from me, Pat, you're scorching me!"

Pat slammed down her book and flounced out of the room. Isabel followed her. All the other girls laughed.

"Idiots!" said Hilary. "Who do they think they are, anyway? Why don't they get some sense? They wouldn't be at all bad if only they would shake down. I vote we knock some of their corners off, else we shall hate them like anything!"

"O.K.," said Vera. "I'm willing. I say, what a shock for them when they find they've got to wait on the top-formers too. I hope they get Belinda Towers. I had to wait on her last term, and my word, didn't she make me skip around! She got it into her head that I was lazy, and I'm sure I lost a whole stone rushing round in circles after her one week!"

The girls laughed. Sheila Naylor spoke haughtily. "The worst of people who think they are somebodies is that so often they are just nobodies. I'm sure I shouldn't even trouble to *know* Patricia and Isabel at home."

"Oh, come off the high horse, Sheila," said Hilary. "The twins aren't as bad as all that. Anyway, there are a few shocks in store for them!"

So there were – and they came the very next week!

4   A LITTLE TROUBLE FOR
THE TWINS

One day, about half-past five, when the twins were writing home, one of the fourth-formers popped her head in at the door.

"Hi, there!" she said. "Where are the O'Sullivan twins? Belinda Towers wants one of them."

Pat and Isabel looked up. Pat went red. "What does

she want us for?" she asked.

"How should I know?" said the messenger. "She's been out over the fields this afternoon, so maybe she wants her boots cleaned. Anyway, jump to it, or you'll get into a row!"

The messenger disappeared. The twins sat still. Hilary looked at them.

"Go on, idiots," she said. "One of you must go and find out what Belinda wants. Don't keep her waiting, for goodness' sake. She's got about as hot a temper as you have, Pat."

"I'll go," said Isabel, and got up. But Pat pulled her down.

"No, don't," she said. "I'm not going to clean anybody's boots! And you're not, either."

"Look here, Pat, don't be goofy," said Janet. "Belinda may want to tell you something. Golly, she might want to ask you if you'll play in a match. She's captain, you know."

"Oh," said Pat. "Well, I shouldn't think it's that because neither Isabel nor I have ever played lacrosse before, and we were pretty bad at it yesterday."

"Well, do GO!" said Hilary. "You've got to go in the end, so why not go now?"

Another girl popped her head in at the door. "I say! Belinda's foaming at the mouth! Where *are* those O'Sullivan twins? They'll get it hot if one of them doesn't go along!"

"Come on," said Pat to Isabel. "We'll go and see what she wants. But I'm not doing any boot-cleaning or fire-lighting, that's certain. And neither are you!"

The two got up and went out of the room. Everybody giggled. "Wish I could go and see what happens!" said Janet. "I love to see Belinda in a rage!"

Belinda Towers was in her study with Pamela Harrison, the girl who shared it with her. Pat opened the door.

"Knock, can't you!" cried Belinda. "Barging in like that! And I should jolly well like to know why you've been all this time coming. I sent for you ages ago."

Pat was rather taken aback, and Isabel did not dare to say anything.

"Well, haven't you a tongue between you?" said Belinda. "My goodness, Pam, did you ever see such a pair of boobs? Well, as you've *both* come, you can both do a spot of work for me. I want my boots cleaned and Pam's too. And make up my fire for me and put the kettle on to boil. You'll find water just down the passage. Come on, Pam – we'll go and collect our prep and by that time the kettle will be boiling and we'll make tea."

The two big girls walked to the door. Pat, very red and angry, stopped them.

"I didn't come to St. Clare's to wait on the older girls," she said. "Neither did my twin. We shan't clean your boots nor put on the kettle, nor make up the fire."

Belinda stopped as if she had been shot. She stared at Pat as if she was some particularly nasty insect. Then she turned to Pam.

"Did you hear that?" she said. "Talk about cheek! All right, my girl – no walks down the town for you. Just remember that!"

The twins stared at Belinda in dismay. The St. Clare girls were allowed to go down to the town in twos to buy anything they needed, or to look at the shops, or even to go to the cinema if they had permission. Surely Belinda hadn't the power to stop them doing that?

"I don't think you've any right to say that," said Pat. "I shall go to Winifred James and tell her what you've said and ask her about it."

"Well, I'm blessed!" said Belinda, flaring up angrily, her red hair seeming to flame too. "You *do* want taking down a peg, don't you? Run off to Winifred, by all means. Tell your little tales and see what happens."

Pat and Isabel went out of the study. Isabel was very much upset, and wanted to stay and do what Belinda had ordered, but Pat was furious. She took hold of her twin's arm and marched her off to Winifred's study. The head-girl had her own study, which she shared with no one. Pat dared not go in without knocking. So, she knocked quietly.

"Come in!" said Winifred's voice. The twins went in. Winifred was working at a table, "What is it?" she said. "I'm rather busy."

"Please, Winifred," said Pat, "Belinda Towers ordered us to clean her boots, make up her fire and put her kettle on. And when we said we wouldn't she said we weren't to go down into the town. So we've come to ask you about it."

"I see," said Winifred. "Well, it's the custom of this school to get the juniors to wait on the seniors within reason. It doesn't hurt them. When you go to Rome, you must do as Rome does, you know."

"But we didn't want to come to St. Clare's, so we don't want to follow silly customs of that sort," said Pat. "Do we, Isabel?"

Isabel shook her head. She couldn't think how Pat could dare to speak to Winifred like that. Her knees were shaking as she stood! She was never so brave as Pat.

"I think I should wait a little while before you call our customs silly," said Winifred. "Now listen – can't you clean boots? Don't you know how to make up a fire? Have you never put a kettle on to boil?"

"We never had to at Redroofs," said Pat, obstinately. "And we don't at home either."

"I don't think I'd know how to clean muddy boots!" said Isabel, thinking that perhaps if she said that, Winifred would let them off.

"Good heavens!" said Winifred in disgust. "To think

you're nearly fifteen and you don't know how to clean boots! How shocking! All the more reason why you should learn at once. Go back to Belinda's study and try to do what she tells you. I know she's hot-tempered and will tick you off properly, but honestly I think you both deserve it. Do have a little common sense."

Winifred turned back to her books. The twins, red in the face, went out of the room and closed the door quietly. They stood outside and looked at each other.

"I shan't clean her beastly boots, even if I have to stay in the school grounds the whole of the term and not go down into the town once," said Pat, angrily.

"Oh, Pat! I do want to get a new set of hair-grips and some chocolate," said Isabel, in dismay. "Come on – we'd better do it. The others will think we're terribly silly if we kick up such a fuss. They laugh at us enough already."

"Well, you can do it if you like, but *I'm* not going to!" said Pat, and she stalked off, her nose in the air, leaving Isabel by herself.

Isabel stood for a little while, thinking. "Supposing I go and do the jobs that Belinda wants done," she thought. "That means that I can go down into the town if I want to – and as Pat is so exactly like me, she can go down too, if we each go at different times, with some-body else. No one will ever know! That will trick Belinda nicely!"

Isabel went to Belinda's study. It was empty. On the floor lay two pairs of very muddy boots. The owners had evidently been across some very clayey fields. Isabel picked them up. Goodness, however did anyone set about cleaning boots like that?

She heard some one passing and went to the door. She saw Kathleen Gregory and called her.

"Kathleen! Look at these awful boots! How do I clean them?"

The Twins marched to Winifred's study

Kathleen stopped at once, looking delighted. She was pleased that Isabel should ask her help. "You want to scrape them first and get all the clay off," she said. "Come on, I'll help you."

Soon the two girls were cleaning the muddy boots thoroughly. They took quite a time. Kathleen talked hard all the time, pouring out all kinds of information about how her mother spoilt her at home, and what a lot of presents she was always getting from her parents, and how much money they sent her for her birthday.

Isabel listened politely, grateful for Kathleen's help, but thinking that she was rather silly. After all, every one got presents for their birthdays, and every one had money on their birthdays! When the boots were finished she put them neatly together on the shoe-shelf, and made up the fire. Kathleen showed her where to fill the kettle and set it on to boil. Just then Belinda and Pam came back.

"Oh, so you decided to be sensible, I see," she said. "Where's your twin? Did she help you?"

"No," said Isabel.

"Well, tell her from me that there's to be no going down to the town till she does her bit," said Belinda, flinging herself down in a chair. "I won't have new girls behaving as if they owned the place! Is the kettle boiling yet? My goodness, the water's cold! How long has this kettle been on?"

"I've only just this minute put it on, Belinda," said Isabel.

"I suppose it didn't occur to you that it would be a good idea to make up the fire and put the kettle on *first*, before you did the boots?" said Belinda, sarcastically. "I suppose you thought it would be a great pity if the kettle boiled whilst you were doing the boots? I don't know what you kids are coming to nowadays. When I was your age I had a lot more common sense. Clear out now. And see that you come running next time I send a message!"

Isabel went out of the room. Just as she was closing the door Belinda yelled to her again. "And mind you tell that obstinate twin of yours what I said. If she disobeys I'll report her to Miss Theobald."

Isabel fled. She felt upset and angry and very foolish. Why, why, why hadn't she put the kettle on first? No wonder that Belinda had thought her stupid.

Isabel told Pat what had happened. "And she says you're not to go down to the town till you do your bit," she said. "But you can, Pat – because no one will know if it's you or me going! I don't think anyone can tell the difference between us yet."

"All right," said Pat, ungraciously. "But I don't think much of you for giving in like that, Isabel. Fancy cleaning those dirty boots!"

"Well, I rather enjoyed it," said Isabel. "Kathleen helped me. First we . . ."

"Oh, shut up," said Pat, rudely. "Go and write an essay about how to clean boots and boil kettles if you want to, but don't preach to me!"

Isabel was hurt. But Pat could not be angry with her twin for long. Before an hour had gone by she had slipped her arm through Isabel's. "Sorry, old thing," she said. "I wasn't really angry with you. I was furious with Belinda, and took it out on you. Never mind! I'll trick Belinda all right and go down to the town whenever I like, pretending that I am you."

Pat was as good as her word! She slipped down to the town with one or other of the girls, pretending that she was Isabel, and nobody knew the difference! How the twins giggled about their trick!

And then something happened. Pat had gone down to the town with Kathleen after tea, when a messenger came to the common-room. Isabel was winding up the gramophone, and she jumped when she heard Pat's name called.

"Patricia O'Sullivan! Belinda wants you!"

"Well – I must pretend to be Pat," thought Isabel. "But why does Belinda want Pat? I'm the one that does her jobs just now. She knows Pat doesn't."

She soon knew what Belinda wanted. The sports-captain was making out a list and she looked up as Isabel came in.

"Pat O'Sullivan, you played well in the lacrosse practice yesterday," she said. "I was watching. You're a silly, obstinate kid, but I'm not counting that against you where lacrosse is concerned. I'm putting you down for the match on Saturday."

Isabel stared in surprise. How pleased Pat would be! Isabel muttered a thank you and sped, longing for Pat to come back so that she might tell her the good news.

When Pat heard she stood speechless. "In a match already!" she cried. "How decent of Belinda! If she'd been spiteful she'd have left me out for months."

Then she became silent and went away by herself. Isabel knew quite well what she was thinking, because she was worrying about the same thing herself

Soon Pat came over and put her arm through Isabel's. "I feel a beast now," said Pat. "I've let you do all the jobs – and I've gone down to the town all I wanted to, just to spite Belinda. I thought we were being rather clever to play a trick like that. But now I don't think so."

"Nor do I," said Isabel. "I just feel mean and dishonest. It was decent of Belinda to stick you in the match, although she must have felt furious with you – but *we* haven't been decent. And, you know, Pat, I don't really mind doing anything for the top-formers. They are awfully good sorts, really. After all, why should anyone mind putting a kettle on to boil and making toast? Belinda talks to me quite a lot now, and I like her, though I'm a bit afraid of her hot temper."

Pat rubbed her nose and frowned. She always did that when she felt uncomfortable. She suddenly got up and went to the door. "I'm going to tell Belinda I've played her a trick," she said. "I'm not playing in the match on Saturday knowing I've been mean."

She ran out. She went to Belinda's study and knocked on the door. Belinda yelled, "Come in!" She looked surprised when she saw Pat.

"Hallo, Isabel!" she said. "I didn't send for you."

"I'm not Isabel, I'm Pat," said Pat. "I've come about the match on Saturday."

"Well, there's nothing more to tell you than I told you just now," said Belinda.

"That's just it. You didn't tell *me* just now – you told my twin, Isabel," said Pat. "I was down in the town. I know you said I wasn't to go – but I'm so like my twin that I knew nobody would ever know."

"Rather a mean trick, Pat," said Belinda, in a scornful voice.

"I know," said Pat, in a troubled voice. "I'm sorry for that. I've come to say thank you for putting me in the match, but of course I don't expect to play now. Anyway, I couldn't have you being decent to me if I was playing a trick just to pay you out. And I'll take my share of the jobs with Isabel now. I was silly before. That's all, Belinda."

"No – not quite all," said Belinda, in an unexpectedly gentle voice. "I've something to say too. You've done something rather mean, but you've been big enough to put it right. We'll say no more about it – but you'll play in the match on Saturday!"

Pat flew off to tell Isabel, her heart leaping for joy. How decent Belinda was! How could she ever have thought her beastly and horrid?

"I'll boil her old kettle and clean her old boots and even scrub the floor now!" thought Pat. "And my word I'll shoot a dozen goals on Saturday, see if I don't!"

She didn't – but she shot one very difficult one – and how pleased she was to hear both Isabel *and* Belinda shout, "Well done, Pat! Oh, good shot, good shot!"

5 A BATTLE WITH MAM'ZELLE

Every week the twin's form had marks for different subjects. Pat and Isabel had been used to being top in most things at Redroofs, and it was with shame and dismay that they found they were nearer the bottom than the top at St. Clare's.

Hilary saw them looking unhappy about it and she spoke to them. "You've got to remember that you are the only new girls in your form," she said. "The rest of us have been in the form at least two terms, and we are used to St. Clare ways. Cheer up!"

It was "Mam'zelle Abominable" who really upset the twins. She would not make allowances for them, and when they sent in badly written French essays, she was very angry.

She had the pile of French books on the desk before her, all neatly marked with *"Très bien"* or *"Bien"* or *"Excellent"*. But when she took out Pat's book and Isabel's they were both marked the same. "Abominable!"

"This will not do!" cried Mam'zelle, banging her big hand down on the books. *"C'est abominable!* You will write the whole essay again today, and you will bring it to me after supper."

"We can't write it again today, Mam'zelle," said Isabel, politely. "We've got art this afternoon, and after tea we've got permission to go to the cinema together. We shan't have time to rewrite it. Can we do it tomorrow?"

"Oh, *que vous êtes* insupportable!" raged Mam'zelle, stamping her foot on the floor, and making the books on her desk jump and slide. "How dare you talk to me like this! You present me with a shocking, yes, a shocking essay, and then you talk of going to the cinema. You will not go! You will stay behind and write the essay for me. And if there is more than one mistake you will write it all over again! That is certain!"

"But – but – we've got the tickets," said Isabel. "We had to book our seats. We . . ."

"I do not care about seats, I do not care about booking!" shouted Mam'zelle, now quite losing her temper. "All I care about is that you should learn good French, which is what I am here for. You will bring me the essays tonight."

Isabel looked ready to cry. Pat looked mutinous, and stuck out her lower lip. Every one else enjoyed the row and a few of the girls were secretly very pleased to see the twins taken down a peg. Nobody dared to be inattentive after that, and the lesson went very smoothly, though Pat was sulky and joined in the lesson as little as she dared.

When the lesson was over the twins had a few words together. I'm going to the cinema!" said Pat.

"Oh, no, Pat!" said Isabel, shocked. "We can't do that. We'd really get into a terrible row. We'd better stay behind and do the work again. For goodness' sake let's!"

"I'm GOING to the cinema!" said Pat, obstinately. "I'll fit in the beastly essay somehow, and you must too. Let's do it directly after dinner. I don't care how badly I do it either."

But after dinner they had to go to a meeting of their

form to plan nature rambles, so there was no time then. Art took up the whole of the afternoon. Isabel began to be worried. Suppose Pat insisted on going to the cinema even if they hadn't rewritten their essays? She could not imagine what Mam'zelle would say.

"Let's miss our tea," said Isabel to Pat as they ran down the stairs after the art lesson. "We could do our essays then."

"Miss my tea! No, thank you!" said Pat. "I'm jolly hungry. I don't know why art makes me hungry, but it always does. And I know Janet has got a big pot of plum jam sent to her that she's opening this tea time. I'm not going to miss my share!"

Isabel was hungry too, and she weakly gave way. She knew that if they were going to get into the cinema in time they wouldn't have a moment to spare for anything after tea, let alone rewriting essays! "I really shan't go to the cinema," she thought. "I daren't. Honestly, I think Mam'zelle Abominable would go up in smoke if she heard we'd gone."

But after tea Pat dragged Isabel off to the dormitory to get her hat and coat. "We're not really going, Pat, surely!" cried Isabel.

"Indeed we are !" said Pat, sticking out her lower lip. "Come on."

"But, Pat – we'll really get into a simply enormous row!" said Isabel. "It isn't worth it. Perhaps Mam'zelle will give us an hour's extra work every day or something like that. Janet told me that once she had to stop in after tea for a whole week and write out French verbs for cheeking Mam'zelle just a little bit. And she wouldn't count this a little thing."

"Don't be a coward, Isabel," said Pat. "I've got a plan. Mam'zelle said we were to take our essays to her after supper, didn't she? But she didn't say what time after supper! So when we're in bed and think the others are asleep, we'll slip down to the common room in our dressing-gowns, rewrite our essays then – and give them to Mam'zelle when they're finished!"

"Pat! I'd never dare to!" cried poor Isabel. "Think of going to find Mam'zelle at that time of night in our dressing-gowns. You must be mad."

"Well, Mam'zelle has *made* me feel mad," said obstinate Pat. "Anyway, I don't care what happens. You know we never wanted to come to St. Clare's – and if it's going to treat us like this, I'm jolly sure I won't stay. I'll get expelled!"

"Pat, you're not to say things like that!" said Isabel. "Think what Mummy and Daddy would say!"

"Well it's their fault for sending us here," said Pat, who really was in a great rage.

"Yes, but, Pat – think how awful it would be if Redroofs heard that we'd been sent away from St. Clare's," said Isabel, in a low voice.

Pat's eyes filled with tears. She didn't want to think of that. "Come on," she said, gruffly. "I'm not going to change my mind now. If you're coming with me, come. If not, you can jolly well be a coward by yourself!"

But Isabel was not going to be left by herself. She put on her hat and coat. Janet came into the room as the twins were going out.

"Hallo, hallo!" she said. "So you *are* going to the cinema after all! Whenever did you find time to rewrite your French?"

"We haven't done it," said Pat. Janet gave a long whistle and stared at the twins in surprise.

"I wouldn't like to be in your shoes tomorrow when you tell Mam'zelle that!" she said. "You really are a couple of idiots. I can't think why you should go out of your way to make things difficult for yourselves!"

The twins did not answer. They ran downstairs and were soon in the town. But neither of them really en-

joyed the show, although it was a fine nature-film. They
had to leave a little before the end to get back to supper
in time. There was a debate afterwards that they had to
go to, and they both wished they could miss it. But it
was taken by Winifred James, the head-girl, and neither
of the twins dared to ask if they might miss it.

Nine o'clock was the bedtime for their form and the
two forms above them. Chattering and laughing, the
girls went upstairs and undressed. Usually a mistress
came to see that all the girls were in bed, and switched
off the lights – but tonight Hilary announced that she
was to see to this.

"Miss Roberts is with Miss Theobald," she said, "so
I'm on duty tonight. Hurry, all of you, because the light
will go off in five minutes' time, and you'll have to finish
in the dark if you're not ready."

Two girls, Joan and Doris, began to have a pillow-
fight when they heard that Miss Roberts was not
coming. Bang-thud went the two pillows, and the girls
shrieked with laughter. But it wasn't quite so funny
when one of the pillows split and feathers poured out
into the air!

"Golly!" said Joan. "Look at my pillow. Hilary, for
goodness' sake don't turn the lights off yet. I *must* pick
up some of these feathers!"

"Sorry," said Hilary. "You'll have to do it in the
morning. Lights are going out now! Miss Roberts will
be along to see we're all right in an hour's time, so let's
hope she won't spot the feathers all over the place. She'll
think the cat's been chasing hens in our dormitory!"

The lights snapped out. All the girls were in bed except Joan and Doris, who were still groping for feathers.
They had to finish undressing and cleaning their teeth
in the dark. Joan upset her tooth-mug and Doris banged
her ankle on her chest-of-drawers and groaned deeply.
Janet giggled, and Kathleen Gregory went off into a

spasm of laughter that gave her hiccups.

"Shut up, Kathleen," ordered Hilary. "You're hiccupping on purpose. I know you!"

"I'm *not*!" said Kathleen, indignantly, and gave such an enormous hiccup that her bed shook. Janet couldn't stop giggling. Every time she tried to stop, poor Kathleen hiccupped again and Janet went off into more gurgles.

Even the twins, anxious though they were to have every one going to sleep quickly, could not help laughing. Hilary lost her temper and sat up in bed.

"You're all meanies!" she cried. "If any one comes along and hears you making this row I'll be blamed because I'm head of the dormitory. Shut up, Janet – and Kathleen, for goodness' sake get a drink of water. How do you suppose we're going to sleep with you hiccupping like that?"

"Sorry, Hilary," said Kathleen, with another hiccup. "I'll get up and get some water."

"Get into bed, Joan and Doris," said Hilary, snuggling down again. "I don't care if you've cleaned your teeth and brushed your hair or not. GET INTO BED!"

In five minutes' time there was peace in the dormitory except for an occasional small and subdued hiccup from Kathleen and a smothered giggle from Janet.

The twins lay awake, listening for the others to go to sleep. They were worried because Miss Roberts was coming in about an hour's time. They could not wait a whole hour before going down to the common room. For one thing, Mam'zelle would have gone to bed by the time they had finished their essays!

"Isabel!" whispered Pat at last. "Isabel! I think they're all asleep. Get up and put on your dressing-gown."

"But Miss Roberts hasn't been in yet," whispered back Isabel.

"We'll put our bolsters down our beds, so that they'll look like our bodies," said Pat. "Come on!"

They got up quietly and slipped on their dressing-gowns. They pushed their bolsters down their beds and hoped that Miss Roberts wouldn't notice anything different when she came. Then out of the door they went, and down the dimly-lit stairs to the common room, which was just below their own dormitory.

Pat shut the door and turned on the light. The two girls sat down and took out their French books. Mam'-zelle had marked all the mistakes, and carefully and laboriously the two girls wrote out the essays again.

"Well, mine had fifteen mistakes before, and I hope it hasn't got more than five now!" said Isabel. "Blow Mam'zelle Abominable! I'm so sleepy. And oh, Pat – *dare* we go and find Mam'zelle now, do you think? My knees are shaking at the very thought!"

"Oh, don't be stupid," said Pat. "What can she say to us, anyway? We've done the essays again – and she said give them to her after supper – and we are going to do that, aren't we?"

The essays were finished. Now they had to find Mam'-zelle. Where would she be? In one of the mistresses' common rooms – or in her own bedroom – or where?

"Well, come on," said Pat, at last. "We must go and find her. Cheer up, Isabel."

The twins slipped out of the common room and went to the first of the mistresses' rooms. The light was out and the room was quite dark. No one was there at all. As they went on their way to the second common room, they heard Mam'zelle's voice in one of the classrooms! What luck!

"She's in the upper third classroom," whispered Pat. "I don't know who's there with her, but it doesn't matter. The art mistress, I expect – Mam'zelle's awfully friendly with Miss Walker."

They knocked at the upper third door. A surprised voice called "Come in! Who's there?"

Pat opened the door and the twins went in. And oh my goodness, who should be with Mam'zelle, studying a big French chart, but the Head, Miss Theobald herself!

The twins were so shocked that they stood and stared with wide eyes. Mam'zelle cried *"Tiens!"* in a loud and amazed voice, and Miss Theobald said nothing at all.

Mam'zelle recovered first. "What is wrong?" she cried. "Are you ill, *mes petites*?"

"No," said Pat, in rather a trembling voice. "We're not ill. We've brought you our re-written essays. You said we were to bring them after supper, so here they are."

"But why bring them so late?" asked Miss Theobald, in her deep, serious voice. "You must have known that Mam'zelle meant you to bring them before you went to bed."

"We hadn't time to rewrite the essays till just now," answered Pat, suddenly feeling very foolish indeed. "We got out of bed and went down to the common room to do them."

"Ah! The bad children! They went to the cinema after all, instead of doing my essays!" cried Mam'zelle, guessing everything at once. "Ah, Miss Theobald, these twins send my hair grey! The work they do! It is impossible that they have gone to a school before they came here! Their work is abominable."

"We *did* go to a school, and it was a jolly fine one!" cried Pat, indignantly. *"Much* better than St. Clares!"

There was a silence after this. Miss Theobald looked thoughtful. Mam'zelle was speechless.

"I think we won't decide anything tonight or talk about this," said Miss Theobald at last. "It is too late. Go to bed, twins, and come and see me at ten o'clock tomorrow morning. Ask Miss Roberts to excuse you for fifteen minutes then."

So back to bed with their French books went the twins, subdued and dismayed. What bad luck to have run into the Head herself like that! Now what was going to happen to them? They didn't like to think of ten o'clock in the morning!

6   POOR MISS KENNEDY!

Hilary was awake when they got back into bed and she sat up and demanded to know where they had been.

"Miss Roberts came in and turned on the light and I woke up," said Hilary. "I spotted that you'd put bolsters down your beds, but Miss Roberts didn't. Whatever have you been doing?"

Pat told her. Hilary listened in amazement. "Whatever will you two do next?" she said. "Honestly, I think you're mad. Nobody would ever think you'd been head-girls in your old school. You behave like a couple of babies!"

The twins were annoyed with Hilary, particularly as they each had a kind of feeling that she was right. They got into bed and lay thinking. It was all very well to be defiant and daring – but it wasn't so funny afterwards!

They asked Miss Roberts to excuse them at ten o'clock. Miss Roberts had evidently been told to expect this, for she nodded her head at once, and did not ask any questions. The twins went off together to Miss Theobald's room.

The head was making out time-tables and she told them to sit down for a minute. It was rather dreadful waiting for her to finish what she was doing. Both the twins felt much more nervous than they pretended. Pat began to wonder if the Head would write home about them to their parents. Much as she had grumbled about going to St. Clare's, she didn't want the Head to report her for misbehaviour at the school.

At last Miss Theobald was ready. She swung her chair round and faced the twins. She looked very serious, but not angry.

"I have been looking through the reports that your father sent me from your last school," the Head began. "They are very good, and you seem to have been responsible and conscientious children there. I can't imagine that you can have completely changed your characters in a few weeks, so I am not going to treat you as naughty irresponsible girls. I know there must be a good reason behind all your queer behaviour last night. Really, my dears, you gave Mam'zelle and me quite a shock when you walked into the classroom in your blue dressing-gowns."

The Head smiled. The twins felt most relieved, and Pat began to pour out what had happened in the French class.

"The French isn't the same as at our old school. It isn't much use our trying to do well, because we always get everything wrong. It isn't our fault. And Mam'zelle was simply furious with us yesterday, and . . ."

Miss Theobald heard Pat patiently to the end.

"Well, your French difficulties can easily be put right," said the Head Mistress. "I have spoken to Mam'-zelle, and she says that you speak well and understand well, but that you have not been well grounded in the writing of French. She has offered to give you half an hour's extra French a day until you have caught up the others. This is very kind of her because she is extremely busy. All this bother has come from the fact that you were behind your class in one thing – and if you are willing to help to put it right by working hard with Mam'-zelle, there is no need to say any more about your rather silly behaviour last night."

The twins stared at Miss Theobald with mixed feelings. They were most relieved that nothing more was to be said – but oh dear, oh dear – extra French each day! How tiresome! And yet how decent of Mam'zelle Abominable to be willing to help them.

"Thank you, Miss Theobald," said Pat at last. "We'll try. Once we catch up the others, we shan't feel so angry and ashamed when we are scolded in front of the class."

"Well, you won't be scolded if Mam'zelle really feels you are trying," said Miss Theobald. "Now go to her and arrange what time will be best each day for the extra lesson. And don't go marching through the corridors in your dressing-gowns at half-past ten any more!"

"No, Miss Theobald," said the twins, smiling at the Head. Things seemed suddenly brighter. What they had done didn't any longer seem a dreadful piece of misbehaviour likely to be punished in dire ways – but just a silly bit of nonsense that they were both heartily ashamed of. They went out of the room, and skipped down the passage to the common room. Mam'zelle was there, correcting piles of French essays, and muttering to herself as she ticked the pages.

"*Très bien, ma petite* Hilary! Ah, this dreadful girl. Joan! Ah . . . come in!"

The twins went into the mistresses' common room. Mam'zelle beamed at them, and patted them on the shoulder. Although she had an extremely quick and hot temper, she was very good hearted and kind.

"Ah, now we will see how clever you can be at catching up the others," she said. "Every day you will work with me, and we shall be good friends, *n'est ce pas?*"

"Thank you, Mam'zelle," said Pat. "We were rather idiots yesterday. We won't be again!"

"And thank you for saying you'll help us each day," said Isabel.

So that was that, and the classes with Mam'zelle went much more smoothly. Mam'zelle was patient with the twins, and they tried hard.

But nobody tried hard with poor Miss Kennedy! Janet was a born tease and leg-puller, and she gave the unfortunate history-teacher a terrible time. Janet had a wonderful collection of trick-pencils, all of which she tried on Miss Kennedy with enormous success.

One pencil had a point that was made of rubber, so that it wobbled to one side when Miss Kennedy took it to write with. Another pencil had a point that slipped right inside the pencil as soon as any one wrote with it. The girls all watched with intense eagerness as the unfortunate mistress unwarily used these pencils, and gazed at them in surprise when they behaved so queerly.

Then Janet produced a pencil that wouldn't write at all, although it appeared to have a most marvellous point. To see poor Miss Kennedy pressing hard with the pencil, trying her best to write "Very good" with it, sent the whole class into fits of giggles.

"Girls, girls! Please make less noise!" Miss Kennedy said. "Turn to page eighty-seven of your history books. Today I want to tell you how the people lived in the seventeenth century."

The class at once began to turn over the pages of their history books in a most feverish manner, making a noise like the whispering of trees in the wind. They went on and on turning over the pages, muttering "eighty-seven, eighty-seven" to themselves all the time.

"What number did you say, Miss Kennedy?" asked Kathleen, innocently, though she knew very well indeed.

"I said page eighty-seven," said Miss Kennedy, politely. She was always polite, never rude like Mam'-

zelle, or sarcastic like Miss Roberts.

"Oh, eighty-seven!" said all the girls at once, and immediately began to turn over their pages the other way, very busy and very serious – until Janet let out a giggle, and then the whole class roared. Miss Kennedy rapped on the desk.

"Please, please," she said, "I do beg you to be quiet and let us get on with the lesson."

"Please, Miss Kennedy, did the people wear clothes in the seventeenth century, or just skins?" asked Janet, in an innocent voice. Miss Kennedy looked surprised.

"Surely you know that they wore clothes," she said. "I have a picture here of the kind of clothes they wore. You should know that they didn't wear skins then, Janet."

"Not even their *own* skins?" asked Janet. This wasn't really at all funny, but the class was now in a state to giggle at anything, and the twins and every one else joined in the laughter.

"Perhaps they had jumped *out* of their skins and that's why they didn't wear any," said Hilary. More giggles followed this, though half the class didn't even catch what Hilary had said.

"Girls, I can't have this, I really can't," said Miss Kennedy. "I shall have to report you."

"Oh, please, please, PLEASE, Miss Kennedy!" chanted the class in a chorus, and one or two girls pretended to sob.

Poor Miss Kennedy! She had to deal with this sort of thing every time, though the upper forms were better behaved. The lower forms did not mean to be cruel or unkind, but they loved a joke and did not stop to think about Miss Kennedy and what she must be feeling. They just thought she was silly and asked for trouble.

One morning, when the class was especially riotous, Janet caught every one's eye. Kathleen giggled, for she knew what had been planned. When Janet gave the signal every girl was to drop her history text book flat on the floor! Janet nodded, and each girl let go her book.

Crash! Miss Kennedy jumped in fright – and the next minute the door opened and in came Miss Roberts! She had been taking a class in the next room, and when the crash of twenty history books had sounded, like a gunshot, she had decided it was time to investigate.

"Miss Kennedy, I don't know if there are any girls' names you would like to report to me," said Miss Roberts, in a very cold voice, "but I shall be glad to have them after morning school. I am sure you find it as difficult as I do to teach with all this noise going on."

Miss Roberts glared at the form, and they sat silent, half the girls going red. Miss Kennedy went red too.

"I'm so sorry for the noise, Miss Roberts," she said. "You see . . ."

But Miss Roberts was gone, shutting the door after her very firmly indeed.

"Kenny won't report any one," whispered Janet to Isabel. "If she did, she'd have to report the whole class, and she would be ashamed to do that."

Miss Kennedy reported no one – but in the secrecy of her bedroom that night she worried and tossed all night long. She had come to St. Clare's because her friend, Miss Lewis, who thought so much of her, was ill – and now Miss Kennedy felt that she was letting her down because the girls were quite out of hand, and she was sure that not one of them had learnt any history worth mentioning that term! And Miss Roberts had come in like that and been so cold and horrid – and had hardly spoken to her in the common room afterwards. Suppose she complained about her to Miss Theobald? It was dreadful to feel herself a failure, and poor Miss

Kennedy did not see how she could possibly turn her failure into anything like success.

"I'm afraid of the girls, that's why!" she said to herself. "And I do hate reporting them, because if I do they will hate me, and then my classes will be worse than ever."

And in the dormitory Janet was planning other tricks to play on poor unsuspecting Miss Kennedy! Janet had brothers, monkeys all of them, and they sent her all kinds of tricks which they themselves tried out in their own classes.

"Pat! Isabel! Are you asleep?" whispered Janet. "I say! My brothers are sending me some fire-cracks! Have you ever heard of them?"

"Never," said the twins. "Whatever are they?"

"Well, you throw them on the fire and they crack and spit and hiss," whispered Janet, in glee. "My seat is next to the fire – so watch out for some fun next week! I expect the parcel will come tomorrow."

The twins giggled. Whatever would Kenny say when the fire began to spit and hiss and crack? They hugged themselves and pictured Miss Kennedy's alarmed expression.

"Janet!" whispered Pat. "Let's . . ."

But Hilary, head of the dormitory, put an end to the whispering. "Shut up!" she said. "You know the rules, don't you? For goodness' sake, go to sleep!"

7   JANET IS UP TO TRICKS

The parcel of "fire-cracks" duly arrived for Janet. She giggled when she took it from the post-rack, and winked at the twins.

"I'll undo it in the dormitory after breakfast," she said. "Say you've forgotten something and get permission to go up before prayers."

So Janet and the twins scurried up stairs to the dormitory immediately after breakfast, and for five minutes they gloated over the contents of the parcel. There was a box inside, and this contained about fifty squib-like crackers small and innocent-looking, coloured red and yellow.

"But will they really make much noise?" asked Pat, taking one up. "I shouldn't think they'd do much more than make a gentle pop."

"Don't worry! I'll throw about a dozen on at a time!" said Janet. "There'll be quite an explosion, I promise you. Golly! We'll have some sport!"

With many giggles the girls hurried downstairs as the bell for prayers went. They could hardly wait for the history-lesson to come. It came after the mid-morning break. Janet told some of the other girls what she was going to do, and the whole form was in a great state of expectation. Even Miss Roberts felt there was something up, though the class tried to work well.

At the end of the maths. lesson, just before break, Miss Roberts spoke a few dry words to her form.

"After break you will have your history lesson as usual. I expect you to work as well for Miss Kennedy as you do for me. If you don't, I shall have something serious to say to you all. There is to be no disturbance at all this morning. DO YOU HEAR ME, JANET?"

Janet jumped. She couldn't imagine why Miss Roberts had suddenly picked her out. She did not know that she had been looking extremely guilty!

"Yes, Miss Roberts," said Janet, thinking that, alas, she would not be able to play her fire-crack trick after all.

But the rest of the form crowded round her during

break, and insisted that she carried out her promise. They couldn't bear not to have the treat of seeing Miss Kennedy jump and stare with wide eyes at the fire's extraordinary behaviour.

"All right," said Janet, at last. "But for goodness' sake don't give me away to Miss Roberts, that's all, if she hears anything. And DO promise not to laugh too loudly. Honestly, we'll get into an awful row if Miss Roberts hears us. And she'll be quite near, you know."

"No, she won't," said Kathleen. "She's taking the sixth for something. I heard her say so. And they're right at the other end of the school! She won't hear a thing."

"Good," said Janet, feeling more comfortable. "Well, watch out! We'll hear some fine spitting and hissing, I can tell you!"

The whole form were in their places as quiet as mice when Miss Kennedy came in to give them their usual history lesson. She was feeling even more nervous than usual, for she had not forgotten how the form had behaved the last time she had taken them. She was most relieved to see them sitting so quietly in their places.

"Good morning, girls," said Miss Kennedy, sitting at her desk.

"Good morning, Miss Kennedy," chorused the form, and the lesson opened. Miss Kennedy had to turn to the blackboard to draw a history chart, and immediately every girl turned her head towards Janet. The time had come!

Janet's seat was just by the fire. The box of fire-cracks was in her desk. Cautiously she lifted the lid, and took out about a dozen. She threw them into the heart of the fire.

Every one waited tensely. For a moment nothing happened at all except that the fire flamed up a little. Then the excitement began!

Crack! Spit! Hiss! Half the fire-cracks went off at once, and sparks jumped up the chimney and leapt out of the fire on to the floor.

CRACK! Sssssssssss! Every one watched and listened, their eyes on poor Miss Kennedy, who looked as surprised and as startled as could be!

"Miss Kennedy! Oh Miss Kennedy! What's happening!" cried Pat, pretending to be frightened.

"It's all right, Pat – it's probably a very gassy piece of coal," said Miss Kennedy. "It's all over now – but it really made me jump."

"CRACK! CRACK!" some more fireworks went off, and a shower of sparks flew out of the fire. Janet jumped up, took the blackboard-cleaner, and began to beat out the sparks with an enormous amount of quite unnecessary noise.

"Janet! Janet! Stop!" cried Miss Kennedy, afraid that the next class would hear the noise.

By this time the class had begun to giggle, though they had tried hard to keep serious and to smother their laughter. When the fire-cracks went off once more the class nearly went into hysterics, which were not made any better by the sight of Janet again pretending to beat out sparks on the floor by flapping about with the blackboard-cleaner, making an enormous dust.

Miss Kennedy went pale. She guessed that some trick had been played, though she couldn't imagine what. She stood up, looking unexpectedly dignified, though bits of straight hair fell rather wildly from the two knots at the sides of her head.

"Girls!" she said. "There will be no history lesson this morning. I refuse to teach an unruly class like this."

She went out of the room, her face white and her eyes swimming with tears.

She would have to go to the Head and give up her job. She couldn't possibly take fees for teaching girls who simply played the whole of the time. But it was no use going when she felt so upset. She would wait until the end of the morning and go then. She hurriedly scribbled a note to Miss Roberts, and sent it to her by one of the school maids.

"Am afraid I feel unwell, and have had to leave your form for a while," said the note.

Miss Roberts was surprised to get the note. She debated with herself whether to let the first form carry on by itself – surely Miss Kennedy would have left them some work to do? Or should she leave the sixth form to get on by themselves, and go back to the first? She decided to give the sixth some questions to answer, and leave them. They would behave themselves, of course – but she wasn't so sure about her own form!

So she began to write out questions on the board, wondering meanwhile what the first form was up to.

They had been rather taken aback when Miss Kennedy walked out. Some of the girls felt guilty and uncomfortable, but when the fire began to hiss and spit again, it all seemed terribly funny once more, and Doris, Joan, Kathleen and the rest began to giggle again.

"*Did* you see old Kenny when the first crack went off?" cried Joan. "I thought I should die, trying not to laugh. I had an awful stitch in my side, I can tell you."

"Janet, those fire-cracks are simply marvellous!" cried Hilary. "Put some more on – Kenny won't be back. All I hope is that she doesn't go and tell Miss Theobald."

"She didn't go towards the Head's room," said Janet. "She went the other way. All right – I'll stick some more on. Watch out, every one!"

Janet shook the box over the fire, meaning to throw out about a dozen of the little squibs – but the whole lot went in! Janet laughed.

"Golly! They've all gone in. We'll have some fun!"

Doris was at the door of the classroom, keeping guard in case a teacher came along. Suddenly she gave a cry.

"Look out! Miss Roberts is coming! Get to your seats, quick!"

Every one scurried to their seats at once. They pulled open their history books, and by the time that Miss Roberts came into the room, the class looked fairly peaceful, though it was rather surprising to see so many bent heads. Miss Roberts became suspicious at once – usually the girls all looked up when she came into the room!

"You seem very busy," she said, drily. "Did Miss Kennedy leave you history work to do?"

Nobody answered. Janet gave an anxious glance at the fire. Those fire-cracks! How she wished she hadn't put so many on! The fire began to flare up a little. Miss Roberts spoke sharply.

"Can't somebody answer me? Did Miss . . ."

But she did not finish her question, because about twenty fire-cracks went off at once with the most tremendous hissing, spluttering and cracking! Sparks flew out and huge flames shot up the chimney.

"Good heavens!" said Miss Roberts. "What in the world is going on there?"

Again nobody said a word. There was no giggling or laughing this time, no smothered gurgles. Everyone looked scared.

Crack! Sssssss! Crack! Some of the fireworks shot themselves up the chimney and exploded there, bringing down showers of soot. It was hot soot, and flew out over the room. Janet and the girls nearest the fire began to cough and choke.

Come away from the fire, Janet," ordered Miss Roberts. "Those sparks will set fire to your tunic."

The soot flew out again, and black specks began to descend on to books, papers, desks and heads. Miss

Roberts' mouth went very straight and thin. She looked round the class.

"Some one has been putting fireworks into the fire," she said. "The class will dismiss. I am going to the common room across the passage. I expect the girl who played this stupid and dangerous joke to come and own up at once."

She left the room. Every one stared in dismay. It was all very well to play a joke on stupid old Kenny – but Miss Roberts was a different matter altogether! Miss Roberts knew a great many most annoying punishments.

"Gosh! I'm in for it now!" said Janet, gloomily. "I'd better go and get it over."

She went to the door. The twins stared after her. Pat ran to the door too.

"Janet! Wait! I'm coming too. I was as much to blame as you, because I egged you on. I'd have put those fire-cracks on if you hadn't!"

"And I'll come as well," said Isabel at once.

"Oh, I say! That *is* decent of you!" said Janet, slipping her arm through Pat's, and holding out her other hand to Isabel.

Then Hilary spoke up too. "Well, I'll come along as well. As a matter of fact, we're all to blame. It's true you got the squibs and put them on – but we all shared the joke, and it's not fair that only you should be punished."

So it ended in the whole of the class going to the common room, looking very downcast and ashamed. Miss Roberts looked up, surprised to see so many girls crowding into the room.

"What's all this for?" she asked, sternly.

"Miss Roberts, may I tell you?" said Hilary. "I'm head of the form."

"I want the person who played the trick to own up," said Miss Roberts. "Who did it?"

"I did," said poor Janet, going rather white. Her knees

shook a little, and she looked on the floor. She could not bear to meet Miss Roberts' sharp hazel eyes.

"But we were all in it," said Hilary. "We wanted Janet to do it, and we shared in it."

"And may I ask if you also treated Miss Kennedy to the same silly trick?" asked Miss Roberts, in her most sarcastic voice.

"Yes," said Janet, in a low voice.

"So that explains it," said Miss Roberts, thinking of the note that Miss Kennedy had sent her. "Well, you will all share the expenses of the chimney being swept and you will all spend two hours each washing down the walls and scrubbing the floor and desks after the sweep has been. That means that you will work in batches of five, each giving up two hours of your free time to do it."

"Yes, Miss Roberts," said the class dolefully.

"You will also apologize to Miss Kennedy, of course," went on Miss Roberts. "And I should like to say that I am ashamed of you for taking advantage of somebody not able to deal with you as I can!"

The form trooped out. Miss Roberts telephoned for the sweep – and Miss Kennedy was surprised to find relays of girls waylaying her, offering her humble apologies for their behaviour. They did not tell her what had happened, so Miss Kennedy had no idea that Miss Roberts had experienced the same startling explosions from the fire, but had dealt with the whole matter with a firm hand. She really thought that the girls were offering their apologies of their own accord, and she felt almost happy.

"I shan't give in my resignation to Miss Theobald after all," she thought. "Anyway, if I did, I would have to say why, and I shouldn't like to give the girls away after they had said they were sorry in such a nice way."

So the matter rested there for a while – and batches of dismal girls washed and scrubbed that afternoon and evening, instead of playing lacrosse, and going to a concert!

One good thing came out of the row – and that was that the twins' form liked them a great deal better.

"It was decent of Pat and Isabel to go after Janet like that and say they'd share the blame," said Hilary. "Good for them!"

8   THE GREAT MIDNIGHT FEAST

Miss Roberts kept a very tight hand indeed on her form for the next week or two, and they squirmed under her dry tongue. Pat and Isabel hated being spoken to as if they were nobodies, but they did not dare to grumble.

"It's simply awful being ticked off as if we were in the kindergarten, when we've been used to bossing the whole school at Redroofs," said Isabel. "I shall never get used to it!"

"I hate it too," said Pat. But all the same, I can't help liking Miss Roberts, you know. I do respect her awfully, and you can't help liking people you respect."

"Well, I wish she'd start respecting *us*, then," said Isabel gloomily, "Then maybe she'd like us, and we wouldn't get such a hot time in class. Golly, when I forgot to take my maths. book to her this morning you'd have thought she was going to 'phone up the police station and have me sent to prison!"

Pat laughed. "Don't be an idiot," she said. "By the way, don't forget to give half a crown towards buying Miss Theobald something on her birthday. I've given mine in."

"Oh, my!" groaned Isabel. "I hope I've got half a crown! I had to give sixpence towards the sweep, and

I gave a shilling to the housemaid for cleaning my tunic for me in case Matron ticked me off about it – and we had to give sixpence to the Babies' Convalescent Home last week. I'm just about broke!"

She went to her part of the shelf in the common room and took down her purse. It was empty!

"Golly!" said Isabel in dismay. "I'm sure I had two shillings in my purse. Did you borrow it, Pat?"

"No," said Pat. "Or I'd have told you. It must be in your coat-pocket, silly."

But the two shillings were nowhere to be found. Isabel decided she must have lost them, and she had to borrow some money from Pat to give towards buying the Head a present.

Then Janet had a birthday, and every one went down to the town to buy a small present for her – all but Hilary, who discovered, to her dismay, that the ten-shilling note that her Granny had sent her, had disappeared out of her pocket!

"Oh, my, a whole ten shillings!" wailed Hilary. "I was going to buy all sorts of things with it. I really must get some new shoelaces, and my lacrosse stick wants mending. Where in the world has it gone?"

Joan lent Hilary a shilling to buy a present for Janet, and on her birthday Janet was most delighted to find so many gifts. She was very popular, in spite of her bluntness. The finest gift she had was from Kathleen Gregory, who presented her with a gold bar-brooch, with her name inscribed at the back.

"I say! You shouldn't have done that!" said Janet, in amazement. "Why, it must have cost you a mint of money, Kathleen! I really can't accept it. It's too generous a gift."

"But you *must* accept it, because it's got your name inside," said Kathleen. "It's no use to any one else!"

Every one admired the little gold brooch and read the

name inscribed on the back. Kathleen glowed with
pleasure at the attention that her gift produced, and
when Janet thanked her again, and slipped her arm
through hers, she was red with delight.

"It was very generous of Kathleen," said Janet to the
twins, as they went to the classroom. "But I can't understand why she went such a splash on me! Usually she's
awfully mean with her gifts – either gives nothing at all,
or something that costs half a farthing! It isn't as if she
likes me such a lot, either. I've gone for her heaps of
times because she's such a goof!"

Janet had a marvellous tuck-hamper sent to her for
her birthday, and she and Hilary and the twins unpacked
it with glee. "All the things I love!" said Janet. "A big
chocolate cake! Shortbread biscuits! Sardines in tom-
ato sauce! Nestlé's milk. And look at these peppermint
creams! They'll melt in our mouths!"

"Let's have a midnight feast!" said Pat, suddenly.
"We once had one at Redroofs, before we were head-
girls. I don't know why food tastes so much nicer in the
middle of the night than in the daytime, but it does!
Oh, Janet – don't you think it would be fun?"

"It might be rather sport," said Janet. "But there's
not enough food here for us all. The rest of you will
have to bring something as well. Each girl had better
bring one thing – a cake – or ginger-beer – or chocolate.
When shall we have the feast?"

"Tomorrow night," said Isabel, with a giggle. "Miss
Roberts is going to a concert. I heard her say so. She's
going to stay the night with a friend and get a train that
brings her back in time for prayers."

"Oh, good! Tomorrow's the night then!" said Janet.
"Let's tell every one."

So the whole form was told about the Great feast, and
every one promised to bring something. Pat bought a
jam sponge sandwich. Isabel, who again had to borrow

from Pat, bought a bar of chocolate. Joan brought candles, because the girls were not allowed to put on the electric light once it was turned out except for urgent reasons, such as illness.

The most lavish contribution was Kathleen's! She brought a really marvellous cake, with almond icing all over it, and pink and yellow sugar roses on the top. Every one exclaimed over it!

"Golly, Kathleen! Have you come into a fortune or something!" cried Janet. "That cake must have cost you all your pocket-money for the rest of the term! It's marvellous."

"The prettiest cake I've ever seen," said Hilary. "Jolly decent of you, Kathleen."

Kathleen was red with pleasure. She beamed round at every one, and enjoyed the smiles that she and her cake received.

"I wish I could have got something better than my silly little bar of chocolate," said Isabel. "But I even had to borrow from Pat to get that."

"And I can only bring a few biscuits I had left from a tin that Mother sent me a fortnight ago," said Hilary. "I'm quite broke since I lost my ten-shilling note."

"Anyway, we've got heaps of things," said Janet, who was busy hiding everything at the bottom of a cupboard just outside the dormitory. "Golly, I hope Matron doesn't suddenly take it into her head to spring-clean this cupboard! She *would* be surprised to see what's in it. Goodness – who brought this pork-pie? How marvellous!"

The whole form was in a state of excitement that day. It was simply gorgeous to have a secret and not to let any of the other forms know. Hilary knew that the upper third had had a midnight feast already that term, and it had been a great success. She meant to make theirs even more of a success!

Miss Roberts couldn't think why the first-form girls were so restless. As for Mam'zelle, she sensed the underlying excitement at once, and grew excited too.

"Ah, now, *mes petites*, what is the matter with you today!" she cried, when one girl after another made a mistake in the French translation. "What is in your thoughts? You are planning something – is it not so? Tell me what it is."

"Oh, Mam'zelle, whatever makes you think such a thing!" cried Janet. "What should we be planning?"

"How should I know?" said Mam'zelle. "All I know is that you are not paying attention. "Now, one more mistake and I send you to bed an hour earlier than usual!"

Mam'zelle did not mean this, of course – but it tickled the girls, who were all longing for bedtime that night, and would have been quite pleased to go early. Janet giggled and was nearly sent out of the room.

At last bedtime came, and every one undressed.

"Who's going to get the stuff out of the cupboard?" said Pat.

"You and I and Hilary and Isabel," said Janet. "And for goodness' sake don't drop anything. If you drop the pork-pie on the linoleum there *will* be a mess."

Every one laughed. They snuggled down into bed. They all wanted to keep awake, but it was arranged that some of them should take it in turns to sit up and keep awake for half an hour, waking the next girl when it was her turn. Then, at midnight, they should all be awakened and the Feast would begin!

First Janet sat up in bed for half an hour, hugging her knees, and thinking of all the things in the cupboard outside. She was not a bit sleepy. She switched on her torch to look at the time. The half-hour was just up. She leaned across to the next bed and awoke Hilary.

At midnight every one was fast asleep except for the

girl on watch, who was Pat. As she heard the big clock striking from the west tower of the school, Pat crept out of bed. She went from girl to girl, whispering in her ear and shaking her.

"Hilary! It's time! Wake up! Isabel! It's midnight! Joan! The Feast is about to begin. Kathleen! Kathleen! Do wake up! It's twelve o'clock!"

At last every girl was awake, and with many smothered giggles, they put on their dressing-gowns and slippers.

The whole school was in darkness. Pat lighted two candles, and placed them on a dressing-table in the middle of the dormitory. She had sent Isabel to waken the rest of the form in the next dormitory, and with scuffles and chuckles all the girls crept in. They sat on the beds nearest to the candles, and waited whilst Pat and the others went to get the things out of the cupboard.

Pat took her torch and shone it into the cupboard whilst the others took out the things. A tin of sweetened milk dropped to the floor with a crash. Every one jumped and stood stock still. They listened, but there was no sound to be heard – no door opened, no one switched on a light.

"Idiot!" whispered Janet to Isabel. "For goodness' sake don't drop that chocolate cake. Where did that tin roll to? Oh, here it is."

At last all the eatables were safely in the dormitory, and the door was shut softly. The girls looked at everything, and felt terribly hungry.

"Golly! Pork-pie and chocolate cake, sardines and Nestlé's milk, chocolate and peppermint creams, tinned pineapple and ginger-beer!" said Janet. "Talk about a feast! I bet this beats the upper third's feast hollow! Come on – let's begin. I'll cut the cake."

Soon every girl was munching hard and thinking that food had never tasted quite so nice before. Janet took

"Talk about a feast!" said Janet

an opener and opened a ginger-beer bottle. The first one was quite all right and Janet filled two tooth-glasses. But the next ginger-beer bottle fizzed out tremendously and soaked the bed that Janet was sitting on. Everyone giggled. It went off with a real pop, and sounded quite loud in the silence of the night.

"Don't worry! No one will hear that," said Janet. "Here, Pat – open the sardines. I've got some bread and butter somewhere, and we'll make sandwiches."

The bread and butter was unwrapped from its paper. Janet had brought it up from the tea-table! Every girl had taken a piece from the plate at tea-time, and hidden it to give to Janet.

"Look – take a bite of a sardine sandwich, and then a bite of pork-pie, and then a spoonful of Nestlé's milk," said Pat. "It tastes gorgeous."

The chocolate was saved till last. By that time the girls were all unable to eat any more and could only suck the sweets and the chocolate. They sat about and giggled at the silliest jokes.

"Of course, the nicest thing of the whole feast was Kathleen's marvellous cake," said Hilary. "The almond icing was gorgeous."

"Yes – and I had one of the sugar roses," said Joan. "Lovely! However much did you pay for that cake, Kath? It was jolly decent of you."

"Oh, that's nothing," said Kathleen. "I'm most awfully glad you liked it."

She looked very happy. There had not been quite enough cake to go round and Kathleen hadn't even tasted the marvellous cake. But she didn't mind at all. She sat quite happily watching the others feast on it.

Then the girls began to press Doris to do her clown-dance. This was a dance she had learnt during the holidays at some special classes, and it was very funny. Doris was full of humour and could make the others laugh very easily. The clown dance was most ridiculous, because Doris had to keep falling over herself. She accompanied this falling about with many groans and gurgles, which always sent the audience into fits of laughter.

"Well, don't laugh too loudly this time," said Doris, getting up. "You made such a row last time I did it in the common room that Belinda Towers came in and ticked me off for playing the fool."

She began the dance with a solemn face. She fell over the foot of the bed, on purpose of course, and rubbed herself with a groan. The girls began to chuckle, their hands over their mouths.

Doris loved making people laugh. She swayed about, making comical faces, then pretended to catch one leg in another, and fell, clutching at Pat with a deep groan.

With a giggle Pat fell too, and knocked against the dressing-table. The table shook violently, and everything on it slid to the floor! Brushes, combs, photograph frames, tooth-mugs, a ginger-beer bottle – goodness, what a crash!

The girls stared in horror. The noise sounded simply terrific!

"Quick! Clear everything up and get into bed," cried Janet, in a loud whisper. "Golly! We'll have half the mistresses here."

The girls belonging to the next dormitory fled out of the door at once. The others cleared up quickly, but very soon heard the sound of an electric light being switched on in the passage.

"Into bed!" hissed Hilary, and they all leapt under the sheets. They pulled them up to their chins and lay listening. Hilary remembered that they had left two ginger-beer bottles out in the middle of the floor – and they hadn't had time to clear up the remains of the pork-pie either. Pork-pies were so untidy, and *would* scatter themselves in crumbs every time a bite was taken!

The door opened, and some one was outlined against the light from the passage outside. Pat saw who it was – old Kenny! What bad luck! If she discovered anything she would be sure to report it after the bad behaviour of the form. But perhaps she wouldn't switch on the dormitory light.

Miss Kennedy stood listening. One of the girls gave a gentle snore, making believe that she was fast asleep – but that was too much for Kathleen, who was already very strung up. She gave a smothered giggle, and Miss Kennedy heard it. She switched on the light.

The first thing she saw were the two ginger-beer bottles standing boldly in the middle of the floor. Then she saw the remains of the pork-pie. She saw the paper from the chocolate. She guessed immediately what the girls had been up to.

A little smile came over her face. What monkeys girls were! She remembered the thrill of a midnight feast herself – and how she and the others had been caught and severely punished. She spoke in a low voice to Hilary, the head of the dormitory.

"Hilary! Are you awake?"

Hilary dared not pretend. She answered in a sleepy voice. "Hallo, Miss Kennedy! Is anything wrong?"

"I thought I heard a noise from this dormitory," said Miss Kennedy. "I'm in charge of it tonight as Miss Roberts isn't here. But I may have been mistaken."

Hilary sat up in bed and saw the ginger-beer bottles. She glanced at Miss Kennedy and saw a twinkle in her eye.

"Perhaps you *were* mistaken, Miss Kennedy," she said. "Perhaps – perhaps – it was mice or something."

"Perhaps it *was*," said Miss Kennedy. "Er – well, I don't see that there's anything to report to Miss Roberts – but as you're head of the dormitory, Hilary, you might

see that it's tidy before Matron goes her rounds tomorrow morning. Good night."

She switched off the light, shut the door and went
back to her room. The girls all sat up in bed at once
and began to whisper.

"My goodness! Kenny's a sport!'

"Golly! She saw those awful ginger-beer bottles all
right! And fancy agreeing that that terrific noise we
made might have been *mice*!"

"And she as good as said we were to remove all traces
of the feast, and she promised not to report anything to
Miss Roberts."

"Though old Roberts is a sport too, in her way," said
Doris.

"Yes, but we're in her bad books at the moment,
don't forget, and anything like this would just about
finish things!" said Isabel. "Good old Kenny!"

9   A LACROSSE MATCH –
AND A PUZZLE

The only bad effects of the Great Midnight Feast, as it
came to be called, were that Isabel, Doris and Vera
didn't feel at all well the next day. Miss Roberts eyed
them sharply.

"What have you been eating?" she asked.

"Only what the others have," answered Doris, quite
truthfully.

"Well, go to Matron and she'll dose you," said
Miss Roberts. The three girls went off dolefully. Matron had some most disgusting medicine. She dosed the
girls generously and they groaned when she made them
lick the spoon round.

Then Joan and Kathleen felt ill and they were sent to
Matron too.

"I know these symptoms," said Matron. "You are suffering from Midnight Feast Illness! Aha! You needn't pretend to me! If you *will* feast on pork-pies and sardines, chocolate and ginger-beer in the middle of the night, you can expect a dose of medicine from me the next day."

The girls stared at her in horror. How did she know?

"Who told you?" asked Joan, thinking that Miss Kennedy had told tales after all.

"Nobody," said Matron, putting the cork back firmly into the enormous bottle. "But I haven't been Matron of a girls' school for twenty-five years without knowing a *few* things! I dosed your mother before you, Joan, and your aunt too. They couldn't stand midnight food any more than you can. Go along now – don't stare at me like that. I shan't tell tales – and I always say there's no need to punish girls for having a midnight feast, because the feelings they get the next day are punishment enough!"

The girls went away. Joan looked at Kathleen. "You know, I simply loved the pork-pie and the sardines last night," she said, gloomily, "but the very thought of them makes me feel sick today. I don't believe I'll ever be able to look a sardine in the face again."

But every one soon forgot their aches and pains, and the feast passed into a legend that was told throughout the school. Even Belinda Towers heard about it and chuckled when she was told how everything fell off the dressing-table at the last.

It was Kathleen who told Belinda. It was rather strange how Kathleen had altered during the last few weeks. She was no longer nervous and apologetic to every one, but took her place happily and laughed and joked like the rest. She could even talk to tall Belinda Towers without stammering with nervousness! She was waiting on Belinda that week, and rushed about quite

happily, making toast, running errands and not even
grumbling when Belinda sent for her in the middle of
a concert rehearsal.

Kathleen was to play in an important lacrosse match
that week, and so was Isabel. They were the only first-
form girls chosen – all the others were second-
formers. At first Pat had been by far the better of the
two, but Isabel soon learnt the knack of catching and
throwing the ball in the easiest way, and had out-
stripped her twin. The match was to be against the
second form of a nearby day school, and the girls were
very keen about it.

"Kathleen's goalkeeper," said Pat to Isabel. "Belinda
told her today. I say, isn't Kath different? I quite like
her now."

"Yes – and she's so generous!" said Isabel. "She
bought some sweets yesterday and shared the whole lot
round without having even one herself. And she
bought some chrysanthemums for Vera – they must
have cost a lot!"

Vera was in the sick-bay, recovering from a bad cold.
She had been very surprised and touched when Kathleen
had taken her six beautiful yellow chrysanthemums. It
was so unlike Kathleen, who had always been rather
mean before.

Kathleen got Isabel to practise throwing balls into
the goal, so that she might get even better at stopping
them. She was very quick. Then she and Isabel practised catching and throwing the ball and running with it
and dodging each other.

"If only, only I could shoot two or three goals on Saturday," Isabel said a dozen times a day. Hilary laughed.
Isabel asked her why.

"I'm laughing at *you*," said Hilary. "Who turned up
her nose at lacrosse a few weeks ago? You did! Who
said there wasn't any game worth playing except

hockey? You did! Who vowed and declared she would never try to be any good at a silly game like lacrosse? You did. That's why I'm laughing! I have to sit and hear you raving about lacrosse now, talking it all day long. It sounds funny to me."

Isabel laughed too, but she went rather red. "I must have seemed rather an idiot," she said.

"You *were* a bit of a goof," said Janet, joining in. "The stuck-up twins! That's what we used to call you."

"Oh," said Isabel, ashamed. She made up her mind to play so well on Saturday that her whole form would be proud of her. The stuck-up twins! What a dreadful name! She and Pat must really do something to make the form forget that.

Saturday came, a brilliantly fine winter's day. The first form were excited. The girls from the day-school were coming to lunch and they had to entertain them. Dinner was to be sausages and mashed potatoes, with treacle pudding to follow, a very favourite meal.

"Now look here, Isabel and Kathleen, just see you don't eat too much," ordered Hilary. "We want you to play your best. You're the only ones from the first form who are playing – all the rest are second-formers. We'll stuff the other school all right – give them so much to eat that they won't be able to catch a ball!"

"Oh, I say! Can't I have two sausages?" said Isabel in dismay. "And I always have two helpings of treacle pudding."

"Well, you won't today," said Janet, firmly. "But if you play well and we win, the whole form will stand you cream-buns at tea-time. See?"

So Isabel cheered up and went without a second helping of treacle pudding quite amiably. It was a pleasant lunch. The guests were all jolly, friendly girls, and how they laughed when they were told the story of the Great Feast!

"We can't have fun like that," said one of the day-girls. "We always go home at night. What's your lacrosse team like? Any good? We've beaten you each time we've played you so far."

"And I bet we'll beat them again," cried the captain, a tall girl with flaming red hair.

"Cream-buns for you if you stop their goals, Kathleen!" cried Janet, and every one laughed.

All the first, second and third forms turned out to watch the match. The fourth form were playing a match of their own away from home, and the sixth rarely bothered to watch the juniors. Some of the fifth turned up, among them Belinda Towers, who arranged all the matches and the players, for she was sports-captain, and very keen that St. Clare's should win as many matches as possible.

The players took their places. Isabel was tremendously excited. Kathleen was quite cool and calm in goal. The match began.

The day girls made a strong team, and were splendid runners. They got the ball at once, and passed it from one to another whenever they were tackled. But Isabel jumped high into the air and caught the ball as it flew from one day girl to another!

Then she was off like the wind, racing down the field. A girl came out to tackle and tried to knock the ball off Isabel's net – but Isabel jerked it neatly over her head into the waiting net of another St. Clare girl – and she was off down the field too. Isabel sped behind – and caught the ball again neatly as the other girl threw it when tackled.

But a very fast girl was after Isabel and took the ball from her. Back the other way raced the day-girl, making for the goal. She passed the ball to another girl, who passed it to a third – and the third one shot straight at the goal, where Kathleen stood on guard. Swift as lightning Kathleen put her net down towards the ball, caught it and threw it to Isabel who was waiting not far off.

"Jolly well saved, Kathleen!" roared every one of the St. Clare girls, and Kathleen went red with excitement and delight.

So the match went on till half-time, when lemon quarters were taken round on plates to all the hot and panting players. How they loved sucking the cool sour lemon!

"The score is three-one," said the umpire. "Three to the day-girls of St. Christopher's and one to St. Clare's."

"Play up, St. Clare's!" cried Belinda. "Play up. Now, Isabel, score, please!"

The second half of the match began. The players were not quite so fast now, for they were tired. But the excitement ran very high, especially when St. Clare's shot two goals in quick succession, one of them thrown by Isabel.

Kathleen hopped about on one leg as the play went on down the other end of the field. She had saved seven goals already. Down the field raced the players, the ball flying from one to another with grace and ease. Kathleen stood tensely, knowing that a goal would be tried.

The ball came down on her, hard and swift. She tried to save the goal, but the ball shot into the corner of the net. Goal! Four-three – and only five minutes to go!

Then St. Clare's scored a most unexpected goal in the next two minutes and that made the score equal.

"Only one and a half minutes more!" panted Isabel to a St. Clare girl as she passed her the ball. "For goodness' sake, let's get another goal and win!"

The ball came back to her. A day girl thundered down on Isabel, a big, burly girl. Isabel swung round and dodged, the ball still in her net. She passed it to another girl, who neatly passed it back as soon as she was tackled. And then Isabel took a look at the goal, which, although a good way away, was almost straight in front. It was worth a shot!

She threw the ball hard and straight down the field. The goalkeeper stood ready – but somehow she missed the ball and it rolled into the net, just before the whistle went for time! How the St. Clare girls cheered! Pat leapt up and down like a mad thing, Belinda yelled till she was hoarse, and Hilary and Janet thumped one another on the back, though neither of them quite knew why!

"Good old Isabel! She saved the match just in time!" cried Pat. "Cream-buns for her!"

Hot and tired and happy, all the girls trooped off the field to wash and tidy themselves before tea. Janet ran to get her purse to rush off on her bicycle to buy the cream-buns.

But her purse only had a few pence inside! How strange! Janet knew quite well that it had had five shillings in it that very morning – and she certainly hadn't spent any of it.

"I say! My money's gone!" she said in dismay. "I can't get the cream-buns. Dash! Where's it gone?"

"Funny," said Isabel. "Mine went a little while ago – and so did Hilary's. Now yours has gone."

"Well, don't discuss it now," said Joan. "We've got to entertain the day-girls. But it's a pity about the cream-buns."

"*I'll* buy them!" said Kathleen. "I'll give you the money, Janet."

"Oh, no!" said Janet. "We wanted to buy them for you and Isabel because you did so well in the match. We can't let you buy them for yourselves!"

"Please do," said Kathleen, and she took some money from her pocket. "Here you are. Buy buns for every one!"

"Well – it's jolly decent of you," said Janet, taking the money. "Thanks awfully." She sped off on her bicycle whilst the other girls got ready for tea.

"Well played, kids," said Belinda Towers, strolling up. "You stopped some pretty good goals, Kathleen – and you just about saved the match, Isabel, though all the rest did jolly well too."

Every one glowed at the sports-captain's praise. Then they sat down to tea, and soon the big piles of bread and butter and jam, currant buns and chocolate cake disappeared like magic. Janet was back in a few minutes with a large number of delicious-looking cream-buns. The girls greeted them with cheers.

"Thanks, Kathleen! You're a brick, Kathleen!" everyone cried, and Kathleen beamed with delight.

"Well, I *did* enjoy today!" said Isabel to Pat, as they went off to the common room together, after seeing the day-girls off. "Simply marvellous! Every bit of it."

"Not quite every bit," said Pat, rather gravely. "What about Janet's money? Somebody took that, Isabel. And that's pretty beastly. Who in the world could it be?"

"I simply can't imagine," said Isabel.

Neither could anyone else. The girls talked about it together, and wondered who had been near Janet's coat. She had hung it on a peg in the sports pavilion, and most of the first and second form had been in and out. But surely, surely no St. Clare girl could possibly do such a thing!

"It's stealing, just plain stealing," said Hilary. "And it's been going on for some time too, because I know others besides myself and Janet and Isabel have lost money. Belinda lost ten shillings too. She made an awful row about it, but she never found it."

"Could it be one of the maids?" said Joan.

"Shouldn't think so," said Hilary. "They've been here

for years. Well – we must all be careful of our money, that's all, and, if we can't *find* the thief, we'll make it difficult for her to *be* one!"

10   A VERY MUDDLED GIRL

One afternoon Rita George, one of the big girls, sent for Kathleen to give her some instructions about a nature ramble she was getting up. Kathleen was head of the nature club in her form. She asked Pat to finish winding the wool that Isabel was holding for her, and ran off.

"Shan't be long," she said, and disappeared. Pat wound the wool into balls and then threw them into Kathleen's work-basket. She looked at her watch.

"I hope Kath won't be long," she said. "We are due for gym. in five minutes. I'd better go and remind her. Coming, Isabel?"

The twins went out, and made their way to Rita's study, meaning to see if Kathleen was still there. But when they arrived outside they stood still in dismay.

Some one was sobbing and crying inside! Some one was saying, "Oh, please forgive me! Oh, please don't tell anyone! Please, please, don't!"

"Gracious! That's not Kathleen, is it?" said Pat, horrified. "What's happened?"

They did not dare to go in. They waited, hearing more sobs, pitiful, heartbroken sobs, and they heard Rita's rather deep voice, sounding very stern. They could not hear what she said.

Then the door opened and Kathleen came out, her eyes red, and her cheeks tear-stained. She sobbed under her breath, and did not see the twins. She hurried towards the stairs that led to her dormitory.

Pat and Isabel stared after her. "She's forgotten about gym.," said Pat. "I don't like to go to her in case she hates any one seeing her cry."

"Oh, let's go and comfort her," said Isabel. "We'll get into a row for being late for gym. – but it's awful to see any one in trouble like that and not see if we can help."

So they ran up the stairs to the dormitory. Kathleen was lying on her bed, her face buried in her pillow, sobbing.

"Kathleen! Whatever's happened?" asked Isabel, putting her hand on Kathleen's shoulder. Kathleen shook it off.

"Go away!" she said. "Go away! Don't come peeping and prying after me."

"We're not," said Pat, gently. "What's the matter? We're your friends, you know."

"You wouldn't be, if I told you what had happened," sobbed Kathleen. "Oh, do go away. I'm going to pack my things and leave St. Clare's! I'm going this very night!"

"Kathleen! Do tell us what's happened!" cried Isabel. "Did Rita tick you off for something? Don't worry about that."

"It's not the ticking off I'm worrying about – it's the thing I did to *get* the ticking off," said Kathleen. She sat up, her eyes swollen and red. "Well, I'll tell you – and you can go and spread it all round the school if you like – and every one can laugh and jeer at me – but I'll not be here!"

She began to cry again. Pat and Isabel were very much upset. Isabel slipped her arm round the sobbing girl. "All right – tell us," she said. "We won't turn on you, I promise."

"Yes, you will, yes you will! What I've done is so dreadful!" sobbed Kathleen. "You won't believe it! I hardly believe it myself. I'm – I'm – I'm a thief!"

"Kathleen! What do you mean?" asked Pat, shocked. Kathleen stared at her defiantly. She wiped her eyes with a hand that shook.

"*I* took all the money that's been missing!" she said. "Every bit of it – even your two shillings, Isabel. I couldn't bear never having any money of my own, and saying no when people wanted subscriptions, and not giving any nice birthday presents to any one, and being thought mean and selfish and ungenerous. I did so want to be generous to everybody, and to make friends. I do so love giving things and making people happy."

The twins stared at Kathleen in surprise and horror. They could hardly believe what she said. She went on, pouring out her troubles between her sobs.

"I haven't a mother to send me money as you and the other girls have. My father is away abroad and I only have a mean old aunt who gives me about a penny a week! I hated to own up to such a miserable bit of money – and then one day I found a shilling belonging to some one and I bought something for somebody with it – and they were so terribly pleased – and I was so happy. I can't tell you how dreadful it is to want to be generous and not to be able to be!"

"Poor Kathleen!" said Isabel, and she patted her on the shoulder. "Nobody would have minded at all if only you had told them you hadn't any money. We could all have shared with you."

"But I was too proud to let you do that," said Kathleen. "And yet I wasn't too proud to steal. Oh, I can't think how I did it now! I took Janet's money – and Hilary's – and Belinda's. It was all so easy. And this afternoon I – I – I . . ."

She began to cry so bitterly that the twins were quite frightened. "Don't tell us if you'd rather not," said Pat.

"Oh, I'll tell you everything now I've begun," said poor Kathleen. "It's a relief to tell somebody. Well, this

afternoon when I went to Rita's study, she wasn't there
– but I saw her coat hanging up and her purse sticking
out of it. And I went to it – and oh, Rita came
in quietly and caught me! And she's going to Miss
Theobald about it, and I shall be known all over the
school as a thief, and I'll be expelled and . . ."

She wept again, and the twins looked at one another
helplessly. They remembered all Kathleen's sudden
generosity – her gifts – the marvellous cake with sugar
roses on it – the fine chrysanthemums for Vera – and
they remembered too Kathleen's flushed cheeks and
shining eyes when she saw her friends enjoying the
things she had bought for them.

"Kathleen – go and wash your face and come down to
gym.," said Pat at last.

"I'm not going to," said Kathleen, obstinately. "I'm
going to stay here and pack. I don't want to see anybody
again. You two have been decent to me, but I know in
your heart of hearts that you simply despise me!"

"We don't, Kath dear," said Isabel. "We're terribly,
terribly sorry for you – and we do understand why you
did it. You so badly wanted to be generous – you
did a wrong thing to make a right thing, and that's never
any good."

"Please go, and leave me alone," said Kathleen.
"Please go."

The twins went out of the dormitory. Halfway to the
gym. Isabel stopped and pulled at Pat's arm.

"Pat! Let's go and find Rita if we can. Let's say what
we can for poor old Kathleen."

"All right," said Pat. The two of them went to Rita's
study, but it was empty. "Blow!" said Pat. "I wonder if
she's gone to Miss Theobald already."

"Well, come on – let's see," said Isabel. So to the
Head's room they went – and coming out of the door,
looking very grim indeed, was Rita George!

"What are you two kids doing here?" she said, and went on her way without waiting for an answer. Pat looked at Isabel.

"She's told Miss Theobald," she said. "Well – dare we go in and speak to the Head about it? I do really think Kathleen isn't an ordinary kind of thief – and if she gets branded as one, and sent away, she may really become one, and be spoilt for always. Come on – let's go in."

They knocked, and the Head called them to come in. She looked surprised to see them.

"Well, twins," she said. "What is the matter? You look rather serious."

Pat didn't quite know how to begin. Then the words came in a rush and the whole story came out about how Kathleen had stolen all the money, and why.

"But oh, Miss Theobald, Kathleen didn't spend a penny on herself," said Pat. "It was all for us others. She certainly took our money – but we got it back in gifts and things. She isn't just an ordinary, contemptible sort of thief. She's terribly, terribly upset. Oh, could you possibly do anything about it – not send her away – not let the school know? I'm quite sure Kathleen would try to repay every penny, and Isabel and I would help her all we could never to do such a thing again."

"You see, it was all because Kathleen got hardly any pocket-money and she was too proud to say so – and she hated to be thought mean and selfish because really she's terribly generous," said Isabel.

Miss Theobald smiled a very sweet smile at the earnest twins. "My dears," she said, "you tell me such a different story from Rita, and I'm so very glad to hear it. Rita naturally sees poor Kathleen as a plain thief. You see her as she is – a poor muddled child who wants to be generous and chooses an easy but a very wrong way. I am sure I would not have got any explanation from Kathleen, and I might have written to her aunt to take her away. And then I dread what might have happened to her, poor, sensitive child!"

"Oh, Miss Theobald! Do you mean that you will let Kathleen stay?" cried Pat.

"Of course," said the Head. "I must talk to her first, and get her to tell me all this herself. I shall know how to deal with her, don't worry. Where is she?"

"In her dormitory, packing," said Pat. Miss Theobald stood up. "I'll go to her," she said. "Now you go off to whatever lesson you are supposed to be at, and tell your teacher please to excuse your being late, but that you have been with me. And I just want to say this – I am proud of you both! You are kind and understanding, two things that matter a great deal."

Blushing with surprise and pleasure, the twins held open the door for Miss Theobald to go out. They looked at each other in delight.

"Isn't she a sport?" said Pat. "Oh, how glad I am we dared to come in and tell her. I believe things will be all right for Kath now!"

They sped off to gym., and were excused for being late. They wondered and wondered how Kathleen was getting on with Miss Theobald. They knew after tea when Kathleen, her eyes still red, but looking very much happier, came up to them.

"I'm not going," she said. "I'm going to stay here and show Miss Theobald I'm as decent as anyone else. She's going to write to my aunt and ask for a proper amount of pocket money to be paid to me – and I shall give back all the money I took – and start again. And if I can't be as generous as I'd like for a little while, I'll wait patiently till I can."

"Yes – and don't be afraid of owning up if you haven't got money to spare," said Pat. "Nobody minds that at all. That's just silly pride, to be afraid of saying when you can't afford something. Oh, Kath – I'm so glad you're not going. Isabel and I had just got to like you very much."

"You've been good friends to me," said Kathleen, squeezing their arms as she walked between them. "If ever I can return your kindness, I will. You *will* trust me again, won't you? It would be so awful not to be trusted. I couldn't bear that."

"Of course we'll trust you," said Pat. "If you go on like that I'll get a hundred pounds out of the bank and ask you to keep it for me! Don't be such a silly-billy!"

11   MISS KENNEDY AGAIN

The twins were really beginning to settle down well at St. Clare's. They were getting used to being in the lowest form instead of in the top one, and they were no longer called the "stuck-up twins". Mam'zelle had helped them a great deal with their French writing, and they had caught up with the rest of the form. Miss Roberts found that they had good brains and occasionally threw them a word of praise, which they treasured very much.

Kathleen was their firm friend. She really was a very generous-hearted girl, and although she now had no longer plenty of money to spend, she gave generously in other ways – mended Pat's stockings for her, stuck together a favourite vase of Mam'zelle's that got broken, and spent what time she could with Doris and Hilary when they had to go to the sick-room with "flu". She knew that she would never be dishonest again, and she held her head high and tried to forget the silly things she had done, which were now put right.

Miss Kennedy had a bit better time, for since she had been so nice over their Great Feast, the first-formers behaved better. But the second form were not so good. They had discovered that Miss Kennedy was terrified of cats, and it was perfectly astonishing the number of cats that appeared at times in the second-form classroom.

The second form found every cat they could lay hands on, and secreted them somewhere in the class-room before their history lesson. They had a big cupboard, and this was a good place to hide a cat.

One morning Miss Roberts was not well. She felt sure that she had "flu" coming, and she retired to bed, hoping to ward it off quickly. So poor Miss Kennedy had to tackle both first and second forms together. The first-formers went into the second-form classroom, as it was much bigger than theirs.

They entered in an orderly line. Miss Jenks, the second-form mistress, was there, and she gave them their places. "Now sit quietly till Miss Kennedy comes," she said, and went off to take needlework with another form.

As soon as she had gone, a perfect babel of noise broke out, and to the enormous astonishment of the first-formers, a large black cat was produced from the passage, where Tessie, a girl of the second form, had hidden the cat in a cupboard.

The cat was most amiable. It arched its back and purred, sticking its tail up in the air. The twins stared at it in surprise.

"Why the cat?" asked Pat. "Is it a member of your class, by any chance?"

"Ha ha! Funny joke, I don't think," said Pam, stroking the cat. "No, Pat – It's just going to give old Kenny a fine surprise, that's all! Didn't you know she was terrified of cats? We're going to shut old Blackie up in our handwork cupboard over there – and then, at a good moment Tessie, who sits near, is going to pull the door open – and out will walk dear old Blackie, large as life and twice as natural – and he'll make straight for Kenny, you see if he doesn't!"

The first-formers began to giggle. This was marvellous – even better than fire-cracks!

"Sh! She's coming!" came a cry from the door, where some one was keeping guard. "To your places! Put the cat into the cupboard, quick, Tessie!"

The cat went into the cupboard with a rush, much to its amazement. The door was shut on it. Kathleen, who was passionately fond of animals, began to object.

"I say – can the cat breathe properly in there? Ought we to . . ."

"Shut up!" hissed Tessie, and at that moment in walked Miss Kennedy, her pile of books under her arm. She smiled at the girls and sat down. She felt very nervous, for she did not like handling two forms at once. Also she felt something was in the air, and did not like the one or two chuckles that she heard from the back row. Her book dropped to the floor and she bent to pick it up – and her belt snapped undone, and flew off.

This really wasn't very funny, but it seemed most humorous to the girls in the front row, and they bent over their books, trying not to laugh. Miss Kennedy knew that they were laughing and she determined to be firm for once.

"Any girl who disturbs the class by laughing or playing will stand the whole of the time," she announced in as firm a voice as she could. Every one was astonished to hear the mild Miss Kennedy make such a statement, and for a while the lesson went smoothly.

Tessie was to let the cat out about half-way through the class – but the cat thought otherwise. It had lain down on the handwork, and had got itself mixed up with the coloured raffia that was used by the girls for their basket-making. It tried to lick the raffia off its back legs, but couldn't.

It stood up and shook itself. It turned round and round – but the more it turned, the more entangled it got, and at last it became frightened.

It jumped about on the shelf, and some curious noises came from the cupboard. At first Miss Kennedy could not imagine what the noise was. The girls knew quite well that it was the cat, and they bent their heads over their exercise books, doing their best not to laugh.

The cat got excited. It leapt into the air and knocked its head against the shelf above. Then it scrabbled about and bit savagely at the entangling raffia.

"What *is* in that cupboard?" said Miss Kennedy at last.

"The handwork, Miss Kennedy," answered Tessie.

"I know that," answered Miss Kennedy, impatiently. "But handwork doesn't make a noise. What *can* be causing all that disturbance? It must be mice."

It certainly wasn't mice. It was just poor old Blackie going completely mad. He tore round and round the big shelf, the raffia catching his legs all the time. The whole class began to giggle helplessly.

"This is too much!" said Miss Kennedy, angrily. She walked quickly to the handwork cupboard and flung open the door. Blackie was thrilled, and leapt out with an enormous yowl. Miss Kennedy gave a shriek when she saw the big black animal springing out, and she rushed to the door. Blackie went with her, thinking she was going to let him out. He rubbed against her ankles and Miss Kennedy went white with fright, for she really was quite terrified of cats.

Blackie and Miss Kennedy went out of the door together, parted, and fled in opposite directions. The girls put down their heads on their desks and almost sobbed with laughter. Tears trickled out of Kathleen's eyes, and as for the twins, they had to hold their sides, for they each got dreadful stitches with laughing so much.

Tessie staggered to the door and shut it, in case any other mistress came by. For at least five minutes the girls let themselves go and laughed till they cried. As soon as they stopped, some one started them off again.

"Oh, I say – *did* you see Blackie when he shot out?" cried Tessie, and every one giggled again.

"It must be mice!" said Doris, imitating Miss Kennedy's voice. Shrieks of laughter again.

"Sh!" said Tessie, wiping her eyes. "Some one will hear us. I say – I wonder what's become of old Kenny? She disappeared into the blue. Do you suppose she'll come back and finish the lesson?"

But no Miss Kennedy came back. She was sitting in one of the empty common rooms, drinking a glass of water, and looking very pale. She was afraid of cats as some people are afraid of beetles or bats – but that was not all that made her feel worried and ill. It was the thought of the girls playing the trick on her, knowing that she would so easily fall into the trap.

"I'm absolutely no good at taking a class," thought Miss Kennedy, putting down her glass. "It was all very well when I coached one or two girls at a time – but this job is too much for me. And yet the money does come in so useful now. Mother is ill. Still, it's no use. I must give it up."

She decided to go down to the town and meet a friend of hers at tea-time. She would talk over the matter with her, then come back and give in her notice to Miss Theobald, confessing that she could neither teach nor keep discipline.

So down to the town she went at four o'clock, after telephoning to her friend, Miss Roper, to meet her at the tea-shop.

Miss Kennedy shrieked when she saw the cat

And to the same shop went the twins and Kathleen, having tea there by themselves as a great treat! The tea-shop was divided into little cosy partitions with red curtains, and the three girls were already sitting eating buttered buns when Miss Kennedy and Miss Roper came in.

They chose the partition next to the three girls, and sat down. The girls could not see them – but it was possible to hear the voices. And they recognized Miss Kennedy's at once!

"Listen! There's old Kenny! I bet she's going to talk about the black cat!" chuckled Kathleen. The girls had no intention of eavesdropping, but they could not help hearing what was said. And, as they thought, Kenny began to talk about the morning's happenings.

But she talked of something else too – of her old mother, ill and poor; of the money that her teaching had so unexpectedly brought in; of the bills she had to pay. She spoke with sadness of her failure to hold the girls in class.

"I'm a fraud," she told her friend. "I take the school's money for teaching the girls, and I don't teach them a thing, because I can't manage them, and they just rag me the whole time. Don't you think I should tell the head this, Clara? It's not honest of me to go on, leaving my classes because they rag me. Miss Lewis, the school's history specialist, can't possibly come back till the end of next term – but I don't see how I can honestly take her place till then."

"But you do so badly need the money to help your mother whilst she's ill," said Miss Roper. "It's bad luck, my dear – those girls must be wretches."

The three girls listened, stricken dumb. They were horrified. What seemed just teasing and ragging to them, meant losing a job to somebody else, meant being a failure – not being able to help a mother when she was ill.

"Let's go," muttered Pat, in a low voice. "We oughtn't to overhear this."

They crept out, unseen by Miss Kennedy, paid their bill and went back to school. They all felt unhappy. They couldn't let Miss Kennedy give up her post. She *was* a silly in many ways, but she was kind, and a real sport. And they, the girls, *were* wretches!

"Oh, dash, I do feel mean!" said Kathleen, sitting down in their common room. "I just hate myself now. I loved the joke this morning – but a joke's not a joke when it means real unhappiness to somebody else."

"We can't let Kenny go to Miss Theobald," said Pat, suddenly. "It would look awful. Look here – we've got to do something, for goodness sake. Think hard!"

Isabel looked up. "There's only one thing to do, really," she said. "We ought to get all our form to sign a letter, and the second form too, apologizing for the trick, and swearing we won't rag Kenny again. And we'll have to stick to that."

"That's not a bad idea at all," said Pat. "Kath, you go to the second form – they're having a meeting – and tell them quite shortly what's happened. I'll write out the letter – and each one of us can sign it."

Kathleen sped off. Pat took a pen and some notepaper, and she and Isabel wrote out the letter. This is what it said:

DEAR MISS KENNEDY,

We are all ashamed of our behaviour this morning, and we do ask you to accept our very humble apologies. We didn't mean the cat to jump out at you. Please forgive us. If you will, we promise never to rag you again, but to behave much better, and work hard. We thought

you were a great sport not to split on us about You
Know What.

Yours sincerely,

and then all the names of the girls were to follow, written
out by each girl.

The second form came in to sign their names.
"What's 'You Know What'?" asked Tessie, curiously.

"It's our Great Midnight Feast," answered Pat. "She
knew we had one and didn't tell. Now, has every one
signed? You haven't, Lorna. Put your name at the
bottom."

All the girls felt rather ashamed when they heard
Kathleen's tale of what they had overheard.

"You shouldn't really have listened," said Hilary, re-
provingly. "It's mean to overhear things."

"I know," said Pat. "But we really couldn't help it,
Hilary. And anyway, I'm glad we did. We can stop Kenny giving up her job, anyway."

It did prevent Miss Kennedy from going to Miss
Theobald when she came in that evening. She saw the
letter on her desk, and opened it. When she read it, the
tears came into her eyes.

"What a nice letter!" she thought. "The girls are not
little wretches after all! If only they keep their promise! I should be happy teaching them then!"

She thanked each form the next morning, and assured them that she forgave them. And, for the first
time that term, her lessons went as smoothly as those
of the other teachers, for the girls had no intention of
breaking their word.

There would be giggles now and then – sly flippings
of paper darts – but no organized ragging, and no un-
kindness. Kenny was happy. She taught well now that
she had no ragging to fight, and the girls became interested and keen.

"I'm glad we did the decent thing," said Pat, one day, after the history lesson. "I asked old Kenny how her mother was today, and she said she's much better, and is coming out of the nursing home tomorrow. Wouldn't it have been awful if she had died because we made Kenny lose her job so that her mother couldn't be nursed back to health?"

"*Awful*," agreed Isabel. And every one in the form thought the same.

12   A BROKEN WINDOW

One morning Hilary came into the common room most excited.

"I say! Did you know that the circus was coming to the field just outside the town? Well, it is! I saw the notices up!"

"Golly! I hope we're all allowed to go!" said Pat, who loved a circus.

"It's Galliano's Circus," said Hilary, and she pulled a handbill out of her pocket. "Look – clowns, acrobats, dancing horses, performing dogs, everything. If only Miss Theobald gives permission for the school to go!"

Miss Theobald did. She said that each evening two of the forms might go, with their teachers. The first form were thrilled. Pat, Isabel, Kathleen and Janet went down to the town to examine the big coloured posters pasted up everywhere.

They did look exciting. Then the girls went to see the big tents set up in the field. They leaned over the gate and watched the sleek satin-skinned horses being galloped round, and saw five clumsy-looking bears ambling along with their trainer. They watched in wonder when a big chimpanzee dressed up in trousers and jersey, came along hand in hand with a small boy, who had a terrier at his heels.

"Gracious! Look at that big monkey!" cried Isabel.

"Sammy's not a monkey. He's a chimpanzee," said the boy, smiling. "Shake hands, Sammy!"

The big chimpanzee solemnly held out his hand to the girls. Isabel and Kathleen were too afraid to take it, but Pat put out her hand at once. Sammy shook it up and down.

"Are you coming to see our show?" asked the boy.

"Rather!" said Pat. "Are you in the circus? What do you do?"

"I'm Jimmy Brown, and I go into the ring with my famous dog, Lucky. That's Lucky, just by your feet. She knows how to spell and count!"

"Oh, no! Dogs can't do that!" said Isabel.

Jimmy laughed. "Well, mine can. You'll see when you come! Look – see that girl over there, riding the black horse – that's Lotta. You'll see her in the ring too. She can ride the wildest horse in the world!"

The girls stared at Lotta. She was galloping round the field on a beautiful black horse. As she came near she suddenly stood up on the horse's back and waved to the astonished girls!

"Isn't she awfully clever!" said Pat. "How I wish I could ride like that! Doesn't she ever fall off?"

"Of course not," said Jimmy. "Well, I must go. Come on, Sammy. We'll look out for you four girls when you come to the show!"

He went off with the chimpanzee and the little dog. The girls made their way back to school. They were longing for the night to come when they might go to the circus with the first and second forms.

"There are two shows each night," said Pat. "One at 6.30 to 8.30, and the second at 8.45 to 10.45. I wish we were going to the later one – it would be sport getting back at eleven o'clock!"

"No such luck," said Isabel. "Come on, hurry – we shall be late for tea."

But a dreadful blow befell the first form the next morning. They came into their classroom, chattering as usual – and saw that one big pane of the middle window was completely broken! Miss Roberts was at her desk, looking stern.

"Gracious! How did the window get broken?" cried Janet in surprise.

"That is exactly what I would like to know," said Miss Roberts. "When I was in the common room I heard a crash, and came to see what caused it. I heard the sound of running feet going round the corner of the corridor – and when I came into the room I saw the broken window!"

"Who did it?" said Pat.

"I don't know," answered Miss Roberts. "But this is what broke the window." She held up a hard rubber lacrosse ball. "I found it still rolling across the floor when I came in. Somebody must have been playing with it in the classroom – and the window was smashed. It's against the rules to take lacrosse balls out of the locker in the gym, unless you go to games, as you know."

Every one listened in silence. They all felt a little guilty when Miss Roberts mentioned that it was against the rules to take lacrosse balls, because it was a rule nobody bothered to keep. Any girl slipped to the locker to borrow a ball to play with at break.

"Now," said Miss Roberts, "I want the girl who broke the window to own up now, or to come to me at break and tell me then. She should, of course, have stayed to own up as soon as the window was broken – but it is quite natural in a moment of fright to run away."

Nobody spoke. All the girls sat perfectly still in their

seats. Nobody looked at any one else. Miss Roberts looked searchingly along the rows, looking for a guilty face.

But as half the girls were blushing with sheer nervousness, that was no help. Practically all the class looked guilty and ill at ease. They always did when anything went wrong.

"Well," said Miss Roberts at last, "it is quite evident that the culprit is not going to own up now. She must come to me at break, without fail. All you girls have a sense of honour, I know, and not one of you is a coward. So I am quite sure that the culprit will be brave enough to come to me. I shall be in the common room, alone."

Still nobody said a word. One or two looked round at each other, and every one wondered who the sinner was. Pat and Isabel smiled nervously at each other. They had been together since breakfast, so they knew that neither of *them* was the sinner!

The first lesson began. It was maths. Miss Roberts was not in a good temper, and nobody dared to utter a word. Dark and fair heads were bent busily over books, and when the form-mistress rapped out an order it was obeyed at once. Every one knew how dangerous it would be to get into trouble when Miss Roberts was on the warpath.

After maths. came French. Mam'zelle came into the room, and exclaimed at the broken window.

"*Tiens!* The window is broken! How did that happen?"

"We don't know, Mam'zelle," said Hilary. "Nobody has owned up yet."

"That is abominable!" cried Mam'zelle, looking round the class with her big dark eyes. "It is not brave!"

The class said nothing. They all felt uncomfortable,

for it was not nice to think that somebody in the class
was a coward. Still, maybe the culprit would own up at
break. Whoever could it be?

Pat and Isabel thought hard. It couldn't be Janet or
Hilary, for both girls were brave-spirited and owned to a
fault at once. It couldn't be Kathleen, for she had been
with them. It might be Vera – or Sheila – or Joan – or
Doris. No, surely it couldn't be any of them! They
wouldn't be cowards.

At break the first form got together and discussed the
matter. "It wasn't *us*," said Pat. "Isabel and I were together all the time after breakfast till we went to the classroom. And Kathleen was with us too."

"Well, it wasn't *me*," said Hilary. "I was doing a
job for Rita."

"And it wasn't *me*," said Janet. "I was cleaning the
bird-table, and Doris was helping."

One by one the girls of the first form all said what
they had been doing between breakfast-time and the
first lesson. Apparently not one of them could have
broken the window – though one must be telling an un-
truth!

After break the girls took their places in their form
room. Miss Roberts came in, her mouth in a thin line
and her hazel eyes cold. She looked round the class.

"I am sorry to say that no one has owned up," she
said. "So I have had to report the matter to Miss Theobald. She agrees with me that the window must be paid
for by the whole class, as the culprit hasn't owned up.
The window is made of vita-glass, and will cost twenty
shillings to mend. Miss Theobald has decided instead
of letting you go to the circus, which would cost one
shilling each, she will use the money for the window."

There was a gasp of dismay from all the girls. Not
go to the circus! That was a terrible blow. They looked
round one another, angry and upset. Why should the

whole class suffer because one person had done a wrong thing? It didn't seem fair.

"I am sure that the one who broke the window will not want her whole class to be punished," went on Miss Roberts. "So I hope she will still own up, before the night comes when our form is due to go to the show – that is, on Thursday. And I trust that if any of you know who it is you will insist that she does her duty by her form."

"But Miss Roberts, suppose nobody owns up," began Hilary, "couldn't we all put a shilling of our own towards the window and still go to the circus?"

"No," said Miss Roberts. "There's no argument, Hilary. What I have said, stands, and will not be altered. Open your books at page eighty-two, please."

What a babel there was after morning school was over, in the quarter of an hour before dinner! How angry and indignant the girls were!

"It's a shame!" cried Janet. "I didn't do it – nor did you, Pat and Isabel – and we jolly well know it. So why should we be punished too?"

"Well, it's the custom in schools to make a whole form suffer for one person in a case like this," said Hilary. "They do it at my brother's school too – though it doesn't happen often. I don't see the point of it myself, but there you are. If only I knew who it was! Wouldn't I take them by the scruff of the neck and give them a shaking!"

"Look here – what about one of us owning up to it, so that the rest can go?" said Kathleen, suddenly. "I don't mind owning up and taking the blame. Then all you others can go."

"Don't be an idiot," said Pat, slipping her arm through Kathleen's. "As if we'd let you do a thing like that!"

"I suppose you *didn't* do it, Kath?" said Sheila, half-laughing.

"Of course she didn't!" cried Isabel. "She was with Pat and me all the time. It's jolly decent of her to offer to take the blame – but I wouldn't dream of it. If I heard she'd owned up to save our skins I'd go straight to Miss Roberts myself and tell her that Kathleen couldn't possibly have done it!"

"Oh, well," said Kathleen, "I shan't say anything, of course, if you feel like that about it. If only we knew which of us had done it!"

The whole of Tuesday slipped by and the whole of Wednesday. Still nobody had owned up. When Thursday came Miss Roberts informed the class that the second form were to go to the circus, but not the first. The class groaned and fidgeted.

"I'm very sorry," said Miss Roberts. "It's most unfortunate. I only hope that the culprit is feeling most unhappy and uncomfortable. Now, no more groaning, please. Let's get on with our geography!"

13   THE FOUR TRUANTS

That afternoon, after tea, four girls of the first form held a secret meeting in one of the little music rooms. They were the twins, and Kathleen and Janet. They were all furious because they were not allowed to go that night to the show in the town.

"Look here! *Let's* go!" said Janet. "We can slip off at a quarter past eight on our bikes without any one noticing, if we go down the path by the lacrosse field. And we can get back in the dark all right."

"But the school doors are locked at ten," said Kathleen.

"I know that, idiot!" said Janet. "But what's the matter with a ladder? There's one alongside the gardener's shed. We can easily get into our dormitory window with that."

"Yes – but the ladder will be seen the next morning, leading up to our window!" said Isabel.

"Oh, golly, haven't you *any* brains!" sighed Janet. *"One* of us can go up the ladder – and undo the side-door to let the others in – and we can all take the ladder back to the shed before we go in. Is that quite clear, or shall I say it all over again?"

Every one laughed. Janet was funny when she was impatient. "I see," said Pat. "But gosh, if we were caught! I don't like to think what would happen to us."

"Well, don't," said Janet, "because we *shan't* be caught! Miss Roberts never puts the light on at night when she comes to our dormitory now. We shall be all right. We must tell Hilary though. She won't come with us because she's head-girl and keeps all the rules – but she won't stop us going."

Hilary didn't stop them. "All right," she said. "Risk it if you want to. I won't stop you. But for goodness' sake don't get caught!"

The second form went off to the circus with Miss Jenks. The first form stayed behind, sulky and angry. Only the four who were going to slip off by themselves looked at all bright. Most of the first form knew what Janet had planned, but nobody else dared to risk it.

"You'll get expelled if you're caught, I shouldn't wonder," said Doris.

"We shan't be expelled and we shan't be caught," said Janet, firmly.

When the time came, the four girls put on their hats and coats and slipped down to the side-door. It was dark outside, but the night was clear. Coming home there would be a moon. They went softly to the bicycle shed.

"Golly! What a noise bikes make!" whispered Janet, as the four machines clanked and rattled. "Now – down the path by the field. Come on."

Off they all rode, their lamps shining in the darkness. When they arrived at the circus field they saw the people streaming out of the gates. They had been to the 6.30 performance.

"Look out! Hide by the hedge till every one's gone!" said Janet. "We don't want to run into Miss Jenks!"

They hid until it was safe. They pushed their bicycles behind the hedge and went to the gate, where people were already going in, under the flare of acetylene lamps. The girls paid and went towards the big circus tent. Soon they had taken their seats, well at the back in case any one saw them. They took off their school hats.

The circus was marvellous. They saw the girl Lotta, now dressed in a sparkling, shining frock, riding bareback round the ring, standing on her horse, kneeling, jumping, smiling all the time. They saw Jimmy and his dog Lucky, and could not imagine how he had been trained to be so clever. They cheered the absurd clowns and the amazing acrobats. They loved big Mr. Galliano, with his cracking whip and big moustaches. It was a gorgeous show and the four girls enjoyed every minute.

"We'd better slip out a bit before the end," whispered Janet, watching Sammy the chimpanzee solemnly undress himself and put on a pair of pyjamas. "I say – isn't he funny? Oh, look – he's getting into bed!"

Just before the show was finished the girls slipped out quietly. Everyone was intent on watching the five bears, who were now playing ring-a-ring-of-roses with their trainer.

"*All* fall down!" chanted the trainer, and just as the four girls went out, down fell the five bears in the ring, for all the world as if they were children!

"What a marvellous show!" said Janet, as they made their way to where they had left their bicycles. "Where's my bike? Oh, here it is."

They mounted their bicycles and rode off. The moon was up now and they could see clearly. They were soon back at the school. They put their bicycles into the shed as quietly as they could, and then, with beating hearts, they tiptoed to the shed, outside which the ladder was kept.

They all felt excited and nervous. Just suppose they were caught now! It would be awful. But nobody was about. A dim light showed from a mistress's bedroom in the eastern wing of the school. It was about eleven o'clock, and all the girls and some of the mistresses would be asleep.

They looked for the ladder. There were two, a small one and a much bigger one. Janet tugged at the smaller one.

"I should think this one will just about reach," she said. So the four of them carried it to where their dormitory windows shone in the moonlight. They kept in the dark shadows and were as quiet as they could be.

They set the ladder up gently against the wall – but to their great dismay it didn't nearly reach to the window-sill!

"Dash!" said Janet. "Look at that! It's much too dangerous to try and climb to the sill from the top of the ladder – it's so far below the window. Well – come on, let's take it back and get the other ladder. That's long enough to reach to the roof, I should think!"

They took the small ladder back and put it down gently. But then they found they could not possibly carry the big ladder! It was enormously heavy and needed two or three gardeners to handle it. The four girls could hardly move it and certainly would not be able to set it up against the wall.

They stood in the moonlight and stared at one another in dismay. "Now what are we going to do?" asked Isabel, her voice quivering. "We can't stay out here all night."

"Of course not, silly," said Janet. "We'll try all the doors. Maybe we'll find one that's unlocked. Cheer up."

So they tiptoed round the school, trying the doors, but every one of them was safely locked and bolted. The maids did their work well!

Kathleen began to cry. She did not want to be caught breaking the rules, because she had tried very hard to be in Miss Theobald's good books since she had been forgiven for her fault. It suddenly seemed a very dreadful thing to her to be out of doors when all the others were in bed and asleep.

"We shall be discovered in the morning," she whispered. "And we shall catch our deaths of cold staying out here."

"Shut up and don't be such a baby," said Janet fiercely.

"I know what we can do! We'll throw little pebbles up to our dormitory window!" said Pat. "They will make a rattling noise and maybe one of the girls will wake. Then she can slip down and open a door for us."

"Good idea!" said Janet. "Pick up tiny pebbles, every one!"

They scooped handfuls up from the gravel, and threw them up. But Kathleen threw very badly and her pebbles rattled against the wrong window – the one above the dormitory, where Mam'zelle slept! And Mam'zelle awoke!

"Quick! Back into the shadows!" whispered Janet, urgently. "Idiot – you hit Mam'zelle's window!"

The big dark head of Mam'zelle looked out, and they heard her mutter to herself. They squeezed together in a corner, hardly daring to breathe, terrified that Mamzelle would see them. But the shadows were black and she could see nothing. Puzzled, and yawning deeply, she went back to her bed. The girls stayed where they were for a few minutes and then began to whisper.

"This is awful! Really awful. What *are* we going to do?"

"I do wish we hadn't slipped off to the circus!"

"I'm so cold my teeth are chattering."

Then Pat clutched hold of Isabel's arm and whispered loudly. "Look – look – isn't that some one looking out of our dormitory window?"

They all looked up – and sure enough a girl's head was peeping from the window. Pat slipped out of the shadows and stood in the moonlight. Hilary's voice came down to her in a whisper.

"Pat! How late you are! Where are the others?"

"Here," whispered Pat. "The ladders aren't any good. Open the side-door here and let us in, Hilary, quick! We're so cold."

Hilary drew in her head and disappeared. A minute later the four girls heard the key turning in the lock of the side-door, and the bolts being slipped back – and the door was open! They crept in quietly and Hilary locked and bolted the door once more.

They all slipped upstairs like mice, and tip-toed in their stockinged feet to their dormitory. Once there they sank on to Janet's bed and began to giggle from sheer excitement and relief.

They told Hilary all that had happened, Doris woke up and joined the little group. The four truants began to feel much better now that they were safe, and boasted of all they had done.

"Did you hear our pebbles rattling on the window?" asked Janet of Hilary. "Why did you come to the window? Golly, wasn't I glad to hear your voice?"

"Your pebbles came rattling on to the floor!" said

Hilary, with a laugh. "The window was open at the bottom. I left it like that for you to climb in. When I heard the sound of pebbles all over the lino I woke up. At first I couldn't imagine what the noise was – then I switched on my torch and saw the bits of gravel. We'll have to sweep those up in the morning."

Janet yawned. "I'm so tired," she said. "The circus was marvellous. I wish you could have seen it, Hilary."

"So do I," said Hilary. "Buck up and get undressed now, for goodness' sake. And don't make too much noise or you'll wake Mam'zelle. Her room's just above, remember."

"We know that all right!" said Pat, giggling as she remembered Mam'zelle's dark head sticking out of the window. "Where's my nightie? Oh, blow, where's it gone?"

"You won't find it on *my* bed, silly," said Isabel, who was already undressed and in her nightgown. "You've got muddled. That's your bed, over there, and there's your nightie on the pillow."

"Oh, yes," said Pat, yawning. "I wish I could go to sleep in my clothes!"

Soon all the dormitory was quiet once more, and every girl was asleep. The four truants slept peacefully – but there was a shock in store for them in the morning!

14   A GREAT DISAPPOINTMENT

The four truants were extremely sleepy the next day. They could hardly wake up. When the dressing-bell went not one of them got out of bed.

"Hi, Janet! Kathleen! Aren't you going to get a move on?" cried Hilary. "You'll be late. And just look at those lazy twins – they haven't even opened their eyes!"

"Another five minutes!" murmured Pat, sleepily. But the five minutes stretched into ten, and still the four girls hadn't moved. Hilary winked at Doris, and the two of them went swiftly to the four white beds and stripped off all the bedclothes, throwing them on the floor.

"Oooooh!" shivered the girls, for it was a very cold morning. "You mean things!"

"Come on, get up, or you'll get into a row," said Hilary. And, very slowly and sleepily the four dressed, yawning all the time. They cheered up a bit when the rest of the form clustered round them, asking what happened the night before. They really felt almost heroines as they related their exciting adventures.

"I don't feel in the least like lessons this morning," said Janet. "Oh, my goodness – Miss Roberts is taking us for algebra, isn't she? I always am stupid about that anyhow, and I shan't be able to understand a thing today. I hope she's in a good temper."

The class went into their form room, and took their places. Janet got out her algebra book and hurriedly glanced through the chapter she had been told to learn. It seemed to her as if she had entirely forgotten every word! But that was just because she had had such a short night.

"Here comes Miss Roberts!" hissed Doris, who was at the door. The girls stood. Miss Roberts came in – and goodness, whatever could have happened! She looked very pleased, and her eyes sparkled so that she looked really pretty.

"Sit, girls," she said, and the girls sat down, wondering why their mistress looked so pleased. Had they done some marvellous prep. or something?

"Girls," said Miss Roberts, "I feel very happy about something this morning. I have found out that it was not any one in my form who broke the window!"

The girls looked at her, amazed. Miss Roberts smiled round the class.

"It was one of the second form," she said. "Apparently the ball bounced in here, the girl rushed for it, tried to catch it, and it was knocked on to the window, which broke."

"But why didn't she own up?" cried Hilary, indignantly. "That was jolly mean of her! We missed going to the circus because of that."

"Wait," said Miss Roberts. "The girl was Queenie Hobart, who, as you know, is now in the sick-room with a bad attack of 'flu'. She was frightened when she broke the window, but meant to own up at the end of the morning. In the middle of the morning she was taken ill and was hurried off to the sick-room where she has been really ill for a few days. Today she is better, and her form-mistress, Miss Jenks, went to see her."

"Did she own up then?" asked Janet.

"Miss Jenks told her that the second form had gone to the circus the night before, but not the first form, and Queenie asked why," said Miss Roberts. "When she heard that you had all been punished for something that was her fault, she was very upset and began to cry. She told Miss Jenks, of course, and Miss Jenks came hurrying to tell me."

"Oh! I *am* glad it wasn't anybody in our form," said Hilary. "I did hate to think that somebody was such a mean coward!"

"And I couldn't understand it either," said Miss Roberts. "I think I know you all pretty well – and although you are sometimes very stupid, aggravating and, in fact, a set of nuisances – I really couldn't believe that any of you were cowards!"

Miss Roberts smiled as she made these remarks, and the class laughed. They were all most relieved.

"Can we go to the circus after all, then?" asked Hilary.

"There's still tonight or tomorrow."

"Of course," said Miss Roberts. "You are to go to morrow, Miss Theobald says – and to make up for your disappointment, which was quite undeserved, I am to take you down into the town and give you a real good tea first! What do you think of that?"

The girls thought a lot of it! They said "Oooh" and "Ah!" and rubbed their hands together, and looked as cheerful as possible. Tea first – a really scrumptious tea – and then the circus – and it was sure to be good fun on the last night of all! What luck that Queenie had owned up in time!

But there were four girls who were feeling most un-comfortable about the whole thing – and they were the twins, and Kathleen and Janet. They had played truant and seen the show! They looked at one another and felt very guilty. Why hadn't they waited?

They went to Hilary about it afterwards. "Hilary! We feel awfully mean now somehow – do you think we ought to go tomorrow?" asked Pat.

"Well, if you don't, what excuse will you make?" said Hilary. "Since you ask me, I say you jolly well oughtn't to go! You've had your pleasure, by breaking the rules – well, every one breaks rules sometimes, so I'm not blaming you for that. The thing is, it's not fair that you should have a second treat. I should feel like that my-self, just as you do. But if you go and tell Miss Roberts why, you certainly will get into a first-class row."

"Could we say we don't feel well?" said Isabel. "I really don't feel awfully well today – I had so little sleep."

"Well, say that tomorrow," said Hilary. "But I say, it's bad luck on you, isn't it! You've done yourself out of a gorgeous tea, and every one knows that a Saturday night is the best night to see a show."

"I wish we hadn't been so impatient now," sighed

Kathleen. "I would so love to go with you tomorrow."

The four were very sad. They talked about it together. "Let's go anyhow!" said Janet. Then almost immediately she changed her mind. "No, we can't. I'd feel mean all the time. And the other girls would think us mean too."

"I only hope Miss Roberts doesn't send us to Matron for some of her disgusting medicine, when we tell her we don't feel well tomorrow," said Kathleen, who was a perfect coward over taking medicine.

But when the next day came there was no question of telling a story about feeling unwell – for all four girls had bad colds! They had caught a chill standing about waiting to get into the school on Thursday night – and how they sneezed and coughed!

Miss Roberts noticed at once. "You'd better spend a day in bed," she said. "You may be in for 'flu'. Go along to Matron and ask her to take your temperatures. Four of you at once! Wherever could you all have caught such bad colds?"

They didn't tell her. They went to Matron, feeling very sad and sorry. Kathleen had a temperature, and as Matron was not at all sure that the whole lot were not going to have "flu" she did the sensible thing and popped them all into bed. She gave them each a dose out of one of her enormous bottles, tucked them up, and left them in the sick-room together.

"A-tish-oo!" sneezed Kathleen. "Golly, weren't we idiots to rush off like that the other night. I do hate having a beastly cold like this."

"And missing that tea," sighed Pat. "Hilary said Miss Roberts had rung up the tea-shop and made sure that they had those special chocolate cakes we like."

"Well – it's no use grumbling!" said Isabel, sensibly. "We brought this on ourselves. Now shut up, you others. I want to read."

The first form went off at five with Miss Roberts and had a gorgeous tea. Miss Roberts bought four of the special chocolate cakes to take back to the girls in the sick-room.

"I think they have been perfect bricks about all this," she said to Hilary. "Not a grumble, not one word of complaint!"

Hilary said nothing. Miss Roberts would have been astonished if she had known the real reason why the four truants were not at the circus! But Hilary was certainly not going to tell her.

The circus was at its best that night – and afterwards the girls were allowed to go behind the ring and see the performers at close quarters. Sammy the chimpanzee was delighted to see them and kept taking off his cap to them most politely. Jumbo, the enormous elephant, blew down Hilary's neck and lifted her curls as if they had been blown by the wind! Lotta let them all stroke her magnificent horse, Black Beauty. Altogether, it was a marvellous evening, the girls went back tired, but very happy and talkative.

Miss Roberts slipped into the sick-room to see if the four girls were awake. Matron was just tucking them up for the night.

"There's nothing much wrong with them," she told Miss Roberts. "Kathleen's temperature is down to normal. They've just got ordinary bad colds, that's all. As tomorrow is Sunday I'll keep them in bed one more day."

"I've brought them some of the special chocolate cakes we always have at the tea-shop," said Miss Roberts. "I suppose they mustn't have them now."

"Oh, they can if they feel like it," said Matron, smiling. "It won't hurt them!"

All four girls felt like chocolate cakes immediately, and sat up. They thought it was jolly kind of Miss Roberts to think of them. They munched their cakes and listened to their teacher's recital of the evening's happenings.

"Didn't you think Sammy the chimpanzee was funny when he undressed himself and got into bed?" asked Kathleen eagerly, quite forgetting that Miss Roberts had no idea she had seen the circus. Miss Roberts stared in surprise.

"Kathleen saw the posters in the town," said Pat, hurriedly, glaring at the unfortunate Kathleen with rage.

"I think it's time the girls settled down now, Miss Roberts," said Matron, coming in, luckily for the four, at that very moment. Miss Roberts said good night at once, and went. They girls lay down, whilst Matron fussed round a bit, then turned out the light, and went.

"Idiot, Kathleen!" said Janet. "You nearly gave us all away!"

"Sorry," said Kathleen, sleepily. "I quite forgot!"

"No more talking!" said Matron, putting her head round the door. "Another word, and I'll come in and give you all a dose of my very nastiest medicine!"

And after that there wasn't a word!

15   A TERRIBLE QUARREL

The weeks went quickly by. Half-term came and went. The twins' mother came to see them at half-term and took them out in the car for the day. She was glad to see them looking so well and happy.

"Well, how are you getting on?" she asked. "I hope you're not finding St. Clare's quite as bad as you feared!"

The twins blushed. "It's not a bad school," said Pat.

"It's quite decent," said Isabel. Their mother smiled to herself. She knew the twins so well – and their few words meant that they liked St. Clare's and were happy.

Every week there were lacrosse matches. Sometimes they were played by the lower forms, sometimes by the upper. The twins became very keen indeed, and used to watch all the upper form matches with great enjoyment. They thought Belinda Towers was marvellous. She was as swift as the wind, and her catching was beautiful to watch.

"Do you remember how rude we were to her at the beginning of the term?" said Pat. "Golly, I wonder how we dared now!"

"We were awful idiots," said Isabel. "Honestly, I wonder how everyone put up with us!"

"Well, there's one person I simply *can't* put up with!" said Pat. "And that's Sheila Naylor. What *is* the matter with her? She's so awfully haughty and conceited – always talking about her marvellous home and the number of servants they keep, and her horse, and their three motor-cars. Always pushing herself forward and airing her opinions – which aren't worth twopence, anyway!"

Everyone found Sheila very trying indeed. She was always doing her best to impress people, and to make them think that she was wonderful. Actually she was a plain and ordinary girl, with rather bad manners, who didn't speak very well. All her clothes were good, and she went to no end of trouble to buy the best of everything – and yet she never brushed her hair really well, and if she could forget to wash her neck, she would!

The most impatient girl in the first form was Janet. She could not bear vanity, or conceit, and Sheila's airs and graces irritated her beyond words. She hadn't the patience to put up with Sheila, and usually Sheila knew this and kept out of her way.

One afternoon, just before tea, the first form were enjoying themselves in their common room. Pat put on the gramophone, and played the same record four times running. Janet looked up.

"For goodness' sake! Are you trying to learn that record by heart, Pat? Take it off and break it! If I have to hear it again I'll scream!"

"You didn't ought to talk like that," began Sheila, in a mincing voice – and Janet flung down her book in a rage.

"Hark at Sheila! 'Didn't ought to!' Good heavens, Sheila, where were you brought up? Haven't you learnt by now that decent people don't say 'Didn't ought to!' My goodness, you talk about your servants, and your Rolls Royce cars, your horse and your lake and goodness knows what – and then you talk like the daughter of the dustman!"

Sheila went very white. Pat hurriedly put on another record. Janet took up her book again, still angry, but rather ashamed. If Sheila had said nothing more, the whole thing might have blown over. But after a while Sheila raised her voice and addressed Janet.

"I'm sure that if my people knew that I had to put up with girls like *you*, Janet, they would never have sent me to St. Clare's," she began. "You've no manners at all, you . . ."

"Manners! *You* talk about manners!" raged Janet, flinging down her book again. "Good heavens! What about your own manners, I should like to know! You can begin to talk about other people's when you know how to wash your neck and brush your hair, and how to eat decently! And then you pretend you are too grand for us! Huh!"

Janet stamped out of the room. Sheila sat perfectly still, very pale. The twins glanced at her, and Pat put on yet another record, setting it at "Loud". What an awful quarrel!

After a while Sheila went out of the room. Pat switched off the gramophone. "Didn't she look awful?" she said to Isabel. "I wish Janet hadn't said all that. "It's true it's what we've all thought, and perhaps said to one another in joke – but its rather awful to blurt it all out like that."

"Well, it's partly Sheila's own silly fault," said Hilary. "If she wouldn't swank as she does, and try to make out she's someone marvellous, we wouldn't notice so easily the stupid things she does and says. I mean to say – if people swank about five different bathrooms, one pink, one blue, one green, one yellow and one mauve, and then don't trouble to wash their necks, you do notice it rather!"

"Yes – she's funny about her bathrooms!" said Isabel. "She's funny altogether. She's the only girl in the form that I really and truly don't know at all. I mean, I don't know if she's generous or mean, kind or unkind, honest or dishonest, truthful or untruthful, jolly or serious – because she's always pretending about herself – putting on airs and graces, swanking, being somebody that she isn't. She might be quite nice, for all we know!"

"I shouldn't think so," said Hilary, who was heartily tired of Sheila and her nonsense. "Honestly, I think she's batty."

Sheila didn't come in for tea, but nobody missed her. When she didn't attend evening preparation in the form room, Miss Roberts sent Pat to find her. Pat hunted all over the place, and at last came across Sheila sitting in a deserted and cold little music room, all by herself.

"Sheila! What in the world are you doing?" asked Pat. "Have you forgotten it's prep. tonight?"

Sheila sat still and said nothing. Pat looked at her

closely. She looked ill.

"Don't you feel well?" asked Pat. "I'll take you to Matron if you like. What's up, Sheila old girl?"

"Nothing," said Sheila.

"Well, what are you sitting here for, all in the cold?" asked Pat. "Don't be an idiot. If you're not ill, come along to prep. Miss Roberts is getting all hot and bothered about you."

"I'm not coming," said Sheila. "I can't face you all again, after what Janet said."

"Well, really! Fancy taking any notice of Janet!" said Pat, feeling worried. "You know how she loses her temper with all of us, and says things she doesn't mean. She's forgotten all about it by now. Come along!"

"She didn't say things she didn't mean. That's the whole point," said Sheila, still in the same quiet, rather queer voice. "She said things she *did* mean! Oh, I hate her!"

"You can't hate old Janet!" said Pat. "She's dreadfully quick-tempered and impatient, but she's very kind too. She wouldn't *really* hurt you, Sheila. Look here – I'm sure you're not well. Come with me to Matron. Perhaps you've got a temperature."

"Leave me alone," said Sheila, obstinately. So in despair Pat left her, feeling very worried. What a pity Janet had flared out like that, and said those really dreadful things! Pat knew how she would feel if anyone sneered at her in that way in front of every one. She wondered what to do. What should she tell Miss Roberts?

On her way back to the form room she passed the head-girl's study. The door was a little open and Pat could just see Winifred James bent over a book. She hesitated outside, as a thought came into her head.

She couldn't tell Miss Roberts about the awful quarrel. But could she tell Winifred? Something had got to be done about Sheila, and she simply didn't know what! She knocked at Winifred's door.

"Come in!" said the head-girl, and raised her serious face as Pat came in.

"Hallo! Is there anything the matter?" asked Winifred. "Oughtn't you to be at prep?"

"Yes, I ought," said Pat. "But Miss Roberts sent me to find somebody. And I'm rather worried about this girl, Winifred, but I can't possibly tell Miss Roberts, so can I tell you?"

"Of course," said Winifred, "so long as it isn't just telling tales, Patricia."

"Of course it's not, Winifred!" said Pat. "I would never tell tales. But I suddenly remembered that you and this girl come from the same town, so I thought maybe you could help a bit."

"This is very mysterious," said Winifred. "What's it all about?"

Then Pat explained about the quarrel, and told the head-girl all that had happened. "And Sheila looks so funny and so ill," she said. "I'm afraid it's something worse than just a silly quarrel."

Winifred listened in silence. "I'm glad you came to me," she said. "It so happens I'm the only person that can help a little, because I know Sheila's history. You are a sensible person, Pat, so I shall tell you a little. And perhaps between us we can help Sheila."

"I hope we can," said Pat. "I don't like her, Winifred – in fact, I hardly know her at all because she's always hidden behind conceit and swank, if you know what I mean. But she's awfully unhappy and I hate to see that."

"Sheila's parents were once very poor," said Winifred. "Her mother was the daughter of our gardener. Her father kept a kind of village stores. He made a great deal of money, an enormous fortune, in fact, so they

rose tremendously in the world. Now they have a wonderful house, almost a mansion, goodness knows how
many servants and cars – and they sent Sheila to the
best schools possible because they wanted their daughter to be a lady."

"Oh," said Pat, suddenly understanding a lot of things.
"So that's why poor Sheila is always swanking and
being haughty and arrogant, and showing off – because
she's afraid we'll not want to be friends with her. She's
afraid we might sneer at her."

"Yes – her stupid haughtiness is just a sort of smoke-
screen to hide the plain, ordinary, rather frightened
person she is underneath," said Winifred. "And now
you see what as happened. Janet has blown away the
smoke-screen and pointed out to every one just those
things that Sheila is always trying to hide – the manners
and speech she learnt when she was very small."

"But how awfully silly of Sheila to pretend like that!"
said Pat. "If she'd told us honestly that her people had
made a lot of money, and how pleased she was to be
able to come to St. Clare's, and all that, we'd have
understood and liked her for it. But all that silly conceit and pretence! Honestly, Winifred, it was awful."

"When people feel that they are not so clever, so good
or so well-born as others, they often behave like that, to
hide their feelings of inferiority," said Winifred,
sounding rather learned to Pat. "Be sorry for them and
help them."

"Well – how can I help Sheila?" asked Pat. "I really
don't see how I can."

"I'll go to her myself," said Winifred, getting up. "All
I want *you* to do – and Isabel too – is to be extra nice to
her for a week or two, and not to laugh at her or point
out anything that might hurt her. Now that Janet has
dragged away the wall Sheila set up round herself, and
shown what a poor thing there is behind it, she will want

a little friendship and understanding. If she's got any common sense she'll drop her airs and graces after this, and you'll have a chance of finding out what the real Sheila is like. But do give her a chance, won't you?"

"Of course I will," said Pat. "Thanks awfully, Winifred. I'll go back to prep. now."

What Winifred said to Sheila the twins never knew. The head-girl was wise beyond her years, and handled the shocked and distressed girl with understanding and gentleness. Sheila appeared in the common room that night, pale and nervous, and would not meet any one's eyes. But Pat came to her rescue at once.

"Sheila! You're just the person I wanted! *Please* tell me where I've gone wrong in this jumper I'm knitting. You're so clever at following patterns and I get all muddled. Look – did I go wrong there – or was it here?"

Sheila gladly went to Pat's side, and was soon showing her how to put the wrong stitch right. When that was done, Isabel called to her. "Hi, Sheila – will you lend me your paints? I can't imagine what's happened to mine."

"Yes, of course," said Sheila, and went to fetch her paints. Janet looked up as soon as she was out of the room.

"Why all this sudden friendship for our haughty Sheila?" she asked.

"To make up a bit for the beastly things you said to her," said Pat. "Give her a chance, Janet. You've hit her hard on her tenderest places, and taken all the stuffing out of her."

"Good thing too," said Janet, gruffly. "She needed it."

"Well, she's had it, so now give her a chance," said Pat. "Don't be small, Janet."

"I'm not," said Janet. "I'm jolly sorry for what I said now, though you may not think it. All right – I'll do my bit. But I'm not going to say I'm sorry. If I do it'll get her all hot and bothered again. But I don't mind *showing* I'm sorry."

"Better still," said Isabel. "Look out – here she comes!"

Sheila came in with the paints. "Thanks," said Isabel. "Golly, what a lovely box!"

Usually Sheila would have said at once what the box had cost, and would have boasted about it. But she said nothing. Janet glanced at her and saw that she was still pale. Janet was kind-hearted and generous, although her tongue could be sharp and bitter, and her temper was hot. She got down a tin of toffees from her shelf and handed them round. Sheila expected to be missed out and looked away.

"Toffee for you, Sheila, old girl?" said Janet, in her clear, pleasant voice. Sheila looked at Janet and hesitated. She still felt sore and angry with her. But Janet's brown eyes were kind and soft, and Sheila knew that she was trying to make peace. She swallowed her feelings, and put out her hand to take a toffee.

"Thanks, Janet," she said, in rather a shaky voice. Then all the girls plunged into a discussion of the play they were going to prepare for Christmas, and in the interest of it all Sheila forgot the quarrel, sucked her toffee, and grew happier.

She thought hard when she went to bed that night. She shouldn't have boasted and bragged – but she had only done it because she knew she wasn't as good as the others and she wanted to hide it. And all the time the girls had seen her weak spots, and must have laughed at her boasting. Well – if only they would be friendly towards her and not sneer at her, she would try not to mind. She was not a brave girl, and not a very sensible one – but that night she was brave enough and sensible enough to see that money and servants and cars didn't matter at all. It was the person underneath that mattered.

"And now I'll do what Winifred said I must do – show the girls the person I am underneath," thought poor Sheila, turning over in bed. "I don't think I'm much of a person really – but anyway, I'll be better than that awful conceited creature I've pretended to be for a year!"

And that was the end of Sheila's haughty and boastful manner. The other girls followed the example of Janet and the twins, and were friendly to Sheila, and gave her a chance. She took the chance, and although, as she had feared, she wasn't much of a person at first, nevertheless the rather mouse-like gentle Sheila was much nicer than the girl she had been before. As time went on, she would become somebody real, and then as Pat said, she would be worth having for a friend.

"I shall always give people a chance now," Pat said to Isabel. "Look at Kathleen – what a brick she is! And Sheila's so different, already."

"Well," said Janet, who overheard, "I should jolly well think you *would* give people a chance! Didn't we all give *you* two a chance! My goodness, you were pretty unbearable when you came, I can tell you. But you're not so bad now. In fact, you're quite passable!"

Pat and Isabel picked up cushions and rushed at the quick-tongued Janet. With squeals and shrieks she tried to get away, but they pummelled her unmercifully.

"We shan't give *you* a chance, you wretch!" giggled Isabel. "You don't deserve one! Ow, stop pinching, you brute."

"Well, get off my middle then," panted Janet. "Wait till *I* get hold of a cushion!"

But they didn't wait! They tore off to gym. with Janet after them, bumping into half a dozen girls on the way.

"Those first-form kids!" said Tessie, in disgust. "Honestly, they ought to be in a kindergarten, the way they behave!"

"Toffee for you, Sheila?" said Janet

Only four weeks remained of the winter term. The girls were busy with plays, songs and sketches, ready for the end of the term. The first form were doing a historical play with Miss Kennedy and thoroughly enjoying themselves.

Miss Kennedy had written the play herself with the girls all helping where they could. Miss Ross, the sewing mistress, was helping with the costumes. It was great fun.

"You know, old Kenny is a good sort," said Pat, who was busily learning her part for the play. "It's funny – I hardly ever think of playing about in her lesson now. I suppose it's because we're all so interested in the play."

"Well, I wish I was as interested in our French play!" groaned Doris, whose French accent drove Mam'zelle to despair. "I simply can NOT roll my *r's* in my throat like the rest of you. R-r-r-r-r-r-r!"

Every one laughed at Doris's funny efforts to say the letter *r* in the French way. Doris had no ear for either music or languages, and was the despair of both the music mistress and Mam'zelle. But she was a wonderful dancer, and her sense of humour sent the class into fits of laughter half a dozen times a day.

It was fun preparing for the Christmas concert. All the different forms were doing something, and there were squabbles over using the gym. for rehearsals. Miss Thomas, the gym. mistress, complained that the gym. was used for everything else but its proper purpose these days!

Lessons went on as usual, of course, and Miss Roberts refused to allow the Christmas preparations to make any difference at all to the work her form did for her. She was very cross with Pat when she found that she was secretly learning her part in the play, when she should have been learning a list of grammar rules.

Pat had copied out her words, and had neatly fitted them into her grammar book. She had a good part in the play and was very anxious to be word-perfect for the rehearsal that afternoon.

"I think, Pat, that you must have got the wrong page in your grammar book," said Miss Roberts, suddenly. "Bring it to me."

Pat went red. She got up with her book. She dropped it purposely on the floor so that it shut, and then picked it up, hoping that Miss Roberts would not notice the words of the play inside. But Miss Roberts did, of course. Her sharp eyes missed nothing!

"I thought so," she said, dryly, taking out the neatly-copied play-words. "When is the rehearsal?"

"This afternoon, Miss Roberts," said Pat.

"Well, you will learn your grammar rules instead of going to the rehearsal," said Miss Roberts. "That seems quite fair to me, and I hope it does to you. If you learn your part in the play during grammar time, then it seems just that you should learn your grammar rules in rehearsal time."

Pat looked up in dismay. "Oh, Miss Roberts! Please don't make me miss rehearsal. I've got an important part in the play, you know."

"Yes, and next year this form has important exams. to take," said Miss Roberts. "Well, I'll give you one more chance, Pat. No more of this, please! Learn those rules now and say them to me at the end of the morning. If they are correct, I'll let you off. Go back to your seat!"

Pat went to the rehearsal, of course! It was just no

good at all trying to play any tricks in Miss Roberts' class, and she had had to learn her grammar in break in order to get it perfect for Miss Roberts by the end of the morning.

But every one liked the form-mistress. She was strict, could be very severe and sarcastic, but she was always perfectly just, and never went back on what she said or promised. Mam'zelle was not always just, but she was so goodhearted that very few of the girls really disliked her.

What with working up for the end of term exams., and the concert, the girls had very little time to themselves, but they enjoyed every minute. Doris was to dance a solo dance that she had created herself. Vera was to play the piano, at which she was extremely good. Five of the girls were in the French play, and most of them in the history play. Everybody was in something.

Except one person! Sheila was in nothing! This happened quite by accident. At first Mam'zelle had said she was to be Monsieur Toc-Toc in the play, so Miss Kennedy didn't put her in the history play – and then Mam'zelle changed her mind and put Joan into the French play instead. So Sheila was in neither, and as she didn't play the piano or the violin, could not recite at all, and was no good at dancing, she felt very left-out.

She said nothing. At first nobody noticed that she wasn't going to be in anything, because it had all happened accidentally. Then Isabel noticed that Sheila was looking mopey and asked her why.

"What's up? Had bad news from home or something?"

"Oh, no," said Sheila. "Nothing's wrong."

Isabel said no more but watched Sheila for a few days. She soon noticed that she was not in either of the plays and was not doing anything by herself either.

"I say! I believe you're miserable because you're not

in the concert!" said Isabel. "I thought you were going to be in the French play."

"I was," said Sheila, uncomfortably. "But then Mam-'zelle chose some one else. I'm not in anything, and every one will notice it, Isabel. I do so hate being left out."

"Well, it wasn't done on purpose, silly," said Isabel, laughing.

"I feel as if it was," said Sheila. "I know I'm not much good at anything, but it doesn't make it any better when I'm not even given the *chance* to do anything."

"Oh, don't be an idiot!" said Isabel. Sheila looked obstinate. Like many weak people she could be really pig-headed.

"Well, I'm fed up!" she said. "I shan't go to the re-hearsal or anything. I'll just go off by myself."

"Well, anyway, you might at least take an interest in what the form is doing, even if you're not doing any-thing yourself!" cried Isabel, indignantly. "That's mean and stupid."

"I'll be mean and stupid then," said Sheila, almost in tears, and she went off by herself.

Isabel told Pat. "Oh blow!" said Pat. "Just as we were getting Sheila to be sensible too, and giving her a chance. Don't let's bother about her! If she wants to feel she's left out and slighted when she isn't, let her!"

Janet came up and listened to the tale. She had been very good to Sheila the last week or two, for she had really felt very guilty over her loss of temper. She looked thoughtful now. "No – don't let's undo the good work we've been trying to do!" she said. "Let's think of some-thing. I know once I was left out of a match when I badly wanted to be in it, and although I'm not such a silly as Sheila, still I did feel pretty awful. I remember thinking that the whole school would be whispering about me, wondering what I had done to be out of the match!"

The twins laughed. Janet was so sensible and jolly that they couldn't imagine her worrying about a thing like that.

"It's all very well to laugh," said Janet. "You are twins and have always got each other to back up and laugh over things with – but when you're a naturally lonely person like Sheila, it's different. Little things get awfully big."

"You *are* sticking up for Sheila all of a sudden," said Pat, in surprise.

"No, I'm not. All I say is – don't let's spoil what we've been trying to *do*," said Janet, impatiently.

"Oh, well – you think of something then," said Isabel. "I can't!"

The twins went off. Janet sat down and began to think. She was impatient and impulsive, but once she had set her hand to anything she wouldn't give up. Sheila wanted help again, and Janet was going to give it.

"Gosh! I've got it!" said Janet to herself. "We'll make her prompter, of course! We need some one at rehearsals with the book, ready to prompt any of us who forgets. And my goodness, I forget my words all right! I'll go and ask Sheila if she'll be prompter at rehearsals and on the concert night too."

She went off to find Sheila. It was some time before she found her, and then at last she ran her to earth in the art room, tidying out the cupboards.

"I say, Sheila! Will you do something for us?" cried Janet. "Will you be prompter for the play? We get into an awful muddle trying to prompt each other, and it would be an awful help to have some one with the book, who will follow the words and help when we go wrong."

"I wouldn't be any good at that," said Sheila, rather sullenly.

"Oh, yes, you would, idiot!" said Janet. "It *would* be such a help, Sheila. Please do. Some of us are sure to be nervous on the concert night too, and it would be nice to know you were at the side, ready to prompt us with the words."

"All right," said Sheila, rather ungraciously. She had felt that if she wasn't in the plays, she jolly well wouldn't help at all. But that was small and mean – and Sheila was doing her best not to be that.

So she became prompter, and attended all the rehearsals with the book of words. She soon began to enjoy it all, and loved the play. She did nothing but stand or sit with the book, prompting those who forgot, whilst the others had the fun of acting. But she didn't grumble or complain, and the twins secretly thought she was behaving rather well.

"Good for Janet to have thought of that," said Pat.

"Yes – she thought Sheila was going to refuse," said Isabel. "I'm not at all sure *I* wouldn't have said no, if it had been me!"

"I shouldn't have let you!" said Pat.

Two weeks before the end of the term an accident happened. Vera, a very quiet girl in the first form, fell during gym. and broke her arm. She broke it just by the wrist and had to be taken off to hospital to have it X-rayed. It was set in plaster, and her parents decided that as it was so near the end of the term, she might as well go home, instead of staying the last two weeks.

"It's her right arm, so she won't be able to write at all," said her mother to Miss Theobald. "It would be just as well for her to be quiet at home."

So poor Vera said good-bye and went, promising to be back the next term with her arm mended again! And then there was consternation in the class, because Vera had an important part in the play!

"Golly! What's to be done?" said Pat, in dismay.

"No one else can possibly learn all the words in time. Vera had such a big part."

Every one stared round in despair. Those who were not in the play felt perfectly certain that they could not possibly learn the big part in so short a time. And then Janet spoke.

"There's some one who *does* know all the words!" she cried. "Sheila, you do! You've been prompting us at every rehearsal, and you know every part! You're the only one who's been following the words page by page in the book. Can't *you* take Vera's part?"

Sheila went bright red. All the girls looked at her expectantly.

"Go on – say you will," said Pat. "You can do it just as well as Vera!"

"I should love to," said Sheila. "I'm sure I could do it! I know every word! Well – I know every word of every part now, of course – but I'd just love to do Vera's part. I like it best of all."

"Good!" cried Pat. "That's settled then. We'll get some one else to be prompter and you must be in the play."

"So at the next rehearsal Sheila was not prompter, but took one of the most important parts. She was quite word-perfect, and because she had so often watched Vera doing the part, she was able to act it very well.

Every one was pleased. They had all known that Sheila was hurt because she had been left out of everything by accident, and had admired her for taking on the rather dull job of prompter – and now that she had had such an unexpected reward the whole form was delighted.

But nobody was more delighted than Sheila herself. She was really thrilled with her good luck. She went about with a smiling face, and was so unexpectedly jolly that the class could hardly believe it was Sheila.

But Sheila did not forget to write and tell Vera how sorry she was to hear about her accident. She remembered some one else's disappointment in the middle of her own pleasure. Yes – Sheila was well on the way to becoming somebody now!

17   KATHLEEN HAS A SECRET

One afternoon, when Pat, Isabel and Kathleen were coming back from the town across the fields, they heard a whining noise from the hedge.

"That's a dog!" said Kathleen at once, and she ran to see. The others followed – and there, in the ditch, they saw a half-grown rough-haired terrier, its chest and face bleeding.

"It's been shot!" cried Kathleen indignantly. "Look at all the pellets in its poor legs! Oh! It's that hateful farmer who lives over the hill. He always swears he'll shoot any dog that goes wandering in his fields."

"But why?" asked Pat, in surprise. "Dogs go all over the fields."

"Yes – but sheep are in these fields, and soon the lambs will be born," said Kathleen. "Dogs chase sheep, you know, and frighten them."

"Well, this poor animal has been shot," said Pat. "What are we going to do with it?"

"I'm going to take it back to school with me and look after it," said Kathleen. She was quite crazy over animals. The twins looked at her in astonishment.

"You won't be able to keep him," said Pat. "And anyway, you ought to ring up the police and report him. Suppose his owner is looking for him?"

"Well, I'll ring up and see if any one has been asking

for him," said Kathleen. "But if you think I'm going to leave a dog bleeding all by itself out in the fields, you're jolly well mistaken!"

"All right, all right!" said Isabel. "But how are you going to take him home? He'll cover you with blood."

"As if I care about that!" said Kathleen, picking the dog up very gently. He whined again, but snuggled down into the girl's arms, knowing quite well that they were kind and friendly.

They walked back to school with the dog. They debated where to put him. No girl was allowed to keep a dog, and if he were discovered he would certainly be sent off. And Kathleen was quite determined that she was going to nurse him till he was better!

"Could we keep him in the bicycle shed?" asked Pat.

"Oh, no. He would be much too cold," said Kathleen, standing behind the bushes with the dog in her arms, pondering how to get him into school without being seen. "Wait a minute – let's think."

They all thought. Then Pat gave an exclamation. "I know! What about that little box-room near the hot tank upstairs in the attics? He'd be warm there, and right away from every one. Nobody ever goes there."

"And we're not supposed to either," said Isabel. "Dash! We always seem to be doing things we oughtn't to do."

"Well, this is for the dog's sake," said Kathleen. "I'm willing to do anything. Poor darling! Don't whine like that. I promise I'll make you better soon."

Janet came round the corner and saw the three of them standing by the bushes. "Hallo!" she said. "What's up? What have you got there? A dog! Goodness gracious, what's wrong with him?"

"He's been shot," said Kathleen. "We're going to keep him in the boxroom upstairs in the attics till he's better. Are you going down to the town, Janet? Well,

They debated where to put the dog

be a sport and ask at the police station if anyone has
reported a lost dog. If they have, ask for their name and
address, and I'll tell them I've got him safely."

"All right," said Janet. "But look out that he doesn't
make a noise or you'll get into trouble. You're quite
batty over animals, Kathleen! Good-bye!"

Janet rushed off to get her bicycle. Kathleen turned to
the twins. "You go and see that the coast is clear," she
said. "And let's think what to have for a bed for him."

"There's an old wooden box in the gardener's shed,"
said Isabel, eagerly. "That would do nicely. I'll get it."

She ran to get it. Pat went indoors to see if it was safe
for Kathleen to take the dog in. She whistled a little
tune, and Kathleen ran in with the dog. The two of
them scurried up the stairs without meeting any one –
but round the corner of the corridor they could hear
footsteps coming and the loud voice of Mam'zelle, talking to Miss Jenks.

"Oh, crumbs!" groaned Kathleen, and she turned to
go down the stairs again. But some one was now coming
up. Pat opened the door of a big broom cupboard and
pushed Kathleen and the dog into it. She shut the door,
and then dropped on one knee, pretending to do up her
shoe. Just as Mam'zelle and Miss Jenks passed her, the
dog in the cupboard gave a whine. Mam'zelle looked
round in surprise.

"*Tiens!* Why do you whine like a dog?" she asked
Pat, and passed on, thinking that girls were indeed
funny creatures. Pat giggled, and opened the door when
the two mistresses had gone by.

"Did you hear what Mam'zelle said?" she asked.
"Come on – it's all right now. We can get up the attic
stairs in a trice!"

They went up to the top of the school. The attics were
just under the roof, and the boxrooms were a peculiar
shape, being small, with slanting roofs, and almost im-

possible to stand up in. Here were kept the trunks and cases belonging to the girls. The boxrooms were only visited twice a term – once when the trunks were put there, and once when they were brought down to be packed.

After a moment Isabel came up with the box and an old rug she had found in the locker downstairs in the gym. The girls chose the little boxroom next to the hot tanks. It was warm and cosy. They set the wooden box down in a corner and tucked the old rug into it. It made a very cosy bed.

Then Kathleen set to work to bathe the dog's wounds. It took a long time, and the dog lay patiently till it was finished, licking Kathleen's careful hands as she bathed him.

"You're awfully good with animals," said Pat, watching her. "And doesn't he love you?"

"I'm going to be a vet when I'm grown up," said Kathleen. "There you are, my beauty. You're all right now. Don't lick off that ointment more than you can help! Lie quietly here now, and you'll soon be all right again! I'll bring you some water and some food."

The bell went for prep. and the three girls hurried downstairs, carefully closing the boxroom door behind them. They met Janet as they went into the classroom.

"I asked at the police station," whispered Janet. "But they said nobody had reported a dog. I had to tell them what he was like and they wanted your name and address."

"Gracious! What an idiot you are!" whispered back Kathleen, as she took her seat. "Whatever will Miss Theobald say if the police ring up the school and ask for me! Really, Janet!"

"Well, I *had* to give it!" whispered Janet. "You can't say no to the police, can you? Anyway, I don't expect the dog will be reported, so don't worry!"

But Kathleen did worry. When she heard the telephone bell ringing that evening she was quite sure that it was the police ringing up the Head Mistress. But it wasn't. The girls breathed with relief when they heard that it was a message for Miss Roberts.

The dog was given water and food. He lay quite quietly in his basket and was as good as gold. "He ought to have a run before we go to bed," said Kathleen, anxiously. "How are we to manage it?"

"Let's bundle him up in a heap of the clothes we are using for the play," said Pat. "If anyone meets us they will think we are just taking a pile of clothes for rehearsal. I'll get some!"

So, five minutes before bedtime the girls crept up the attic stairs with a heap of clothes. The surprised dog was carefully tucked up in them, with just his nose showing so that he could breathe.

Then Kathleen carried him downstairs, whispering to him so that he would lie quiet. He did not want to be quiet at all, and struggled violently, but luckily the girls met nobody except Matron. She was in a hurry, and hardly glanced at them.

"You won't be in time for bed if you aren't quick!" she called. The girls giggled, and went out into the garden by a little-used door. They set the dog free in a tiny yard where the gardeners chopped firewood and logs, and he limped about joyfully. Then they packed him up in the pile of clothes again, and scurried indoors.

This time they were not so lucky. They met Belinda Towers! She stopped and glared at them.

"Don't you know that your bed-time bell has gone? What are you doing wandering about here? And what on earth is that in those clothes?"

The dog struggled to get out and its head came out with a jerk. "Oh, we've been trying so hard not to let any one see him!" said Kathleen, almost in tears. "Belinda, he's been shot, he's . . ."

"Don't tell me anything about him and I shan't know," said Belinda, who was very fond of animals too. "Go on – take that pile of clothes away – and go to your dormitory quickly."

"Good old Belinda!" said Pat, as the three of them ran up the stairs to the boxroom. "Isn't she a sport? Talk about Nelson turning the blind eye – she turned a blind eye on our dog all right! Do hurry, Kath. We really shall get into a row if we're much longer!"

They tucked the dog up again in his basket. He licked their hands and wuffed a very small bark. "Isn't he clever?" cried Kathleen, in delight. "He even knows he must whisper a bark."

"Well, it was a pretty loud whisper," said Pat. "Come on. Let's go down and hope that Hilary won't say a word. It's about the first time we've been late, anyway. I hope the dog doesn't bark the place down in the night!"

"Of course he won't!" said Kathleen, shutting the boxroom door carefully. "He'll sleep all night – and in the morning, very early, I'll take him for a run again."

They tore down to their dormitory, to find Hilary getting most exasperated with them. "Where *have* you been?" she demanded. "You know it's my job to see you're here on time at nine o'clock. It's too bad of you."

"We've been putting a dog to bed," whispered Kathleen. Hilary stared in surprise.

"*What* did you say?" she asked. "Putting *what* to bed?"

"Shall I tell every one?" said Kathleen to the twins. They nodded. It was lovely to have a secret – but it was great fun to surprise every one and tell it!

So Kathleen explained about the hurt dog, and every one listened in amazement. "Fancy taking a dog to the boxroom!" cried Doris. "Well, I'd never dare to do that! Suppose Matron went up there! She'd soon find him!"

"Well, we shall only keep him for a day or two till he's quite better," said Kathleen. "Then we'll have found out where he belongs to and can take him back."

But it wasn't quite as easy as all that!

18   THE SECRET IS OUT!

The dog made no noise at all in the night. Kathleen managed to wake very early, and creep up to the box-room to take him for a run in the little wood-yard. He completely refused to be taken down all wrapped up again, so Kathleen had to put a bit of string round his neck and lead him down the stairs. He made rather a noise flopping down, but nobody came to see what was the matter.

It was marvellous the way his legs and chest and face had healed during the night. Kathleen was very pleased. The dog fawned round her legs in the yard, and tried to jump up to lick her hand. The girl thought he was a marvellous dog, and hoped against hope that no one would claim him.

"If only I could keep him until the end of term, and then take him home!" she thought. "Wouldn't it be lovely!"

She took him back to the boxroom again. This time he didn't want her to leave him, and after she had shut the door and gone back to the dormitory she felt sure she could hear him whining and scraping against the door.

The first-form's classroom was just underneath the boxrooms. The room where the dog was was not ex-actly overhead but more to the right. Kathleen listened anxiously to see if he was making any noise during school time. Her sharp ears heard the patter of feet and small whines, but Miss Roberts apparently heard nothing.

When Mam'zelle came to take a French lesson, however, she heard the dog quite plainly! Her ears were exceedingly keen. The first time that the dog whined, she looked up in surprise.

"What can that noise be?" she said.

"What noise, Mam'zelle?" asked Isabel, with an innocent face.

"The noise of a dog!" said Mam'zelle, impatiently. "The whine, the bark! Is it possible that you have not heard it, Isabel!"

All the class pretended to listen hard. Then the girls shook their heads.

"You must be mistaken, Mam'zelle," said Doris, gravely.

"There surely isn't a dog in the school," said Joan. "Only the kitchen cats."

Mam'zelle was really most astonished to think that she was the only one who heard the strange noises.

"Ah, it must be something wrong with my ears, then," she said, and she shook her big head vigorously. "I will get the doctor to syringe them for me. I cannot have dogs barking and whining in my head."

The class, already in a state of giggle, was glad to burst into laughter at this. Mam'zelle rapped on the desk.

"Enough! I made no joke! Take down *dictée*, please."

The class went on with its work. The dog in the box-room explored the place thoroughly, and, judging by the noise, tried a good deal of scratching at the door and the walls. Mam'zelle looked extremely puzzled once or twice, and glanced at the girls to see if they too had noticed the noises – but one and all went serenely on with their work, and appeared to hear nothing – so Mam'zelle pressed her ears thoughtfully, and made up her mind to see the doctor that véry same day.

The twins and Kathleen spent most of their free time in the boxroom with the dog. It was always so pleased to see them, and they all grew very fond of it indeed. The only exasperating thing was that when they left it, it *would* bark and whine after them, and try to scratch the door open. They were always afraid that somebody would hear it then.

But two days went by safely, and it was not discovered. The girls fed it, gave it water, and took it down secretly for runs in the woodyard. Kathleen really adored the little creature, and indeed it was a very intelligent and affectionate animal.

"As nobody has claimed to be its owner, I really think I might keep it for myself, don't you?" asked Kathleen, anxiously, as she and the twins stroked the dog up in the boxroom one free half-hour. "I do love him so. He really is a darling. I couldn't bear to take him to the police-station now and leave him there. You know, if nobody claimed him at all the police would have him put to sleep."

"Well, you keep him then," said Pat. "There isn't much longer till the end of the term. But you'll have to move him out of here when the maids come up to get down our boxes for us. That's very soon. I don't see what you're going to do, really I don't!"

However, the twins and Kathleen did not need to bother about what was going to happen because the dog soon decided things for himself.

One morning, about four days after he had been found, he lay down in a bit of wintry sunshine that came slanting through the attic window. It made him feel restless and he jumped up and prowled round. He came to the door and stood sniffing at it. Then he began to jump at the handle.

After a while he managed, quite by chance, to jerk the catch back – and the door opened! The dog was delighted. He pushed it wide open with his nose and trotted down the attic stairs.

Now all might still have been well if one of the school cats had not been lying fast asleep on a mat underneath one of the corridor radiators. The dog sniffed the cat-smell, and trotted up in delight. What! A cat! And what was more, a cat asleep!

With a loud wuff the dog leapt on the cat in play. It was only a puppy and would not really have hurt it – but the cat was in a most terrible fright. It leapt up, gave an anguished yowl, and fled down the corridor, its tail straight up in the air. The dog gave chase at once, prancing along on all four puppy-legs! And that was how Miss Theobald met the dog.

She was going along to one of the classrooms when first the cat and then the dog shot round her legs. She turned in amazement. Cats there were in the school, because of mice – but where in the world did a dog suddenly appear from?

The cat leapt out of a window. The dog paused, surprised that the cat had disappeared so suddenly. Then he decided to go and find Kathleen. He thought he had smelt her somewhere along the passage. So off he trotted again, and soon came to the first-form classroom. He stood up on his hind legs and whined and scratched.

Mam'zelle was once again giving a French lesson, and the whole class was busy correcting its French prep., and writing out various mistakes. When the dog jumped up at the door and whined, Mam'zelle leapt to her feet.

"*Tiens!* This time it is not my ears! It is in truth a

dog!" She marched to the door and opened it. In ran the dog, his tail wagging nineteen to the dozen, and went straight to Kathleen. How all the class stared!

And after him came Miss Theobald, determined to unravel the mystery of the dog! She looked into the classroom and saw Mam'zelle stamping up and down, and Kathleen doing her best to quiet the excited dog!

"What is all this disturbance?" asked Miss Theobald, in her quiet, serious voice. Mam'zelle turned to her at once, her hands wagging above her shoulders as she poured out how she had heard a dog some days ago, and how he had come to the door and scratched.

"I think perhaps Kathleen knows more about him than any one," said Miss Theobald, noticing how the animal fawned on the girl, and how she stroked and patted him. "Kathleen, come with me, and perhaps you can give me an explanation."

Kathleen, rather pale, stood up. She followed the Head to her room, the dog trotting amiably at her heels. Miss Theobald made her sit down.

"I didn't mean to do any wrong," said Kathleen, beginning her tale "But he was so hurt, Miss Theobald, and I do so much love dogs, and I've never had any pet of my own, and . . ."

"Begin at the beginning," said the Head. So Kathleen told the whole story, and Miss Theobald listened. At the end she reached for the telephone and took off the receiver. She asked for the police station. Kathleen's heart stood still! Whatever was the Head going to say!

Miss Theobald enquired if any dog had been reported missing. Apparently none had. Then she asked what would happen if a dog was kept, that had been found hurt. "It had no collar when it was found," she explained.

After a while she put down the receiver and turned to Kathleen, who now had the dog on her knee.

"I can't imagine how you have kept the dog hidden all this time," she said, "and I am not going to enquire. I know you are fond of animals. Well, apparently there is no reason why you should not keep the dog for yourself, if no one claims it within a certain time. So I propose to let you keep it until you return home for the holidays, and if your aunt will let you have it, you can take it back. But it must be kept in the stables, Kathleen. For once in a way I will relax the rule that says no pet must be kept, and let you have the dog until the holidays."

If Kathleen had not been in such awe of the Head she would certainly have flung her arms round her neck! As it was she could hardly swallow a lump that suddenly appeared in her throat, which made it very difficult for her to say anything. But she managed to stammer out her thanks. The dog was not in awe of Miss Theobald, however – and he went to her and licked her hands solemnly, for all the world as if he knew what had been said!

"Take him to the stables now, and get one of the men to find a good place for him," said Miss Theobald. "And next time you want to do anything peculiar, Kathleen, come and ask either me or Miss Roberts first! It really would save quite a lot of trouble!"

Kathleen hurried off, her eyes shining. The dog trotted after her. Before she went to the stables the girl ran back to her classroom and burst in, her cheeks flushed and her eyes sparkling.

"I say!" she cried. "I'm to keep the dog. I'm to take him home if my aunt . . ."

"Kathleen! I will not have my class interrupted in this scandalous way!" cried Mam'zelle, rising in wrath from her desk. Kathleen took one look at her and disappeared. She went to the stables and found one of the gardeners. He soon gave the dog a place, and Kathleen left him, happy in the thought that now she could come and take him for a walk whenever she wanted to.

On her way back to her form she met Belinda Towers, off for a practice in the lacrosse field. "Belinda!" she cried. "The dog escaped and came to me in the classroom! And he chased a cat and Miss Theobald saw him and came after him – and she's letting me keep him!"

"Good for you!" said Belinda. "Now buzz off back to your form. You first-form kids always seem to be doing something extraordinary!"

Kathleen buzzed off. She went very, very quietly back to the French lesson and sat down. Mam'zelle still had a lot to say, but the words rolled off Kathleen's head like water off a duck's back. She sat and dreamed of the dog who was really to be her very own.

"And if you do not pay more attention to me I will give you a three-page essay to write about dogs in French!" she suddenly heard Mam'zelle say, and pulled herself together. The whole class was grinning at her. Mam'zelle was glaring, half-angry, half-amused, for the girl had really not heard a word until then.

Kathleen didn't at all want to write a three-page essay in French. Good gracious! She wouldn't be able to take the dog for a walk. So for the next twenty minutes she worked harder than any one in the class, and Mam'zelle said no more!

And during the half-hour between morning school and dinner, four girls crowded round an excited dog and quarrelled as to what name he should be given!

"I'm his owner and I'm going to choose!" said Kathleen, firmly. "His name is Binks. I don't know why – but he looks like a Binks to me."

So Binks he was, and Binks he remained till the last day of term came and he went home with Kathleen.

What a time he had till then, with dozens of girls clamouring to take him for walks, and bringing him so many things to eat that he grew as fat as a barrel! Even the mistresses loved him and gave him a pat when they met him out with Kathleen.

All but Mam'zelle, who thought that school was no place for dogs! "He is abominable!" she said, whenever she saw him. "That dog! How he disturbed my class!" But there was a twinkle in her eye, so nobody took her seriously!

19   A SHOCK FOR ISABEL

Exams. began. The twins were very anxious to do well in them, for they badly wanted to be top in something. They had caught up well with the rest of their form, but as most of the other girls had been there a good deal longer than they had, Miss Roberts told them that they could not expect to come out top that term.

The maths. exam. came first. It was quite a stiff one, for Miss Roberts had taught her form a good deal that term and expected them to make a good showing. Pat and Isabel groaned over it, but did their best.

"I know I got questions 3, 4 and 5 quite wrong," said Isabel, when they compared their papers afterwards. "I think I got the problems right though, but they took me so long to puzzle out that I didn't do them all."

"I bet I'll be bottom," said Pat, dismally. She still at times resented being a "nobody", as she put it, though she was rapidly forgetting all the high-and-mighty ideas she had held at first.

French wasn't so bad. Thanks to "Mam'zelle Abominable's" coaching the twins were now well up to the

average of their class in writing. It was poor Doris who
"fell down" in French. She stammered and stuttered in
the oral exam. and drove Mam'zelle nearly frantic.

"Have I taught you three terms already and still you
speak French like a four-year-old in the kindergarten?"
she stormed. "Now repeat to me again one of the French
verses you learnt this term."

The crosser Mam'zelle got, the worse poor Doris became. She gazed hopelessly round the class, and winked
at the twins.

"Ah! You wink! You will soon wink the other side
of your face!" cried Mam'zelle, getting all mixed up.
"You will have nought for your oral French."

As Doris had expected to be bottom anyhow this did
not disturb her a great deal. She sat down thankfully.
Joan was next, and as she was good at French, Mam-
'zelle calmed down a little.

The exams. went on until only the geography one
was left. The twins examined the lists each morning and
were sad to see that they were not top in anything at all.
They were not even second in anything! Pat managed
to get third in nature, and Isabel fifth in history, but
that was the highest they reached!

"Golly! Our exam. marks won't look too good on
our reports," sighed Pat. "We were always top in most
things at Redroofs, long before we were head of the
school. Mother and Daddy won't like us not being top in
a single thing here."

"They'll think we did what we said, and didn't try at
all," said Isabel. "Oh, blow! And we have been trying.
What a pity we said all we did before we came. I don't
see how Daddy can help feeling we've slacked all this
term. He's so used to getting reports that show us top in
nearly everything."

"Well – there's only the geography exam. left," said
Pat. "We might be top in that – but I doubt it! I don't

feel I know an awful lot about Africa, though we've been studying the wretched place all term. Which part of it do the Zulus live? I never can remember."

"I wish we *could* just be top in it," said Isabel, getting out her geography text-book, and turning over the pages. "Pat — let's cram hard all tonight and really see if we can't do well. Come on!"

So the two of them bent their heads over their text-books and solemnly began to read through the whole of the lessons they had had that term on Africa. They looked at the maps they had drawn, and drew them roughly again two or three times. They made lists of towns and ports and said them to one another. They pored over the rivers and learnt those too, and read up about the peoples of Africa, the animals and the products.

"Well, I really feel I know something now," said Isabel, with a sigh. "I especially know all the products of Africa, and the rivers."

"And I especially know all about the climate," said Pat. "But I bet we shan't get asked questions about those things! Exam. questions always seem to deal with the things you missed because you were ill, or forgot to look up, or for some reason simply can't remember at all!"

"Well, I can't do any more work tonight," said Isabel. "I want to finish the sleeve of the jumper I'm knitting. I've only got a few more rows to do. Where did I put the pattern book?"

"Can't imagine," said Pat. "You're always losing it. I think you took it into the form-room with you this afternoon."

"Blow!" said Isabel. "So I did."

She got up and went out of the common room. She quite forgot that she and the others had been told not to go to the first form room that evening, because the exam.

papers were to be set out there. She sauntered along to the room, opened the door and went in. She walked over to her desk and opened it.

Yes – there was the pattern-book. Good! Isabel took it, and then picked up a pencil that belonged to Miss Roberts. She went to the teacher's big desk and put it in the groove that held pencils and pens.

And there, staring up at her from the desk were the exam. papers for tomorrow! A list of geography questions was written out very neatly on a sheet of paper. Isabel stared at them with a beating heart.

If only she knew what the questions were she could cram them up and answer them so perfectly that she would be top! Without thinking she hurriedly read down the questions. "State what you know about the climate of South Africa. What do you know about the race called Pygmies? What do you . . ."

Isabel read the questions from top to bottom, and then went out of the room. Her face was flushed and her heart was beating. "All those questions are what we've both been looking up this evening," she said to herself. "It doesn't matter me seeing the paper at all. I've already crammed up the answers."

Pat looked up as Isabel came back into the common room. "Got the pattern book?" she asked.

Isabel looked down at her empty hands. No – she had left the pattern book behind after all.

"Didn't you find it?" said Pat, surprised.

"Yes – I did," said Isabel. "But I've gone and left it behind after all."

"Well, aren't you going to go and get it?" asked Pat, still more surprised. Isabel hesitated. She could not bear to go back into the form room again.

"What *is* the matter, Isabel?" asked Pat, impatiently. "Have you gone dumb? What's up?"

"Pat, the geography paper questions were on Miss

Roberts' desk," said Isabel. "I read them."

"Isabel! That's cheating!" said Pat.

"I didn't think about whether it was cheating or not," said Isabel, in a troubled voice. "But it's all right, Pat – the questions were all about what we've been looking up this evening. So it won't matter."

Pat stared at Isabel. Isabel would not look at her. "Isabel, I don't see how in the world you're going to sit for the geography exam. tomorrow when you know you've already seen the questions," she said at last. "I dare say you could answer them all quite perfectly without any further looking up at all – but if any one knew about this they'd think you were a cheat. And you're not – you've always been straight and honourable. I just don't understand you."

"I did it all in a hurry," said poor Isabel.

"Well, you'd better tell Miss Roberts," said Pat.

"Oh, I *can't*!" said Isabel, in horror. "You know how strict she is. I can't."

"Well, you must answer all the questions so badly that Miss Roberts will be angry with you, and then you can tell her why you've done it," said Pat. "If she knows you haven't taken advantage of seeing the questions she can't think you're a cheat. You'll have to own up before or after. Go on now, Isabel, you know you must."

"Well – I'll own up afterwards," said Isabel. "I'll sit for the exam. and do the answers so badly that I'll be bottom. Then when Miss Roberts rows me I'll tell her why. Oh, blow! Why was I so silly? I did it all in a hurry. I might even have been top, you know – because all the questions were ones I could answer quite well."

"Don't tell me what they were," said Pat. "I don't want to know, else I'll feel awkward about answering them. Cheer up, Isabel, I know you well enough to know you didn't mean to cheat! Anybody can be silly!"

Isabel was not very happy that night. She tossed and turned, wishing to goodness she hadn't seen the geography questions. She could so easily have answered them correctly and got high marks! What an idiot she had been!

The geography exam. was to be held first thing after prayers next day. At nine o'clock all the first form filed into their room, and took their places. Isabel saw that the exam questions were still on the desk. Pat saw them there too, though of course it was impossible for any one to read them.

Miss Roberts came in. "Good morning, girls!" she said. "Good morning, Miss Roberts," chorused the class, and sat down.

"Geography exam. this morning," said Miss Roberts, briskly. "Do well, please! Joan, come and give out the questions."

Isabel watched Joan go up for the slips of paper. She felt miserable. It was not nice to have to do badly on purpose, but there was nothing else to do.

Just as Joan was taking up the papers Miss Roberts gave an exclamation and stopped her. "Wait! I don't believe these are the right papers! No – they're not! How stupid! They are the exam. questions for the second form, who have been doing Africa too. Go to Miss Jenks with these, and ask her to give you the papers I left on her desk. Tell her I've left the first form's exam. questions there, and that these are for her form."

Joan took the papers and disappeared out of the room. Isabel looked at Pat. Pat was smiling in delight. When Miss Roberts turned to write something on the board Pat leaned across and whispered to Isabel.

"What luck! Now you can do your best instead of your worst, old girl! You saw the wrong questions! Hurrah!"

Isabel nodded. She was really delighted too. It seemed

too good to be true. Miss Roberts turned round. "No talking! If I catch any girls whispering during exams. I shall deduct ten marks from their papers. Do you hear me, Pat?"

"Yes, Miss Roberts," said Pat, meekly. Joan came back with the right papers and distributed them round the class. Isabel read hers quickly. Yes – they were quite, quite different from the questions she had read last night. How marvellous! Now she could set to work and really do her best to be top. She would never be such an idiot again. She hadn't meant to be a cheat, but it was horrible to feel like one.

But poor Isabel was rather nervous now after her experiences, and did not do nearly such a good paper as Pat. Her hand shook as she drew the maps required, and she made some silly mistakes. So when the papers were gathered up and corrected Isabel was nowhere near the top! She was sixth – but Pat was top! Isabel was as pleased to see Pat's name heading the list as she would have been to see her own. She squeezed her twin's arm hard.

"Good for you, Pat!" she said. "I'm jolly glad! One of us is top in something anyhow!"

Pat glowed with pleasure. It was marvellous to see her name heading the list. Miss Roberts came up and patted her on the back.

"You did an excellent paper, Patricia," she said. "Eighty-three per cent is very good. But I was surprised that Isabel didn't do better? Why was that, Isabel?"

But Isabel did not tell her and Miss Roberts laughed and went on her way. Surprising things happened in exams. – probably next term those O'Sullivan twins would be top in nearly everything!

And now the end of the term was indeed drawing near. Miss Theobald and the other mistresses were busy making out reports, putting up lists, helping the girls with the great concert, and going through exam. papers. The girls themselves were restless, looking forward to the holidays, getting ready for the concert, wondering what their reports would be like, and nearly driving Mam-'zelle mad with their inattention.

Miss Roberts was more lenient, but even she grew impatient when Isabel told her that there were fourteen ounces in a pound.

"I know you all go *slightly* mad at the end of term," she said, "but there really is a limit to my patience. Isabel, if there was a lower form than this I'd send you to it for the rest of the morning!"

The last two weeks were really great fun. For one thing all the cupboards had to be turned out, washed, dried and tidied. The twins had never done this at Red-roofs School, and at first were inclined to turn up their noses at such work. But when they saw the others tying handkerchiefs round their hair, and putting on overalls, they couldn't help thinking it would be rather fun, even though the cleaning had to be done in their free time.

"Come on, Pat, come on, Isabel! Don't stand looking stuck-up like you used to!" cried Janet, who sensed at once the twins hadn't done work like this before. "You'll get dirty, but you can always bath and wash your hair! Come on, high-and-mighties!"

This was not a name that the twins liked at all, so they climbed down at once. They found big hankies and tied up their hair. They put on overalls, and went to join the others. Hilary was in charge of the first-form cleaning.

It really was fun. Everything had to be taken out of the cupboards, and there were squeals and shrieks of delight when things long-lost came to light again.

"Oh! I thought I'd never see that penknife again!" squealed Doris, pouncing on a small pearl-handled knife in delight. "Wherever has it been all this time?"

"Golly! Here's Miss Roberts' fountain-pen!" cried Hilary, a little later. "Look – tangled up in this bundle of raffia. Oooh! I know how it got there. Do you remember, Janet, when you dumped a whole lot of it on to Miss Roberts' desk in handwork one day, and she objected, and you carted it all off to the cupboard again? Well, I bet you took the pen with you! My word, what a hunt we had for it."

"Well, for pity's sake don't remind her that it might have been *me*," said Janet. "She's always going off the deep end about something now. Look – take her the pen, Isabel, and say we found it in the handwork cupboard. You've been in her bad books today, so maybe you'll get an unexpected smile!"

Isabel did! Miss Roberts was delighted to see her pen, and beamed at Isabel with pleasure. Isabel wondered if Miss Roberts was in a good enough temper to be asked something. She tried.

"Miss Roberts! I'm so sorry I made a mess of my maths. this morning. If I promise to do better tomorrow, need I do those sums all over again? I've such a lot to do today."

But Miss Roberts was not to be caught like that! "My dear Isabel!" she said, "I am delighted that you have been able to give me back my pen – but I think you'll agree with me that that isn't any real reason why I should forgive you for shockingly bad work! And even if you find me my best hat, which unaccountably flew from my head last Sunday and completely disappeared over the fields, I should still say you must do your sums again!"

The class chuckled. Miss Roberts could be very dry when she liked. Isabel laughed too and went back to the cleaning and tidying.

"I wish I *could* find her hat for her!" she said. "She's jolly strict, but she's an awful sport!"

There was great excitement when the night of the concert came. For the last few days before the concert the girls had been in a state of great excitement, getting their lines perfect, and rehearsing everything. Each form was to do something, and the concert was to last three hours, with a break in between for refreshments.

Mam'zelle had taught French plays and songs to each form, and pestered the girls continually to make sure that they were word perfect. The sixth form were doing a short Greek play. The fifth were doing an absurd sketch that they had written themselves, called "Mrs. Jenkins Pays a Call", and borrowed all kinds of queer hats and clothes from the mistresses, and even from the school cook!

The fourth form had got up a jazz band, which sounded simply marvellous, though Mam'zelle said that she could easily do without the side-drum, which could be heard rat-a-tat-tatting from a music room at all kinds of odd hours. The third form were doing part of a Shakespeare play, and the second and first were doing plays and odd things such as Doris's solo dance, and Tessie's recitations.

Sheila was tremendously excited. She knew that if she had been given a part in the history play at the beginning she would never have had the chance of such a big part. Now, because of Vera's accident, she had a fine part. She practised it continually, thinking about it, putting in actions that Vera had never thought of, and astonishing every one by her acting.

"She's going to be jolly good!" whispered Janet to Pat. "I'm quite getting to like old Sheila now. Who would have thought there was a hardworking, interesting little person like that underneath all those old posings and boastings of hers!"

Pat and Isabel worked their hardest for the concert too. All the mistresses and the staff were coming and the whole school would be watching. Nobody must forget their words or do anything silly. Each form had its own honour to uphold!

The great night came. There were gigglings and whisperings all day long. Lessons slacked off that day, except Mam'zelle's French classes. Mam'zelle would surely not allow even an earthquake to spoil her lessons! No wonder that the girls were such excellent French scholars by the time that they reached the top form.

The sewing mistress worked at top speed to alter dresses at the last moment. Matron proved unexpectedly good at providing a real meal in one of the plays, instead of the pretend-one that Hilary had arranged for.

"Golly! Isn't that decent of her!" said Hilary, looking at the jug of lemonade and the currant buns that Matron had presented her with. "I *shall* enjoy my part in the play now!"

"Well, don't stuff your mouth so full that you can't speak," grinned Janet. "I say – what about asking Mam'zelle to let us have a meal of some sort in the French play too."

But nobody dared to mention such a thing to Mam'zelle!

At six o'clock the concert began. Everyone had filed into the gym., where benches and chairs had been set ready. The stage had its curtains and footlights, and looked fine. There were pots of plants borrowed from Miss Theobald's hothouse at the sides.

The mistresses sat in the three front rows leaving their forms to look after themselves for once. The kitchen staff sat behind the mistresses. The girls were on benches at the back, completely filling the gym.

Everyone had a programme, designed and coloured by the girls themselves. Pat was terribly proud to see that Miss Theobald had the one that she herself had done. She saw the Head looking carefully at the design of the cover, and she wondered if Miss Theobald would see her name in the corner – Pat O'Sullivan.

Every form knew when its turn was coming and knew when it must rise quietly and go to the back of the stage to dress and await its turn. The fifth form were acting their play first, and as soon as the curtains swung aside and showed the girls dressed up most ridiculously in odd hats and coats and shawls, the audience went off into fits of laughter. The school cook squealed out, "Oh, there's my old hat! I never thought I'd see it on a stage!"

The sketch was really funny and the audience loved it. Then came the Greek play by the sixth which was really a serious and difficult thing to understand. The first-formers listened politely and clapped hard at the end, but they secretly thought that the fifth form were very much better!

The fourth form came on with their jazz band, and this was an instant success. The drummer was simply marvellous and Mam'zelle quite forgave the constant irritation that the practising of the drum had given her. Swinging dance tunes were played, and the audience roared the choruses. They kept clapping for encores, but as it was now half-time, the jazz band had to stop at last!

How the girls enjoyed the trifles and jellies, cream-buns, sandwiches and lemonade! When they went into the dining-room to have their meal, they gasped at the sight of so much food.

"Golly! We'll never, never eat all that!" cried Pat.

"Patricia O'Sullivan, you don't know what you're talking about!" said Janet, lifting up a plate of asparagus sandwiches. "Speak for yourself! Have one – or two whilst they're here."

And sure enough Pat didn't know what she was talking about – for in twenty minutes not a thing was left on the dishes! The girls made a clean sweep of everything – and, hidden under the long cloth of the table, sat some one as hungry as the girls – Binks, the puppy-dog!

Kathleen had let him out secretly and had tied him to a leg of the big table. She gave him bits of sausage roll, which he ate eagerly. He was sensible enough not to poke his nose out in case he was discovered, and nobody guessed he was there except Isabel, who had been filled with astonishment at the amount of sausage rolls that Kathleen was apparently able to eat.

Then she suddenly realized what was happening. "Oh – you monkey, Kath! You've got Binks there."

"Sh!" said Kathleen. "Don't say a word. I didn't see why he should miss the fun. Isn't he good?"

Binks had a marvellous time after that, for there were two people feeding him instead of one!

The concert began again in half an hour. The first form gave their two short plays, and Sheila acted so magnificently that the audience actually roared her name and made her come and give a special bow. The girl was happier than ever she had been in her life, and looked quite pretty as she stood on the stage, flushed and excited. Winifred, the head-girl, smiled across at Pat to let her know how pleased she was, for she guessed that Pat and the others had been giving Sheila the chance she had begged for her.

The French play was a success too, and Mam'zelle

beamed round with pleasure when she heard it clapped so heartily. "Those first-form kids aren't half bad," Isabel heard Belinda Towers say, and she stored it up in her mind to tell the others later on.

Doris did her dance, which was really excellent. She too was encored, and came on again in a clown's dress. She proceeded to do the clown dance which had ended so disastrously on the night of the Great Feast, and this time it ended in plenty of cheers and clapping. Just as she was finishing, a disturbance arrived in the shape of Binks!

He had bitten through his lead and had come to join his mistress. Kathleen was in the wings at the side of the stage, watching Doris dancing. Binks leapt up on to the stage joyfully, to join Kathleen, and tripped Doris up very neatly, for all the world as if he were joining in the dance!

Doris promptly fell over just as the music ended. How the audience laughed and cheered! Binks turned round as he heard them, his pink tongue hanging out, and his tail wagging joyfully. Then he went to Kathleen, who, fearful of being scolded, rushed off at once to put him back into the stables.

But nobody scolded her, not even Mam'zelle, who had never ceased to say that she thought it was "abominable" and "insupportable" to allow "that dog" in the school!

The concert ended with the whole school singing the school song, a very swinging, heartening tune that the twins heard for the first time. They were the only ones who did not know it.

"We'll sing it *next* time!" whispered Pat to Isabel. "Oh, Isabel! What a lovely evening! It beats Redroofs hollow, don't you think?"

Then yawning hugely, for it was an hour past their usual bedtime, the first-formers went up to bed. They chattered and laughed as they undressed, and were just as long as they liked – for this was the last evening of term, and tomorrow they were breaking up and going home!

21   THE LAST DAY

Next day the trunks were dragged down from the loft. Each had its owner's name on in white paint, and soon they were being packed. Matron bustled to and fro, giving out clothes, and seeing that the girls packed at least moderately well. She made Doris take out every single thing and begin again.

"But Matron, I'll never have time!" said Doris laughing at Matron's annoyed face.

"If you stay here till next week you will pack properly!" said Matron, grimly. "Doris Elward, your mother and your two aunts came here years ago, and they never learnt to pack – but *you* are going to! It is *not* sensible to put breakable things at the bottom of your trunk, and shoes and boots on the top of your best things. Begin again!"

"Kath! What's your home address?" yelled Pat. "You said you'd give it to me and you haven't. I want to write to you for Christmas."

Kathleen went red with pleasure. No one had even bothered to ask for her address before. She wrote it down for Pat. Then there was a general exchange of addresses, and promises to telephone, and invitations for parties after Christmas if so-and-so could only manage to come

The school didn't seem like school any more. Everywhere there was babbling and chattering and giggling, and even when mistresses came into the classrooms and dormitories nobody thought of being quiet. The mistresses were excited too, and talked laughingly among themselves.

"I'm pleased with my lot this term," said Miss Roberts, watching Sheila throw something across to Pat. "Two or three of them have altered so much for the better that I hardly know them."

"What about those O'Sullivan twins?" asked Miss Jenks. "I thought they were going to be a handful when they came. They were called the 'stuck-up twins', you know, and at first I couldn't bear the look of their discontented faces."

"Oh, they're all right," said Miss Roberts at once. "They've settled down well. They've got good stuff in them. One of these days St. Clare's will be proud of them, mark my words! They're monkeys, though. Look out when you get them in your form some time next year!"

"Oh, they'll be all right after a term or two in your tender care!" laughed Miss Jenks. "I never have any trouble with girls that come up into my form from yours. It's only the new girls that come straight into my form that I have bother with."

Mam'zelle sailed by, beaming. She always entered every girl's address in a little black holiday note-book, and most conscientiously wrote to every one of them in the holidays.

"Good old 'Mam'zelle Abominable'!" whispered Pat as she went by. Mam'zelle's sharp ears heard what she said.

"What is that you call me?" she demanded, towering over Pat as she knelt packing her trunk.

"Oh – nothing, Mam'zelle," said Pat, horror-struck to think that Mam'zelle might have overheard. The other girls looked round, grinning. They all knew the twins' name for Mam'zelle.

"You will tell me, please. I demand it!" insisted Mam'zelle, her eyes beginning to flash.

"Well," said Pat, reluctantly, "I only call you 'Mam'zelle Abominable' because at first you called me and Isabel and our work abominable so often. Please don't be cross!"

But Mam'zelle was not cross. For some reason the name tickled her sense of humour, and she threw back her head and roared.

"Ha! 'Mam'zelle Abominable'! That is a fine name to call your French mistress. And next term your work will be so fine that I shall say you are *'magnifique!'* and you will then call me 'Mam'zelle Magnifique', *n'est ce pas?*"

At last all the packing was done. Each girl went to say a polite good-bye to Miss Theobald. When the twins went in together, she looked at them seriously, and then smiled an unusually sweet smile at them.

"I don't think you wanted to come to St. Clare's, did you?" she said. "And now somehow I think you've changed your minds?"

"Yes, we *have* changed our minds!" said Pat honestly. She never minded owning up when she altered her ideas. "We hated coming here. We were going to be really awful, and we did try to be. But – well – St. Clare's is fine."

"And we shall simply *love* coming back again next term," said Isabel, eagerly. "It's hard work here, and things aren't a bit the same as at our old school, and it's odd being one of the young ones after being top of the school – but we've got used to it now."

"One day maybe you'll be one of the top ones at St. Clare's," said Miss Theobald.

But the thought of being as grand and great as Winifred James was too much for the twins. "Oh, no!" said Pat. "We could never, never be that!"

But Miss Theobald smiled a secret smile. She knew far more about the girls than they knew about themselves, and she felt sure that she was right. These troublesome twins had the makings of fine girls, and she and St. Clare's would see to it that they fulfilled the promise they showed.

"Here are your reports," she said, and gave one to each girl. "Give my love to your mother and tell her that I haven't had to expel you yet!"

"I hope our reports are good," said Pat. "We told Daddy we weren't going to try a bit – and if they're bad he'll think we were jolly mean."

"Well, you'll see when you get home!" said Miss Theobald, smiling. "But – I wouldn't worry very much, if I were you! Good-bye!"

The twins said good-bye to every one, and received fat kisses on each cheek from Mam'zelle, who seemed unaccountably fond of every girl that day. Miss Roberts shook hands and warned them not to eat too much plum pudding. Miss Kennedy looked rather sad as she said good-bye, for her friend, Miss Lewis, was now quite well, and was coming back to take up her old post the next term.

"I shan't see you again," said Kenny, as she said good-bye to the twins. "I'm going to miss you all very much."

"Good-bye, Kenny," said Pat. "We were pigs to you at first – but you do forgive us for being piggy, don't you? And I do promise to write. I won't forget."

"Neither will I," said Isabel, and then Janet and Hilary and the rest came crowding up, and Miss Kennedy grew quite tearful as the girls poured good-byes and good wishes on her. What a good thing it was that she hadn't been a failure after all!

The most uproarious person that day was Binks. He was set free and spent his time taking chocolate from his friends, and going round licking people's hands and faces as they knelt to pack. No mistress had the heart to complain about him and he had a marvellous time.

"He *will* hate leaving me when I come back to school again!" said Kathleen, as she patted his wiry head. "But never mind – we shall have a whole month together. Miss Theobald wrote to my aunt, and Aunt is going to see if he behaves."

"Of *course* he'll behave!" said Janet. "But I expect he'll take after you, Kathleen – sometimes he'll behave well – and sometimes he won't!"

Kathleen laughed and gave Janet an affectionate punch. She didn't live a great way from the twins and they had already made plans to cycle over and see one another. She was very happy.

The bell rang to say that the first coach was ready to take the girls to the station. That was for the first form. Shouting good-byes to their teachers, the girls ran helter-skelter down the stairs and piled into the big motor-coach. What fun to be breaking up! What fun to be going home to Christmas jollities, parties and theatres! There were Christmas presents to buy, Christmas cards to send, all kinds of things to look forward to.

Pat and Isabel got into the train together and sat down with the others to wait for the rest of the school to come down in the coaches. Before very long the engine gave a violent whistle and the carriages jerked. They were off!

The twins craned their heads out of the window to see the last of the big white building they had grown to love.

"Good-bye!" said Pat under her breath. "We hated you when we first saw you, St. Clare's! But now we love you!"

"And we'll be glad to see you again!" whispered Isabel. "Oh, Pat – it's marvellous that we'll be going back in four weeks' time, isn't it? Good old St. Clare's!"

And then the school disappeared from sight, and the train rattled on its noisy way, singing a song that seemed to say over and over again, "We're pleased we're coming back again-TO-ST.-CLARE'S! We're pleased we're coming back again TO-ST.-CLARE'S!"

A funny song, but quite a true one, thought the twins!

THE O'SULLIVAN
TWINS

CONTENTS

'MOTHER! Did you know that Cousin Alison, who was at Redroofs School with us, is going to St. Clare's next term?' said Pat O'Sullivan, looking up from a letter she was reading. Her twin, Isabel, was reading it too, the two dark heads side by side at the breakfast table.

'Yes, I knew,' said their mother, smiling. 'Your Aunt Sarah wrote and told me. When she heard how much you liked St. Clare's, she decided to send Alison there too—and you can look after her a little, the first term.'

'Alison is a bit stuck-up,' said Pat. 'We saw her these hols., Mummy—full of airs and graces. And she has had her hair permed—think of that!'

'Shocking! At her age!' said Mrs. O'Sullivan. 'Quite time she went to St. Clare's!'

'I remember two girls who were terribly stuck-up last summer holidays,' said Mr. O'Sullivan, looking up from his newspaper. His eyes twinkled as he looked at the twins. 'My goodness—*they* didn't want to go to St. Clare's! They thought it would be a dreadful school—really horrid.'

Pat and Isabel went very red. 'Don't remind us of that, Daddy,' said Pat. 'We were idiots. We

behaved awfully badly at St. Clare's at first—every
one called us the Stuck-Up Twins.'

'Or the High-and-Mighties!' said Isabel, with a
giggle. 'Gracious—I can't think how any one put
up with us.'

'Well, we had a pretty bad time to start with,' said
Pat. 'And serve us right too. I hope Alison won't
be as stuck-up as we were.'

'She'll be worse,' said Isabel. 'She's so vain!
Mummy, couldn't you get Alison to come and stay
here for two or three days before we have to go back
to St. Clare's? Then we could tell her a few things.'

'Well, that would be very kind of you,' said Mrs.
O'Sullivan.

'It's not *alto*gether kindness,' said Isabel, with a
smile. 'Neither Pat nor I want to be saddled with a
cousin who's going to be silly and vain—and we may
be able to prepare her a bit if we have her a few days.'

'Lick her into shape, you mean?' said Mr. O'Sullivan, over the top of his paper. 'Well, if you can
make that conceited little monkey into somebody nice,
I shall be surprised. I never saw any one so spoilt
in all my life.'

'It's a good thing she's going to St. Clare's,' said
Pat, spreading marmalade on her toast. 'Don't you
think Isabel and I are nicer since we went there,
Daddy?'

'I'll have to think a little about that,' said their
father, teasingly. 'Well—yes—on the whole I'm
pleased with you. What do you say, Mother?'

'Oh, I think they settled down very well indeed
at St. Clare's,' said Mrs. O'Sullivan. 'They did so

hate going—and they vowed and declared they wouldn't try a bit—but Miss Theobald, the Head Mistress, said some very nice things on their report. They will be very happy there this term.'

'I don't want the hols. to end, but I can't help feeling quite excited when I think of seeing old Mam'zelle Abominable again,' said Pat, 'and Miss Roberts, and . . .'

'Mam'zelle *Abominable* !' said Mr. O'Sullivan, in astonishment. ' Is that really her name ? '

'Oh, no, Daddy—we only call her that because she says " *C'est abominable !* " to so many things ! ' said Pat. 'Isabel and I were awfully bad at French grammar at first and Mam'zelle used to write " Abominable " across our books. But she is a kind old thing, really.'

' It will be fun to see all the girls again too,' said Isabel. 'Mummy, write and tell Aunt Sarah to let Cousin Alison come next week before we go back.'

So Mrs. O'Sullivan wrote to her sister-in-law and Cousin Alison arrived two days before the girls were due back at school.

She was a very pretty girl, with curled red-brown hair, a rose-bud mouth, and big blue eyes.

' A bit like that doll we used to have, really,' said Pat to Isabel. ' We called her Angela, do you remember ? I wish Alison wouldn't smile that silly smile so much.'

' Oh, I expect some one has told her what a sweet smile she has, or something,' said Isabel. ' Really, she seems to think she's a film-star, the way she behaves ! '

Alison was pleased to be with her cousins so that she might go to St. Clare's with them, for, like most girls, she felt nervous at going for the first time to a new school. It didn't take long to settle down—but it felt rather strange and new at first.

'Tell me a bit about the school,' she said, as she sat down in the old schoolroom that evening. 'I hope it isn't one of these terribly sensible schools that make you play games if you don't want to, and all that.'

Pat winked at Isabel. 'Alison, St. Clare's is just about the most sensible school in the kingdom!' she said, in a solemn voice. 'You have to know how to clean shoes . . .'

'And make tea . . .' said Isabel.

'And toast,' went on Pat. 'And you have to know how to make your own beds . . .'

'And if you tear your clothes you have to mend them yourself,' said Isabel, enjoying Alison's look of horror.

'Wait a minute,' said Alison, sitting up. 'What do you mean—clean shoes, make tea—and toast? Surely you don't do that!'

The twins laughed. 'It's all right,' said Pat. 'You see, Alison, the first form and second form have to wait on the top-formers in turn. When they shout for us we have to go and see what they want, and jolly well do it.'

Alison went pink. 'It sounds pretty awful to me,' she said. 'What are the girls like? Are they awful too?'

'Oh, dreadful,' said Pat, solemnly. 'Very like Isabel and me, in fact. You'll probably hate them!'

' It doesn't sound a bit like Redroofs, the school
you went to with me only a term ago,' said Alison,
sadly. ' What's our form-mistress like ? Shall I be
in the same form as you ? '

' Yes, I should think so,' said Pat. ' We are in the
first form—we certainly shan't be moved up into the
second yet. Our form-mistress is Miss Roberts. She's
a good sort—but my word, she's sarcastic ! If you
get the wrong side of her you'll be sorry.'

' And Mam'zelle is hot stuff too,' said Isabel. ' She's
big, with enormous feet—and she's got a fearful temper
and she shouts.'

' Isabel, she sounds dreadful,' said Alison, in alarm,
thinking of the mouse-like French mistress at Redroofs.

' Oh, she's not a bad sort really,' said Pat, smiling.
' She's got a 'kind heart. Anyway, you needn't worry,
Alison—you'll have Isabel and me to look after you
a bit and show you everything.'

' Thanks,' said Alison, gratefully. ' I hope I'm in
the same dormitory as you are. What's Matron
like ? '

' Oh, Matron has been there for years and years and
years,' said Pat. ' She dosed our mothers and aunts,
and our grandmothers too, for all I know ! She knows
when we've had Midnight Feasts—she doesn't stand
any nonsense at all. But she's nice when you're ill.'

Alison learnt a great deal about St. Clare's during
the two days she stayed with the twins. She thought
they had changed since they had left Redroofs. She
stared at them and tried to think how they had
changed.

' They seem so sensible,' she thought. ' They were

always rather up in the air and proud, at Redroofs.
Oh well—they were head-girls there, and had something to be proud of—now I suppose they're among
the youngest in the school—and I shall be too.'

The day came for the three to leave for their boarding-
school. Everything had been packed. Mrs. O'Sullivan had got the same cakes and sweets for Alison's
tuck-box as she had bought for the twins. Everything was neatly marked and well-packed, and now
the three big trunks and the three tuck-boxes stood
ready in the hall, marked in white paint with the
names of the three girls.

Mrs. O'Sullivan was to see them off in London.
Pat and Isabel were excited at the thought of seeing
all their friends again. Alison was rather quiet. She
was very glad that she had the twins to go with.

They arrived on the platform from which their
train was to go—and then what an excitement there
was! 'There's dear old Janet! Hie, Janet, Janet!
Did you have good hols.? Oh, there's Hilary. Hallo,
Hilary—look, this is our Cousin Alison who's coming
to St. Clare's with us this term. Oh, there's Doris—
and Sheila!

Every one crowded round the twins, talking and
laughing. Alison was made known to them all, and
she felt very grateful to the twins for helping her in
this difficult first meeting with unknown girls.

A pleasant-faced mistress bustled up with a notebook
in hand. 'Good morning, Pat, good morning, Isabel!
Still as like as two peas, I see! Is this your cousin,
Alison O'Sullivan? Good—I'll tick her off in my list.
How do you do, Alison? I'm Miss Roberts, your

form-mistress. No doubt the twins have told you exactly how fierce and savage I am!'

She smiled and passed on to the next group. It was her job to see that all the first- and second-formers were there, and to get them into the train in time.

'Any new girls this term?' wondered Pat, looking round. 'I can't see any—except Alison, of course.'

'Yes—there's one over there—look!' said Isabel, nudging Pat. Pat looked, and saw a tall, rather good-looking girl standing by herself. She had a bad-tempered face, and was not trying to make friends with anyone at all. No one had come to see her off.

'She's new,' said Pat. 'I wonder if she'll be in our form. My word, I should think she's got a temper —I wonder what would happen if she and Janet had a row!'

Janet was very quick-tempered, and flared up easily. But it was soon over with her; this new girl, however, looked sulky, as well as bad tempered. The twins did not take to her at all.

'There's another new girl, too—look, just walking on to the platform!' said Isabel. 'She looks jolly nice! She'll be in our form, I should think.'

The second new girl was quite different from the one they had just seen. She was small, with dancing black curls, and she had deep blue eyes that sparkled and shone. Her father and mother were both with her.

'Her father must be an artist or a musician or something, his hair's so long!' said Pat.

'*I* know who he is,' said Hilary Wentworth, who was standing just nearby. 'He's Max Oriell—the famous painter. My aunt has just had her portrait painted by him—it's simply marvellous. I saw him once or twice when I went with her to a sitting. That must be his daughter. They're awfully alike.'

' She looks clever,' said Pat. ' I hope she's in our form.'

' Get into your carriages, please ! ' called Miss Roberts, in her clear voice. ' The train goes in three minutes. Say your good-byes now.'

So good-byes were said and the girls scrambled into their carriages, trying to sit by their own special friends. Alison thought that the top-formers, walking sedately along the platform, were very grown-up and dignified. She felt small when she saw them.

' There's Winifred James, our head-girl,' whispered Pat, as a tall, serious-looking girl went by. ' She's frightfully clever, and most awfully nice.'

' I should be afraid to say a word to her ! ' said Alison.

' We felt like that at first too,' said Isabel. ' Look —that's Belinda Towers, the sports captain. Pat and I got into a row with her last term—but we soon found she was a good sort. Golly, I hope she puts us down for a few matches this term, don't you, Pat ? '

The whistle blew. Handkerchiefs waved from windows. The train puffed out slowly, full to bursting-point with all the girls of St. Clare's. They were off to school again !

2   SETTLING IN

THE first day or two of a new term is always an exciting time. There are no proper time-tables, rules are not kept strictly, there is a lot of unpacking to be done—and best of all there are tuck-boxes to empty !

The twins missed their home and their mother at first, as did most of the girls—but there was so much to do that there was no time to fret or worry. In any case every one soon settled down into the school routine. It was fun to greet all the teachers again, fun to sit in the same old classroom, and fun to see if the ink-spot that looked like a cat with two tails was still on Janet's desk.

There were new books to be given out, and new pencils, rubbers, rulers and pens.

' Ah, the nice new books ! ' said Mam'zelle, her large eyes gleaming with pleasure as she looked round the class. ' The nice new books—to be filled with beautiful French compositions. Did you groan, Doris ? Surely you are not going to make my hair grey this term as you did last term ? Ah-h-h ! See this grey lock, *ma chère* Doris—it was you who caused that last term ! '

Mam'zelle pulled out a bit of grey hair from her thick thatch, and looked comically at Doris.

'I'll do my best, Mam'zelle,' promised Doris. 'But I shall never, never be able to say the French r's in the right way. Never!'

'R-r-r-r-!' said Mam'zelle, rolling the r in her throat in a most marvellous manner. The class giggled. Mam'zelle sounded remarkably like a dog growling, but nobody dared to say so.

The other teachers welcomed the girls in their own manner. Miss Roberts had already seen most of her girls in the train. Alison couldn't help liking her very much, though she was a little afraid of Miss Roberts's sharp tongue. Miss Roberts had a way of making an offender feel very small indeed.

The form-mistress had a special word for the twins. 'Well, Pat and Isabel, I can see by your faces that you've made up your minds to do well this term. You've got determination written all over you, Pat— and I know that Isabel always follows your example! What about being top in a few things this term?'

'I'd like to be,' said Pat, eagerly. 'We always were at Redroofs—the school we went to before, you know. Now that we've got used to St. Clare's we'll be able to work more quickly.'

Matron was in her room, giving out towels, sheets and pillow-cases, and warning everyone that any buttons would have to be sewn on by the girls themselves, and any tears would have to be neatly mended in sewing-class.

'But I can't mend sheets and things,' said Alison, in dismay.

'Maybe that's one of the things your mother sent you here to learn?' suggested Matron with her wide smile. 'You hope to be happily married one day, don't you—and run your own home ? Well, you must learn to take care of your own linen and mend it, then. But it doesn't seem to me that you need worry much—your mother has sent you all new things. So unless you *try* to kick holes in your sheets, and tear the buttons off there won't be much for you to do in the way of mending *this* term ! '

All the girls had to go and see Miss Theobald in turn. Alison went with Pat and Isabel. She felt very nervous as she stood outside the drawing-room with them, waiting to go in.

'What do I *say* ? ' she whispered. 'Is she very solemn ? '

The door opened and Janet and Hilary came out. ' You next,' said Hilary, and the waiting three went in. Alison liked Miss Theobald, the Head Mistress, at once. She had a very serious face that could break into a really lovely smile. She smiled now as she saw the three cousins.

' Well, Pat and Isabel, I am glad to see you back again, looking so happy,' she said. ' I remember last term, when I first saw you, you scowled and said hardly a word ! But this term I know you better. You will do your very best for your form, and for the school too.'

' Yes, of course, Miss Theobald,' said the twins, beaming.

Miss Theobald turned to Alison. ' And this is another O'Sullivan, a cousin ! ' she said. ' Well, with three O'Sullivans all working hard in the same form, Miss Roberts ought to be pleased ! You are lucky to have two sensible cousins to help you along in this first term, Alison.'

'Yes, Miss Theobald,' gasped Alison, still very nervous.

'You may go now,' said Miss Theobald. 'And remember, Pat and Isabel, that I am here to help in any difficulty, so don't be afraid to come, will you?'

The three went out, all a little awed, but all liking the Head Mistress immensely. They rushed to the common room, which Alison had not yet seen.

'Don't we have studies to ourselves here?' said Alison, in disappointment, looking round the big room that was shared by the first- and second-formers together. 'What an awful row!'

Certainly there was a noise. Girls were talking and laughing. Some one had put the gramophone on, and some one else, at the other end of the big room, was tinkering with the wireless, which kept making most extraordinary noises.

'You'll soon get used to the noise,' said Pat, happily. 'It's nice and friendly, really. Look—you can have this part of the shelf here for your belongings, Alison —your cake-tins and biscuit-tins—and your sewing or knitting and the library book you're reading. The next part belongs to me and Isabel. Keep your part tidy or you'll take up too much room.'

The twins showed their cousin over the school—the big classrooms with the lovely view from the windows —the enormous gym—the fine art-room, high up under the roof, with a good north light—the laboratory— even the cloakrooms, where each girl had a locker

for her shoes, and a peg for her out-door things and
her overall.

'Am I in the same dormitory as you, Pat?' asked
Alison, timidly, as she peeped in at the big bedrooms,
where eight girls slept in eight little cubicles each
night.

'I'll ask Hilary,' said Pat. 'She's head-girl of our
form, and she'll know. Hie, Hilary—do you know if
our Cousin Alison is in with us, or not?'

Hilary took out a list of names. 'Dormitory 8,'
she read out. 'Hilary Wentworth, Pat and Isabel
O'Sullivan, Doris Elward, Kathleen Gregory, Sheila
Naylor, Janet Robins and Alison O'Sullivan. There
you are—that's our dormitory list—same as last term,
except that Vera Johns has gone into number 9—to
make room for Alison, I suppose.'

'Oh, good,' said Pat. 'You're with us, Alison
That's a bit of luck for you.'

The three new girls were in the first form with Miss
Roberts. The tall bad-tempered-looking girl was called
Margery Fenworthy. She looked old enough to be in
the second form, but the girls soon saw that her work
was poor—not even up to the standard of the first
form, really.

'Isn't she a funny creature?' said Pat to Isabel,
after a morning in class with Margery. 'She simply
doesn't seem to care a bit what she does or says. I've
an idea she can be awfully rude. Goodness—there'll
be a row if she gets across Mam'zelle!'

Margery Fenworthy kept herself to herself. She
was always reading, and if anyone spoke to her she
answered so shortly that nobody said any more. She

would have been very good looking if she had smiled —but, as Pat said, she always looked as if she wanted to bite somebody's head off!

Lucy Oriell, the other new girl, was the complete opposite of Margery. She was brilliantly clever, but as she was only fourteen and a half, she was put into the first form for that term at any rate. Nothing was difficult to her. She had a wonderful memory, and was always merry and gay.

'The way she gabbles French with Mam'zelle!' groaned Doris. 'The way she draws in the art class! The way she recites yards and yards of Shakespeare, and it takes me all my time to learn two lines properly.'

Every one laughed. Doris was a duffer—with one great talent. She could make people laugh! She could dance well and comically, and she could mimic others perfectly, which made it all the more strange that she could not imitate Mam'zelle's French accent. Every one liked Doris.

'An absolute idiot—but such a nice one!' as Janet said.

'What do you think of the three new girls, Janet?' asked Hilary, biting the end of her pencil as she tried to think out a problem in arithmetic set by Miss Roberts.

Pat and Isabel were nearby, listening. Janet shook back her dark hair, and gave her judgment.

'Lucy Oriell—top-hole! Clever, responsible, kind and gay. Margery Fenworthy—a bad-tempered, don't-care creature with some sort of PAST.'

'Whatever do you mean?' said Pat, astonished.

'Well, mark my words, there's something behind

that funny way Margery has of keeping herself to herself, and of not caring tuppence for anything or anybody,' said Janet, who could be very far-seeing when she wanted to. 'And what does a girl of fifteen want to be so bad-tempered for? I'd just like to know how she got on at her last school. I bet she didn't make any friends!'

The twins stared across at Margery, who, as usual, had her nose buried in a book. Janet went on to the third new girl, Alison.

'I suppose I mustn't say much about Alison, as she's your cousin—but if you want my real opinion it's this—she's a conceited, stuck-up little monkey without a single idea in her pretty little head!'

'Thanks for your opinions, Janet,' said Hilary, with a laugh. 'You have a wonderful way of putting into words just exactly what every one else is thinking—and doesn't say!'

3 ALISON LEARNS A LESSON

THE Easter term opened very cold and dreary. The girls shivered when they got up in the morning. Alison simply hated getting up. Time after time Hilary stripped the clothes from her, and Alison almost wept with anger. Nothing like that had ever happened at her old school !

' Don't do that ! ' she cried, each time. ' I was *just* going to get up ! '

Every one grinned. They thought Alison was very silly sometimes. She spent ages doing her hair and looking at herself in the glass—and if she had a spot on her face she moaned about it for days till it went.

' As if anybody would notice if she had twenty spots ! ' said Janet, in disgust. ' She's not worth looking at, the vain little thing ! '

In a week or two it seemed to the twins as if they had been back at school for months ! Each form was now working steadily to its own time-table. Lacrosse games were played three times a week, and any one could go to the field and practise in their spare time. Gym was held twice a week, and the twins loved that. The new girl, Margery, was excellent at all the things they did in gym.

' She's strong, isn't she ? ' said Pat, admiringly, as

they watched her climbing up the thick rope that
hung down from the ceiling.

'She plays games and does gym as if she was fighting
somebody fiercely all the time!' said Janet, hitting
the nail on the head, as usual. 'Look at her gritting
her teeth as she climbs that rope. My word, I don't
like marking her at lacrosse I can tell you. She's
given me some bruises across my knuckles even though
I wear padded gloves!'

Janet showed the bruises. 'She's a savage creature!' said Doris. 'Belinda ticked her off yesterday
for deliberately tripping me up on the field. All the
same, she'd be a good one to have in a match! If
she wanted to shoot a goal she'd jolly well shoot one,
even if she had to knock down every single one of
the other side!'

Lucy Oriell was a fine lacrosse player too. She had
been captain of the lacrosse team at her old school,
and she was as swift as the wind.

'She's good at everything, the lucky creature!'
said Hilary. 'Have you seen some of her pictures?
They really are lovely. She showed me some water-
colours she'd done in the hols. with her father. I
couldn't believe they were hers. Of course, she gets
that from him. He must make a lot of money from
his portraits—no wonder all her dresses are so
good.'

'It's a pity that silly cousin of yours doesn't try
a bit harder at games,' said Janet, watching Alison
trying to catch a lacrosse ball in her net. It was
a very easy throw sent by Kathleen. But Alison
muffed it as usual.

'Alison, haven't you ever played games before?'
cried Janet.

'Yes,' said Alison, flushing. 'But I played hockey
—much better game than this stupid lacrosse. I'd
always rather hit a ball than catch it! I was jolly
good at hockey, wasn't I, Pat, at Redroofs?'

Pat did not remember Alison ever being good at
any game, so she said nothing. Belinda Towers came
up and spoke to the twins.

'I say, can't you do something about that silly
little cousin of yours? She just stands and bleats at
me when I order her to practise catching and throwing!
She wants a bit of pep in her.'

Pat laughed. Alison did bleat—that was just the
right word for it.

'I'll try and take her in hand,' she said. 'After
all, I was pretty awful myself at first, last term—and
I'll try and knock some sense into Alison, in the same
way that it was knocked into me and Isabel.'

'She thinks too much about herself,' said Belinda,
in her direct way. 'Stupid sickly smile, big blue eyes,
bleating little voice—make her skip around a bit,
can't you? I really can't stand much more of her.'

So Pat and Isabel made Alison skip around a bit!
She was very indignant indeed.

'Why do you always make me go and practise this
silly catching just when I want to finish my book!'
she grumbled. 'Why do you hustle me out for a
walk when it's so cold and windy? If you call this
looking after me I'd rather you stopped!'

Soon it was Alison's turn to wait on the two top-
formers, Rita George and Katie White! They sent

a runner for her at tea-time one day. Alison had just finished her own tea when the message came.

'Alison! Rita wants you. Buck up. It's your turn to do her jobs this week.'

'What jobs?' said Alison, crossly, swallowing her last mouthful of cake.

'How do I know? Making her tea, I expect. And I think the fire's gone out in her room. You'll have to rake it out and lay it again for her.'

Alison nearly burst with indignation. 'What, me light a fire! I've never lighted one in my life! I don't even know how to lay one.'

'If you don't go, Alison, you'll get into a row,' said Isabel. 'Katie White isn't as patient as Rita. Go on. Don't be a ninny.'

Alison, grumbling under her breath all the while, went slowly off to Rita's study. Rita looked up impatiently as she came in.

'Good heavens, are you always as slow as this! What bad luck to have *you* waiting on us this week. We won't get a thing done!'

'Rake out the fire and lay it again quickly,' said Katie White, in her deep voice. 'There's some paper and sticks in that cupboard. Go on, now—we've got some other girls coming in for tea.'

Poor Alison! She raked out the fire as best she could, got the paper and sticks from the cupboard and put them higgledy-piggledy into the grate. The grate was hot and she burnt her hand when she touched it. She let out a loud squeal.

'What's the matter?' said Rita, startled.

'I've burnt my hand on the hot grate,' said Alison,

nursing her hand against her chest, though really it hardly hurt at all.

'Well, really—did you imagine the grate would be stone-cold after having had a fire in it all day?' asked Rita, impatiently. 'For goodness' sake hurry up and light the fire. There's a box of matches on the mantelpiece.'

Alison took down the matches. She struck one and held it to the paper; it flared up at once. At the same moment three more big girls came in, chattering. One was Belinda Towers. No one took any notice of the first-former lighting the fire. Alison felt very small and unimportant.

The paper burnt all away. The sticks of wood did not catch alight at all. Bother! There was no more paper in the cupboard. Alison turned timidly to Rita.

'Please, where is there some more paper?'

'On the desk over there,' said Rita, shortly, scowling at Alison. The top-formers went on talking and Alison went to a nearby desk. She looked at the papers there. They were sheets covered with Rita's small neat handwriting.

'I suppose it's old work she doesn't want,' thought Alison, and picked it up. She arranged the sheets in the fire-place, and then set a match to them. At the same moment she heard a loud exclamation from Rita.

'I say! I say! You surely haven't taken my prep. to burn? She has·! Oh, the silly donkey, she's taken my French prep.!'

There was a rush for the fire. Alison was pushed

out of the way.   Rita tried to pull some of the blazing
sheets out—but the flames had got a good hold of
them and she could not save any of her precious prep.
It was burnt to black ashes.

'Alison!   How dare you do a thing like that,'
cried Rita, in a rage.   'You deserve to have your
ears boxed.'

'I didn't mean to,' said poor Alison, beginning to
cry all over the fire-place, near which she was still
kneeling.   'You said—take the paper on the desk
over there—and . . .'

'Well, can't you tell the difference between yesterday's newspaper and to-day's French prep. ? ' stormed
the angry fifth-former.   'Now I shall have to do an
hour's extra work and rewrite all that French !'

'*And* she hasn't even lighted the fire yet !' said
Belinda Towers.   'Just as stupid at doing household
jobs as you are in the sports field, Alison.'

'Please let me go,' wept Alison, feeling half-dead
with shame before the accusing faces of the big girls.
'I can't light a fire.   I really can't.'

'Then it's just about time you learnt,' said Rita,
grimly.   'Now, where's that paper ?   Put it like this
—and like this.   Now get the sticks.   Arrange them
so that the flames can lick up them and set the coal
alight.   Now put some coal on the top.   Good heavens,
idiot, what's the good of putting an enormous lump
like that on top ?   You've squashed down all the
sticks !   Take little lumps to start a fire with—like
this.'

Alison wept all the time, feeling terribly sorry for
herself.   She held a match to the paper with a shaking

hand. It flared up—the sticks caught—the coal burnt —and there was the fire, burning merrily.

'Now put the kettle on the hob just there, and you can go, baby,' said Katie. 'Where do you get all those tears from? For goodness' sake, come away from the fire or you'll put it out again!'

Alison crept out of the room, tears running down her cheeks. She stopped at a mirror and looked at herself. She thought that she looked a most sad and pathetic sight—rather like a film-star she had seen crying in a picture. She went back to the common room, sniffing, hoping that every one would sympathize with her.

But to her surprise, nobody did—not even kind-hearted Lucy Oriell. Pat looked up and asked her what was up.

Alison told her tale. When she related how she had burnt Rita's French prep. papers the first-formers looked horrified.

'Fathead!' said Janet, in disgust. 'Letting down our form like that! Golly, the big girls must think we are mutton-heads!'

'It was *awful* being rowed at by so many of the big girls,' wept Alison, thinking that she must look a very pathetic sight. But every one was disgusted.

'Stop it, Alison. You're not in a kindergarten,' said Hilary. 'If you want to behave like an idiot, you must expect the top-formers to treat you like one. For goodness' sake stop sniffing. You look simply awful, I can tell you. Your eyes are red, your nose is swollen, your mouth has gone funny—you look just as ugly as can be!'

That made Alison weep really bitterly. Janet lost her temper. ' Either stop, or go out,' she said roughly to Alison. ' If you don't stop I'll put you out of the room myself. You've no right to disturb us all like this.'

Alison looked up. She saw that sharp-tongued Janet meant what she said. So she stopped crying at once, and the twins grinned at each other.

' Lesson number one ! ' whispered Pat.

4   TESSIE HAS A SECRET

THE first real excitement of the term was Tessie's birthday. Tessie was a lively girl in the second form, fond of tricks and jokes. She and Janet were a pair ! The girls often laughed when they remembered how the term before Janet had thrown fire-works on the schoolroom fire, and given poor Miss Kennedy such a fright.

' And do you remember how Tessie hid the big black cat in the handwork cupboard, and it jumped out at Miss Kennedy and made her rush out of the room ? ' giggled Doris. ' Oh, golly—I've never laughed so much in all my life.'

Miss Kennedy had gone, and in her place was Miss Lewis, a first-class history-teacher. The girls liked her very much, except for one thing—she would not allow the slightest inattention or cheekiness in her classes. Even free-tongued Janet was a model of good behaviour in Miss Lewis's classes. Only surly Margery seemed to care nothing for anything the history teacher said.

Tessie had great ideas for her birthday. She knew she would have plenty of money sent to her, and plenty of good things to eat. She was a generous girl, and wanted every one to share.

But there would not be enough for every one. If

Tessie put all her things on the table at tea-time there would only be a tiny bit for each of the forty or fifty first- and second-formers.

Tessie thought about it. She talked to her great friend, Winnie Thomas.

'Winnie, don't you think it would be better to share my things amongst a few of my *best* friends—and not give every one only a taste?' said Tessie.

'Yes, I do think that,' said Winnie. 'But when can we give the party? We can't very well just ask a few of the ones we like, and leave the rest to stare jealously!'

'Well, we'll have to have the party when there's no one there except the ones we ask,' said Tessie. 'And that means—at night! On my birthday night!'

'But we can't have it in the dormitory,' said Winnie. 'The others would know then. We must keep it a secret. It won't be any fun if we don't.'

'We won't have it in the dormitory,' said Tessie. 'But where in the world *can* we have it, without being found out?'

'I know! We'll have it in that little music-room not far from our dormitory!' said Winnie, her eyes shining. 'It's just the place. No one ever goes there at night. If we pull down the blinds, and shut the door no one will ever know we are there. We mustn't make much noise though—it's rather near Mam'zelle's study.'

'It'll be all the more fun if we mustn't make much noise,' giggled Tessie. 'How can we warm that room? It's awfully cold in there. I know, because I had to practise there last week.'

'Let's borrow an oil-stove out of the cupboard

downstairs ! ' said Winnie. ' Some of them have oil in, I know, because they're not emptied when they are put away in that cupboard.'

' Good idea ! ' said Tessie, who liked everything to be as perfect as possible when she planned anything. Then a thought struck her—' Oooh, Winnie—do you think we could fry sausages on the top of the oil-stove if I could buy some ? I could get some of those tiny little sausages—I forget what they're called—the kind people often have to put round chickens ? '

Winnie stared at Tessie in delight. ' I don't believe ANY ONE has ever fried sausages at a birthday party in the middle of the night before ! ' she said. ' Not any one. It would be a most marvellous thing to do. Can we get a frying-pan ? '

' You bet ! ' said Tessie. ' I'll ask young Gladys, the scullery-maid, to lend me one for the night. She's a good sport and won't tell. And if I can't borrow one, I'll jolly well buy one ! '

' Tessie, this is going to be awful fun,' said Winnie, dancing about. ' What do you suppose you'll have for your party—besides your birthday cake and the sausages ? '

' Well, Mother always sends me a big fruit cake, a ginger cake, sweets, biscuits and home-made toffee,' said Tessie. ' And I'll have plenty of money to buy anything else we want. I'll get some tins of peaches. We all like those.'

The two girls went into corners and whispered excitedly every day. Mam'zelle noticed their inattention in class and scolded them for it.

' Tessie ! Winnie ! Do you wish me to send you

down into the first-form ? You sit there staring out
of the window and you do not pay one small piece
of attention to all I am saying ! What mischief are
you planning ? '

This was so near the mark that both girls went red.
' It's my birthday soon, Mam'zelle,' said Tessie, meekly,
knowing that Mam'zelle usually understood an excuse
like that.

' Ah, I see—and I suppose it is dear Winnie's birthday also ? ' said Mam'zelle. ' Well, unless you both
wish to write me out a ver-r-r-ry nice composition in
your best French all about birthdays you will please
pay attention to *me*.'

The two girls decided to ask only six more girls to
the party. Tessie didn't see why they should all be
from the second-form. ' You know, I like those
O'Sullivan twins awfully,' she said. ' I'd like to ask
them. They're good sports.'

' Yes—but for goodness' sake don't ask that awful
cousin of theirs, always strutting about like a peacock,'
said Winnie.

' Of course not,' said Tessie. ' I simply couldn't
bear her. No—we'll ask Pat and Isabel—and Janet.
And out of our own form we'll ask Hetty, Susan and
Nora. What do you think of that ? '

' Yes—fine,' agreed Winnie.

' We'll have to be careful not to let that sneaky
Erica guess about our party,' said Tessie, thoughtfully.
' She's such a Paul-Pry—always sticking her nose into
things that don't concern her. She's an awful tell-tale
too. I'm sure she sneaked about me to Miss Jenks,
when I lost that lacrosse ball.'

'We'll tell every one to keep it a close secret,' said Winnie. 'I say—won't it be fun ? '

Tessie got hold of the twins that day and took them to a corner. 'Listen,' she said, 'I'm having a small birthday party on Thursday—just you and five others. Will you come ? '

'Oh, yes, thanks,' said Pat, pleased at being asked by a second-former.

'What time ? ' asked Isabel.

'Twelve o'clock at night,' giggled Tessie. The twins stared in surprise.

'Oh—is it a midnight feast, like we had last term ? ' asked Pat, eagerly.

'No—not quite,' said Tessie. 'It's not going to be held in the dormitory, like a midnight feast—we are going to have it in that little music-room not far from my dormitory. You know the one I mean ? '

'Yes,' said Pat. 'I say—what fun ! It will be a proper midnight party, all by ourselves. Who else are you asking ? '

'Four from my form, not counting myself,' said Tessie, 'and you two and Janet from your form. That's all. Now mind you come at twelve o'clock. And oh—I say ! '

'What ? ' asked the twins.

'Don't say a word to any one, will you,' begged Tessie. 'You see, I can't ask every one, and some of the girls might be a bit annoyed they haven't been asked.'

'Of course we won't say a word,' said Pat. The twins went off together, and waited until Tessie had told Janet. Then the three of them whispered together excitedly about the twelve-o'clock party! It was fun to have a secret. It was fun to be asked by a second-former—chosen out of all the girls in their form!

Alison was very curious, for she knew quite well that her cousins had a secret. She kept badgering them to tell her.

'Oh, shut up, Alison,' said Pat. 'Can't we have a secret without telling the whole form?'

'It wouldn't be telling the whole form, if you only told *me*,' said Alison, opening her blue eyes very wide and looking as beseeching as she could.

'My dear Alison, telling you would be quite the quickest way of telling the whole *school*!' said Pat. 'You can't keep your mouth shut about anything. You just go round and bleat out every single thing.'

This wasn't very kind but it was perfectly true. Alison couldn't keep anything to herself at all, and had so often given away little things that the twins had told her that now they left her out of all their secrets.

Alison went away, pouting. Erica, from the second form, saw her and went up to her. She was just as curious as Alison about other people's plans and secrets.

'It's a mean trick, to have plans and keep every one in the dark,' said Erica. 'I know Tessie and Winnie have got some sort of plan too—it's about Tessie's birthday, I think. I wish we could find out about it. That would just serve them right.'

Alison didn't like Erica. Few people did, for she really was a sneak. Not even the mistresses liked her, for they much preferred not to know what was going on rather than have Erica come telling tales.

So Alison would not take Erica's hint and try to find out what was up, though she really longed to do so. Erica asked her again and again if she had discovered anything, but Alison stubbornly shook her head. Silly little vain thing as she was, she was not going to find out things to tell Erica.

Hetty, Susan and Nora kept their mouths shut too, about the party. Winnie, of course, did not say a word to any one except the four in her form who knew. So it was very difficult for Erica really to find out anything much. She guessed that it was to do with Tessie's birthday—and she guessed it was a party—but how, where and when she had no idea.

The plans went steadily forward. Gladys, the little scullery maid, giggled when Tessie asked her for the loan of a frying-pan. She put one under her apron and went to find Tessie. On the way she met Erica.

'Whatever are you hiding under your apron, Gladys?' said Erica, with the high and mighty air that the servants so much disliked. Gladys tossed her neat little head.

'Nothing to do with you, miss,' she answered pertly. Erica was angry. She pulled Gladys's apron aside and saw the pan.

'Oho! For Miss Tessie's party!' she said. It was only a guess—but Gladys at once thought that Erica knew.

'Well, miss, if you knew, why did you ask me?' she said. 'I'm to take it to the little music-room near Miss Tessie's dormitory.'

Erica watched Gladys slip inside the music-room and put the pan into a cupboard, under a pile of music. It was Tessie's birthday to-day. So the party was near—probably at night. The inquisitive girl burned with curiosity and jealousy.

Tessie was having a marvellous birthday. She was a popular girl, for she was amusing and lively. The girls gave her small presents and wished her many happy returns of the day. Tessie handed round a big box of chocolates to every one in her form. Her grandmother had sent it for her—and Tessie meant to share something with *all* her friends, even though she could not share her party with every one.

Erica kept as close as she could to Tessie and Winnie that day, hoping to find out something more about the party. She saw Tessie go to the cupboard where the oil-stoves were kept—and fetch out a big stove!

She did not dare to ask Tessie what she was doing with it, for Tessie had a sharp tongue for Erica. But she hid behind a door and watched Tessie through the crack.

Into the music-room went Tessie, carrying the heavy stove. Erica's eyes shone with delight. She felt sure that the party was to be held there. 'It will have to be after eleven,' thought the girl. 'I know pretty well everything now—serves Tessie right for leaving me out! Nasty, sharp-tongued creature! I've a good mind to spoil the party!'

It is quite likely that Erica would have done nothing more, now that she was satisfied she knew the secret, if Winnie and Tessie had not caught her taking a chocolate from the big box that Tessie had handed

round. Tessie had left it in her classroom, meaning
to ask Miss Lewis, the history teacher, to have one.
Erica had seen it there, and had not been able to stop
herself from lifting the lid to look at the layers.

She could not resist taking one of the chocolates
and popping it into her mouth. After all, there were
plenty ! But just at that moment Tessie and Winnie
came running into the room.

They stopped in amazement when they saw Erica
hurriedly shutting the lid of the box. It was quite
plain that she had a chocolate in her mouth.

'You are simply disgusting, Erica,' said Tessie,
coldly. 'If you'd wanted another and had asked me
I'd have willingly given you as many as you wanted.
But to sneak in and take one like that—you really
are a disgusting creature.'

The two girls went out. Erica had not been able
to say a word. A chocolate was only a chocolate—
how dared Tessie speak to her like that ? Erica's
cheeks burned and she longed to throw the whole
box of sweets out of the window.

But she did not dare to. She went to her desk
and slouched down into the seat. 'Calling me disgusting !' said the girl, in a fury. 'I won't have it !
I'll pay her out for this ! I'll spoil her precious party !
I'll keep awake to-night till I see them going out of
the dormitory—then I'll find a way to have them all
caught !'

5   WHAT HAPPENED AT THE PARTY

EVERYTHING was ready for the party. Tessie had even been into the little music-room and lighted the oil-stove to get the room warm for her guests !

'No one ever goes in there at night,' she said to Winnie, who was afraid that somebody might see the stove, if they went in. 'The room will be lovely and warm by the time we are ready ! '

The two girls were in a great state of excitement. Tessie had had *two* birthday cakes sent to her, which pleased her very much. She had been able to put the bigger one of the two on the tea-table for all her form to share—and had kept the other for the midnight party.

There were biscuits, sweets, chocolates, a big fruit cake, and four tins of peaches, with a tin of Nestle's milk for cream ! There were also the strings of little sausages to fry. It was going to be great fun !

'We haven't anything to drink ! ' whispered Winnie to Tessie, in arithmetic at the end of that morning.

'Yes, we have. I've got some ginger-beer,' whispered back Tessie. Miss Jenks caught the word 'ginger-beer'.

'Tessie, how does ginger-beer come into our arithmetic lesson ? ' she enquired, coldly.

'Well—it doesn't,' said Tessie, at a loss what to say. 'Sorry, Miss Jenks.'

Susan, Hetty and Nora winked at one another. They knew quite well where the ginger-beer came in! Erica saw the winks and smiled to herself. She was going to spoil that party, ginger-beer and all!

Everything was hidden in the music-room, ready for that night. The eight girls were in a great state of excitement. They had all been in to peep at the things in the cupboard. The music-mistress would have been most surprised if she had taken a peep too —for instead of the usual piles of old music, a metronome or two, old hymn-books and so on, she would have seen a big birthday cake with 'Happy returns to Tessie!' on it, and a big tin full of other goodies —to say nothing of eight fat brown ginger-beer bottles!

'How are we going to keep awake till twelve o'clock?' said Pat to Isabel and Janet.

'Oh, I'll be awake at twelve,' said Janet, who had lately got the idea that she could wake at any time she liked, merely by repeating the hour to herself half a dozen times before she went to sleep. 'I shall simply say "twelve o'clock" firmly to myself before I go to sleep. And then I shall wake on the first stroke of midnight! You just see.'

'Well, Janet, I hope you're right,' said Pat, doubtfully. 'I've tried that heaps of times but it never works with me. I just go on sleeping.'

'It's will-power,' said Janet. 'You needn't worry. I shall wake you all right!'

So the twins went peacefully to sleep as usual at

half-past nine, trusting to Janet to wake them. Janet went to sleep too, saying ' twelve o'clock, twelve o'clock ' steadily to herself, as she dropped off.

But alas for Janet ! Midnight came—and she slept on ! Her will-power must have been a little weak that night ! The three first-formers would certainly have missed the party if the second-formers hadn't sent to see why they didn't turn up !

Pat was awakened by some one tugging at her arm, and a torch being flashed into her face. She woke with a jump and was just about to give a squeal of fright when she saw that it was Winnie who held the torch. In a flash she remembered the party.

' Pat ! For goodness' sake ! Aren't you three coming ? ' whispered Winnie.

' Of course,' said Pat. ' I'll wake the others.' She threw off the bed-clothes, slipped her feet into her slippers and put on her warm dressing-gown. She went to wake Isabel and Janet. Soon the three of them were creeping out of the room, down a few stairs, round a corner past the second-form dormitory, and into the music-room.

The door opened and shut quietly and the three girls blinked at the bright electric light. The blinds had been drawn and the oil-stove had made the little room as warm as toast. The other five girls were busy opening tins and setting out cake and biscuits.

' Whatever happened to you ? ' said Tessie, in surprise. ' It's a quarter-past twelve. We waited and waited. Then we sent Winnie.'

' It was my fault,' said Janet, looking ashamed of

herself, a most unusual thing for Janet. ' I promised
I'd wake them—and I didn't. I say—what a marvellous cake ! '

The girls set to work to eat all the good things,
giggling at nothing. It was so exciting to be cooped
up in the little music-room, gobbling all sorts of goodies
when every one else was fast asleep.

' Oh, Susan—you've spilt peach-juice all over my
toes,' giggled Janet.

' Lick it off then,' said Susan. ' I bet you can't ! '

Janet was very supple. She at once tried to reach
her foot up to her mouth to lick off the juice from
her bare pink toes. She overbalanced and fell off her
music-stool.

' Janet ! You've sat on the sausages ! ' hissed
Tessie, in dismay. ' Get up, you idiot. Oh, the poor
sausages—all squashed as flat as pan-cakes ! '

The girls began to giggle helplessly. Tessie tried
to press the little sausages back into their ordinary
shape again.

' When are we going to fry them ? ' asked Isabel,
who loved sausages.

' Last thing,' said Tessie. ' That is, if there is
anything left of them when Janet has finished with
them ! '

The ginger-beer was opened. Each bottle had a top
that had to be taken off with an opener, and each
bottle gave a pop as it was opened.

' If any one hears these pops they'll wonder whatever's happening in this music-room,' said Susan.

' Well, nobody *will* hear,' said Tessie. ' Every one
is fast asleep. Not a soul in our own dormitory knows

Soon they were creeping down the stairs

that we slipped out. Not a single person knows our secret ! '

But Tessie boasted too soon. Some one was already outside the closed door, with her eye to the keyhole and her sharp ears trying to catch all that was said. Erica knew quite well all that was going on. Soon she caught her own name, and she stiffened outside the door, as she tried to hear what was said.

It was Tessie who was speaking. She was handing round chocolates. ' We caught that nasty little sneak Erica helping herself to the chocolates this afternoon,' she said, in her clear voice. ' Isn't she the limit ? '

' Oh, she's always doing things like that,' said Pat. ' You can't trust her an inch.'

Erica felt the tears coming into her eyes. The girls had often told her unpleasant things to her face —but somehow it was horrible hearing them spoken behind her back. But the tears passed into tears of rage.

' I'll give them a few frights ! ' thought Erica, furiously. ' And then I'll go and fetch Miss Jenks. It will serve the wretches right.'

Erica knocked softly on the door, and then, quick as lightning, darted into a nearby cupboard. She hoped that her knocking would give the girls a shock.

It gave them a most terrible shock ! They all stopped talking at once, and Tessie put down the box of chocolates with a shaking hand. They stared at one another, round-eyed.

' What was that ? ' whispered Tessie.

' A knock at the d-d-d-door,' stuttered Winnie.

There was dead silence. Every one waited to see if the door would open. But it didn't.

Erica was still hidden in the cupboard. As nothing happened, she crept out again and knocked once more on the door, this time quite smartly. Then back she hopped to the cupboard again, beginning to enjoy herself.

The eight girls in the music-room jumped almost out of their skins when the second knocking came. 'There must be somebody there,' said Tessie, quite pale with fright. 'I'll go and see.'

She went bravely to the door and opened it. There was no one there! Tessie shone her torch into the passage. It was perfectly empty. The girl shut the door and went back to her seat, looking frightened.

'It wasn't any one,' she said.

'Stuff and nonsense,' said Janet, beginning to recover from her fright. 'Doors don't knock by themselves! It must be some one having a joke.'

'But, Janet, no one knows we are here,' said Isabel.

'Shall we get back to bed—and not fry the sausages?' asked Tessie.

That was too much for Isabel. 'What, not fry the sausages when I've been looking forward to them all the evening!' she said, indignantly.

'Shut up, idiot! Do you want to wake the whole school?' said Pat, giving her a nudge that nearly sent her off her chair. 'Fry the sausages, Tessie, old girl. I think that knocking must have been the wind!'

So the sausages were fried, and sizzled deliciously in the pan on the top of the oil-stove. Tessie turned them over and over with a fork, trying not to squeal when the hot fat jumped out and burnt her.

Erica had crept out of the cupboard again. She heard the sizzling of the sausages, and the lovely smell made her feel hungry. She wondered what to do next. A noise made her scurry back to her cupboard. What could it be ?

Then Erica knew. It was Mam'zelle in her study, having one of her late nights ! The French mistress sometimes stayed up very late, reading and studying —and tonight she was still in her study ! Erica smiled to herself. She knew what she was going to do now. She wouldn't tell Miss Jenks ! She would let hot-tempered Mam'zelle find out—and she herself wouldn't come out into the open at all !

' I'll go and knock at Mam'zelle's door,' said Erica to herself. ' Then I'll skip back to the dormitory. Mam'zelle will open her door in surprise—and when she finds no one there she'll go and prowl around, if I know anything about her ! And it won't be long before she smells those sausages ! '

So Erica slipped up the passage to the door of the little room that Mam'zelle used as a study. She knocked smartly on it three times—rap-rap-rap !

' *Tiens !* ' came Mam'zelle's voice, in the greatest surprise. ' Who is there ! '

There was no answer, of course, for Erica had slipped as quietly as a mouse away from the door—not into the cupboard this time, but back into her dormitory. She guessed there would soon be trouble about, and she wasn't going to share in it !

Mam'zelle slid back her chair and went to the door,

puzzled. She threw it open, but there was no one there. She stood there for a moment, wondering if she could possibly have been mistaken—and then she heard, from somewhere not very far off, a subdued giggle. And down the passage crept the unmistakable smell of—frying sausages !

6   MAM'ZELLE MAKES A DISCOVERY

MAM'ZELLE could not believe her senses. What—frying sausages at a quarter to one at night! It was not possible. She must be dreaming. Mam'zelle gave herself a hard pinch to see if she *was* dreaming or not. No—she was not. She was wide awake! There would be a bruise tomorrow where she had pinched herself.

'But who should be frying sausages at night!' wondered Mam'zelle in amazement. 'And where did that laugh come from? Surely not from the dormitory nearby?'

She went to see, shuffling along in her old comfortable slippers. She looked into the dormitory where Tessie and the others slept. She switched on the light. Five of the beds were empty!

Mam'zelle had not been at all good-tempered lately. She had not been sleeping well, and she had been difficult in class. She was tired now, with her hours of studying and correcting, and she felt really angry with the five truants.

'It is too much!' she said to herself, as she switched out the light. 'The bad girls! How can they do their lessons well if they are awake to such hours of the night? And they are working for the scholarship exam. too—ah, I shall report them to Miss Theobald ! '

Mam'zelle stood in the passage, sniffing. She simply could not imagine where the smell of sausages came from. Then she heard a scuffle and a giggle. It came from the music-room nearby !

Mam'zelle went to the door. She flung it open and glared into the warm little room.

There was a deep silence. Every girl stared in dismay at the large form of the angry French mistress.

' Oh—Mam'zelle—Mam'zelle,' stammered Tessie, at last.

' Yes, it is I, Mam'zelle ! ' said the mistress, her eyes flashing. ' And what have you to say for yourselves, acting in this manner at this time of night ! '

Tessie couldn't think of a word to say and at last in despair she held out a fried sausage on a fork to Mam'zelle.

' Wouldn't you—wouldn't you have a sausage ? ' she asked, desperately.

That was too much for Mam'zelle. She didn't see that Tessie was very frightened, she only thought that the girl was being cheeky. And the English ' cheek ' was something that always made Mam'zelle see red !

She swept the sausage off the fork, and for half a moment Tessie thought that Mam'zelle was going to box her ears. She ducked—and heard Mam'zelle's booming voice above her head.

' So that is the way you would treat your French mistress ? Why did I ever come to England to teach such ungrateful girls ? You will come straight to Miss Theobald now, all of you ! '

There was a moment's intense astonishment and fright. Go to Miss Theobald now—in the middle of the night—when she was asleep in bed ! It couldn't be true !

' Please, Mam'zelle,' said Janet, who was recovering herself more quickly than the others, ' please don't make us do that. Tomorrow morning would do, wouldn't it ? We don't want to disturb Miss Theobald now. We're sorry we disturbed you—we thought every one was asleep.'

' But one of you knocked on my door ! ' said Mam'zelle in astonishment. ' So—rap-rap-rap.' She rapped on the table as she spoke.

' None of us did that,' said Janet, more and more astonished. ' Somebody came and knocked on our door too. Whoever could it have been ? '

But Mam'zelle was not interested in that. Her rage was gradually dying down as she looked at the white, scared faces of the eight girls. She realized that it was impossible to take them all into Miss Theobald's bedroom. It must wait till tomorrow.

' We will not after all disturb Miss Theobald tonight,' she said. ' You will all go back to bed—and in the morning you will expect to be called in front of the Head Mistress to explain this dreadful behaviour.'

' Could—could we just finish the sausages ? ' asked Isabel, longingly. But that roused Mam'zelle's anger again. She caught Isabel firmly by the arm and pushed her out of the music-room. ' You—a first-form girl—daring to do a thing like this ! ' she cried. ' Go ! You should be well slapped, all of you ! Go, before I begin to do it ! '

The girls were half afraid that Mam'zelle might be as good as her word. They slipped down the passage and into their dormitories, climbing into bed, shivering with fright. What a dreadful ending to a midnight party !

Mam'zelle turned out the light. Then she saw the glow of the oil-stove and turned out that too. ' These girls ! ' she said, pursing up her big lips, ' these English girls ! How they behave ! '

Mam'zelle would never have dared to behave in such a free and easy way at her school in France when she had been a girl. She had worked much harder than any of the girls at St. Clare's. She had played no games, had been for hardly any walks, and had never even seen the inside of a gym until she had come to England. She did not really understand the girls at St. Clare's although she had been there for years, and had taught them well. She was quite determined to have every one of the truants well punished.

She reported them to Miss Theobald before breakfast the next morning. She even took the surprised Head Mistress to the little music-room to show her the remains of the feast. Miss Theobald looked at the ginger-beer bottles, the frying-pan with its congealed fat and few sausages left in it, and the crumbs on the floor.

' I will see the girls at break,' said the Head. ' This kind of thing cannot be allowed, Mam'zelle— but at some time or other most school-girls attend a midnight feast ! Do not take too serious a view of it ! '

' In my school-days such a thing was not even

thought of ! ' said Mam'zelle. ' Ah, we knew how to work, we French girls ! '

' But did you know how to play, Mam'zelle ? ' asked Miss Theobald, softly. ' It is just as important to know how to have good fun—as how to do good work, you know ! '

Mam'zelle snorted when Miss Theobald left her. She thought that the Head was far too lenient with the girls. She went into the big dining-hall to have breakfast. She glanced round the table where the first and second form sat.

It was easy to pick out the eight girls who had been caught the night before. They were pale and looked tired. Isabel and Susan could not eat any breakfast, partly because they had eaten too much the night before, and partly because they were scared at what might be going to happen to them.

Mam'zelle stopped the eight girls when they filed out of the dining-hall. ' You, Janet—and you, Winnie —and you, Susan, and you . . . you will all eight go to Miss Theobald at break.'

' Yes, Mam'zelle,' said the girls, and went to the assembly room for morning prayers and roll-call, feeling rather shaky about the legs !

' Pity we were caught,' said Pat to Isabel, in the middle of the hymn. ' Now Miss Theobald will think we didn't mean to try to do our best this term. Oh blow, Mam'zelle ! Mean old thing ! I won't try a bit in French this term now.'

The eight girls were bad at their lessons that morning. Erica watched the five in her form, all trying not to yawn, as they did their arithmetic under Miss Jenks's eagle eye.

It was French next, and Tessie put on a sulky face when Mam'zelle entered the room. She felt that she really hated the French mistress that morning. She wasn't going to try a bit !

It wouldn't have mattered if she *had* tried—for poor Tessie was really woolly-headed that day ! She had not been able to go to sleep until about five o'clock the night before, and was now so sleepy that her thoughts kept running into one another in a most annoying manner. She was really half asleep.

Mam'zelle chose to think that Tessie was defying her. She scolded the girl roundly, and gave her such a lot of extra prep. to do that poor Tessie was almost in tears.

' But I can't possibly get all that done, Mam'zelle, you know I can't,' she protested.

' We shall see ! ' said Mam'zelle, grimly. And Tessie knew that she would have to do it somehow.

At break the eight girls met together outside the Head Mistress's door. They were all nervous, even Pat who was usually bold. Tessie knocked.

' Come in ! ' said Miss Theobald's clear voice. They trooped in and shut the door.

Miss Theobald faced them, and looked at each girl seriously. They all felt upset, and Susan began to cry. Then the Head talked to them, and pointed out that it was impossible for good work to be done on half a night's sleep, and that rules must be kept. She said many other things in her low, calm voice, and the listening girls took it all in.

'Now please understand,' said Miss Theobald, 'that although you have broken the rule forbidding any girl to leave her dormitory at night, your escapade is not in the same rank as, for instance, meanness, lying, or disloyalty. Those are serious things—what you have done might be serious if you were allowed to do it often—but I regard it more as silly mischief. But even silly mischief has to be punished—and so you will not be allowed to go down into the town for two weeks. That means no walks together, no shopping, and no visits to the tea-shop or to the cinema.'

There was a silence. This was a horrid punishment. The girls really loved their privilege of going down to the town in twos, spending their pocket-money, and going to the tea-shop for tea. Two weeks seemed a very, very long time.

But nobody dared to protest. They all knew that Miss Theobald was absolutely just. 'You see,' the Head went on, 'if you behave like small children instead of senior girls, I shall have to treat you as small children, and take away your senior privileges. Now you may go. Tessie, see that the mess in the music-room is cleared up before dinner-time, please.'

'Yes, Miss Theobald,' said Tessie, meekly, and all eight girls filed out of the room.

'Well, I'm glad that's over,' said Pat, when they were out of ear-shot of the drawing-room. 'And there's another thing I'm glad about too—that Miss Theobald made that distinction between mischief and mean things. I wouldn't like her to think we'd do anything mean or rotten. A joke's a joke—ours went too far, that's all.'

'Yes,' said Isabel, thoughtfully. 'But there's one very mean thing about this, Pat—and that is—the knocking on Mam'zelle's door, that told her something was up! That's the meanest thing I ever heard of! We'll have to find out who did it—and punish them!'

ERICA was pleased when she heard of the punishment meted out to the eight girls. She did not dare to say much because she was so afraid that she might be found out. She knew quite well that the girls must wonder who had made the knocking on the doors.

The girls meant to find out who the tale-teller was. They met that evening, and discussed the matter.

'She shan't get away with it,' declared Tessie, fiercely. 'Golly, wasn't I astonished when Mam'zelle let out that she had been disturbed by some one knocking at her door! It must have been the same horrible person who came knocking at ours to give us a fright and spoil the party. I'm sorry I asked you all now. It was my fault.'

'It was jolly decent of you to think of giving us a treat,' said Pat. 'Don't apologize for that! Nobody would have known a thing about it if it hadn't been for that wretched spoil-sport.'

'Pat,' said Tessie, suddenly, 'you don't think it would have been that silly cousin of yours, do you? You know how she bleats everything all over the place. You didn't tell her anything, did you?'

Pat flushed. 'Not a word,' she said, 'and look here, Tessie, though you've got a pretty poor opinion

of Alison—and so have I—she's not the sort to sneak.
Honestly she isn't.   She can't keep her tongue still—
but she wouldn't do a thing like giving us away to
Mam'zelle.'

' All right,' said Tessie.   ' Well—I simply don't know
who it was—and I don't see how we're to find out !
Every one in our dormitory seemed to be asleep when
we got back.'

' And so did every one in ours,' said Pat.   ' It's a
puzzle.   But I'm going to find out who it was, Tessie.
I feel so angry when I think about it.   I shan't rest
till I know who it was.'

They all felt like that, but it was impossible to find
out—or so it seemed !   Every one denied even having
known that the party was to take place—though most
of the girls said that they guessed something was up.

Alison denied absolutely that she knew anything.
' And if I had, I wouldn't have split for worlds,' she
said, an angry flush on her cheek.   ' You might know
that.   You don't seem to have much opinion of me
lately, you two—but you might at least know that.'

' We do know that,' Pat hastened to say.   ' But it
is funny, Alison, that although nobody seems to know
anything about the party, somebody knew enough to
scare us and to bring Mam'zelle out on the war-
path ! '

It was quite by accident that the truth came out.
Gladys, the little scullery-maid, came upstairs to find
the frying-pan she had lent to Tessie.   It had not been
brought back to her, and she was afraid that the cook
might miss it.

She couldn't find Tessie, but she met Pat on the

stairs. 'Oh, Miss Patricia,' she said, 'could you get me back the frying-pan I lent Miss Tessie for the party ? I can't find her. I could have asked Miss Erica, but she disappeared before I could speak to her.'

'Miss Erica wouldn't have known anything about it,' said Pat. 'She didn't go to the party.'

'Oh, but Miss Patricia, she *did* know about it,' said the small scullery-maid. 'I met her when I was bringing it upstairs—and she pulled aside my apron and saw the frying-pan, and she said, in that haughty way of hers—" Oho, for Miss Tessie's party ! " '

Pat was astonished. It might have been a guess on Erica's part, of course—but anyway, she had seen the frying-pan—and, if she knew anything about sneaky Erica, she would certainly have kept watch, and have put two and two together—and found out everything without difficulty !

'I said to Miss Erica, I said " Well, miss, if you knew what the frying-pan was for, why did you ask me ? " ' said Gladys, quite enjoying this talk with Pat. 'Oh dear, miss—I heard you'd got into trouble over the party, and I'm so sorry.'

'I'll get you the frying-pan,' said Pat, and she went to the music-room, where the pan sat solemnly on top of the piano, cleaned by one of the second-formers, but otherwise forgotten.

Gladys took it and scuttled downstairs thankfully. She was just as much in awe of the cook as the girls were in awe of Miss Theobald !

Pat went to find Isabel. She told her what Gladys had said. 'It was Erica all right,' said Pat, fiercely: 'I'm not a bit surprised either, are you ? Every one

says she's a sneak. That's almost one of the worst
things you can be. Whatever will Tessie say ? '

Tessie said a lot. She was angry and indignant.
To think that a girl who had shared her chocolates and
her birthday cake could have played such a mean
trick !

' We'll jolly well tackle her about it,' said Tessie.
' After tea today. You come into the common room,
Pat—and we'll have it out with her. I'll tell the
others.'

' Yes, but every one else will be there,' said Pat,
uneasily. ' Is it quite fair to let every one hear ? '

' Why not ? ' said Tessie, angrily. ' A sneak deserves
to be denounced in public. Anyway, we can't go anywhere else.'

So after tea that day Erica was called by Pat. She
was sitting in a corner, writing a letter home.

' Erica, come over here. We want to speak to you,'
said Pat, in a cold voice. Erica looked up. She went
pale. Could the girls have discovered her mean trick ?

' I'm busy,' she said, sulkily. ' I've got to finish
this letter.'

She went on writing. Pat lost her temper and
snatched away the letter. ' You jolly well come ! ' she
said, fiercely. ' Do you want me and Isabel to lug you
over ? '

Erica saw that there was nothing for it but to go
to the corner of the common room where the six other
girls were waiting for her.

She went, looking pale and sulky. She was determined to deny everything.

' Erica, we know that it was you who knocked on

the music-room door the other night,' said Pat. 'And it was you too who gave the game away to Mam'zelle and got us punished. You're a mean pig, a horrid sneak, and you're jolly well going to be punished ! '

' I don't know what you are talking about,' said Erica, in a trembling voice, not daring to meet eight pairs of accusing eyes.

' Yes, you do. It's no good pretending,' said Tessie. ' Pat has found out everything. Every single thing. We know that you met Gladys on the stairs when she was bringing up something for us.'

' I don't know anything about the frying-pan,' said Erica.

Pat pounced at once. ' How do you know that it was a frying-pan that Gladys was bringing us ? There you are, you see—you do know. You've convicted yourself out of your own mouth ! '

The other girls in the common room, curious to hear what was going on, came round, peeping. Alison came too, her big blue eyes almost popping out of her head.

' Oh, was it Erica who gave you away ? ' she said. ' Well, I might have guessed ! She was always bothering me to find out from you and Isabel, Pat, what the secret was.'

' Well, it's a good thing for you, Alison, that for once you had the common sense not to give anything away,' said Pat, grimly. ' Now, Erica—you're a horrible sneak—but at least you might have the decency to own up ! '

' I don't know anything about it,' said Erica, stubbornly. ' It's no good your going on at me like this— I just simply don't know anything about it.'

'Go on, Erica, own up!' cried half a dozen voices from members of the second form, who were now all crowding round in the greatest curiosity.

But Erica wouldn't. She hadn't the sense to see that if she owned up frankly and could even bring herself to say she was sorry, the other girls would at least respect her for confessing.

As it was, she made them all intensely angry. 'Very well,' said Pat. 'Don't own up. But you'll have two punishments instead of one, that's all. You'll be punished for sneaking—and you'll be punished for not owning up too!'

'Yes,' said Tessie. 'And the punishment for sneaking is that you jolly well won't go down into the town for two weeks, like us. See?'

'I shall,' said Erica.

'Well, you won't,' said Tessie. 'I'm head of the second form, and I forbid *any* one to go with you— and you know you are not allowed to go alone. So there!'

Erica was beaten and she knew it. No girl dared to go to the town alone, for that was strictly forbidden. She flushed and said nothing.

'And the punishment for not owning up decently we leave to the first and second forms,' said Pat, her eyes flashing round. 'I am sure that not one of us, Erica, wants to speak to you, or have anything more to do with you than we can help! That's always the punishment for your sort of behaviour!'

'*I* shan't speak to her,' muttered several girls around. Every one felt disgusted with the miserable Erica. She would have a bad time! It is hard to see glances of contempt and dislike wherever you look, and to have nobody saying a jolly word.

Erica went off to her corner, but her hand trembled as she tried to finish her letter. She was ashamed—but she was angry too—and with Pat most of all!

' So she found out, did she, and told all the others ! ' thought Erica. ' All right, Pat—I'll pay you out for that—and your silly twin too ! '

8   MARGERY GETS A CHANCE

THE first form did not really see very much of Erica, because she did not have lessons with them. But if ever they met her in a passage or in the art room or gym, they looked the other way. In the common room at night Erica had a miserable time. Not one of the second-form girls would have anything to do with her.

Loud remarks about sneaks and cowards were made in her hearing. The only person who ever threw her a word at all was the bad-tempered Margery Fenworthy. Erica did not like Margery, any more than the other girls did, but she was so grateful to be spoken to, even by the surly first-former, that she almost began to like the girl.

'I'm surprised you speak to Erica, Margery,' said Pat, when she had heard Margery ask to borrow Erica's paints.

'Mind your own business,' said Margery, in her usual rude way. 'You're none of you friendly to me, and I know what it is to have people being beastly to you.'

'But Margery, it's your own fault,' said Pat, in surprise. 'You're so rude and sullen. You never smile and joke.'

'Well, people never smile and joke with *me*,' said Margery. 'You don't give me a chance.'

'Oh, Margery, what a fib!' cried Pat. 'It's you who never give *us* a chance to be decent to you. You scowl and glower and frown all the time.'

'If you're going to pick me to pieces you can save yourself the trouble,' said Margery, fiercely. 'I don't care tuppence for any of you. And if I want to speak to that wretched Erica, I shall. Who cares for a pack of silly girls, and a crowd of stuck-up teachers? I don't!'

Pat was astonished. What a strange girl Margery was! Did she really want a chance of being friends with the others? Was she terribly shy—what was behind that funny manner of hers?

Pat talked about it with her twin. 'Margery is always making enemies,' she said, 'I spoke to her today about it—and she accused us of never giving her a chance. Do you think we ought to do something about it?'

'Ask Lucy,' said Isabel, seeing Lucy coming up to show them a picture she had just finished. 'Oh, Lucy —what a marvellous drawing! It's Mam'zelle to the life!'

Lucy had a clever pencil with portraits. She could, with a few strokes of her pencil, draw any girl or teacher so that every one knew at once who it was. The drawing she held out was excellent.

'It's exactly how Mam'zelle looks when she says, "Ah, Dorrrrr-is, you are *insupportable*!"' said Pat. 'Lucy, listen, we've been talking about Margery.'

'I'll draw her,' said Lucy. She sat down and

sketched Margery's sullen good-looking face—and then, in a few strokes she sketched another Margery—a smiling one, most delightful to see.

'Before taking a course of St. Clare's—and after!' laughed Lucy.

'Golly—that's clever,' said Isabel. 'It's a pity Margery can't always look like that second drawing. Listen now, Lucy. She told Pat this morning that we've never given her a chance to be friendly.'

'All wrong,' said Lucy, beginning to draw again. '*She* has never given *us* a chance!'

'Exactly what I said,' said Pat, eagerly. 'Oh, Lucy, is that Erica? Goodness, what a poor creature she looks!'

'And is,' said Lucy. 'I'll be glad when we can speak to her again, in a way. I hate to be beastly to anyone even if they deserve it. It makes me feel horrible myself.'

'Lucy, do you think we'd better give Margery a chance, even though she's so jolly difficult?' asked Pat. 'You know—Isabel and I were simply awful last term—and every one was decent to us. It seems only fair for us to be decent to somebody else who's new, and who seems awful too.'

'I'm all for it,' said Lucy, shaking back her dark curls from her friendly, pretty face. 'My father says "Always give the under-dog a chance"—and for some reason or other poor Margery seems to think she's an under-dog—every one's hand against her—that sort of thing. Goodness knows why she's got that idea, but she has. All right—I'll go out of my way to be friendly, if you will.'

'We'll tell the others, as well,' said Pat. So the first-formers were told about the idea, and although most of them thought it was stupid, because they really did dislike Margery, they all agreed to back up Lucy and the twins. Even Alison said she would—and she had suffered very much from Margery's rudeness. Margery thought Alison a silly little feather-head, and had said so, many times.

So, what with avoiding Erica, and trying to be nice to Margery, things were quite exciting. The first time that Margery showed any signs of being pleased was when the first form were in the gym. Margery was excellent at climbing, jumping, and any kind of exercise. When she did an extra good jump in the gym, the girls clapped.

Margery glanced round, surprised. She gave a half-smile, and stepped to her place. The mistress spoke a few words of praise too. Margery tried not to look too pleased, but she couldn't help going red with pleasure.

Afterwards Pat spoke to her. 'Margery, you're jolly good at gym,' she said. 'I wish I could climb and jump like you.'

'I like anything like that,' said Margery, in a civil tone. 'As for games, I simply adore them. I only wish we could play three times as much as we do! I wish we went riding more here too. I used to love that at my old school.'

'What school did you go to before you came here?' asked Isabel, pleased to see that Margery could really talk quite normally!

But for some reason or other Margery would not

say any more. She turned away and her old scowling look came over her face. The twins were disappointed.

All the same, Margery felt that every one was giving her a chance, and she did respond in many ways. She didn't give so many rude answers, and she did occasionally offer to help any one in difficulties. She even offered to give silly little Alison some practice at catching the ball in lacrosse, because she saw that the twins were really ashamed of their cousin's stupidity at games.

But Alison refused. 'Why does every one keep badgering me to practise catching ?' she grumbled. 'I hate lacrosse. I hate all games. I hate having to run across a dirty field and get hot and out of breath. We all look awful when we've finished playing !'

'Alison ! Is there ever a time when you don't think about how you look ?' cried Janet. 'You're as vain as a peacock. I hope you get a whole lot of spots tomorrow !'

'Don't be mean !' said Alison, the easy tears coming into her eyes.

'Well, for goodness' sake act more like a senior girl and not like a baby,' grumbled Janet. 'Your cousins were bad enough when they came last term—but at least they didn't turn on the water-tap like you do, at any minute of the day !'

'I should think not !' said Pat, hotly, ready to attack Janet, who was in one of her sharp-tongued moods. But Janet gave her a friendly punch. She never wanted to quarrel with the twins, whom she sincerely liked.

Although Margery seemed to be much more friendly

with the girls, she was no better with the mistresses, to whom she was really rude. She did not try at all with her lessons—and the curious thing was that all the mistresses seemed to have endless patience with the sulky girl.

'Golly! If any of us were half as rude to Miss Roberts as Margery is, we'd soon hear about it,' said Pat, half a dozen times a week. 'I can't understand it. Did you see the work that Margery handed in to Miss Lewis too? She only did half a page, and her writing was awful.'

'Well, what about her arithmetic!' said Hilary. 'Honestly, I don't think she got a single sum right this morning—and Miss Roberts never said a word.'

'She won't say how old she is,' said Pat. 'I believe Margery's sixteen! And most of us in the first form are fourteen or just fifteen.'

'Oh well—never mind. She can't help being stupid, I suppose,' said Lucy. 'Anyway, she's jolly good at games—and when we play that match against the Oakdene girls next week, I bet we'll be glad of Margery. She's been put into the match-team, you know.'

'Has she?' said Pat. 'Golly! I wish I'd been put in it too. I haven't seen the list.'

'Well, you're not in it,' said Janet. 'I've looked. No first-former except Margery is in it—and only two second-formers! The rest are all third-formers. It's an honour for Margery to be chosen—but honestly, she's frightfully good at games, and most awfully quick and strong.'

'Well, if she's sixteen, as you say, she *ought* to be quick and strong,' said Alison, cattily.

'Shut up, Alison,' said Pat. 'We don't *know* that she's sixteen. Now don't you go round bleating about *that* !'

'I *don't* bleat,' began Alison, in her pathetic voice, making her blue eyes very wide and hurt. But half a dozen exasperated girls yelled at her and threw cushions—so Alison thought it better to say no more. No one could bear Alison when she went 'all goofy' as Janet described it.

When the two weeks were nearly up, and the eight girls were looking forward to being allowed to go down into the town again, the Big Row happened. It all centred around Margery, who in ten minutes, destroyed the new friendliness that had begun to grow up around her.

It happened in history class, and blew up all in a minute. The girls were horrified—and ever afterwards it was spoken of as the Big Row.

9   THE BIG ROW

MISS LEWIS was taking the history lesson, and the class were learning about the discovery of America, and its conquest. As usual the class was giving the history teacher close attention, for if there was one thing that Miss Lewis would not put up with, it was inattention.

Even Margery usually attended to Miss Lewis more than to the other teachers—partly because she was interested in history, and partly because she was a little afraid of Miss Lewis and her sharp eyes.

But this morning something seemed to have happened to Margery. The girls had noticed it from the time that she had sat down to breakfast. There had been a letter by her plate which Margery had not opened until she had been by herself. From that time onwards Margery had gone back to her most sullen and don't-care self—though nobody imagined that it was anything to do with the letter, of course.

She had been careless and inattentive in Miss Roberts's arithmetic class, and Miss Roberts had been, as usually, patient with her. In the French class, after a sharp look at her, Mam'zelle had taken no notice of Margery, but had let her sit and sulk to herself.

She had cheered up a little in the history class, but had not taken any part in the discussion that Miss

224

Lewis sometimes allowed at the beginning of the lesson.

Then Hilary had come out with a good idea. 'Miss Lewis! There's a play on in the next town, at the Royal Theatre—and it's called " Drake ". Would it be about the same period of history that we're doing ? '

' Oh, yes,' said Miss Lewis. ' It's a fine play. Just the right period.'

' Oh, Miss Lewis—do you think you could possibly take us to see it ! ' cried Hilary, who adored plays of any kind.

' Oh, yes, Miss Lewis ! ' cried the rest of the form, eagerly. ' An outing to the next town would be marvellous.'

' Hush,' said Miss Lewis, rapping on her desk. ' Do remember there are other classes going on. ·When is the play being performed, Hilary ? '

Hilary had a notice of it in her desk. She rummaged about and found it. ' There's a special performance on Saturday afternoon, this week,' she said. ' Oh, Miss Lewis—do, do take us ! I'd so love to see it.'

' That's my week-end off,' said Miss Lewis, regretfully. ' I'd arranged to go for a walking-tour with Miss Walker. We've got it all planned.'

Each mistress had a week-end off during the term, and they looked forward to this very much. The class knew how precious the week-ends were to the staff, and they stared in disappointment at Miss Lewis. What a pity ! Just the Saturday the play was on. It would have been such fun to go and see it.

' Oh, blow ! ' said Pat. ' Wouldn't that just be the way ! Never mind, Miss Lewis—it can't be helped.'

'Well—I don't know,' said Miss Lewis, slowly. 'Perhaps it *can* be helped! You've been good workers this term, and maybe I could give up the Saturday to take you—and go home on the Sunday morning, for one day instead of two. Miss Walker can find some one else to go walking with, I daresay.'

'Oh, I say—we wouldn't let you do that,' said Janet, at once. 'We're not quite such selfish pigs, Miss Lewis.'

Miss Lewis laughed. She liked the outspoken first-formers. 'I'll arrange it,' she said. 'I'll speak to Miss Theobald—and the whole class can go with me in the school bus. We'll book seats at the Royal Theatre, and go and have a lovely time seeing the play —and we'll have a marvellous tea afterwards.'

There were sighs and squeals of delight. Shining eyes looked at Miss Lewis, and every one beamed with joy. What an unexpected treat! Even Margery Fenworthy looked pleased.

'Miss Lewis, you're a sport!' said Janet. 'You really are! Thanks most awfully. Are you really sure you don't mind taking us on your precious week-end?'

'Oh, I mind awfully,' said Miss Lewis, with a twinkle in her eye. 'Do you suppose it's any pleasure to me to take charge of twenty noisy first-formers with no manners at all?'

Every one laughed. Miss Lewis might be sharp at times—but she really was a good sort!

'Now mind—' said Miss Lewis, warningly. 'You will all work well to show me that you really do appreciate the treat! No slacking this term!'

' Of course not ! ' said the girls, quite determined to work better for Miss Lewis than they had ever done before.

Ten minutes later came the Big Row. Each girl had her history book open, and was following the map there that Miss Lewis was explaining—all except Margery. She had her book open it was true—but into the open pages she had slipped the letter she had received that morning, and she was re-reading it, a scowl on her face.

Miss Lewis spoke to Margery and got no answer. The girl didn't hear the question at all. She was so engrossed in her own thoughts. Miss Lewis spoke again, sharply.

' Margery ! You are not paying the least attention ! What is that you have in your book ? '

' Nothing,' said Margery, with a jump. She tried to slip the letter out of the pages. Miss Lewis looked angry.

' Bring me that letter,' she said.

' It's mine,' said Margery, with her sullenest look.

' I know that,' said Miss Lewis, irritably. ' You can give it to me till the end of the morning. Then there will not be any temptation for you to read it in another lesson. You certainly will not do a thing like that in *my* lesson again. Bring me the letter.'

' What ! For you to read ! ' flared up Margery in a rage. ' Nobody's going to read my private letters ! '

' Margery ! You forget yourself,' said Miss Lewis, coldly. ' Do you suppose I should read the letter ? You know better than that. But I shall certainly confiscate it for the rest of the day now. You will bring me the letter, and you will come to me for it this evening, and apologize for your behaviour.'

' I shan't do anything of the sort,' said Margery, rudely. All the girls stared in horror.

' Shut up, Margery,' said Pat, who was sitting next to her. ' Don't you dare to speak like that ! '

' *You* shut up ! ' said Margery, turning a look of rage on Pat. ' I won't be interfered with by anybody—no, not even by Miss Theobald herself ! As for Miss Lewis, with her sharp eyes and her sharp nose sticking into my private business, she won't get anything out of *me* ! '

' Margery ! ' cried half a dozen voices in the utmost horror. Nobody could believe their ears. Margery was flushed a bright red, and her eyes flashed angrily. She was in her worst temper, and she didn't care in the least what she said.

Miss Lewis was very angry. She was white, and her nose looked suddenly rather thin, as it always did when she was cross. But this morning she was more than cross. She stood up.

' Leave the room, Margery,' she said, in a cold quiet voice. ' I shall have to consider whether or not I can have you in my history classes again.'

' I'll leave the room all right,' said Margery. ' I'd leave the whole school if I could ! I didn't want to come. I knew what would happen ! I hate the lot of you ! '

The angry girl walked out, her head held high. But once outside she leaned her head against the wall and cried bitterly. She was shocked and upset.

Miss Theobald happened to come along just as

Margery was wiping her eyes, and wondering where to go. She looked at Margery in silence.

' Come with me, my dear,'she said. ' Something has happened, hasn't it ? You must tell me about it.'

' It's no good,' said Margery. ' I'll be sent away from here. And I don't care. I don't care a bit.'

' Yes, you do care,' said Miss Theobald. ' You care a lot. Margery, come with me. Come along, please. We can't stand out here like this. The girls will be pouring out of the classrooms in a little while.'

Margery took a look at Miss Theobald's calm, serious face. The Head looked at Margery with a wise and compassionate glance in her deep eyes. The angry girl gave a sob, and then went with the Head Mistress.

Inside the classroom there was a babel of furious voices.

' The beast ! How could she behave like that ! '

' Just after Miss Lewis had said she'd give up her Saturday too ! '

' It's waste of time to be nice to a creature like that ! I'll never speak to her again ! '

' She deserves to be expelled ! I shouldn't be surprised if she is ! '

' Miss Lewis ! We all apologize to you for Margery ! We do, really.'

' Girls, girls, be quiet, please,' said Miss Lewis, putting on her glasses and looking round the room. ' There is no need to make a noise like this. We have only five minutes of this lesson left. Turn to page fifty-six, please. I don't want to hear another word about Margery.'

So no more was said in class—but plenty was said

outside ! How they raged against her ! The second
form heard about it too, and they were amazed and
aghast that any one should dare to behave like that to
Miss Lewis.

' I wish I'd been there,' said Tessie, who always
enjoyed a row, so long as she wasn't the centre of it.
' Golly ! Miss Lewis must have been furious ! '

' Where's Margery. now ? ' asked Pat.

Nobody knew. She didn't appear again at all that
morning or afternoon—but after tea she came into the
common room, rather white, and looking defiant, for
she guessed how the girls felt about her.

' Here comes the meanie ! ' said Janet. ' I hope
you're ashamed of yourself, Margery ! '

But Margery refused to say a single word. She sat
in a corner, reading—or pretending to read—and would
not answer anything said to her. The girls gave her
a bad time. Even Erica was forgotten. In fact
Erica seemed quite harmless, somehow, after the
dreadful way Margery had behaved !

' I wonder if Margery will be allowed to come to the
history lesson tomorrow,' said Janet. ' I bet Miss
Lewis won't let her ! '

But there was a surprise in store for the class when
Miss Lewis came to take history next day. Margery
was there too !

' Good morning, girls,' said Miss Lewis, as she came
into the room. ' Margery, will you go and speak to
Mam'zelle for a minute ? She is in her study and
wants a word with you. Come back when she has
finished.'

Margery went out, looking surprised. Miss Lewis

turned to the girls. ' I just want to say that Margery has apologized for her bad behaviour,' said Miss Lewis. ' She had a talk with Miss Theobald who found her, outside the classroom, and she came to me yesterday evening to apologize. I have accepted her apology and am taking her back into my class. I hardly think such a thing will happen again, and I would like you all to forget it as soon as possible, please.'

' But, Miss Lewis—isn't she going to be punished ? ' asked Janet, indignantly.

' Perhaps she has been,' said Miss Lewis, putting on her glasses. ' I think we can safely leave things to be decided by the Head Mistress, don't you ? Now, not a word more about the subject, please. Turn to page fifty-six.'

The class were turning to page fifty-six when Margery came back. Mam'zelle had wanted her about a very small thing, and the girl could not help feeling that she had been sent out for a few minutes so that Miss Lewis could say something about her. She walked to her desk, red in the face, and found her place. She paid great attention to the lesson, and Miss Lewis hadn't the slightest reason to find fault with her that morning.

But at break the girls had a great deal to say about Margery again ! ' Forget it as soon as possible ! ' snorted Janet. ' How could Miss Lewis say a thing like that ? Golly, I think Margery ought to have been expelled from the school ! After we'd tried to be so decent to her too. You just simply CAN'T help a girl like that.'

So once more Margery was sent back to her lonely,

friendless state. No one spoke to her if they could help it, and nobody even looked at her.

' It's a pity she's playing in the match,' said Pat. ' Well—*I* shan't clap if she shoots a goal !'

THE days went quickly by. The first form were taken to the play, and enjoyed every minute of it. They had a wonderful tea afterwards, for Miss Lewis really did do things well !

' Buns and jam ! Fruit cake ! Meringues ! Chocolate éclairs ! ' said Janet, describing it all to the envious second-formers when they got back. ' Golly, it *was* a spread ! I don't know which I enjoyed most—the play or the tea. They were both marvellous.'

' Did Margery go too ? ' asked Tessie, curiously. Every one, of course, had heard of the Big Row. Even the top-formers knew about it.

' Yes—she went,' said Pat. ' Though if it had been me I wouldn't have had the cheek to have gone. She didn't say a word the whole time—but she thanked Miss Lewis for taking her. Personally I think it was jolly sporting of Miss Lewis even to *think* of having her ! '

' So do I,' said Tessie. ' I heard Belinda say yesterday that if Margery wasn't so awfully good at lacrosse, she would strike her out of the match. She's very fond of Miss Lewis, you know, and she was furious when she heard how Margery had cheeked her.'

' Well, it's about the only good thing you can say.

of Margery—that's she's good at games,' said Tessie. 'But my word, she's fierce, isn't she! I hope Belinda will give her a word of warning before the match. If she tackles the Oakdene team too savagely she'll be sent off the field. And then we shall be one man short.'

Belinda did warn Margery. The match was to be played on the home-field, and the whole school was to watch, if it was fine. Oakdene and St. Clare's were well-matched. There wasn't much to choose between them. So far the score was eleven matches won by each, so this match would be rather exciting.

'Margery, don't be hauled up on a foul, please,' said Belinda to the girl, as she was changing into her gym things before the match. 'You lose your head sometimes and forget you're so strong. Play fairly, and you'll be jolly useful. Lose your temper and you'll probably be sent off the field!'

Margery scowled and said nothing. She bent over to put on her shoes. Pat and Janet came into the changing room to look for Isabel and Alison.

'Oh, there you are!' said Pat, seeing the other two. It was dark in the changing-room and she did not see Margery, bending down over her shoes. 'Now don't forget, everybody, if that miserable Margery shoots a goal, we don't clap and we don't cheer. See?'

'Right, Pat,' said the others. 'She doesn't deserve even a whisper—and she won't get it!'

'You horrid beast, Pat!' said Margery, suddenly, standing up in anger. 'So that's what you've planned to do, have you! Just like you!'

The four girls stared in dismay. None of them had known that Margery was there.

'I don't want your claps or your cheers,' said Margery, stalking out. 'One day, Pat, I'll get even with you! You see if I don't!'

The bell rang for the players to take their places. Margery went on to the field, a tall and scowling figure.

'I'm sorry for the girls she's got to play against!' said Belinda to Rita. 'My word, she's an extraordinary girl!'

The whistle went for the game to begin. It was a fine afternoon, rather cold, but with no wind. The watching girls had on their warm coats and felt hats. They put their hands in their pockets as they sat on the forms, and prepared to shout and cheer and clap when the right times came.

It was always fun to watch a match. It was lovely to be able to yell as loudly as they liked, and to dance about and cheer if anything really exciting happened. The school was always glad when the match was an at-home one, then they could see every goal, and watch all that happened, instead of having to wait until the team came back from an away match.

The game was a bit slow at first. The players hadn't warmed up to it, and every one was playing rather cautiously. No one above the third form was playing in either school. The Oakdene girls did not look a very big lot, but they were wiry and ran fast. They soon got into the game, and the running, tackling and catching began to get very swift and exciting.

'Go it, Susan! Go it, Tessie!' yelled the second-formers, anxious to cheer on their members. Except for the first-former, Margery, all the rest but Tessie and Susan were third-form girls. Margery was the tallest, strongest girl of the home team, even bigger than the third-formers.

'Well run, Mary! Shoot, shoot!' yelled the school, seeing a swift third-former catch the ball from Tessie and tear down the field to the goal. But the Oakdene girl marking her was swift too. She tried to knock the ball from Mary's lacrosse net. Mary swung her net in front of her. The Oakdene girl tried to out-run her but couldn't. She yelled to another girl.

'Tackle her, tackle her!'

Like a hare another Oakdene girl shot out from her place and ran straight at Mary. The two met with a clash. Mary went spinning, and the ball rolled from her net. The Oakdene girl picked it up neatly and tore back in the opposite direction.

'On her, Margery!' yelled Belinda, from the on-lookers. 'Go on, go on—run. You can do it?'

Margery Fenworthy shot up like a bullet from a gun! She could run faster than anyone on the field. She raced across to the running girl and did a neat turn round her to get to her lacrosse net. She slashed upwards viciously with her own net—the ball jerked out and Margery caught it deftly. The Oakdene girl slashed back at Margery's net to get the ball, but Margery had already thrown it hard across the field to where Tessie was waiting for it. Down to the goal sped Tessie. She shot—but alas, the ball rolled wide, and the whistle blew.

' My word, that girl Margery plays well,' said Rita.
Nobody, however, had cheered Margery on as she had
tackled the girl and got the ball. But how they yelled
to Tessie when she had tried to shoot !

The match went on its exciting way. The school
yelled itself hoarse as the battle went first this way and
then that way. The teams were beautifully matched,
there was no doubt about that.

Margery stood out among all the players. She
always played well—but today she seemed inspired.
Pat knew why, and felt a little uncomfortable.

' She always plays extra well when she's angry,'
said Pat to her twin. ' Have you noticed that ? She
seems to make the game into a fight and goes all out
for it. Perhaps it helps her to work off her bad
temper.'

Margery soon got the ball again by a swift piece of
running. She dodged a girl running at her, and looked
for some one to pass to. Susan was ready. Margery
threw the ball to her. Susan caught it, was tackled,
and threw back to Margery. There was a clear space
to goal. Should she run nearer and shoot, risking
being tackled—or should she try one of her long hard
shots ?

A girl shot out to tackle her. Margery raised her
net, and shot the ball hard and strong down the field.
It went like a bullet ! The tackling girl tried to stop
it but failed. The goal-keeper saw it coming and put
out her net—but the shot was so hard that she couldn't
stop it ! The ball was in the goal !

' Goal ! ' yelled the school. And then there was a
silence. There was no clapping. No cheering. No

Margery shot up the field like a bullet

shouts of 'Well done, Margery!' It was strange, because after a goal every one usually yelled their loudest. The watching mistresses looked at one another with pursed lips and raised eyebrows. No girl had ever been so unpopular before as not to be cheered in a match!

Half-time came. Pat ran out with a plate of lemon quarters for the thirsty players. How good they tasted! So sour and clean.

'You've got a good player in your team this term,' said the captain of the other side, to Pat, as she took her piece of lemon. 'But golly, isn't she big? I should have thought she was a top-former.'

'Well, she's not,' said Pat. 'She's in the first form!'

'Gracious!' said the girl, staring at Margery in surprise. Margery was not speaking to any of her team, and no one was speaking to her. 'She doesn't seem very popular,' said the Oakdene girl. 'What's up?'

'Oh, nothing,' said Pat, who was not going to talk about Margery's affairs to any one else. 'Have another piece of lemon?'

'Thanks,' said the girl. 'My word, this is a good match. Anybody's game, really. You're one goal up —but I bet we get even this half!'

The whistle blew. Pat scurried off the field. The players took their places, at opposite ends to the ones they had had before. The game began again.

It was fast and furious. Every one was now well-warmed-up and enjoying the game. The Oakdene captain scored an unexpected goal, which Bertha, in goal, should have been able to stop and didn't. The whole school groaned. Poor Bertha went as red as fire.

'One all! Play up, St. Clare's!' yelled every one.

If Margery had played well the first half, she played even better in the second half. She ran like the wind, she tackled fearlessly, she caught accurately and threw well. But she unfortunately lost her temper with an Oakdene girl who neatly dodged her with the ball, and brought down her net with such force on the girl's hand to make her drop the ball that the Oakdene girl squealed in pain. The referee blew her whistle and called Margery to her.

'Gosh! Is she going to send her off the field for a foul?' groaned Belinda, who badly wanted her team to win. 'She deserves it, I know—she's such a savage when she gets excited—but we can't afford to lose her just now!'

But Margery fortunately was not sent off. She was severely reprimanded, and walked back to her place with the usual sullen look on her face. She was much more careful after that, for she hadn't the slightest wish to be sent off in the middle of such an exciting match.

She got the ball again within the next few minutes, and ran for goal. She passed to Mary, who passed back. Margery shot—and the ball rolled straight into the corner of the goal, though the goal-keeper frantically tried to stop it.

'Goal!' yelled the whole school. But again there was that curious silence afterwards. No cheering, no

clapping. Margery noticed it at once, and her eyes
flashed with anger. The beasts! She was playing her
best for the school—and yet they wouldn't even give
her a cheer! All because of that hateful Pat
O'Sullivan!

The girl felt a fury of anger rising up in her. Somehow it gave her even more swiftness and strength than
before. She was a miracle of swiftness as she darted
about the field, tackling and dodging, getting the ball
when it seemed almost impossible.

'If only Oakdene don't shoot again!' cried Pat,
in the greatest excitement. 'Oh, golly—they're going
to. Save it, Bertha, save it!'

But poor Bertha couldn't possibly save the goal
that time, though she threw herself flat down on
her front to do so. The ball trickled by and came to
rest in the goal. Two goals all—and five minutes to
play!

And in that five minutes Margery managed to shoot
two of the finest goals that any of the school had ever
seen. The first one was one of her long shots, straight
and true, from half-way down the field. The second
was extraordinary. She could not shoot because two
girls tackled her just near the goal, and Margery rolled
over and over on the ground. The Oakdene girls tried
to get the ball from her net but somehow or other
Margery managed to hold it safely there—and suddenly, from her position flat on the ground, her nose
almost in the mud, Margery jerked her lacrosse net!
The ball flew out—and landed in the goal right through
the surprised goal-keeper's legs!

At first nobody knew it was a goal—and then the

umpire shouted 'Goal! Four goals to St. Clare's, two goals to Oakdene. One more minute to play!'

But before the ball was in play again, time was up. The whistle blew and the players trooped off the field. What a match it had been!

11 ERICA GETS HER OWN BACK

USUALLY, after a match, the girls who had shot the winning goals were surrounded, patted and cheered. If any one deserved to be cheered that afternoon it was certainly Margery, for she had done the hardest work, and had stood out as the finest player in the team.

Belinda muttered 'Well done!' as Margery came by. But nobody else said a word. No one went to Margery to clap her on the shoulder. No one shouted 'Well played, old girl!' No one, in fact, took any notice of her at all.

The Oakdene girls couldn't help noticing this curious behaviour, and were surprised. They stared hard at Margery, who stared back, her head held high.

'I'm glad we won the match—but I wish it hadn't been Margery who did it all,' said Pat. 'I feel a bit uncomfortable now about not cheering her a bit. Do you think we ought to go and say a word to her, Janet?'

'Of course we ought!' said Janet, 'but you know jolly well what would happen if we did! She'd bite our heads off—and I don't wonder! No—we've started this uncomfortable game of sending some one to Coventry—and we've got to stick to it.'

Brave as Margery was, she could not face the school-

tea with the teams.   Usually after a match the two
opposing teams had a special tea to themselves, apart
from the rest of the school, though in the same dining-
hall of course.   At the long team-table they chattered
and laughed and discussed the match with one another.
The home team acted as hostesses to the visiting team,
and it was all great fun.

' It's so lovely when you're tired and happy to sit
down to buns and butter and fruit cake and chocolate
biscuits and big cups of tea ! ' sighed Tessie.   ' And to
talk as much as you like about the match.   Come on,
Susan.   I'm ready.'

Every one noticed that Margery was not at the table.
No one liked to say anything about it.   The visiting
team were quite aware that there was something queer
in the air and did not like to discuss it.   The St. Clare
team wondered where Margery was, and looked to see
if she was at the table where the first-formers were
sitting eating their own tea.

But she wasn't.   She had gone to the changing-room
and changed.   Then she had slipped into the deserted
class-room and gone to her desk.   She was tired, angry
and miserable.   She wanted a cup of tea to drink, and
she was hungry too.   But not for anything would she
have faced the hostile looks of the other girls that
afternoon.   She had played so well—and won the
match for her team—and if they couldn't even say
' Well played ! ' she didn't want anything to do with
them !

Miss Roberts noticed that Margery was missing.
She guessed what had happened.   She had heard all
about the Big Row, and knew that Margery was being

punished by the girls for her misbehaviour. Well—
people always *were* punished for that kind of thing, by
being disliked. Miss Roberts could not do anything
about it.

Erica's meanness had been almost forgotten in the
excitement of the Big Row, and the match. But
Erica had not forgotten that she meant to pay back
Pat for finding out her trick, and punishing her for it.
She had spent a good deal of time wondering how to
get even with her. It was not so easy as it had seemed
at first, because the two girls were in different forms.

But Erica soon found one or two things to do. She
saw that Pat was making herself a red jumper, with
which she was very pleased. She waited her chance,
and then, one evening when she saw that Pat had put
the knitting back into her bag on the shelf, she made
up her mind to spoil it.

There was a school meeting that evening. ' If I go
in late for it, I can sit at the back,' thought Erica.
' Then I can slip out half-way through for a few
minutes, and come back without any one noticing.
That will just give me time to get to the common
room and back.'

So that evening, at half-past seven, when the meeting
had just begun, Erica slipped in at the back. No one
noticed her, for Miss Walker was speaking, and every
one was listening. Margery Fenworthy was at the
back too. That was usually her place now—at the
back—for it was horrid to be anywhere where people
had the chance of looking disdainfully at you! No
one saw you if you sat at the back.

Erica sat for a while, listening. When Miss Walker

sat down, and Miss Lewis got up to speak, Erica slipped out. No one saw her at all. She ran at top speed to the empty common room. She went to Pat's corner of the shelf and took down her knitting bag.

In it was the half-finished jumper, knitted most beautifully, for Pat was very proud of it. Erica took out the knitting and pulled the needles from the wool. She wrenched at the jumper, and half the even knitting came undone. Erica, with a feeling of real spite, tore at the wool again—and it broke in half a dozen places ! The girl hurriedly pushed the knitting into the bag, and then ran back to the meeting. Miss Lewis was still speaking, in her clear, sharp tones.

No one saw Erica slip in—no one except Margery, who paid no attention, for she was lost in her own thoughts. Erica hugged herself secretly, pleased with what she had done. In her mean little soul she rejoiced that she had harmed some one who had brought her to justice.

The meeting finished. The girls yawned and stretched. Pat looked at her watch.

' Eight o'clock,' she said. ' Time for a game or something in the common room. Come on.'

' There's dance music on the wireless,' said Doris. ' Let's put that on. I want to dance ! '

' I've got some French to finish,' groaned Sheila. ' Blow ! I wish I'd done it before. I daren't leave it. Mam'zelle always seems in such a bad temper these days.'

' Yes, doesn't she,' said Isabel, who had noticed the same thing. ' I'm getting quite scared of her ! '

They all went back to the common room. The third-

formers went to the big room they shared with the
fourth form, and the top-formers went to their studies.
The time before bed was always cosy and friendly and
jolly.

'What are you going to do, Isabel?' asked Pat.
'Shall we finish that jigsaw puzzle Tessie lent us?'

'No,' said Isabel. 'I want to mend a stocking. I
shall have Matron after me if I don't. She told me to
do it three days ago and I forgot.'

'All right. I'll talk to you and knit,' said Pat,
reaching up to the shelf for her bag. 'I'm getting on
so well with my red jumper. I can't imagine what
Mother will say when she sees it! I've never stuck at
knitting so long before.'

'Let's see what it looks like,' said Janet, coming up.
Pat took out her knitting and undid it. The needles
dropped to the floor. The wool hung torn and
unravelled.

'Pat!' gasped Isabel, in horror. 'Pat! It's all
undone! It's spoilt!'

'Gracious goodness!' said Janet, taking a glance
at Pat's horrified face as she saw her ruined work.
'Who's done that?'

'Oh, Pat—I'm so sorry about it,' said Isabel, who
knew what hard and careful work Pat had put into the
jumper. 'Oh, Pat—whatever *has* happened to
it?'

Pat stared at her spoilt work. It was a shock to
her, and she was near tears. She blinked hard and
swallowed the lump that suddenly came into her throat.

'Somebody's done this to me,' she said, in a low
voice. 'Somebody's done it to pay me out.'

'Margery!' said Isabel, at once. 'She overheard what you said about not clapping or cheering her in the match—and this is her way of paying you out. Oh, the mean, mean thing!'

Janet flushed with anger, She hated meanness of any kind. 'Well, if she's done that, she'll jolly well have to be hauled up about it!' she said. 'Look here, girls—come and look at Pat's knitting.'

The first- and second-formers crowded round, Erica came too, pretending to be surprised and shocked. She was enjoying herself very much. If only nobody guessed it was she who had done it!

But every one thought it was Margery. No one imagined it was Erica, for by now they had half-forgotten her mean behaviour. They crowded round Pat and sympathized with her.

'It *is* rotten luck,' said Tessie. 'I know what it feels like even to drop a stitch when you're trying to make something really nice. But to have it all spoilt and pulled out like that—and broken in so many places—that's dreadful. What will you do? Can you do anything about it?'

'I shall just have to undo it all and begin again, that's all,' said Pat. It had given the girl a great shock to think that any one could play such a mean trick on her. Real spite is always horrible—and Pat had never come across it directed at herself before.

'Well, what are we going to do about Margery?' said Janet, fiercely. 'She's got to be dealt with, hasn't she?'

'Where is she?' said Hilary. Just as she spoke Margery came into the room with a book. She had been to the school library to get it. Janet rounded on her at once.

'Margery! Come here! We've all seen your latest display of bad temper!'

Margery looked surprised. 'What do you mean, Janet?' she asked, coldly.

'Oh, don't pretend like that!' said Janet. 'Look here—do you dare to say you didn't do that to Pat's knitting?'

She held up the ruined jumper. Margery stared at it in amazement. 'Of course I didn't,' she said, with a queer dignity. 'I'm bad-tempered and sulky, and there's not much that's good about me, according to all of you—but I don't do mean tricks like that. I dislike Pat, and I'd like to get even with her for some of the unkind things she's done to me—but not in that way.'

The girls stared at her. Nobody believed her. Pat went red, and put the knitting back into her bag.

'You *did* do it, Margery, you know you did!' cried Isabel, quite beside herself because her twin had been hurt. 'You must have slipped out whilst we were at the meeting and done it then!'

'No, I didn't,' said Margery. 'It's true I was at the back—but what's the good of being anywhere else when you all send me to Coventry, as you do? But I tell you quite honestly I didn't play that trick. I could *not* do a trick like that. I might slap Pat or box her ears, or slash her at lacrosse—but I wouldn't do a hole-and-corner thing like that.'

'You'd do anything!' said Janet, scornfully. 'I

bet you wouldn't stick at anything once you got your knife into somebody!'

'You're just proving the truth of the old saying "Give a dog a bad name and hang him," ' said Margery. 'Because I'm bad in some things you think I'm capable of doing anything horrid. I'm not.'

Her eyes suddenly filled with tears and she turned away to hide them. Tears were weak. She could not bear any one to see them. She walked out of the room and left a surprised and furious crowd behind her.

'Well, would you think *any*one would have the nerve to deny it like that?' demanded Kathleen.

'She's absolutely brazen!' declared Tessie.

'Oh, shut up about it,' said Pat. 'Let's not say any more. We can't prove it—and though we're all jolly sure she did it, it's no good going on and on about it. It's hateful, but it's best forgotten.'

'Well, it's decent of you to feel like that,' said Doris, going to the wireless. 'I wish I knew exactly how and when she did it. Who'd like a little dance music to cheer us up?'

Soon the wireless was blaring out dance tunes and Doris and Janet were fox-trotting round the room, doing all sorts of ridiculous steps to make the others laugh. And the one who laughed the loudest was Erica.

'What luck!' she thought, 'No one even thought of me—and they've pinned the blame on to Margery! Now I can think of something else to do to Pat, and nobody will imagine it's any one but that bad-tempered Margery!'

12 THE TWINS HEAR A SECRET

THAT week-end was half-term. Most of the parents who could do so came by train to see their girls, or motored down to them. Those girls whose parents were not able to visit them either went out with their friends, or were taken into the next town to see a cinema or play.

Mrs. O'Sullivan came by car, and took out Pat and Isabel, and also Alison, whose mother could not come. Janet went joyfully with her parents on a long picnic ride, and took Hilary with her. Margery's parents did not come at all—and no one asked her to go out with them, so she went with Miss Roberts and four other girls to see the cinema show in the next town.

Isabel was still full of how Pat's jumper had been ruined. She poured it all out to Mrs. O'Sullivan, and Alison chattered about it too. Pat said very little. She had been shocked and hurt by it, for she was a friendly girl and had had few enemies in her life.

Mrs. O'Sullivan listened. 'You are quite sure that Margery did it?' she asked. 'Don't you think you ought to withhold your judgment until you are quite certain! There is nothing so dreadful as to accuse a person wrongly, you know. It makes them very bitter —and from what you tell me poor Margery must have already had some unhappiness of some sort in her life.'

Mrs. O'Sullivan's remark made the three girls feel a little uncomfortable.   They did feel sure that Margery had spoilt the jumper—but it was quite true that they hadn't any real proof.

No one said anything more—but privately Pat and Isabel decided to do as their mother said—and not judge Margery until they actually had some real proof. After all, although she was bad-tempered and rude, she had never shown before that she could be either mean or deceitful.   Alison looked at the twins and thought she would do as they did—if they told her what that would be !   Alison was getting a little better now and hadn't quite such a good opinion of herself.

But their good intentions were quite ruined by a chance meeting with an old friend of theirs that afternoon.   They were having lunch in a big town some twenty miles away from the school, and afterwards were going to see a play there.   And, having lunch at a nearby table was Pamela Holding, a girl who had been at Redroofs for a year or two whilst the twins had been there.

' Hallo, Pam ! ' cried Isabel, seeing her first.   ' Are you having half-term holiday too ? '

' Hallo, Pat, hallo, Isabel—and is that Alison ! ' cried Pam.   ' Yes—I'm at school at St. Hilda's, and Mother is taking me to the play here this afternoon for my half-term treat.   Don't say you're going too ! '

' Well, we are ! ' said Pat, pleased.   ' Let's all go together, and have tea with one another afterwards.'

The two mothers knew and liked each other, so

they approved of this idea. The four girls and the two grown-ups set off to the theatre at half-past two, chattering and laughing, exchanging all their news.

Unfortunately their seats were not side by side in the theatre, so they had to part there – but arranged to meet for tea. And it was at tea that the twins heard some queer news about Margery Fenworthy.

Pamela was telling the twins and Alison about some one in her school who had just won the record for long distance running.

'Well, we've a girl at our school who could win any records she liked, I should think,' said Alison. 'She's just a miracle at games and gym. Her name's Margery Fenworthy.'

'Margery Fenworthy!' said Pamela, her eyes opening wide. 'You don't mean to tell me *she's* at St. Clare's! Golly! We all wondered where she'd gone.'

'Why – was she at St. Hilda's with you last term then?' asked Pat, in surprise. 'She never will say anything about the schools she has been to.'

'No wonder,' said Pamela, scornfully. 'She's been to about six already!'

'Why so many?' asked Isabel in amazement.

'Can't you guess?' said Pam. 'She's been expelled from the whole lot, as far as I can make out. I know that St. Hilda's stuck her for two terms – and then out she went! She was just too unbearable for words. So rude in class that no mistress would have her!'

The twins stared at Pamela. Yes – that was Margery all right! So she had been sent away from one school after another. What a disgrace!

'Good gracious!' said Alison, finding her tongue first. 'Well, I should think she'll be sent away from St. Clare's soon too. Do you know what she did to Pat?'

And out came the whole history of the spoilt jumper —and then the story of the Big Row. Pamela listened, her eyes wide with interest.

'Well, I must say the Big Row sounds just exactly like Margery,' she said. 'I could tell you things that are more or less the same about her—but the affair of the jumper doesn't sound quite like Margery. I mean —she might in a temper snatch it out of Pat's hand and pull it to pieces in front of her—but as far as I know Margery never did anything behind anyone's back at St. Hilda's. She must be getting worse.'

'What was she expelled from other schools for?' asked Alison, eagerly.

'Oh, bad temper—rudeness—insubordination they called it,' said Pamela. 'She wouldn't work at all at St. Hilda's. She's sixteen, you know. I bet she's only in your form, Pat and Isabel.'

'Yes, she is,' said Pat. 'We thought she must be sixteen. Her work isn't even up to our form's, though. She is always bottom—when Alison isn't!'

Alison flushed. 'Don't be mean!' she said. 'I haven't been bottom for three weeks! I've been trying hard lately.'

'All right, featherhead,' said Pat, good humouredly. 'I think you *have* been trying. Well—it's a race between you and Doris and Margery who'll be bottom the oftenest this term—so you'd better buck up and try a bit harder!'

The three cousins had plenty to talk about as they went back to school in the car. They sat at the back whilst Mrs. O'Sullivan drove.

'So Margery is sixteen!' said Isabel. 'Golly, isn't she a dunce? And fancy being expelled so many times! I wonder that St. Clare's took her.'

Mrs. O'Sullivan chimed in unexpectedly. 'If any school can help that miserable girl you keep talking about it should be St. Clare's. Miss Theobald prides herself on getting the best out of the worst—and I'm quite sure she knows all about Margery Fenworthy, and is hoping that St. Clare's will be the one school that will keep her.'

The three girls were silent. Secretly they had all been hoping that there might be the excitement of Margery being expelled from St. Clare's too. But now the twins' mother had put the matter in rather a different light. It *would* be a score for St. Clare's if it could keep Margery.

'Mother—do you think we'd better not tell the other girls about Margery?' asked Pat, at last, voicing what the others had been thinking too.

'I certainly think there's no doubt about it,' said Mrs. O'Sullivan. 'Why should you spread tales about the girl, when, for all you know, she is simply dreading any one knowing her secret? You say she will not tell you what schools she has been to. She doesn't boast about being expelled—so she is evidently ashamed of it. She hasn't behaved well, but I think you shouldn't give her away.'

The twins felt the same. Much as they disliked Margery they didn't want to spread round the news they had heard. But Alison was rather disappointed.

'It would have been such a bit of news!' She couldn't help saying.

'Now, Alison, if you start to bleat this all over the place——' began Pat, crossly, but Alison gave her a push.

'Be quiet! I shan't tell a soul. And will you STOP saying I bleat? I just hate that word! I've tried not to bleat lately, but you just go on and on saying it.'

Alison's eyes were full of the tears she could call up at a moment's notice. But Pat knew the girl was really upset, so she gave her a friendly pinch.

'Shut up, silly! I know you won't say a word. We can trust you all right, I know.'

But although the three girls did not say a word to any one they could not help feeling that such a bad record was terrible—and they felt that Margery might be anything bad—she might be capable of doing the meanest, horridest things. Each of the girls believed she had ruined the jumper, and when any one said so in their hearing, they all agreed.

Margery took no notice of any one. She was always reading, and she did not seem to hear the remarks made by the girls in front of her. Her good-looking face was even more sullen than usual, and she was the despair of all the mistresses!

ERICA was eagerly on the look-out for another trick to play on Pat or Isabel. If she could make it appear that it was done by Margery, so much the better!

But it was not very easy to play a trick without drawing attention to herself. She waited for a week, and then chance put the opportunity in her way.

There was a nature-walk one afternoon. All the first- and second-formers had to go. They were to take their satchels with them, with their nature notebooks, and their tins for collecting specimens.

Miss Roberts and Miss Jenks were going too. The woods were to be visited, and the ponds. There should be quite a lot of things to observe, draw and collect.

The twins were excited about the outing, which was to take up the whole of one afternoon. It was a brilliantly fine day and the sun was quite warm.

' There might be early tadpoles or frog-spawn in the ponds,' said Pat. ' I think I'll take a little jar in case.'

All the girls prepared their satchels and put into them their nature books, their tins and jars. Pat was proud of her nature notebooks. She had done some beautiful drawings in them, and Miss Roberts had said they were good enough to be exhibited at the end of the term.

'I've just got one more page to fill,' she said to Isabel. 'I'll do it this afternoon. Are you ready? You're walking with me, aren't you?'

'Of course!' said Isabel. It was no good any one else asking to walk with either of the twins because they always went with each other. They preferred each other to any of the other girls, much as they liked Janet and Hilary and Lucy.

All the girls paired off. No one wanted to go with Erica or Margery, and so it came about that those two found themselves together. They did not like one another and walked in silence. Some of the girls nudged each other and giggled when they saw the silent pair.

'Two bad eggs together!' giggled Winnie. 'I hope they're enjoying each other's conversation! Doesn't Margery's face look black—she's in one of her tempers, I expect.'

Margery *was* feeling rather ill-tempered, for she had hoped to walk by herself. She did not like being paired off with the mean little Erica. So she said nothing, hoping that Erica would take the hint and leave her to herself as much as possible.

The afternoon went on happily in the yellow sunshine. The girls wandered over the woods, and made notes and sketches, and collected twigs and moss. Some of them found early primroses and stuck them into their button-holes.

Then they went down to the ponds, and exclaimed in surprise to see frog-spawn already floating at the top of the water.

'I *must* get some!' said Pat at once.

'You can't,' said Isabel. 'It's too far in. You'll get your shoes wet.'

Pat took a quick glance round. 'Where are Miss Roberts and Miss Jenks? Look—they're still at the top of the hill. I've time to take off my shoes and stockings and wade in!'

The girls giggled. 'Pat, you do do some awful things!' said Janet. 'Miss Roberts will *not* be pleased with you—and your feet will be as muddy as anything.'

'Feet can be cleaned,' said Pat. She took off her satchel and hung it on a post not far off. She took out her little jar and put it down on the bank. Then she stripped off her shoes and stockings and waded into the pond.

'Oooooh! The water's jolly cold!' she said. 'And it's mud at the bottom—horrid! Oh—I've trodden on a snail or something!'

Pat made every one laugh. All the girls crowded round, laughing, watching her as she waded here and there.

She reached the frog-spawn and bent down to get it. It slipped through her fingers back into the pond. Isabel laughed.

'Try again, old girl!' she cried. Pat did her best to catch the slippery spawn, but time after time it slipped down into the water. Soon all the watching girls were in a state of giggle, and did not see Miss Roberts or Miss Jenks coming to the pond!

'Pat!' suddenly cried Miss Roberts's voice, in horror. 'What in the world are you doing? Oh, you naughty girl—you'll get your death of cold, wading into the icy water like that! Come out at once!'

'Oh, Miss Roberts—please, Miss Roberts, let me get some frog-spawn first,' begged Pat, snatching another handful, that promptly slithered between her fingers back into the pond again.

'Pat! *Will* you come out!' cried Miss Roberts. 'Really, I can't leave you first-formers for a single minute!'

All the girls but two were watching the scene with the greatest interest and amusement. Those two were Erica and Margery. Margery had stayed behind in a field to watch some horses ploughing—and Erica had dawdled too.

Erica heard the laughter going on and hastened to see what the excitement was. Before she got to the pond she saw Pat's satchel hanging on to the post. On it was Pat's name—P. O'Sullivan.

Erica took a quick look at the pond. Not a single girl was looking her way. Anyway, she was out of sight, behind the hedge. She looked to see where Margery was. But Margery was still up in the field, watching the horses.

Quick as lightning Erica took the satchel off the post and opened it. Down into the mud she flung all Pat's precious nature books, and her tins of nature finds. She ground the books into the mud with her heel and stamped on the tins.

She flung the satchel into the hedge. Then, as silently as she could, she ran behind the hedge and came up to the pond from the opposite direction. No one noticed her. When Tessie saw her there she imagined that Erica had been there all the time.

Pat was wading out of the water. Her feet were terribly cold. She took out her handkerchief and dried them, and Miss Roberts slapped them well to get the circulation back. Then she made Pat put on her shoes and stockings and run up the hill and back to warm herself.

'And after all that I didn't get any frog-spawn!' said Pat, sorrowfully, as she rejoined the others, her feet tingling. 'Where's my satchel? Where did I put it?'

'Over there on the post,' said Isabel, turning to point. But the satchel wasn't there.

'Well, that's funny,' said Isabel. 'I saw you put it there. Look—there's Margery nearby. Margery! Bring Pat's satchel over with you if you can see it.'

'What's that in the hedge?' suddenly said Sheila, pointing. Her sharp eyes had seen the big brown satchel there.

'Golly! It's my satchel!' said Pat, in astonishment. 'How did it get there?'

She ran to get it—and then saw the note-books stamped down into the mud—and the dented tins with their little collections spilt on the ground. She said nothing, but there was something in her face that made the girls run towards her.

'What's up, Pat?' asked Isabel—and then she too saw what had happened. There was absolutely no doubt at all but that some spiteful hand had done the mischief. There was the half-imprint of a muddy

Everyone watched as Pat waded in the pond

foot on the exercise book—and some one had stamped on the tins !

' It—it couldn't have been a cow or something, could it ? ' said Isabel, hating to think that some one had done this to her twin.

Janet shook her head. ' No, of course not. I think we all know who did it—though we didn't see.'

All the girls looked at Margery, who was standing nearby, looking as surprised as the others. ' Who was the only one not at the pond ? ' said Janet. ' Margery ! Why did she stay behind ? To play this beastly trick, I suppose ! '

' Girls ! What is the matter ? ' asked Miss Roberts, coming up. ' Oh, Pat—are those your books in the mud ? How careless ! And all your beautiful drawings spoilt too. How did that happen ? '

' I don't know, Miss Roberts,' said poor Pat, red with dismay. She could not bring herself to sneak on Margery, even at that moment. Miss Roberts saw that something serious was the matter, and could hear Margery's name being whispered around her.

' Well, pick up your things quickly,' said Miss Roberts, looking at her watch. ' You have made us late with your paddling. Hurry now. This matter can be settled later on.'

The girls walked quickly home. Erica had to walk with Margery. She was pleased that her mean trick had come off so well, and that Margery had once again been blamed for what was not her fault. Margery walked as if she was in a dream. She simply could not understand who had done these things, for she knew quite well that *she* had not! Who could be so amazingly mean as to do them—and let some one else take the blame? Not even Erica, surely!

She took a glance at Erica, walking by her side. There was something in the smug look on the girl's face that made Margery begin to suspect her. She remembered suddenly how she had noticed Erica slipping back into the meeting the night the jumper was spoilt. *Could* it be Erica! She was a mean little sneak—every one knew it—but could she be so hateful as that?

'Well, it's some one,' thought Margery, bitterly, 'and as usual I get all the blame. What an unlucky creature I am!'

That evening after tea the girls talked about the latest trick on poor Pat. Margery could not bear their scornful glances and went to the school library to pretend to choose a book.

And whilst she was there Alison let the cat out of the bag!

'We didn't mean to tell this,' she began, looking all round, 'but now that we've seen this fresh bit of spite from Margery, I'm going to tell you all a bit of interesting news.'

'Shut up, Alison,' said Pat.

'I'm not going to shut up,' said Alison, with spirit. 'Do you think I'm going to stand by and see these things happen without getting back on Margery if I can? Now just you listen everybody!'

All the girls were silent, listening eagerly. What *could* Alison be going to tell them?

'We met an old friend of ours at half-term,' said

Alison. ' She goes to St. Hilda's—and Margery went there—and she was expelled from there ! '

There was a buzz of horror. Expelled ! What a dreadful disgrace ! And to think she was at St. Clare's ! No wonder she would never say what school she had been to !

' Not only that,' went on Alison, her eyes flashing round, ' but she has been to five or six schools altogether—and has been sent away from each one ! Do you wonder she's backward ? Do you wonder she's still in the first form when she's *sixteen* ! '

A loud chatter broke out. The girls were amazed. They couldn't believe it—and yet it was so easy to believe, knowing Margery !

' Well, why should *St. Clare's* have to have her ! ' cried Tessie, in indignation. ' Why have *we* got to put up with her, I'd like to know ? '

' Turn her out ! ' cried Hilary.

' Let's go to Miss Theobald and say we don't want to have a girl like that here ! ' cried Winnie.

' My mother wouldn't let me stay here if she knew there was a girl like Margery here ! ' said Erica.

' You be quiet,' said Tessie, giving Erica a push. She wasn't going to let mean little Erica give herself airs.

' Well, now we know all about dear Margery ! ' said Doris. ' The girl who has been expelled from six schools—and will soon be expelled from the seventh ! And a jolly good thing too. She won't be able to wreak her spite on Pat any more.'

There was a sound at the door. The girls turned. Margery was there, as white as chalk. She had heard

what Doris had said, and was fixed to the spot with
horror. So her poor secret was out. She didn't know
how the girls had learnt it—but evidently some one
had found out about her. And now she would have
to leave St. Clare's.

Margery stared at the girls out of her deep brown
eyes. She opened her mouth to say something but
no words came. She turned round and left the silent
girls there; they heard her foot-steps tip-tapping
uncertainly along the passage.

'Well, we've done it now!' said Isabel, feeling
rather scared. 'The secret's out—and the whole
school will know tomorrow!'

THE twins felt most uncomfortable about Margery. Yet they could not blame their cousin for telling the girl's secret. Alison had been very indignant about the trick that had been played on Pat, and it was her way of backing up her cousin, to talk against Margery.

' I say—you don't think Margery will run away or anything like that, do you ? ' said Pat, to Isabel. ' You know, Isabel—if that sort of thing happened to me, I couldn't stay one moment more at St. Clare's. I simply couldn't. I'd have to go home.'

' Maybe Margery hasn't much of a home to go to,' said Isabel. ' You know, she never talks about her home as we all do—she never says anything about her mother and father, or if she has any brothers or sisters. Does she ? It seems rather queer to me.'

' I don't think we can leave things like this,' said Lucy Oriell, looking grave. ' I think Miss Theobald must have known all about Margery—and her bad reputation—and I think she must have said she would let her try here, at St. Clare's. And I think something else too—I think that all the mistresses were in the secret, and knew about Margery—and that they have been asked to be lenient with her to give her a chance.'

The girls stared at Lucy's serious little face. She
was such a sweet-natured girl that every one listened
to her willingly. No one had ever known Lucy say
anything horrid about any one.

'I think you're right, Lucy,' said Pat. 'I've often
wondered why Margery seemed to get away with rudeness and carelessness—whilst we got into hot water if
we did the same things. · I knew of course it wasn't
favouritism, for no mistress could possibly *like* Margery. Now I understand.'

'Yes—Lucy's right,' said Hilary. 'All the mistresses were in the secret, and were trying to help
Margery, hoping she'd turn over a new leaf, and be
all right at St. Clare's. What a hope!'

'It's this meanness I can't stand,' said Pat. 'I can
put up with bad manners and rudeness and even
sulkiness, but I just hate meanness."

'Yes, I agree with you there,' said Janet. 'You
can't do much with a mean nature. Well—what are
we going to do about Margery? Lucy, you said we
couldn't leave things as they are now. What do you
suggest doing?'

'I suggest that we all sleep on it, and then one or
more of us should go to Miss Theobald tomorrow and
tell all we know,' said Lucy. 'If Margery can't face
us after what has happened, then she ought to be
given the chance to go. But if she still wants to
stay, and face it out, then she ought to have the
chance to do that. But Miss Theobald ought to
decide—not us. We don't know enough. Miss Theobald probably knows the reason for Margery's funny
behaviour. We don't.'

'All right. Let's sleep on it,' said Janet. 'My mother always says that's a good thing to do. Things often seem different after a night's sleep. Well—we'll do that—and tomorrow we'll go to Miss Theobald and tell her all we know.'

'Lucy must go,' said Hilary. 'She's good at that sort of thing. She's got no spite in her and can tell a story fairly. Pat and Isabel had better go too—because after all, it's against Pat that these hateful tricks have been directed.'

'All right,' said Lucy. 'I'd rather *not* go really, because I hate being mixed up in this sort of thing. But somebody's got to go. Well, that's decided then.'

But although the girls had laid their plans seriously and carefully, they were not to be put into action. For something happened that night that upset them completely, and that changed everything in a few hours.

The girls all went to bed as usual. Erica had complained of a sore throat and had been sent to Matron. Matron had taken her temperature, and found that it was a hundred. So into the sanatorium went Erica, where two other girls were, with bad chills.

'You've just got a chill too,' said Matron. 'Now drink this, and settle down quickly into bed. I'll pop in and see you later. You'll probably be normal tomorrow, and can go back to school the next day if you're sensible.'

Erica didn't mind at all. She rather liked missing lessons for a day or two—and she felt that it was lucky to be away when all the fuss was being made

about Margery.   Erica was a mean soul—but even she
had been horrified at the look on Margery's face when
she had overheard what the girls were saying about
her.

'I wouldn't have played those tricks and made it
seem as if they'd been done by Margery if I'd known
the girls were going to find out about her being expelled
—and blame the tricks on to her as well as despise her
for her disgrace,' thought Erica, her conscience beginning to prick her for the first time.   'I wish I hadn't
done them now.   But I do hate that horrid Pat.   It
does serve her right to have her jumper spoilt and all
her nature books!'

Erica got undressed and into bed.   She was alone
in a little room at the top of the sanatorium, which
was a separate building on the west side of the school.
In the san. were put any infectious cases, any girls
with measles and so on, or who had perhaps sprained
an ankle.   Here Matron looked after them and kept
them under her eye until they were well enough to
go back to their forms.

Erica was put into a room alone because Matron
was not quite sure if her cold was going to turn to
something infectious.   There had been a case of measles
among the Oakdene girls who had played the match
against St. Clare's, and the mistresses had been on
the watch in case any of their own girls should have
caught it from the Oakdene girl.

So Erica was not put with the two girls who had
chills, in case by any chance she was beginning measles,
which she hadn't had.

It was a nice little room, well-tucked away at the

top of the san. Erica looked out of the window before she got into bed and saw a sky full of stars. She drew back the curtains so that the sun could come in the next morning and then got into bed.

Matron came along with a hot-water bottle and some hot lemon and honey. Erica enjoyed it. Then Matron tucked her up, switched off the light, and left her to go to sleep.

Erica was soon asleep. Her conscience did not keep her awake, for it was not a very lively one. If Pat or Isabel had done the things that Erica had done lately, neither of them would have been able to sleep at night because of feeling mean and wretched. But Erica went sweetly off to sleep, and slept as soundly as any of the girls in her form.

But one girl did not sleep that night. It was Margery. She lay in her dormitory, wide awake, thinking of what she had heard the girls say about her. Always, always, wherever she went, her secret was found out, and sooner or later she had to go. She didn't want to be at school. She didn't want to stay at home. She wished with all her might that she could go out into the world and find a job and earn her own living. It was dreadful going from school to school like this, getting worse every time!

The other girls slept soundly. Someone snored a little. Margery turned over to her left side and shut her eyes. If only she could go to sleep! If only she could stop thinking and thinking! What was going to happen tomorrow? Now that all the girls knew about her, things would be terrible.

She couldn't go home. She couldn't run away

because she only had a few shillings. There was simply nothing she could do but stay and be miserable —and when she was miserable she didn't care about anything in the world, and that made her rude and careless and sulky.

'There isn't any way out for me,' thought the girl. 'There's simply nothing I can do. If only there was something—some way of escape from all this. But there isn't.'

She turned over on to her right side, and shut her eyes again. But in a moment they were wide open. It was impossible to go to sleep. She tried lying on her back, staring up into the dark. But that didn't make her sleepy either. She heard the school clock chime out. Eleven o'clock. Twelve o'clock. One o'clock. Two o'clock. Was there ever such a long night as this? At this rate the night would never never be over.

'I'll get myself a drink of water,' said Margery, sitting up. 'Maybe that will help me to go to sleep.'

She put on her dressing-gown and slippers and found her torch. She switched it on. Its light showed her the sleeping forms of the other girls. No one stirred as she went down between the cubicles to the door.

She opened the door and went out into the passage. There was a bathroom not far off, with glasses. She went there and filled a glass with water. She took it to the window to drink it.

And it was whilst she was standing there, drinking the icy-cold water that she saw something that puzzled her. She forgot to finish the water, and set the glass down to peer out of the window.

The bathroom window faced the sanatorium, which was a four-storey building, tall and rather narrow. It was in complete darkness except at one place.

A flickering light showed now and again from high up on the third storey. It came from a window there. Margery puzzled over it. She tried to think what it could be.

'It looks like flickering firelight,' she thought. 'But who is sleeping on the third storey, I wonder? Wait a minute—surely that isn't the window of a bedroom? Surely it's the little window that gives light to the stairway that goes up to the top storey?'

She watched for a little while, trying to make certain. But in the darkness she couldn't be sure if it was the staircase window or a bedroom window. The light flickered on and on, exactly as if it were the glow of a bedroom fire, sometimes dancing up into flames and sometimes dying down.

'I'd better go back to bed,' said Margery to herself, shivering. 'It's probably the room where Erica is— and Matron has given her a fire in her bedroom for a treat. It's the flickering glow I can see.'

So back to bed she went—but she kept worrying a little about that curious light—and in the end she got out of bed once more to see if it was still there.

And this time, looking out of the bathroom window, she knew without any doubt what it was. It was Fire, Fire, Fire!

AS soon as Margery saw the light for the second time, she gave a shout. The whole of the staircase window was lighted up, and flames were shooting out of it!

'Fire!' yelled Margery, and darted off to Miss Roberts's room. She hammered on her door.

'Miss Roberts! Miss Roberts! Quick, come and look! The san. is on fire! Oh, quick!'

Miss Roberts woke with a jump. Her room faced on to the san. and she saw at once what Margery had just seen. Dragging on a dressing-gown she ran to the door. Margery clutched hold of her.

'Miss Roberts! Shall I go across and see if Matron knows! I'm sure she doesn't!'

'Yes, run quickly!' said Miss Roberts. 'Don't wake any of the girls in this building, Margery—there's no need for them to know. Hurry now. I'll get Miss Theobald and we'll join you.'

Margery tore down the stairs and undid the side door. She raced across the piece of grass that separated the san. from the school. She hammered on the door there and shouted.

'Matron! Matron! Are you there!'

Matron was fast sleep on the second floor. She didn't wake. It was Queenie, one of the girls in bed with a chill who heard Margery shouting. She ran to the window and looked out.

' What is it, what is it ? ' she cried.

' The san. is on fire ! ' shouted Margery. ' Flames are coming out on the storey above you. Wake Matron ! '

The girl darted into the Matron's room. She shook her hard, calling to her in fright. Matron woke up in a hurry and pulled on a coat.

Miss Theobald appeared with some of the other mistresses. Some one had telephoned for the fire-engine. Girls appeared from everywhere, in spite of mistresses' orders to go back to bed.

' Good gracious ! Go back to bed when there's a perfectly good fire on ! ' said Janet, who, as usual, was eager to enjoy any experience that came her way. ' Golly, I've never seen a fire before ! I'm going to enjoy this one. Nobody's in any danger ! '

Girls swarmed all over the place. Matron tried to find the three who had had chills—Queenie, Rita, and Erica. ' They mustn't stand about in this cold night air,' she said, very worried. ' Oh, there you are, Queenie. You are to go at once to the second-form dormitory and get into the first bed you see there. Is Rita with you—and where is Erica ? '

' Rita's here,' said Queenie, ' and I think I saw Erica somewhere.'

' Well, find her and take her to bed at once,' ordered Matron. 'Where are the two maids ? Are they safe ? '

Yes—they were safe. They were shivering in their coats nearby, watching the flames getting bigger and bigger.

'Matron, is every one out of the sanatorium?' asked Miss Theobald. 'Are you sure? All the girls? The maids? Any one else?'

'I've seen Queenie,' said Matron, 'and Rita—and Queenie said she saw Erica. Those are the only girls I had in. And the two maids are out. They are over there.'

'Well, that's all right then,' said Miss Theobald, in relief. 'Oh, I wish that fire-engine would hurry up. I'm afraid the fourth storey will be completely burnt out.'

Queenie had not seen the right Erica. She *had* seen a girl called Erica, who was in the fourth form, and she had not known that Matron meant Erica of the second form. Erica was still in the san.

No one knew this at all until suddenly Mam'zelle gave a scream and pointed with a trembling hand to the window of the top storey.

'*Oh, que c'est terrible!*' she cried. 'There is some one there!'

Poor Erica was at the window. She had been awakened by the smell of smoke, and had found her bedroom dark with the evil-smelling smoke that crept in under and around her door. Then she had heard the crackling of the flames.

In a terrible fright she had jumped up and tried to switch on her light. But nothing happened. The wires outside had been burnt and there was no light in her room. The girl felt for her torch and switched it on.

She ran to the door—but when she opened it a great roll of smoke unfolded itself and almost choked her.

There was no way out down the staircase. It was in flames.

The fire had been started by an electric wire which had smouldered on the staircase, and had kindled the dry wood nearby. The staircase was old and soon burnt fiercely. There was no way out for Erica. She tried to run into the next room, from whose window there was a fire-escape—but the smoke was so thick that it choked her and she had to run back into her own room. She shut the door and rushed to the window.

She threw it open, and thankfully breathed in the pure night air. ' Help ! ' she shouted, in a weak voice. ' Help ! '

No one heard her—but Mam'zelle saw her. Every one looked up at Mam'zelle's shout, and a deep groan went up as they saw Erica at the window.

Miss Theobald went pale, and her heart beat fast. A girl up there ! And the staircase burning !

' The fire-engine isn't here,' she groaned. ' If only we had the fire-escape to run up its ladder to that high window ! Oh, when will it come ? '

Some one had found the garden-hose and was playing water on the flames. But the force of water was feeble and made little difference to the fire. Erica shouted again.

·'Help'! Save me! Oh, save me ! ' She could see all the crowd of people below and she could not think why some one did not save her. She did not realize that the fire-engine had not yet come, and that there was no ladder long enough to reach her.

'Where is the long garden ladder ? ' cried Margery,

suddenly, seeing a gardener nearby. 'Let's get it. Maybe we can send a rope up or something, even if the ladder isn't long enough!'

The men ran to get the longest ladder. They set it up against the wall and one of them ran up to the top. But it did not nearly reach to Erica's window.

'It's no good,' he said, when he came down. 'It's impossible to reach. Where's that fire-engine? It's a long time coming.'

'It's been called out to another fire,' said one of the mistresses, who had just heard the news. 'It's coming immediately.'

'Immediately!' cried Margery. 'Well, that's not soon enough! Erica will soon be trapped by the flames.'

Before any one could stop her the girl threw off her dressing-gown and rushed to the ladder. She was up it like a monkey, though Miss Theobald shouted to her to come back.

'You can't do anything, you silly girl!' cried the Head Mistress. 'Come down!'

Every one watched Margery as she climbed to the very top of the ladder. The flames lighted up the whole scene now, and the dark figure of the climbing girl could be clearly seen.

'What *does* she think she can do?' said Miss Roberts, in despair. 'She'll fall!'

But Margery had seen something that had given her an idea. To the right side of the ladder ran an iron pipe. Maybe she could swarm up that and get to Erica's window. What she was going to do then she didn't know—but she meant to do *some*thing!

She reached the top of the ladder. She put out a hand and caught hold of the strong iron pipe hoping that it was well nailed to the wall. Fortunately it was. Margery swung herself from the ladder to the pipe, clutching hold of it with her knees, and holding for dear life with her hands.

And now all her training in the gym stood her in good stead. All the scores of times she had climbed the ropes there had strengthened her arms and legs, and made them very steady and strong. It was far more difficult to climb an unyielding pipe than to swarm up a pliant rope, but Margery could do it. Up the pipe she went, pulling herself by her arms, and clinging with her knees and feet. Erica saw her coming.

'Oh, save me!' cried the girl, almost mad with fright. Margery came up to the window. Now was the most difficult part. She had to get safely from the pipe to the window-sill.

'Erica! Hold on to something and give me a hand!' yelled Margery, holding out her hand above the window-sill. 'If you can give me a pull I can get there.'

Erica gave her hand to Margery. She held on to a heavy book-case just inside the room, and Margery swung herself strongly across to the sill from the pipe. She put up a knee, grazing it badly on the sill, but she did not even feel the pain. In half a moment she was inside the room. Erica clung to her, weeping.

'Now don't be silly,' said Margery, shaking herself free and looking round the room, filled with dense black smoke. The flames were already just outside the door and the floor felt hot to her feet. 'There's no time to lose. Where's your bed?'

Erica pointed through the smoke to where her bed was. Margery ran to it, choking, and dragged the sheets and blankets off it. She ran back to the window, and leaned her head outside to get some fresh air. Then she quickly tore the sheets in half.

'Oh, what are you doing?' cried Erica, thinking that Margery was quite mad. 'Take me out of the window with you!'

'I will in a moment,' said Margery, as she knotted the sheet-strips firmly together. There were four long strips. Margery looked for something to tie one end to. As she looked, the door fell in with a crash, and flames came into the room.

'Oh, quick, quick!' cried Erica. 'I shall jump!'

'No, you won't,' said Margery. 'You're going to be saved—and very quickly too. Look here—see how I've knotted this sheet—and tied it to the end of your bed. Help me to drag the bed to the window. That's right.'

Margery threw the other end of the sheet-strips out of the window. The end almost reached the top of the ladder! There was no need to climb down the pipe this time!

Margery sat herself on the window-sill and made Erica come beside her. Below, the crowds of girls and mistresses were watching what was happening, hardly daring to breathe. One of the gardeners had gone up the ladder, hoping to help.

'Now do you think you can climb down this sheet-

rope I've made ? ' said Margery to the trembling Erica.
' Look—it should be quite easy.'

' Oh, no, I can't, I can't,' sobbed Erica, terrified.
So Margery did a very brave thing. She took Erica
on her back, and with the frightened girl clinging
tightly to her, her arms holding fast, she began to
climb down the sheet-rope herself. Luckily the sheets
were new and strong, and they held well.

Down went Margery and down, her arms almost
pulled out of their sockets with Erica's weight. She
felt with her feet for the ladder, and oh, how thankful
she was when at last she felt the top rung, and a loud
voice cried, ' Well done, miss ! I've got you ! '

The gardener at the top of the ladder reached for
Erica, and took hold of her. He helped the weeping
girl down, and Margery slid down the few remaining
feet of the sheet-rope.

What happened next nobody ever knew. It was
likely that Margery was tired out with her amazing
climb and equally amazing rescue, and that her feet
slipped on the ladder—for somehow or other she lost
her balance, and half slid, half fell down the ladder.
She fell on the gardener, who helped to break her fall
a little—but then she slid right off the ladder to the
ground seven or eight feet below.

People rushed over to her—but Margery lay still.
She had struck her head against something and was
quite unconscious. Careful hands carried her into the
big school just as the fire-engine rumbled up with a
great clangour of its big bell. In one minute strong
jets of water were pouring on to the flames, and in
five minutes the fire was under control.

But the top storey, as Miss Theobald had feared, was entirely burnt out. The room where Erica had been sleeping was a mass of black charred timbers.

The girls were ordered back to bed, and this time they went ! But there was one name on every one's lips that night—the name of a real heroine.

' Margery ! Wasn't she wonderful ! She saved Erica's life. Fancy her climbing that pipe like that. Let's pray she isn't much hurt. Margery ! Well, wasn't she *wonderful* ! '

THE next morning every one wanted to know how Margery was. A few remembered to ask about poor Erica, but it was Margery that people worried about.

'She's broken her leg! Poor old Margery! And she's hurt her head too, but not very badly. She's in the dressing-room off Miss Theobald's own bedroom. Miss Theobald is terribly proud of her!'

'I don't wonder!' said Janet, who always intensely admired bravery of any sort. 'I don't care now what Margery has been like in the past few weeks. I've forgotten it all! A girl who can do a big thing like that can be as rude and sulky as she likes, for all I care!'

'And now I find it more difficult than ever to think that Margery can have played any mean tricks!' said Lucy. 'I simply can't help thinking we made a mistake over that. It *must* have been some one else! Courage of the sort that Margery showed last night never goes with a mean nature—never, never, never! It's impossible.'

'I wish we knew for certain,' said Alison, who was now feeling very guilty because she had told Margery's secret, and had let the girls know that she had been expelled from so many schools.

They did know, very soon, who was the guilty one. It was Lucy who found out. She went to see Erica who was in a little room off one of the dormitories, not much the worse for her adventure except that she was very sorry for herself.

Something had happened to Erica besides the fire. She had lain awake all that night, thinking of it—and thinking of Margery, who had rescued her.

And her conscience had come very much alive! To think that the girl who had so bravely saved her life was the girl who had been taking the blame for Erica's own meanness! Erica's cheeks burned when she thought of it. She wished it had been any other girl but Margery who had rescued her.

Lucy came to see her at the end of morning school. Nobody had been allowed to see Margery, who was to be kept quite quiet for a few days. No one had wanted very much to see Erica—but kind-hearted Lucy, as usual, thought of the girl lying alone in the little room, and asked Matron if she could see her.

'Yes, of course,' said Matron. 'She's normal this morning and there's nothing wrong with her except a bit of a cold and shock. It will do her good to see you.'

So Lucy went into the little room and sat down beside Erica. They talked for a while, and then Erica asked about Margery. She did not look at Lucy as she asked, for she felt very guilty.

'Haven't they told you about Margery?' said Lucy, in surprise. 'Oh, poor thing, she's broken her right leg. That means no more gym or games for her for some time—and as they are the only things she cares about, she's going to have a pretty thin time. She hit her head on something too, but not very badly. She *was* a heroine, Erica !'

Erica was terribly upset. She had thought that Margery was quite all right, and had pictured her receiving the praise of the whole school. And now after all she was in bed with a broken leg and a bad head !

Erica turned her face to the wall, trying to think the matter out. She looked so miserable that Lucy was touched. She didn't like Erica, but misery of any kind must be comforted.

She took Erica's hand. 'Don't worry about it,' she said. ' Her leg will mend—and she will be quite all right again. We are all very proud of her.'

' Do you—do you still think she did those mean things ? ' asked Erica, not looking at Lucy.

' No, I don't,' said Lucy at once. ' Those kind of tricks don't go with a strong and fearless nature like Margery's. She's got plenty of faults—and bad ones too—but she has no petty, mean faults, as far as I can see.'

Matron popped her head round the door. ' Come along now, Lucy,' she said. ' Your ten minutes is up.'

' Oh, don't go yet, don't go yet ! ' said Erica, clutching Lucy's hand, and feeling that she did not want to be left alone with her own thoughts. But Lucy had to go.

And then Erica had a very bad time indeed. It is hard enough when any one thinks contemptuously of us—but far worse if we have to despise ourselves. And that is what poor Erica found herself doing. She saw herself clearly—a mean, small, spiteful little creature, insincere and dishonest, and she didn't like herself at all.

She turned her face to the wall. She would not eat any dinner at all, and Matron took her temperature, feeling worried. But it was still normal.

' Are you worrying about something ? ' she asked. Erica's eyes filled with tears at the kind voice.

' Yes,' she said desperately. ' I'm worrying terribly. I can't stop.'

' Tell me all about it,' said Matron, gently.

' No,' said Erica, and turned her face to the wall again. But she knew she could not keep all her thoughts to herself much longer. She had to tell some one, she simply had to. She called to Matron as she was going out of the room.

' Matron ! I want Lucy ! '

My dear child, she's in class ! ' said Matron. ' She can come and see you at tea-time, if you like.'

Erica burst into floods of tears, and sobbed so heartrendingly that Matron hurried over to her.

' Whatever *is* the matter ? ' she said.

' Matron, fetch Lucy,' sobbed Erica. ' Oh, do fetch Lucy.'

Matron went out of the room and sent some one for Lucy. There was something queer about Erica's face, and the sooner she told somebody what was worrying her, the better ! Lucy came along in surprise.

' Erica has something on her mind, Lucy,' said Matron. ' Try to get her to tell you, will you ? Her temperature will shoot up and she'll be really ill if she goes on like this.'

Lucy went into the little room and sat down on Erica's bed. Erica had stopped crying, and her face was white and pinched. She stared dry-eyed at Lucy.

'What's up, old girl?' asked Lucy, her kind little face glowing with friendliness.

'Lucy! I've got to tell somebody or I'll go quite mad!' said Erica, desperately. '*I* did all those awful things to Pat. It wasn't Margery. It was me.'

'Oh, Erica!' said Lucy, deeply shocked. 'Poor, poor Margery!'

Erica said nothing. She turned her face to the wall again and lay still. She felt ill.

Lucy sat for a moment, taking in what Erica had said. Then, with an effort, she took Erica's cold hand. She knew that she must try to be kind to the girl, though she could hardly bring herself to be, because of her pity for what Margery must have gone through.

'Erica! I'm glad you told me. You know that I must tell the others, don't you? We mustn't for one moment more think that Margery did those things. We have accused her most unjustly, and treated her very unfairly. You see that I must tell the others, don't you?'

'Must you?' said Erica, her eyes filling with tears again. 'But how can I face them all, if you do?'

'I don't know, Erica,' said Lucy. 'That's for you to decide. You have been awfully mean and spiteful. Why don't you tell Miss Theobald, now that you've told me, and see what she says?'

'No. I daren't tell her,' said Erica, trembling as she thought of Miss Theobald's stern face. 'You tell her, Lucy. Oh, Lucy—I want to leave here. I've done so badly. Nobody has ever liked me much—and nobody will ever, ever like me now. And there won't be a chance for me to try properly if nobody feels friendly towards me. I'm a coward, you know. I can't stand up to things.'

'I know,' said Lucy gravely. 'But sooner or later, you'll have to learn to face things that come along, Erica, and you'll have to get that meanness and spite out of your character, or you'll never be happy. I'll see Miss Theobald. Now don't worry too much. I'm very glad you told me all you did.'

Lucy left Erica to her thoughts. She went to Matron. 'Matron,' she said, 'Erica has told me what's worrying her—but it's something I ought to tell Miss Theobald. Can I go now?'

'Of course,' said Matron, thinking that Lucy Oriell was one of the nicest girls who had ever come to St. Clare's. 'Hurry along now. I'll send a message to Miss Roberts for you.'

And so it came about that Lucy went to Miss Theobald with Erica's guilty secret, and related it all to the Head Mistress in her clear, friendly little voice. Miss Theobald listened gravely, not interrupting her at all.

'So Margery was accused wrongly,' she said. 'Poor Margery! She is a most unlucky child! But she did behave amazingly last night. What a plucky girl she is! She has two sides to her character—and the finer side came out very strongly yesterday.'

'Miss Theobald, we know that Margery has been expelled from many schools,' said Lucy, looking the Head straight in the eyes. 'And we have guessed that the mistresses have been asked to be lenient with her to give her a chance at St. Clare's. And although I'm a new girl too I do see that any girl with a bad record would have a fine chance here to do better, because there's a wonderful spirit in this school. I've felt it and loved it. I'm so very glad my parents chose this school to send me to.'

Miss Theobald looked at Lucy's honest and sincere face. She smiled one of her rare sweet smiles.

' And I too am glad that your parents sent you here,' she said. ' You are the type of girl that helps to make the spirit of the school a living powerful thing, Lucy.'

Lucy flushed with pleasure, and felt very happy. Miss Theobald went back to the matter they had been discussing.

' Now we have to decide one or two things,' she said, and at that word ' we ', Lucy felt proud and delighted. To think that she and Miss Theobald together were going to decide things !

' About Margery. You shall go and see her and tell her what you have told me. She must know as soon as possible that you have all been wrong about her, and that you know it and are sorry. She must know it was Erica too. How strange that the girl she rescued should be the girl who did her so much wrong ! Erica must have felt very upset about it.'

' This will make a great difference to Margery,' said Lucy, her eyes shining. ' Every one will think of her as a heroine now, instead of as a sulky, rude girl. What a chance for Margery ! '

' Yes—I think things may be easier for her now,' said Miss Theobald. ' You may have guessed that

Margery's home is not quite a normal one, Lucy, and that has made things hard for her. I can't tell you any more. You must just be content with that! And now—what about Erica?'

They looked at one another gravely, and Lucy felt pride swell up in her as she saw how Miss Theobald trusted her opinion.

'Miss Theobald—things won't be easier for Erica,' said Lucy. 'She's awfully weak, you know. She won't be able to stand up to the girls' unfriendliness after this. If she only could, it would be the making of her. But I'm quite sure she can't. I think it would be better for her to go away and start all over again at another school. I don't mean expel her in disgrace—but couldn't something be arranged?'

'Yes, of course,' said the Head Mistress. 'I can explain things to her mother—she has no father, you know—and suggest that Erica goes home for the rest of the term, and then is sent to a fresh school in the summer—perhaps with the determination to do a great deal better! Poor Erica! What a good thing she at least had the courage to tell you.'

Lucy left the Head Mistress feeling contented. It was good to know that some one wise and kindly had the handling of matters such as these. By this time it was teatime and Lucy went to the dining-hall feeling terribly hungry.

'Where *have* you been?' cried a dozen voices, as she came in. 'You missed painting—and you love that!'

'Oh, dear—so I did!' said Lucy, sadly. 'I forgot about that. Well—I couldn't help it.'

' But, Lucy, where have you been and what have you been doing ? ' asked Pat. ' Do tell us ! You look all excited somehow.'

' I've heard some interesting things,' said Lucy, helping herself to bread and butter and jam. ' I'll tell you in the common room after tea. I'm too hungry to talk now. You must just wait ! '

THE first- and second-formers crowded into their common room after tea, eager to hear what Lucy had to say. They knew quite well it was something exciting.

Lucy sat on a table and told them everything in her clear, calm voice. There were many interruptions, for the girls were intensely angry when they heard that it was Erica who had spoilt Pat's jumper and books—and had allowed the blame to rest on Margery.

'The beast! The hateful beast!'

'I'd like to pull all her hair out! I do feel a mean pig to think I blamed poor old Margery!'

'Oh, the spiteful creature! I'll never speak to her again as long as I live!'

'Just wait till she comes back into class! I'll give her an awful time. And to think that Margery broke her leg rescuing *that* mean creature!'

'Now listen,' said Lucy, trying to stop the yells and shouts. 'Do LISTEN! I've got something else to say.'

Every one was quiet. Lucy then told them that Erica was to go home—not to be expelled in disgrace, but simply to go home and start again somewhere else. 'And let's hope she's learnt her lesson and won't be quite so mean in future,' said Lucy.

' She'd learn her lesson all right if only Miss Theobald made her come back into class,' said Janet, grimly.

' Yes, but she'd learn it in the wrong way,' argued Lucy. ' She'd just be scared and frightened out of her life, and terribly miserable. And honestly nobody can ever do much good if they are scared and unhappy.'

' Lucy is always for giving the under-dog a chance ! ' said Pat, giving Lucy a warm hug. ' You're a good sort, Lucy, old thing. You're quite right, of course.'

And so it came about that Erica was not seen again at St. Clare's, except once by Lucy who went to say good-bye to her. That was two days later when Erica was up again, looking pale and unhappy. She was glad to be going away—but dreaded all that her mother would say.

' Now you just tell your mother honestly that you've been a mean and spiteful girl ! ' said Lucy. ' And tell her you know it and you're going to start all over again and be just the opposite. You can, you know ! Write to me next term and tell me how you're getting on.'

So poor, mean little Erica disappeared from St. Clare's to start again somewhere else. Nobody missed her, and nobody waved to her as she went down the school drive in a taxi with her trunks. She had made her own punishment, which is always much harder to bear than any other.

' How's Margery getting on ? ' Matron was asked a dozen times a day, and at last in despair she put up a bulletin on her door, which read :—

' Margery is getting on nicely.'

' Golly ! Just like royalty ! ' said Janet, when she

saw the bulletin. 'You know—when the king is ill they put a notice outside the gate about him.'

Lucy and Pat were the first two allowed to see Margery. They brought flowers and grapes and went into the cosy little dressing-room, which was lighted by a dancing fire.

'Hallo, old girl!' said Pat, presenting the flowers. 'How's the heroine?'

'Don't be an idiot!' said Margery. 'Oh, what glorious daffodils! And oh, how did you know that my favourite grapes were those big purple ones!'

'Here's something from Isabel,' said Pat, bringing out a jigsaw puzzle. 'And Janet sent you this. Everybody's got something for you, but Matron won't allow too much at once.'

Margery flushed with pleasure. She looked at the jigsaw from Isabel and the book from Janet. She forgot the pain in her leg in her delight at being spoilt like this.

'How's Erica?' she asked.

'She's gone,' said Lucy. 'She's not coming back again.'

'Gone!' said Margery, startled. 'Why? Is she ill?'

'No,' said Lucy. 'She's gone because she couldn't face the school now that they know it was she who ruined Pat's jumper and spoilt her books.'

Margery stared in the utmost amazement. 'But you said it was I who did those things,' she said. 'How did you find out it was Erica?'

Lucy told her. 'And we all owe you a humble apology for being so unjust,' she said. 'Please accept it, Margery. We will make it up to you when you are out and about again.'

Margery seldom cried, but the tears came shining into her eyes now. She blinked them away in shame. She did not know what to say for a minute.

' Well, I don't wonder you thought I was the one who did those spiteful things,' she said at last. ' I've been so awful. And it's perfectly true I've been expelled from about six schools for rudeness and sulkiness. But you see—nobody cares about me at home— and so I'm miserable, and I'm always badly-behaved when I'm miserable.'

' Don't tell us if you don't want to,' said Lucy. ' But if it's going to help—*do* tell us. We'll understand, you may be sure.'

' Well—there's nothing much to tell, really, I suppose,' said Margery, looking into Lucy's friendly eyes. ' It's probably my own silly fault. You see— my mother died when I was little. She was such a darling. And my father married again and my stepmother didn't like me. She said awful things about me to my father and he ticked me off like anything. I—I loved him awfully—I still do, of course. I'd give anything in the world to make him have a good opinion of me. He's so marvellous.'

Margery stopped and bit her lip. The others said nothing.

' My stepmother had three boys, and my father was terribly pleased. He always wanted boys. So I was pushed into the background and made to feel I wasn't wanted. And of course I got worse and worse and more and more unbearable, I suppose. I gave my stepmother a bad time, I was so rude and hateful. And that made my father angry. So I'm the black sheep of the family, and I just got to feel I didn't care about anything at all.'

'And so you were sent to boarding-school and went on being unpleasant there,' said Lucy, taking Margery's big strong hand in her little one. 'Oh, Margery—I'm terribly sorry. You haven't had a chance.'

'But won't your father be awfully bucked when he hears how you rescued Erica!' cried Pat.

'I shan't tell him,' said Margery. 'He won't know. He wouldn't believe it if anyone did tell him! He thinks I'm no use at all. You know, he's wonderful— so brave and courageous. He climbed Mount Everest.'

'Golly!' cried Pat, in astonishment. 'I say, he must be marvellous—and you take after him, don't you? You are so strong, and so good at games and gym—and so frightfully brave too.'

Margery's eyes suddenly lighted up. She lay looking up at Pat as if Pat had said something simply miraculous.

'I never, never thought of that before,' she said. 'But I believe I *do* take after him! It's lovely to think that. Yes—I'm awfully strong—and I suppose I *am* brave too, though that's not much to my credit really, because strong people ought always to be brave. Oh, you made me happy by saying that, Pat. I think my father would think a lot more of me if he knew I was like him!'

Matron came in as the conversation reached this interesting point. She was pleased to see Margery's happy face. 'You've done her good,' she said. 'But

you must go now. My word, what lovely flowers!
Tell Isabel that she and Janet can come tomorrow,
Lucy.'

The two of them said good-bye and went out. Pat
caught hold of Lucy's arm as soon as they were outside
the door. Her eyes were bright.

'Lucy! Oh, Lucy! I've got a most marvellous
idea.'

'What?' asked Lucy.

'Listen!' said Pat. 'You know that there's a
picture of Margery in the local paper, don't you—
and a long bit telling all about how she saved Erica?
Well—I'm going to cut that out and send it to Margery's
father—with a letter telling all about her and how very
proud we are of her at St. Clare's!'

'I say—that really *is* a good idea!' said Lucy. 'I
wish I'd thought of it. We can get the address from
Miss Theobald. My word—that will make Margery's
father sit up a bit—to think that St. Clare's is so proud
of her! That will be a bit different from the opinion
of the other schools she's been to. Well—it's time
Margery had a bit of luck. I expect it was partly her
own fault she didn't get on with her stepmother,
because she *is* difficult—but the treatment she had at
home only turned her from bad to worse. How silly
some parents are! When I think of my own—so kind
and understanding—I feel jolly sorry for Margery.'

After this long speech the two girls said nothing till
they reached the common room. Then Pat took the
local paper and snipped out the paragraph about
'Brave Schoolgirl Heroine' with Margery's picture.

'What are you doing?' said Isabel, curiously.

' I'll tell *you*, but no one else,' said Pat. So she told Isabel, and she and her twin and Lucy set to work to compose the letter to Margery's father.

Here it is, just as it was written by the three of them.

DEAR MR. FENWORTHY,

We know that you are a very brave man, because Margery has told us about you. Perhaps you have heard how brave Margery is too, though you may not have been told all the details. Well, here they are.

Margery climbed up an iron pipe to the window-sill of a burning room, and rescued a girl called Erica. She tore sheets into strips and tied them to the bed. She climbed down them with Erica over her shoulder. She fell from the ladder and broke her leg and hurt her head. She saved Erica's life, and is a real heroine.

Margery is awfully strong. You should see her at gym, and she is almost the best in the school already at games. She won the last match for St. Clare's. We think that she must take after you, because we are quite sure she is already strong and courageous enough to climb mountains or anything like that. She is getting a bit better now, but we think she is rather lonely, so it would be lovely if you had enough time to spare to come and see her.

We are all as proud of her as we can be, and we hope she will stay at St. Clare's till she leaves school altogether. We thought you ought to know all this so that you could be proud of her too.

With kind regards from three of Margery's friends.

PAT and ISABEL O'SULLIVAN, and LUCY ORIELL.

The girls were quite pleased with this letter, and

they posted it off the same day. It had an immediate effect—for the next day Margery had a telegram that excited her very much. It was from her father.

'Very, very proud of you. Coming to see you today. Love from Daddy.'

Margery showed the telegram to Isabel and told her to tell Pat and Lucy. 'I'm so happy,' she kept saying. 'I'm so awfully happy. Fancy my father sparing the time to come and see me. He's proud of me too! It's simply marvellous!'

The girls all watched eagerly for Margery's father to arrive. He was a fine-looking man, tall, broad-shouldered and good-looking. He was very like Margery. He was shown into Miss Theobald's room, and then taken to Margery.

What happened between Margery and her father nobody ever knew for certain, for Margery guarded her precious secret jealously. She could not even tell Lucy of those wonderful minutes when her father had taken her into his arms and praised her and loved her. Everything had come right. She had at last what she wanted and had missed so much, and in a few short minutes all that was best in Margery's character came up to the surface—and stayed there.

'Pat—Isabel—Lucy—you wrote to my father!' said Margery, next day, her eyes shining brightly. 'He showed me your letter. You're dears, all of you. It's made all the difference in the world! He didn't know a bit what I was like—and now he does—and he's terribly pleased to know I am so exactly like him! I'm going mountaineering with him next hols.!

Think of that ! And he's going to let me stay on at
St. Clare's, and then, when I'm eighteen, I'm to go to
a training college to train to be a games-mistress.
I've always wanted to do that.'

'Margery—you do look different !' said Pat,
marvelling at the glow in Margery's good-looking face.
All the sullenness was gone.

'I'll be able to work well and happily now,' said
Margery. 'I shan't be at the bottom of the form any
more !'

'No—you'll be shot up into the top form, I expect,
and send for us poor first-formers to make your tea
and clean your boots !' laughed Lucy. 'Don't you
get too swollen-headed, my girl ! You'll hear about it
from Janet, if you do !'

MARGERY was allowed to hop about on one leg fairly
soon, with crutches. Although she had to miss games
and gym she didn't fret at all. Nothing seemed to
matter to her now, she was so contented and happy.
She worked well, and the mistresses began to like this
new, cheerful Margery.

Lucy and she made firm friends. Margery could not
do enough for the merry, friendly Lucy, who only came
up to her friend's shoulder. They were always
together, and it was good to hear them joking and
laughing.

'Lucy ought always to be happy,' said Pat, as she
watched her helping Margery down the passage with
her crutches. 'There's something simply lovely about
her—she's one of those people you just can't help
liking.'

'Well, there's no reason why she shouldn't be
happy,' said Isabel. 'She's got a lovely mother—and
a famous father—and she's very clever and pretty.
She just loves St. Clare's too. She told me yesterday
that she means to be its head-girl someday. I bet she
will too.'

But ill fortune came swiftly to poor Lucy the next
week. A telegram came to Miss Theobald and Lucy

Pat and Isabel helped Margery along

was sent for out of the history class. She went to the Head Mistress's study, feeling rather frightened. What was the matter?

Miss Theobald was looking grave. She held out her hand to Lucy as the girl came in, and drew her to her.

'Lucy,' she said, 'I have some rather bad news for you. Can you be brave?'

'Yes,' said Lucy, her lip trembling. 'Tell me quickly.'

'Your father has been in a motor accident,' said Miss Theobald. 'He is badly hurt. He wants you to go to him.'

'He won't—die—will he?' said Lucy, her face very white.

'I hope not,' said Miss Theobald. 'Go and ask one of the girls to help you to pack a small bag, and then I will take you to the station. I'm so sorry, my dear— but things may not be so bad as they appear. Be brave.'

Lucy hurried off and asked Margery to help her. The bigger girl was unhappy to see Lucy so upset. She put her arm round her and hugged her. 'Cheer up,' she said. 'You may find things are all right. I'll pack your bag for you. Just you tell me what you want to take.'

Very soon poor white-faced Lucy was driving to the station with Miss Theobald. The first-formers were sad and subdued, and Margery missed her friend terribly. It seemed all wrong that anything like this should happen to merry, friendly Lucy.

'I'm going to pray hard for Lucy's father,' said Janet. 'As hard as I can.'

All the girls did the same, and thought a great deal of Lucy and wondered what was happening. Margery had a letter in four or five days. She told the others what it said.

'Lucy's father is out of danger,' she said. 'But an awful thing has happened to him. He'll never be able to use his right hand properly again—and he's a painter !'

The girls listened in dismay. 'It's terribly hard luck on him,' said Margery, 'and hard luck on Lucy too—because if he can't make money by his portrait-painting, there won't be any ! So Lucy won't be able to stay on at St. Clare's.'

'What a shame !' cried Tessie. 'She's the nicest girl that ever came here !'

'And she had planned to be head-girl one day,' said Pat. 'Oh gosh—what bad luck ! Poor old Lucy. She must be so terribly upset about her father—and then to see all her future changed in a moment like that—it must be terrible.'

'She'll have to leave school and take a job, I suppose,' said Hilary. 'St. Clare's is expensive. What a pity she can't win a scholarship or something.'

'She could if she was in the third form,' said Tessie. 'There's a scholarship set there, sitting for an exam. at the end of next term—and the winner has the right to go to one of a dozen special schools, free of fees.'

'But Lucy is only in the first form,' said Pat. 'Oh dear—I wish something could be done. Margery, is she coming back this term at all ?'

'Yes, when her father leaves the nursing home in two days' time,' said Margery, looking at the letter.

' We mustn't be all over her when she comes back. That would only upset her. Let's be quite ordinary and friendly. She'll know we are feeling for her all right.'

Lucy got a great welcome when she came back. She was pale and her face had gone thin, but she held her head up and smiled her old sweet smile. She could be as brave in her way, as Margery !

The girls did not say too much to her, and Margery took her off to show her what the class had done during the week she had been away. Lucy took her friend's arm and squeezed it.

' You're so nice to me, Margery,' she said. ' Thank you. You sent me a lovely letter. It did help. Poor Daddy—you can't think how brave he is. He knows he will probably never be able to paint again—but he means to try with his left hand. He's so brave. He blames himself terribly now because he never saved any money—so Mummy and I have got hardly any. You see, he always made as much as he wanted to— and spent it all ! We none of us bothered about saving. We thought Daddy could always get as much as he wanted.'

' Will you really have to leave St. Clare's after this term ? ' asked Margery.

' Of course,' said Lucy. ' We couldn't possibly afford the fees. If I could only have stayed on I might have won a scholarship to some other school. As it is I'm going to leave and Mummy is looking out for some sort of job for me. I'm quite quick, you know, and I could learn to be a secretary, I'm sure.'

' I shall miss you dreadfully,' said Margery, ' Just

as I've got a friend for the first time in my life! Oh,
I wish I could do something about it!'

Margery was not a person to sit down lightly under
misfortune, and she puzzled and puzzled about how
she might do something to help Lucy. And then she
suddenly got an idea. If only, only it would work!
She told nobody about it at all, not even Lucy, but
went straight to Miss Theobald.

The Head Mistress had some one with her. She
called out ' Come in!' when Margery knocked, and
the girl went in. Her good-looking face was bright
with her idea, and Miss Theobald marvelled to see the
difference in her looks.

' Oh, Miss Theobald—I didn't know you had any
one with you,' said Margery, in disappointment. ' I
did want to ask you something very badly.'

Miss Walker, the art mistress was there. She
had been talking to the Head Mistress and had not
yet finished. Miss Theobald looked at Margery and
saw her eagerness.

' What do you want to speak to me about ?' she
asked. ' Is it anything private ?'

' Well—yes, it is rather,' said Margery. ' It's about
Lucy.'

' How strange!' said Miss Theobald. ' Miss Walker
has also been speaking to me about Lucy. Well—I
think you can say what you want to with Miss Walker
here. You know that she is very interested in Lucy,
because she is so good at art.'

' Miss Theobald—you know Lucy is going to leave
after this term, don't you ?' said Margery. ' Well, she
is awfully unhappy about it, because she does so love

St. Clare's—and she is exactly the sort of girl you want, isn't she ? We all love her. Well, Miss Theobald, I've got an idea.'

' And what is that ? ' asked the Head, trying not to smile as Margery almost fell over her words in her eagerness to get them out.

' Miss Theobald, you do think Lucy is awfully clever, don't you ? ' said Margery. ' She's always top of our form, and she's got the most wonderful memory. Why, she's only just got to *look* at a page and she knows it by heart ! '

' That is a gift,' said Miss Theobald. ' I know Lucy has it. She is very lucky. Well—go on, Margery.'

' Don't you think that Lucy is clever enough to sit for the scholarship exam. with the third form next term ? ' said Margery, her eyes shining. ' I'm sure she'd win it, because she'd work so awfully hard ! Couldn't you give her a chance to do that, Miss Theobald ? She's worth it, honestly she is.'

' You needn't tell me that,' said Miss Theobald. ' We all know that Lucy is worth helping. I would keep her on at St. Clare's at reduced fees—but her parents will not hear of that. But, Margery, my dear— Lucy is only fourteen—and all the other girls going in for the exam. are sixteen. I know she's clever—but I doubt if she is as clever as that. It would only mean a great deal of very hard work—and probably a bitter disappointment at the end. There are one or two clever girls in the third form, you know.'

Margery looked dismayed. She had set her heart on her idea. She had felt so certain that Lucy was clever enough to win any scholarship, if only she had a few months to prepare for it !

Miss Walker joined in the conversation. ' I don't quite see how going in for the scholarship exam. will help Lucy to stay on at St. Clare's ! ' she said.

' Oh, but Miss Walker, it *will* ! ' cried Margery. ' I've looked at the list of schools that are open to scholarship girls free of fees—and St. Clare's is one of them this year ! So of course Lucy would choose St. Clare's, if she won the scholarship.'

Miss Theobald began to laugh.   Margery was so very determined about it all. ' Really, the running of this school is being taken out of my hands ! ' she said. ' What with Lucy deciding what was to be done about Erica—and writing that letter to your father, Margery —and now you telling me how we can manage to keep Lucy on—I feel a Head Mistress is not really needed at St. Clare's.'

' Oh, Miss Theobald, we all know that it's you that makes the school what it is,' said Margery, going red. ' But you've no idea how popular Lucy is, and how we all want to keep her. She's the first friend I've ever had—and I've been puzzling my brains how to help her. I did think this idea might be some good.'

' Well, Margery, I don't somehow think it will work,' said Miss Theobald. ' I'm not going to overwork a brilliant brain like Lucy's, two years below the scholarship exam. age unless there is a very great hope of her winning it. Miss Walker has also been to me with ideas about Lucy—and we have been talking them over.'

' Oh, how nice of you, Miss Walker ! ' said Margery, who had never very much liked the art-mistress before—

entirely her own fault, for she had never tried at all
in Miss Walker's excellent classes ! Now she felt that
she would do anything for Miss Walker because she
had taken an interest in Lucy.

' Well, my idea was that we should try to keep Lucy
here for a couple of years somehow—and then let her
go in for an art scholarship,' said Miss Walker. ' Her
art is so brilliant already, that she is bound to be an
artist of some sort. She must go to the best art-school
in the country—but she is too young yet. I didn't
somehow feel I wanted her to go in for shorthand and
typing and get a job as a junior clerk somewhere,
when she could make such good use of her time here—
and then win a place at a London art-school.'

' I've already offered to let Lucy stay here at reduced
fees for two years, so that she might try for an art
scholarship then,' said Miss Theobald, ' but her parents
will not hear of it—neither will Lucy either, Margery,
though I don't suppose she has told you that. She
apparently wants to do her bit in helping to keep her
family now that her father can't paint.'

' Miss Theobald—couldn't you keep Lucy just one
more term and let her try for the scholarship ? ' said
Margery, eagerly. ' Then she could be here for two or
three years if she won it—and then try for an art
scholarship. She'd get that easily enough ! '

' Well, Margery, we'll see what can be done,' said
Miss Theobald. ' It's certainly an idea I hadn't
thought of—and I'm still not sure it can possibly be
carried out. I shall have to talk to the other mistresses
and find out more about Lucy's capabilities. I'll tell
you as soon as we have decided something. In the

meantime—thank you, my dear, for trying to be so helpful.   I am more glad than I can say that you came to St. Clare's.   We have helped you, I know—and now you are going to help us tremendously.'

MARGERY left the drawing-room on her crutches, her face bright with hope. Surely, surely, something would be arranged for Lucy now! She did not say a word to anyone about what she had suggested, least of all to Lucy, in case nothing came of it.

' I know Miss Theobald will keep her word and look into the idea thoroughly,' thought Margery, as she looked across the classroom at Lucy's rather sad little face. Lucy was brave—but she could not help feeling sad now. Things looked so different. All her bright future was gone.

Miss Theobald kept her word. She called a meeting of the first-, second- and third-form mistresses, and of Mam'zelle and Miss Lewis, the history teacher, too. She told them shortly what Margery had suggested.

They talked the matter out thoroughly. All the teachers liked Lucy Oriell and admired her quick brain and wonderful memory. Miss Lewis said at once that she could coach Lucy for the history section of the exam., and she was certain that Lucy would excel in that, whatever she did in other subjects.

' And her French is already perfect ! ' said Mam'zelle. ' She has spent many of her holidays in France, and she speaks French almost as well as I do ! '

Mathematics were Lucy's weak point. She did not like them and found them difficult, though even here her quick brain helped her over difficulties. But mathematics were Miss Theobald's specialty. She was a wonderful teacher where they were concerned.

' I could give her special coaching there,' she said. ' The child is worth extra trouble. I know I do no coaching now, because the running of the school takes all my time—but I would make an exception for Lucy Oriell.'

The meeting ended after an hour and the mistresses went to their various rooms. Margery, who knew that the mistresses had been summoned to Miss Theobald's room, wondered and wondered if they had been talking about Lucy. She soon knew, for Miss Theobald sent for her.

' Well, Margery,' said the Head, coming to the point at once. ' We've been discussing Lucy's future—and we think you are right—we think it *is* possible that she might win the scholarship. So I have written to her parents and put the idea before them. We must see what they say.'

The answer came by telephone the next day. Mrs. Oriell had been delighted with the Head's suggestion. She knew how very much Lucy had wanted to stay on at St. Clare's—and if there really was a chance that the girl could win a scholarship and stay there without the payment of fees, going on to an art-school afterwards, then she should certainly be given the chance.

' I'm so glad you think that, Mrs. Oriell,' said Miss

Theobald, pleased. 'Thank you for letting me know so soon. I will tell Lucy tonight.'

Miss Theobald sent for Lucy and in a few words told her what was suggested. The girl listened with shining eyes. It all seemed too good to be true, after her terrible disappointment and shock.

'Oh, Miss Theobald—thank you very very much!' she said. 'I'll do my best, I promise. I'll work terribly hard—all the holidays too. I'll win that scholarship somehow, and stay on here. It nearly broke my heart to think I'd have to leave just when I was so happy!'

'Well, that's settled then,' said Miss Theobald. 'I have discussed the whole thing with the other mistresses, and they are going to give you special coaching. I shall take you for maths. myself, and we must begin this very week, for every day's work will count. I will draw up a special time-table for you, because you will be taking different classes now. You must not be foolish and work *too* hard, though! I think I must tell Margery Fenworthy to keep an eye on you and make you take a rest when you get overtired!'

'Oh—won't Margery be pleased!' cried Lucy, thinking of her friend with pleasure. 'I shall tell her first of all.'

'Yes—she will be delighted,' said Miss Theobald. 'Go and find her now.'

Lucy rushed off and found Margery in the common room with one or two others. She pounced on her friend and made her jump.

'Margery! Listen! I've got the most marvellous

news ! ' she cried. ' You won't believe it ! I'm staying on at St. Clare's ! '

' Oh *Lucy* ! Are you going to be allowed to go in for the scholarship exam. then ? ' cried Margery, wishing her leg was better, so that she might dance around.

' Why, Margery—what do *you* know about it ? ' said Lucy, in astonishment.

' Because it was all my idea ! ' said Margery, happily. ' I thought of it. I went to Miss Theobald about it. But I couldn't say a word to you till I knew it was decided, in case you might be disappointed. Oh, Lucy —I'm so terribly pleased ! '

' What a friend you are ! ' said Lucy, wonderingly, as she looked into Margery's strong, determined face. ' How lucky I am to have you ! Fancy you going to all that trouble for me. Oh, Margery, I'll never never forget this. I'll remember your kindness all my life long.'

' Don't be silly,' said Margery. ' I'm the lucky one, not you ! Why, now I shall have you here at St. Clare's with me, instead of being all alone. The only thing is—you will have to work so terribly hard. I shall have to keep my eye on you and see that you get some fun sometimes ! '

' How funny—that's just what Miss Theobald said ! ' said Lucy, laughing. ' Well, with the mistresses looking after my work and you looking after my play, I should be all right, shouldn't I ? '

' What's the matter ? ' cried Pat, from her corner of the room. ' What are you two talking about in such excitement ? Has one of you got a " Very Good " from Mam'zelle ? '

'Not likely, these days!' said Margery. It was quite a joke that Mam'zelle never gave any one a Very Good now. 'No—the excitement is—that Lucy is staying on here after all—and going in for the third-form scholarship exam. at the end of next term. What about *that*?'

All the girls came over to say how glad they were. Lucy was happy again. It was lovely to be liked so much. It was lovely to have a friend who would do so much for her. If only her father's poor hand would get right, she would be even happier than she had been before the accident.

'Lucy,' said Margery, that night, just before they went up to bed. 'I've thought of something.'

'Gracious—not another idea so soon!' said Lucy, teasingly.

'Yes—but about me, this time, not you,' said Margery, rather soberly. 'You know, I'm sixteen, and I've no right to be so low down in the school. It's only because I've never been able to settle for long in any school, so my education has been a sort of hotch-potch, all mixed-up. But my brains aren't too bad if only I'll use them. Well, I'm going to use them like anything now—so that I can go up in form, and keep with you a bit. I couldn't bear to be in the first form whilst you forged ahead and became one of the top-formers, although you are two years younger. It's so difficult to be friends, proper friends, if we are in different forms.'

'Oh, Margery—that would be splendid!' said Lucy at once. 'Yes—I suppose I shall go up next term, and keep up in a higher form, if I *do* win that scholar-

ship—and it would be lovely if you got put up too.
Do work hard ! '

And so, to every mistress's enormous astonishment,
Margery Fenworthy, the dunce of the first form, suddenly produced excellent brains, and worked so much
harder that one week she actually tied for top place
with Lucy.

' Miracles will never cease ! ' said Miss Roberts, when
she read out the marks to the form.   ' Margery, you'll
be in the second form before you know where you are !
Good gracious, what a surprise this is.   Doris, perhaps
you will give me a nice surprise next.   You have been
bottom for three weeks.   What about tying for top
place with Lucy and Margery *next* week ? '

Every one laughed, Doris too.   The first form was a
very pleasant place to be in those last few weeks of
term.

20   JANET IS UP TO TRICKS AGAIN

IT was Mam'zelle who seemed to spoil things each day. She had always had a very hot temper—but nowadays she seemed to be unusually irritable, and the girls felt the rough edge of her tongue in every lesson.

Janet got tired of it. She was very hot-tempered herself, and she found it difficult to control herself when Mam'zelle made some specially biting remark.

' Ah, Janet ! Once more you have made the same mistake that you have made at least one hundred times this term ! ' said Mam'zelle one day, scoring a sentence with a blue pencil, and pressing so hard that it almost tore the page. ' I have no pleasure in teaching a stupid careless girl like you.'

' Well, I've no pleasure in being taught ! ' muttered Janet, angrily. She said it half under her breath, but Mam'zelle caught enough of it to look up with flashing eyes.

' *Que dites-vous ?* ' she cried. ' What is that you said ? You will please repeat it.'

The class listened breathlessly. Mam'zelle was in one of her rages. That was exciting—providing it was some one else who was getting into trouble !

Janet was bold enough to repeat what she had said, and she said it loudly, so that all the class could hear.

' I said " I've no pleasure in being taught ! " ' she repeated.

' *Méchante fille* ! ' cried Mam'zelle. ' What has happened to all you girls this term ? You are rude and careless and sulky.'

The class knew that it was really Mam'zelle's fault, not theirs. She was so bad-tempered. They looked mutinous, and said nothing. Even Lucy would not look at Mam'zelle when her eyes flashed round the class.

' Janet, you will learn the whole of the French poem in this book, and you will write it out for me three times ! ' said Mam'zelle, her voice trembling with rage. The class gasped. The poem was three pages long !

' Oh, Mam'zelle ! ' said Janet, startled. ' You know I can't do that. It would take me ages and ages. Besides, I'm not good at learning French poetry. It's as much as I can do to learn eight lines—and there must be about a hundred in that poem.'

' Then it will make you think twice before you are rude to me again,' said Mam'zelle. She took up her spectacle case and put her glasses on her big nose. Her face was flushed an angry red, and her head was aching. Ah, these English girls ! They were terrible ! How was it she had liked them so much before ? She could not bear them now.

After the class Janet talked angrily about her punishment. ' It's not fair,' she said. ' It's all Mam'-zelle's own fault, the wretch ! Can't she see that we won't stand her sarcastic remarks when we don't deserve them ? I'm sure we work just as hard as we did last term—and look at Lucy, how good she is in

French, and yet Mam'zelle scolded her like anything
yesterday.'

'Wasn't she always as bad-tempered as this then?'
asked Lucy, in wonder.

'Gracious no,' said Janet. 'This is the fourth term
I've been in the first form—and Mam'zelle has always
been quite a brick before—well, she always did have a
hot temper—but she wasn't *bad*-tempered, like she is
now.'

'Janet, I'll copy out that poem once for you,' said
Kathleen. 'My writing is a bit like yours. Mam'zelle
won't know, You can't possibly do it three times
yourself today.'

'Oh, thanks, Kath, you're a brick,' said Janet.
'That *will* be a help. I wouldn't let anyone take on a
part of my punishments if I could help it. But goodness me, Mam'zelle must be mad if she thinks I've
enough time to do all she said!'

Kathleen copied out the poem once in Janet's French
book. Sheila did it once too, for her writing was not
unlike Janet's. Janet scribbled it out the third time
and, with much trouble and pains, learnt it by heart.
The whole class was sick of the poem by the time that
Janet had it perfect.

She went to Mam'zelle at seven o'clock to take the
written work and to say the poem. She said it in a
sulky voice and would not look at the French teacher
at all. By this time Mam'zelle had recovered a little
and was half-sorry she had given the girl such a long
punishment. But Janet would not smile at Mam'zelle,
and would not even say good night to her when she
went from the room.

Ah, these impolite English girls ! ' said Mam'zelle, with a sigh.   ' They should go to school in France— then they would know what good behaviour and hard work are ! '

Janet did not forgive Mam'zelle for her hardness. She was a dreadful girl for playing tricks and practical jokes, and had got into great trouble the term before for throwing fireworks into the classroom fire.   She had not done anything very bad this term—but now she determined to make Mam'zelle ' sit up ', as she called it, the last two or three weeks of term.

She told the others.   ' If Mam'zelle thinks she can treat me like that without my getting a bit of my own back, she's jolly well mistaken ! ' said Janet.   ' I'm going to pay her out—so look out for some fun ! '

The class was pleasantly excited.   They knew Janet's tricks and appreciated them, for Janet was clever and original with her jokes.   What would she be up to now ?

' You know, it was terribly funny last term when she threw the fireworks into the fire,' said Pat to Margery and Lucy.   ' We really meant to play that joke on Miss Kennedy, a timid sort of mistress who took Miss Lewis's place for history last term.   Well, Miss Roberts came along just when Janet had thrown about fifty in—and golly, we had fireworks from Miss Roberts then too, I can tell you ! '

' I wonder what Janet will do ? ' said Doris, hugging herself, for she adored a joke, and was pretty good herself at playing them.   ' I've got a funny trick my cousin gave me at Christmas—it's a thing that looks exactly like spilt ink ! '

'Oh, why haven't you shown it to us?' cried Janet, in delight. 'I know the thing you mean—it's awfully good. Have you got it?'

'Well, I brought it to school meaning to give somebody a shock with it,' said Doris, 'but I couldn't find it. It must be somewhere about.'

'Go and look, Doris. Go and look now,' begged Pat, giggling. 'Look where you haven't looked before. In your tuck-box for instance. You haven't opened that since the beginning of the term, when we ate everything.'

The joke *was* in the neglected tuck-box! Doris pounced on it with glee. It was a thing which, when put down flat on a book looked exactly like a big, irregular, shiny ink-blot—almost as if the ink-pot had been spilt.

Janet took it in delight. 'This is fine!' she said. 'Lend it to me, there's a sport!'

'Rather!' said Doris. 'What will you do with it?'

'Wait and see, tomorrow,' said Janet. So the class waited impatiently till the French lesson came, and Mam'zelle bustled in, out of breath as usual.

It was French dictation that morning. Mam'zelle looked round the class, which was suspiciously good and docile all of a sudden.

'Take down *dictée*,' she said. 'Get out your exercise books, and begin.'

Every girl had to take her book to Mam'zelle to be corrected after *dictée*. Janet took hers up when her turn came and laid it flat on the desk. Mam'zelle took up her fountain pen—and then, before her eyes, there

Mam'zelle stared in horror at the enormous ink blot

appeared on Janet's perfectly clean book, a very large and shiny ink-blot !

'Oh, Mam'zelle ! ' cried Janet, in a doleful voice. 'Look what you've done on my book ! It must have been your fountain pen ! Is it leaking ? Oh, and I did try so hard with my *dictée* this morning ! '

Man'zelle stared in horror at the enormous blot. She couldn't believe her eyes.

'Janet ! What can have happened ! ' she cried. She looked at her fountain pen. It seemed all right. And yet there was the tremendous blot, right across Janet's neat book.

'I'll go and blot it, Mam'zelle,' said Janet, and took her book away carefully, as if she were trying not to let the blot run across the page. The class saw it clearly and buried their heads in their hands or under their desks to stifle their giggles.

Janet slipped the trick-blot into her pocket and then pretended to be very busy with blotting-paper. Mam'zelle was shaking her pen with a puzzled air. She simply could not imagine how so much ink had run out of it so suddenly.

Janet took back her book, which was now absolutely clean. Mam'zelle stared at it in the greatest amazement.

'But where is the smudge ? ' she asked in astonishment. 'You cannot have cleaned it so well ! '

'Well, I've got some special blotting-paper, Mam'zelle,' said Janet, in a solemn voice. 'It cleans ink like magic.'

'Ah, but it is indeed magic ! ' said Mam'zelle, pleased. 'Your *dictée* is now not spoilt at all. Thank you, *ma chère* Janet ! I was so sorry to have spoilt your work.'

One or two muffled giggles could be heard from Doris and Kathleen. Mam'zelle looked up sharply. ' There is nothing to laugh at,' she said. ' *Taisez-vous !* '

But, of course, there *was* something to laugh at—and when Janet cleverly managed to slip the ink-blot on to Doris's desk, just as Mam'zelle was leaning over to look at her work, the class nearly had hysterics !

' Oh, Mam'zelle—that wretched pen of yours ! ' said Doris, in a reproachful voice, looking at the blot. ' It's messed up my desk now.'

Mam'zelle stared at it in surprise and horror. Blots seemed to be following her round this morning. She looked at her fountain-pen again and shook it violently. A shower of ink-drops flew over the floor. Doris cried out loudly.

' It *is* your pen ! Look at all the blots it has made on the floor ! Oh, Mam'zelle, please may I borrow Janet's wonderful blotting-paper to wipe up the mess ? Miss Roberts will be so angry with me if she sees it there next lesson.'

' I cannot understand it,' murmured poor Mam'zelle, feeling she must be in some sort of a dream, as she looked at the large and shiny blot on Doris's desk. ' I have never made such blots before.'

The class went off into giggles that spread round uncontrollably. Mam'zelle lost her temper.

' Is it so funny that I make blots ? ' she cried. ' Silence ! Another giggle and I will keep the whole class in for break.'

That was enough to keep the class quiet for a while,

though there were many handkerchiefs stuffed into mouths when the urge to laugh became too great. Janet was pleased with the success of her joke, and already she was planning another.

'I'm going to put beetles into Mam'zelle's spectacle case,' she giggled to the others, when they were in the common room after tea, discussing with enjoyment the success of the ink-blot. The second-formers had enjoyed the tale immensely and had groaned because they hadn't been able to share in the joke.

'Janet! Not *beetles*!' shuddered Sheila. 'How could you possibly pick them up to put them in?'

'And anyway, how are you going to get them there?' said Pat.

'Easy enough,' said Janet. 'Mam'zelle is always leaving her spectacle case around. The first time she leaves it in our class-room I grab it and put the beetles into the case! What ho for a squeal from Mam'zelle! That will teach her to make me learn her horrid French poems!'

The very next day Mam'zelle left her glasses in their case on the first-form desk. Janet winked at the others. She saw them at once. Immediately Mam'zelle was out of the room on her way to the second-form Janet whipped out of her seat and took the case from the desk. She slipped it into her pocket and got back to her seat just as Miss Roberts came in to take arithmetic.

The lesson had hardly been going for more than four minutes when a girl from the second form came in.

'Please, Miss Roberts, Mam'zelle is sorry to inter-

rupt you, but may she have her glasses ?　She left them
in a case on your desk.'

Miss Roberts looked round the big desk and then
opened it.　No spectacle case was to be seen, which
was not surprising considering that it was safely in
Janet's pocket.

' It doesn't seem to be here,' said Miss Roberts.
' Mam'zelle will probably find that they are in her
pocket.'

The class giggled to itself.　They knew quite well
that Mam'zelle would find nothing of the sort !　Janet
looked quite solemn.　It made the others giggle to look
at her.

' Girls !　What is the joke, please ? ' asked Miss
Roberts, impatiently.　She did not like giggles.　' Is
there anything funny in Mam'zelle losing her glasses ? '

As it happened, there was—but Miss Roberts, of
course, didn't know it.　The class sobered down.

' Well, Miss Roberts, it's only that Mam'zelle is
always leaving her glasses about,' said Doris.

' Quite,' said Miss Roberts, drily.　' Turn to page
forty-seven, please. KATHLEEN !　If you stare round
the class any more I'll put you with your back to it !
What *is* the matter with you this morning ? '

The class had to behave itself.　Miss Roberts made
it work so hard that most of them thought no more of
the next trick Janet was going to play, until break
came.　Then they all crowded round Janet to see her
put the poor surprised beetles into the spectacle case !

21   MAM'ZELLE GETS
ANOTHER SHOCK

JANET collected various kinds of beetles and grubs from underneath fences at break. Giggling loudly the first- and second-formers watched her take out Mam'-zelle's spectacles and carefully put in the wriggling insects. They were half-dazed with their winter sleep. Janet shut the case with a snap.

' I hope the beetles can breathe,' said Kathleen, in a troubled voice. She was passionately fond of animals, and her kindness extended even to spiders, beetles and moths.

' Of course they can breathe,' said Janet. ' This spectacle case is as big as a room to them ! '

' What are you going to do with the case ? ' asked Hilary. ' Are you going to put it back on the desk so that Mam'zelle can open it next day ? '

' Of course, silly,' said Janet. ' We all want to see the fun, don't we ? '

' I say, Janet—won't Mam'zelle be absolutely furious ? ' said Lucy. ' She'll tell Miss Theobald, I should think. Better be careful—you don't want to get into a fearful row just before the end of term. You might get a bad report.'

' I don't care,' said Janet. ' I'm going to get even with Mam'zelle, the bad-tempered thing ! '

The beetles and grubs passed quite a pleasant time in the spectacle case, and didn't seem to mind at all, though Kathleen kept worrying about them and opening the case to give them a little air. In the morning Janet placed the case on Miss Roberts's desk just before Mam'zelle came to give her daily French lesson. The whole class was in a state of fidget and excitement. They had tried to keep it under whilst Miss Roberts was teaching them, for she was very clever at sensing anything wrong with the class.

She had been rather sharp with them, but had not seemed to suspect anything. She left to go to the second form—and Mam'zelle came in. Mam'zelle had had a bad night. She was not sleeping well these days, and her eyes were circled with big black rings.

' *Bon jour !* ' she said, as she came in. She went to the desk, and put down her books. The girls wished her good morning and sat down. Mam'zelle turned to the blackboard and wrote down a few questions which the class had to answer in writing, in French.

Then suddenly Mam'zelle spotted her spectacle case. She pounced on it with delight.

' Ah ! Here are my glasses ! Now this is a strange thing ! I sent to ask for them yesterday and was told they were not here ! All day long I looked for them ! '

The girls watched in the most intense excitement. The ones at the back craned their necks round the girls in front of them, trying their hardest to see. The girls at the front were thrilled to have such a good view.

Mam'zelle sat down. She did not open the case at once. She looked round the class. ' *Dépechez-vous !* '

she cried. 'Why are you so slow at beginning your work today!'

The class took up their pens. Mam'zelle yawned and tapped her big white teeth with her pencil. Why, oh why didn't she open her spectacle case?

Ah! Now she was going to. She stretched out her hand and picked up the case. She opened it slowly—and out scrambled the quick-legged beetles, and out crawled the grubs, wide awake now because of the warmth of the room!

Mam'zelle stared at them. She took out her handkerchief and rubbed it across her eyes. Then she looked cautiously at the spectacle case again. She simply could not believe her eyes.

'It is impossible!' thought poor Mam'zelle. 'My eyes tell me that there are beetles and grubs crawling over my desk, but my sense tells me that my glasses should be there. And no doubt they *are* there. It is because I am tired that I see these insects crawling out of my case!'

The girls were trying to smother their giggles. Mam'zelle's face was so funny! It was quite plain that she was immensely astonished and couldn't believe her eyes.

Mam'zelle was trying to think calmly. She hated anything that crawled, and one of her favourite nightmares was that beetles were crawling over her. And now here they were walking out of her spectacle case. It was quite impossible. Beetles did not live in spectacle cases. Her eyes must be wrong. She must go to the occulist again and get fresh glasses. Perhaps that was why she had such head-aches lately! All these thoughts passed through poor Mam'zelle's mind, and the first formers peered over their books and watched eagerly to see what would happen.

'It cannot be that these insects are real,' Mam'zelle was thinking firmly to herself. 'They are in my imagination only! My glasses must be in the case, although it appears to me that there are insects there instead. I must be brave and put my hand into the case to get my glasses. Then, when they are safely on my nose I shall see that the beetles are not really there!'

The girls began to giggle, though they tried their hardest to stop. Mam'zelle was so puzzled and so amazed. It did not seem to enter her mind for one moment that it was a trick. She put out her hand to feel for the glasses she felt sure must really be in her case.

And, of course, all she got hold of were beetles and grubs! When she felt them in her fingers she gave a loud scream. The girls watched in enjoyment. This was simply marvellous!

'What's the matter, Mam'zelle?' asked Doris, demurely, winking round at the others.

'Ah, Doris—Janet—come up here and tell me what there is on my desk,' said poor Mam'zelle, looking down in horror as one beetle ran round and round the ink-pot and finally fell right into it.

Doris and Janet leapt up at once. Janet stared solemnly at Mam'zelle. 'Your glasses are in your case,' said the naughty girl. 'Put them on, Mam'zelle, and maybe you will see properly.'

'My glasses are not there!' cried Mam'zelle. 'But do you not see those insects, girls!'

'What insects?' asked Doris, innocently, and the whole class exploded into stifled giggles. But Mam'-zelle hardly noticed them.

'Ah, there is something wrong with me!' she groaned. 'I have feared it all these weeks. I am not the same. My temper is so bad. I am so irritable. And now my eyes are wrong. I see things! I see beetles on this desk! If only I could find my glasses!'

Janet picked up the empty case, quickly slipped Mam'zelle's glasses into it, from her pocket, and then took them out of the case as if they had been there all the time. She handed them to the astonished French mistress.

'Ah, this is worse than ever!' cried Mam'zelle. 'So they were there all the time and I could not even see them! And alas, alas—still the beetles they crawl over my desk! I am ill! I must leave you! You will go on with your French quietly, please, and wait till Miss Roberts comes back. I am ill—*très malade, très malade!*'

Mam'zelle left the room stooping like an old woman. The class were startled and dismayed. This was not the right ending for a joke at all! Mam'zelle had taken it really seriously. She had believed Janet and Doris when they had assured her that the insects were not there. The girls stared at one another in dismay. Janet picked the insects off the desk and put them carefully out of the window.

'Janet, I don't much like this,' said Lucy, in her clear voice. 'We've given Mam'zelle a real shock. It sounded to me as if she hadn't been feeling well for

ages and thought that our joke was all part of her
illness. I wish we hadn't done it now.'

Everyone wished the same. Nobody giggled. Janet
wished that Mam'zelle had seen through the joke and
had punished her. This was much worse than any
punishment. The girls took up their pens and got on
with their work, each feeling decidedly uncomfortable.

In about ten minutes Miss Theobald came in. The
girls stood up at once. The Head Mistress glanced at
the board and at the girls' books. She saw that they
were working and she was pleased.

' Girls,' she said, in her low, pleasant voice, ' I am
sorry to tell you that Mam'zelle is sure she is ill, so she
will not come back to you this morning. I have sent
for the doctor. Please get on with what work you can,
and wait until Miss Roberts returns.'

She went out. The girls sat down. They felt more
uncomfortable than ever. Janet was very red. She
kicked herself for playing such a trick now. She
thought about Mam'zelle and her bad temper. Could
it have been because she was feeling ill ?

The first form were so subdued that morning that
Miss Roberts was quite astonished. She kept looking
at the bent heads and wondering what was the matter.
But nobody told her.

At the end of the morning there was a regular buzz
of talk in the common room. ' Did you know that
Mam'zelle is very ill ? Whose form was she in when
she was taken ill ? Oh, yours, Margery ? What happened ? Did she faint or something ? '

Nobody gave Janet away. They all felt that she
was sorry about the trick, and they were ashamed

too—so they said nothing about the joke at all. It had gone very wrong and goodness knows how it could be put right.

Mam'zelle was put to bed, and Matron went to see to her. Poor Mam'zelle was more worried about her eyes than about anything else. She kept telling Matron about the insects she had seen, and she declared she was afraid to go to sleep in case her nightmare came back.

Janet went to ask Matron how Mam'zelle was after tea. The doctor had been, so Matron was able to tell the girl all the news.

'It's overwork and strain,' she told Janet. 'Poor Mam'zelle's sister was ill all the Christmas holidays and she went to nurse her. She nursed her day and night, and got very little rest or sleep herself. So she came back tired out, and instead of taking things easy, she worked herself all the harder. I know you girls thought her very bad-tempered and irritable this term—but that's the explanation!'

'Did she—did she say anything about her spectacle case?' asked Janet.

Matron stared at Janet in surprise. 'What do *you* know about her spectacle case?' she said. 'As a matter of fact something seems to be worrying poor Mam'zelle terribly. She keeps saying that her eyes are going wrong because she saw insects coming out of her spectacle case—and she daren't go to sleep and get the rest she needs because she is so afraid she will dream that insects are crawling over her. She is in a very over-tired state!'

Janet went away to tell the others. So that was the

explanation of Mam'zelle's bad temper that term! She had been nursing her sister day and night—and, knowing Mam'zelle's zeal and thoroughness, Janet could well imagine that she had spared herself nothing in the holidays. Mam'zelle had the kindest heart in the world, in spite of her hot temper.

' I do feel simply awful about that trick,' said Janet to Pat. ' I really do. I've a good mind to go into Mam'zelle's room and tell her about it to set her mind at rest. I simply daren't tell Miss Roberts or Miss Theobald.'

' Well, go and tell Mam'zelle then,' said Pat.

' That's a good idea. Take her some flowers from me. And some from Isabel too.'

Every girl in the class put money towards flowers for Mam'zelle. As the next day was Saturday they were able to go down into the town to buy them. They bought daffodils, narcissi, anemones and prim-roses. They all felt so guilty that they spent far more money than they could really afford.

Miss Roberts saw the girls coming back with their flowers, and stared in amazement.

' What's this—a flower-show ? ' she asked.

' They're for Mam'zelle,' said Hilary, which aston-ished Miss Roberts all the more, for she had heard the bitter complaints of her form about the amount of work set by Mam'zelle that term, and her bad temper when it was not done properly.

' These first-formers have really kind hearts,' thought Miss Roberts. She spoke aloud to them. ' This is very nice of you. Mam'zelle will be pleased. She had a very bad night, so I don't expect any of you will be

allowed to see her. But you can take the flowers to
Matron to give to her.'

But that wasn't Janet's plan at all ! She was going
to see Mam'zelle somehow, whatever Matron said !

PAT and Isabel kept watch for Matron after tea that day. They were to tell Janet when she was not about so that Janet might slip in by herself. Janet was not going to take the flowers in with her. They were outside the room in a cupboard and Janet meant to go and fetch them as a kind of peace-offering when she had confessed everything to Mam'zelle.

Poor Janet was rather white. She didn't at all like the idea of facing Mam'zelle, even when she was ill. But it had to be done. Pat and Isabel saw Matron come out of Mam'zelle's bedroom with her tea-tray and they went to her.

' Matron, please may we have a clean towel ? '

' What have you done with yours ? ' asked Matron, bustling along with the tray. ' Come along and get it then, I haven't much time.'

Pat looked back over her shoulder and winked at Janet to tell her that Matron wouldn't be back for a few minutes. The twins meant to keep her talking and give Janet a clear field.

Janet slipped to Mam'zelle's door. She knocked and a voice said ' Entrez ! ' Janet went in. Mam'zelle was lying in bed, looking up at the ceiling. She looked very unhappy, because she was still worrying about what was suddenly and mysteriously the matter with her eyes. She expected to see insects crawling all over the ceiling. Poor Mam'zelle—she would not have thought these things if she had not been so overworked.

She looked with surprise at Janet. Matron had told her there were to be no visitors that day.

'Mam'zelle,' said Janet, going to the bed. 'Are you better? I had to come and see you. I wanted to tell you something.'

'It is nice to see you, *ma chère* Janet!' said Mam'-zelle, who was always touched by any kindness. 'What have you to tell me, *ma petite*?'

'Mam'zelle—Mam'zelle—I don't know how to tell you,' said Janet, 'you'll be so angry. But please believe me when I say I'm terribly sorry—so are we all—and we wouldn't have done it if we'd known you'd been feeling ill—and . . .'

'My dear child, what are you trying to say?' asked Mam'zelle, in the utmost astonishment. 'What is this terrible thing you have done?'

'Mam'zelle—we—I—I put those beetles and things into your spectacle case to pay you out for punishing me the other day,' blurted out Janet, desperately. 'And I put a trick ink-blot on my book too. You see . . .'

Mam'zelle looked at Janet as if she couldn't believe her ears. 'Those—those crawling insects were *real*, then?' she said, at last.

'Yes, Mam'zelle,' said Janet. 'Quite real. I got them from places under the fence. I—I didn't think you'd believe it was your eyes that were wrong. Now you're ill we feel awful.'

Mam'zelle lay quite still. So her eyes and her mind were quite all right. Those insects were not in her imagination, they were real. It was only a joke! If she had been well and quite herself she would have guessed that! But she was tired and could not think properly. How thankful she was that Janet had told her!

She turned to speak to the girl but Janet was not there. She had slipped out to get the flowers. She came back with her arms full of them, and Mam'zelle gasped to see them.

' Mam'zelle, these are from all of us in the first form,' said Janet. ' We are sorry you're ill—and please forgive us, won't you? Honestly we'd have put up with all your rages and everything if we'd known you were so tired! '

' Come here,' said Mam'zelle, and reached out a large hand to Janet. The girl took it shyly. ' I have been *abominable* this term! ' said Mam'zelle, a smile coming over her face. ' *Insupportable* and *abominable*! You will please tell the O'Sullivan twins that, Janet. I know the nickname they had for me last term—Mam'-zelle Abominable, which they gave me because I said so often that their work was abominable! But this term I have really earned that name.'

' You were awfully cross with us lots of times,' said Janet, honestly. ' But we don't mind now. We understand.'

' Ah, you English girls! There is nobody like you when you are nice! ' said Mam'zelle, quite forgetting all the dreadful things she had thought and said about them that term. ' You will give my love to the others,

Janet—and my best thanks for these beautiful flowers
—and you will tell them that if they will forgive me I
will forgive them also—and you too, of course!
Méchante fille! Wicked girl! Ah—but how brave
and good of you to come and tell me!'

Janet stared at Mam'zelle and Mam'zelle looked at
Janet with her big dark eyes. She began to laugh,
for she had a great sense of humour at times.

' To think you put those beetles there—and I did
not know it was a trick—and that ink-blot! What
bad children you are! But how it makes me laugh
now!'

And Mam'zelle went off into a loud burst of laughter.
Matron was passing by the door at that moment and
heard it in amazement. Thinking that Mam'zelle
must have gone mad for a minute, Matron quickly
opened the door and went in. She looked in astonishment when she saw the masses of flowers—and Janet!

' Janet! What are you doing in here? You
naughty girl! I didn't give you permission to come.
Go at once.'

' No, Matron, I will not have Janet sent away,' said
Mam'zelle, most surprisingly. ' She stays here to put
my flowers in water! She has brought me good news.
I feel better already. She makes me laugh, this
méchante fille!'

Mam'zelle certainly looked better. Matron looked
at her and then nodded to Janet that she might stay
and put the flowers in water. Janet swiftly arranged
them as well as she could. Mam'zelle watched her.

' The lovely flowers!' she said, contentedly.
' Matron, do you see what beautiful bunches the girls

have sent to their bad-tempered, insupportable old Mam'zelle ? '

' I see them,' said Matron. ' Now, Janet, you must go. And if you come here again without permission I shall spank you ! '

Janet went, with a grin. She ran straight to the common room to tell the others all that had happened. How glad they were to know that Mam'zelle had been such a brick about it all—and had actually laughed.

' Perhaps things will be better this last week of term,' said Doris, who had suffered very much that term from Mam'zelle's rough tongue. ' If Mam'zelle is well enough to come back for a few days at the end of term she'll be nicer—and if she doesn't I shall be jolly glad to miss French.'

' This term *has* gone quickly ! ' said Pat. ' It seems no time at all since half-term—and here we are almost at the Easter hols. What a lot has happened this term—almost as much as last term.'

' More,' said Isabel. ' We didn't have a fire last term—or a heroine either ! '

Margery blushed. She was getting very clever at using her crutches, and her leg was mending marvellously. Lucy twinkled at her.

' It always makes Margery go red if you say the word " heroine " ! ' she said. ' Pat, Margery is coming to stay with me for a week of the hols. We shan't have any maids or anything, because we are poor now, but Margery's going to help in the house all she can—isn't she a brick ? I shall be working hard most of the time, but I shall take time off to be with Margery too.'

' And then I'm going on a holiday with my father,'

said Margery. ' What are you twins doing for the hols.? '

Holidays were certainly in the air. Every one was making plans for Easter. Some were going shopping to get new clothes. Alison was full of this, of course.

' Vain little creature ! ' said Pat, pulling Alison's pretty hair teasingly. ' Well, you're coming to stay with us part of the hols. and you can bring your new pretties to show us—but we'll only allow you to boast *once* about them. After that—not a word ! '

' All right, Pat,' said Alison, who was really learning to be much more sensible. ' I'll have one good glorious boast—and then be the strong silent girl ! '

' You couldn't be silent ! ' said Isabel, who now liked her silly little cousin very much better. ' If your own tongue couldn't talk, the tongues of your shoes would do it for you ! '

The last week of term was very happy. Mam'zelle got much better, and the girls went into her room to see her and play a game with her. She was the same old jolly Mam'zelle she used to be, now that she had had a rest, and had changed her ideas about ' these English girls '. She was already making plans for next term's work—but the girls refused to listen !

Lucy had been working hard to prepare for the scholarship exam. next term. She had had good news of her father and this made her work with much more zest and happiness. Miss Theobald and the other teachers had worked out her holiday tasks and praised her for the progress she had already made. So Lucy looked much happier, and laughed and joked like her old self.

The twins were happy too. Things had gone well that term. They were top in five subjects. Lucy did not go in for the class exams. as she was doing so much extra work, or she would, of course, have been top in everything except maths. Doris and Alison were bottom in most things, but they were both quite cheerful about it.

'Somebody's got to be bottom,' said Doris to Alison, 'and I think it's rather sweet of us to be willing to take such a back seat in everything!'

'Willing! You jolly well can't help it, you duffer!' said Pat. 'But who cares? You can make us laugh more than anybody else in the form—so you go on being bottom, old girl!'

The last day came, and the excitement of packing and saying good-byes. Mam'zelle was up once more, making jokes and writing down everyone's address. There was laughter everywhere, and occasionally Miss Roberts's voice was lifted in complaint.

'Kathleen! Is it necessary to yell like that? Sheila, you don't look at all elegant rolling on the floor to do your packing. PAT! PAT! Stop pummelling Janet. What a bear-garden! I shall set you all a hundred lines to write out in the train home and send me tomorrow!'

There were giggles and squeals at this. It was fun to be going home—fun to look forward to Easter and Easter eggs, to long walks through the primrose woods, and reunions with dogs and cats and horses at home, to say nothing of mothers and fathers and little sisters and brothers.

'See you next term!' called Pat. 'Don't forget to

write, Janet. Be good, Doris ! Oh, Isabel, don't drag
me like that—I'm coming ! We're off in the first
coach, everybody ! Good bye ! See you all next
term ! '

Yes—see you all next term.   That's what *we* will
hope to do—see them all next term !

SUMMER TERM AT ST CLARE'S

CONTENTS

1   GOING BACK TO SCHOOL

' FOUR weeks' holiday ! ' said Pat O'Sullivan, as she sat up in bed the first morning of the Easter holidays. ' How lovely !   Hope it's good weather ! '

Her twin yawned and turned over. ' How nice not to have to get up as soon as the school-bell goes,' she said, sleepily. ' I'm going to have another snooze.'

' Well, I'm not,' said Pat, hopping out of bed. ' Oh, Isabel—it's a simply perfect day !   Do get up and let's go round the garden.'

But Isabel was asleep again. Pat dressed and ran downstairs. She felt happy and excited. The first day of the holidays was always grand.   Everything at home looked so new and exciting and welcoming.   Even the staid brown hens in the yard seemed to cluck a welcome !

' School is lovely—but holidays are grand too,' thought Pat. ' Oh, there s the first daffodil coming out—and look at those scyllas—exactly the colour of the April sky ! '

Both the twins enjoyed the first day of the holidays in their own way.   Isabel lazed round, peaceful and happy. Pat rushed here, there and everywhere, seeing everybody and everything.   Their mother laughed to see the different ways in which they enjoyed themselves.

' You're as like as two peas to look at,' she said, ' but you often act in quite the opposite way. I hope this lovely weather goes on—you'll be quite nice and brown ! Well—make the most of it, my dears, because your four weeks will soon go ! "

' Oh, Mother—four weeks is a lovely long time—simply ages ! ' said Pat.

But although it seemed ages at first, it began to slip by

very quickly after the first few days! The twins were astonished to find that a week had gone by—and then ten days—and then a fortnight!

'Cousin Alison is coming to spend the last two weeks with us, isn't she, Mother?' said Pat. 'When is she coming? This week?'

'On Thursday,' said Mrs. O'Sullivan. 'By the way, her mother said to me on the telephone yesterday that she is much better for being a term at St. Clare's—not nearly so vain and silly.'

'That's quite right,' said Isabel, thinking of the teasing and scolding her feather-headed cousin had had at St. Clare's the last term. 'She learnt quite a lot of lessons—well, so did we the first term too. I'm glad you sent us there, Mother. It's a fine school. I'm already beginning to look forward to going back. Summer term ought to be grand!'

'Two more weeks,' said Pat. 'I say—won't it be fun to play tennis again? I wonder if we'll play any matches? Isabel and I were tennis captains at Redroofs, our old school. But I expect St. Clare's tennis is a pretty high standard.'

'Let's mark out the court and play a few games,' said Isabel, eagerly. But Mrs. O'Sullivan shook her head.

'Not in April,' she said. 'You would spoil the lawn. Ring up Katie Johnston and see if you can fix up a four on her hard court.'

It was all because of poor Isabel's eagerness to have a few practice games at tennis that the rest of the holidays were spoilt! They went over to Katie Johnston's, and played a tennis four there, with another girl, Winnie Ellis. Winnie played a very poor game, and quite spoilt it for the others.

Katie apologized for Winnie when she had the twins alone for a minute. 'Can't think what has happened to her today,' she said. 'She usually plays such a good game. She's sending everything into the net. She says her head aches, so maybe she isn't very well.'

Poor Winnie was certainly not well. She went down with mumps that evening, and her mother rang up Katie's parents at once.

' I'm so very sorry,' she said, ' but Winnie has mumps ! I hope Katie has had it.   Otherwise she will be in quarantine, I'm afraid.'

' Yes, Katie's had it, thank goodness,' said Mrs. Johnston.   ' But I don't know about the other two girls who were here playing tennis today—the O'Sullivan twins.   I must ring up their mother and tell them.'

The telephone rang that evening as the twins were having supper with their parents. Mrs. O'Sullivan went to answer it. She soon came back, looking a little worried.

' What's the matter ? ' asked Mr. O'Sullivan.

' That was Mrs. Johnston,' said the twins' mother. ' Pat and Isabel went over to Katie's to play tennis today —and the fourth girl was Winnie Ellis. She has just developed mumps this evening—and the twins haven't had it ! '

' Well, Mother, we didn't breathe her breath or anything,' said Pat. ' We shall be all right.'

' I hope you will, dear,' said her mother. ' But the thing is—you'll both be in quarantine now—and the quarantine for mumps is rather long. You won't be able to go back to school at the beginning of the term, I'm afraid.'

The twins stared at her in dismay. ' Oh, Mother ! Don't let's miss the beginning of term ! It's one of the nicest parts. Can't we possibly go back in time ? '

' Well, you certainly can't, of course, if you get the mumps,' said Mother. ' I'll see the doctor and find out exactly how long you will have to be away.'

Alas for the twins ! The doctor said firmly that they

could not go back to school for just over a week after the beginning of term. Pat and Isabel could have cried with disappointment.

' Well, well—anyone would think you liked school, the way you are looking,' said their father, laughing at their gloomy faces. ' I should have thought you would have been pleased at the chance of an extra week's holiday.'

' Not when everyone else is back at school bagging the best desks and hearing all the holiday news and seeing if there are any new girls,.' said Pat. ' The first week is lovely, settling in together. Oh, blow Winnie Ellis ! What did she want to go and have mumps for, and spoil things for us ? '

' Well, these things do happen,' said Mother. ' Never mind. Try to enjoy your extra week. Keep out in the open air as much as you can, and let's hope you don't develop the mumps, either of you ! '

During their quarantine time the twins could not go out to tea, and could have no one in to play with them, so they felt rather dull. They were glad to have each other, especially when the day came for all the girls to return to St. Clare's for the summer term.

' I wonder if they'll miss us ? ' said Pat.

' Of course they will,' said Isabel. ' Our Cousin Alison will tell them what's happened to us. Lucky for Alison she didn't come and stay with us before we were in quarantine, or she'd have been caught like this too ! Oh blow, blow, blow ! What's the time ? They'll all be catching the train now, and gabbling like anything in the carriages.'

' Wonder if there are any new girls ? ' said Pat. ' Or any new teachers ? Oh dear—do you remember the tricks that Janet played on poor old Mam'zelle last term ? I nearly died of laughter ! '

' We shan't be able to share the tuck-boxes,' said Isabel, gloomily. ' All the cakes and things will be eaten before we get back. Oh, how I wish we were back today. Old Janet will be there—and Hilary—and Doris—and Kathleen—and Lucy and Margery—though *they* may have gone up into the second or third form, I suppose—and Sheila will be back, and Tessie.'

'Let's not think about it,' said Pat. 'Do you feel as if you are getting the mumps, Isabel? Have you got a headache or a pain in the jaw or neck or anything?'

'Not a thing,' said Isabel. 'I say, wouldn't it be perfectly awful if we got mumps on the very last day of our quarantine and couldn't go back even then!'

'Anyone would think you disliked your home thoroughly!' said Mrs. O'Sullivan, coming into the room. 'Well, it's nice to think you look forward to school so much. But do be sensible girls and make the most of this last week. I don't think you will get the mumps, so just be happy and look forward to going back next week.'

They tried to take their mother's advice. It was lovely weather, and they were out in the garden all day long, helping the gardener, or lazing in the hammock. But the time went very slowly, and each night the twins looked anxiously at each other to see if they had any sign of the mumps.

At last the final day of their quarantine came and in the evening the doctor arrived to make quite sure they could go back to school. He smiled cheerfully at them as he examined them, and then made their hearts sink with his next words.

'Well, my dears—I'm afraid—I'm very much afraid—that you'll have to go back to school tomorrow!'

The twins had looked full of dismay at his first words—but as he finished the sentence they beamed, and yelled with delight.

'Hurrah! We can go to school tomorrow. Hurrah! Mother, can we go and pack?'

'It's all done,' said Mrs. O'Sullivan, smiling. 'I

thought you were quite all right—so I packed today for you. Yes—even your tuck-boxes ! '

So the next day up to London went the twins with their mother, and were put into the train for St. Clare's. They were happy and excited. They would soon see all their friends again, and be lost in the excitements of school-life. They would sit in class under Mam'zelle's stern eye, they would giggle at Janet's tricks, and they would hear all the latest news. What fun !

The train sped away from the platform. It seemed to take ages to get to the station that served St. Clare's. At last it drew up, and out got the two girls, shouting to the porter to get their luggage. Usually the mistresses saw to the luggage and looked after everything, tickets included—but as they were by themselves, the twins had to do all this. They quite enjoyed it.

They got a taxi, had their luggage put in, and set off to the big white building in the distance, whose tall twin towers overlooked the beautiful valley.

' Good old St. Clare's,' said Pat, as she saw the building coming nearer and nearer. ' It's nice to see you again. I wonder what all the girls are doing, Isabel ? '

They were at tea when the twins arrived. It was strange to arrive alone, and to have the great front door opened to them by Jane the parlour-maid, looking very smart indeed.

' Hallo, Jane ! ' cried the twins. ' Where's every one ? '

' Having tea, miss,' answered Jane. ' You'd better go along in before everything's eaten up ! '

The twins ran to the big dining-hall and opened the door. A great babel of sound came to their ears—the girls all talking together happily. No one saw them at first. Then Janet happened to glance up and saw the twins standing at the door, still in their coats and hats.

' Pat ! Isabel ! ' she yelled. ' Look, Hilary, look Kathleen, they're back ! Hurrah ! '

She jumped up and rushed to greet them.   With a look
at the astonished Miss Roberts, the mistress who was at
the head of the first-form table, Kathleen and Hilary did
the same.   They dragged the twins to their table, and
made room for them.   Miss Roberts nodded at them and
smiled.

'Glad you're back !' she said.   'You can take off your
hats and coats and hang them over your chairs for now.
I don't know if these greedy first-formers have left much
for you to eat, but I've no doubt we can get more from the
kitchen if not !'

How good it was to be back among the girls once more !
What fun to have questions hurled at them, and to call
back answers !   How friendly every one was, clapping
them on the back, and smiling with welcoming eyes !
The twins felt very happy indeed.

'How are the mumps ? '

'So you've turned up at last !'

'Your Cousin Alison told us the news.   Bad luck you
couldn't come back the first day !'

'Mam'zelle has missed you terribly—haven't you,
Mam'zelle ? '

'Ah, *ma chère* Pat, the French class is no longer the
same without you and Isabel.   There is now no one to
shout at and say " *C'est abominable !* " ' said Mam'zelle,
in her deep voice.

'It's good to be back !' said Isabel, helping herself to
bread and butter and jam.   'I say—we've got our tuck-
boxes with us.   We must open them tomorrow.'

'We've finished all that was in ours,' said Hilary.
'Never mind—two or three of us have birthdays this term
and you can have a double share of birthday cake to make
up for missing our tuck-boxes !'

Only four or five girls around the big table said nothing.
They were all new girls, and they did not know the twins.
They stared at them in silence, thinking that the two

must be very popular to get such a welcome. Pat and
Isabel took a quick look at the strange girls, but had no
time to size them up for they were so busy exchanging
news and eating.

'Plenty of time to know the new girls afterwards,'
thought Pat. 'My, it's good to be back at St. Clare's
again!'

2   SETTLING DOWN AGAIN

IT really was lovely to be back at school again, and to
hear the familiar chattering and laughing, to see the piles
of books everywhere, and to hear the familiar groans of
'Who's taken my pen?' or 'Gracious, I'll never get all
this prep done!'

It was good to see the smiling mistresses, and to catch
a glimpse of Winifred James, the dignified head-girl. It
was fun to have a word with Belinda Towers, the sports
captain. The twins greeted her with beaming smiles, for
they liked her immensely. She was one of the top-
formers, but because she arranged all the matches for the
whole school, she was much better known to the lower
forms than the other big girls.

'Hallo, twins!' she said, stopping to greet them after
tea. 'What about tennis this term? I hope you're
good. We want to play St. Christopher's and Oakdene,
and beat them hollow. Have you played any in the hols.?'

'Only once,' said Pat. 'We used to be good at our old
school, but I don't expect we shall shine much at St.
Clare's.'

'My word, haven't you changed since you first came
two terms ago!' said Janet, with a sly smile. 'The
stuck-up twins would at once have said that they were
champions at tennis!'

' Shut up, Janet,' said Pat, uncomfortably. She never liked being reminded of the way she and Isabel had behaved the first term they had arrived at St. Clare's. They had been called the ' stuck-up twins ' then, and had had a very difficult time.

' Don't mind Janet's teasing,' said Lucy Oriell, slipping her arm through Pat's. ' You know her bark is worse than her bite. Pat, I shan't see as much of you this term as I'd like, because I've been moved up into the second form.'

' I thought you would be,' said Pat, sadly. She and Isabel were very fond of Lucy. Lucy's father had had an accident the term before, which meant he could no longer do his usual work, and for a while every one had thought that the popular, merry-eyed Lucy would have to leave. But there was a chance that she could win a scholarship and stay on at St. Clare's, for she was very clever and quick. So she had been moved up and would now work with the scholarship girls.

' Margery's been moved up too,' said Lucy. Margery came up at that moment, a tall, older-looking girl. She gave the twins a slap on the back.

' Hallo ! ' she said. ' Did Lucy tell you the sad news ? I'm in the second form too, and I feel very superior indeed to you tiddlers ! And gosh—I'm working hard ! Aren't I, Lucy ? '

' You are,' said Lucy. Margery was her friend, and the two had been glad to be moved up together.

' Who else has been moved up ? ' asked Isabel, as they all went to the common room together.

' Vera Johns, but that's all,' said Janet. ' Otherwise our form is the same—except for the new girls, of course. By the way, your Cousin Alison has palled up with one of them—an American girl, stiff-rich, called Sadie Greene. There she is, over there.''

The twins looked for Sadie. There was no mistaking

her. Although she wore the school uniform it was plain
that her mother had got the very best material possible
and had had it made by the very best dressmaker! It
was plain too that her hair was permed, and her nails
were polished so highly that each small finger-tip shone
like a little mirror.

'Golly!' said Pat, staring. 'What a fashion-plate.
What's she been sent to St. Clare's for?'

'Can't imagine,' said Janet. 'She thinks of nothing
but her appearance, and nearly drives poor Mam'zelle
mad. She has the most atrocious French accent you ever
heard, and her American drawl is worst Hollywood. You
should hear her say " Twenty-four! " The best she can
manage is " Twenny-fourr-r-r-r-r! ' no matter how many
times Miss Roberts makes her repeat it. Honestly we've
had some fun in English classes, I can tell you. Sadie's
not a bad sort though—awfully good-tempered and
generous really. But she's jolly bad for that silly cousin
of yours. They walk together whenever we go out and
talk of nothing but dresses and perms and film-actresses!'

'We'll have to take Alison in hand,' said Pat, firmly.
'I thought she looked a bit more feather-brained than
usual when I saw her just now. I *say*—who's that?
What a wild-looking creature!'

'That's our Carlotta,' said Hilary with a grin. 'She's
half-Spanish, and has a fiercer temper than Mam'zelle's,
and that's saying something! She speaks very badly,
and has the most awful ideas—but she's pretty good fun.
I can see a first-class row boiling up between her and
Mam'zelle someday!'

'Oh, it *is* good to be back,' said Pat, thoroughly enjoying hearing all this exciting news. 'The new girls sound
thrilling. I did hope there would be some. But I'm
sorry the other three have gone up into the second form—
I shall miss Lucy and Margery especially.'

Pat and Isabel had no prep to do that night but they

had to unpack and put away their things instead. They left the noisy common room and went upstairs to their dormitory.

Hilary called after them. 'You're in Number Six, twins. I'm there, and Janet, and Prudence Arnold, a new girl, and Carlotta Brown. And Kathleen and Sheila are there too. You'll see which are your cubicles.'

The twins went up the broad stairway and made their way to the big dormitory. It was divided into eight cubicles, which had white curtains hung around them that could be pulled back or drawn round, just as the girls wished. Pat found their cubicles at once. They were side by side.

'Come on, let's be quick,' said Pat. 'I want to get down and have a talk again. There are still three new girls to hear about. I rather liked one of them—the one with the turned-up nose and crinkly eyes.'

'Yes, I liked her too,' said Isabel. 'She looked a monkey. I noticed she and Janet ragged each other a lot. I bet she's good at tricks too. I say—it looks as if we'll have some fun this term, Pat!'

They unpacked happily, and stowed their things away in the drawers of their chests. They hung up their dresses and coats in the cupboard, and set out the few things they had for their dressing-table. They put out the pictures of their father and mother, and their brushes and mirrors.

'I expect we'd better go and see Matron and Miss Theobald,' said Pat, when they had finished. So down they went and made their way to Matron's room. She was there, sorting out piles of laundry. 'Come in!' she called in her cheerful voice. She looked up and beamed at the twins.

'Two bad eggs back again!' she said. 'Dear dear— and I've had such a peaceful time without you for a whole week of term. Why couldn't you get the mumps and give me a little longer spell ? Well—all I say is—don't you dare to go down with the mumps now, and start an epidemic of it ! '

The twins grinned. Every one liked Matron. She was full of common sense and fun—but woe betide any one who lost too many hankies, tore their sheets, or didn't darn their stockings at once ! Matron descended on them immediately, and many a time the twins had had to go to Matron's room and try in vain to explain away missing articles.

' We're glad to be back,' said Pat. ' We're looking forward to tennis and swimming, Matron.'

' Well, remember that your bathing-costumes have to be brought to me after swimming,' said Matron. ' No screwing them up and stuffing away into drawers with dry things ! Now run away, both of you—unless you want a dose out of a nice new bottle of medicine ! '

The twins laughed. Matron had the largest bottles of medicine they had ever seen anywhere. There was a big new one on the mantelpiece. Matron picked it up and shook it. ' Try it ! ' she said.

But the twins fled. Downstairs they went to see Miss Theobald, the wise and kindly Head Mistress. They knocked at the drawing-room door.

' Come in ! ' said a voice, and in they went. Miss Theobald was sitting at her desk, writing. She took off her glasses and smiled at the blushing twins. They liked the Head Mistress very much, but they always felt nervous in front of her.

' Well, twins ? ' she said. ' I still don't know which is which ! Are *you* Patricia ? ' She looked at Isabel as she said this and Isabel shook her head.

' No, I'm Isabel,' she said, with a laugh. ' I've got a few more freckles on my nose than Pat has. That's about the only way to tell us at present.'

Miss Theobald laughed. ' Well, that's an easy way to

tell one from the other when you are both in front of me,' she said, ' but it wouldn't be very helpful when there was only one of you. Now listen, twins—I want you to work hard this term, because Miss Roberts thinks you should go up into the second form next term. So just see what you can do! I should like you to try for top places this term. You both have good brains and should be able to do it.'

The twins felt proud. Of course they would try! What fun it would be to go up into the next form—and how pleased their parents would be.

They went out of the room determined to work hard— and to play tennis hard and swim well. ' Thank goodness we didn't get the mumps,' said Pat, happily, as they went back to the common room. ' Wouldn't it have been awful to have missed more weeks of the summer term ? '

It was supper-time when they reached the common room and the girls were pouring out to go to the dining-hall, chattering loudly. Janet was arm-in-arm with the new girl, the one with the turned-up nose and crinkly eyes.

' Hallo, Pat, hallo, Isabel,' she said. ' Come and be introduced to the Bad Girl of the Form—Bobby Ellis ! '

Bobby grinned, and her eyes became more crinkled than ever. She certainly looked naughty—and there was a sort of don't-care air about her that the twins liked at once.

' Is your name really Bobby ? ' asked Pat. ' It's a boy's name.'

' I know,' said Bobby. ' But my name is Roberta and the short name for Robert is Bobby, you know—so I'm always called Bobby too. I've heard a lot about you two twins.'

' Good things I hope, not bad,' said Isabel, laughing.

' Wouldn't you like to know ! ' said Bobby, with a twinkle, and went off with Janet.

It was fun to sit down at supper-time again and hear

the familiar chatter going on, fun to take big thick slices
of bread and spread it with potted meat or jam. Fun
to drink the milky cocoa and yell for the sugar. Everything was so friendly and jolly, and the twins loved it all.
Afterwards the girls returned to the common room and
put on the wireless or the gramophone. Some of the girls
did their knitting, some read, and some merely lazed.

By the time that bedtime came the twins felt as if they
had been back at school for weeks! It seemed quite
impossible to think they had only been there a few hours.

They went upstairs yawning. 'What's the work like
this term?' asked Pat, poking her head into Janet's
cubicle as they undressed.

'Fierce,' said Janet. 'It always is in the summer
term, don't you think so? I suppose it seems extra
difficult because we all so badly want to be out in the
sunshine—but honestly Miss Roberts is driving us like
slaves this term. Some of us will have to go up into the
second form next term, and I suppose she doesn't want
us to be backward in anything. My goodness, the maths
we've had the last week! You just wait and see.'

But not even the thought of Miss Roberts being fierce
with maths could make the twins feel unhappy that first
night! They cuddled down into their narrow beds and
fell asleep at once, looking forward to the next day with
enjoyment.

3   BACK IN MISS ROBERTS'S CLASS

THE twins awoke before the dressing-bell went the next
morning. They lay whispering to each other whilst the
May sunshine shone warmly in at the window. Then the
bell went and the eight girls got out of bed, some with a
leap, like Carlotta and the twins, some with a groan like

Sheila, who always hated turning out of her warm bed, winter or summer.

They met their Cousin Alison coming out of her dormitory arm-in-arm with the American girl, Sadie Greene. They stared at her, because she had done her hair in quite a different way.

' Alison ! What have you done to your hair ? ' said Pat. ' It looks awful. Do you think you are a film-star or something ? '

' Sadie says I look grand like this,' said Alison, setting her little mouth in an obstinate line. ' Sadie says . . .'

' That's all Alison can say nowadays,' remarked Janet. ' She's like a gramophone record always set to say " Sadie says. . . . Sadie says . . . Sadie says . . ." '

Every one laughed. ' It's sure a wunnerful way of fixing the hair,' said Doris, with a very good imitation of Sadie's American accent. Sadie laughed. She was very good tempered.

' I don't know what Miss Roberts will say though,' went on Doris. ' She isn't very keen on fancy hair styles, Alison.'

' Well, but Sadie says . . .' began Alison, in an injured sort of voice—and at once all the girls took up the refrain.

' Sadie says . . . Sadie says . . . Sadie says ! ' they chanted in a sort of chorus, whilst Doris jumped up on to a nearby chair and beat time for the chanting. Alison's eyes filled with the easy tears she always knew now to shed.

' You can see your cousin can turn on the water-tap just as easily as last term,' said Janet, in her clear voice. Alison turned away to hide her face. She knew that the girls had no patience with her tears. Sadie slipped her arm through hers.

' Aw, come on, sugar-baby,' she said. ' You're a cute little thing, and I won't let them tease you ! '

' I can't think how your cousin can make friends with

that vulgar American girl,' said a soft voice at Pat's side.
' It's a good thing you've come. Sadie has a very bad
influence on the class.'

Pat turned and saw the girl called Prudence Arnold.
She didn't know whether she liked the look of her or not.
Prudence was pretty, but her mouth was hard, and her
eyes, set too close together, were a pale brown.

The breakfast-bell went and saved Pat the bother of
answering. She ran down the stairs with the others and
whispered to Janet. ' Is that Prudence ? She looks
awfully goody-goody.'

' Yes, you'd better mind your P's and Q's with her ! '
said Janet. ' She's so good she'll burst with it one day
—and as for playing a trick on anyone, well the thought
of it would send her into a fit. You should have seen
her face one day last week when I flipped a rubber at
Hilary in class. It was enough to turn the milk sour.
Oh and by the way—according to her she's related to
half the lords and ladies in the kingdom. Get her on to
the subject—she's funny ! '

' No talking now please,' said Miss Roberts as the girls
stood for grace to be said. Pat took a quick look at
Prudence. The girl was standing with her head bent and
her eyes shut, the very picture of goodness.

' Now Lucy Oriell is *really* good,' thought Pat, glancing
at Lucy, ' and I like her awfully, and did from the first—
and yet I don't take to Prudence at all, and *she* sounds
good too. Perhaps it is because she hasn't any sense of
fun, and Lucy has. I wonder if she's as clever as Lucy
at lessons. Well, we shall soon see.'

That morning Miss Roberts read out the class-marks
for the week, and the last new girl, Pamela Boardman,
was top with ninety-three marks out of a hundred.
Prudence Arnold was only half-way down the list. Sadie,
Alison, Carlotta and Doris vied for places at the bottom.

' Pamela, you have done very well for the first week,'

said Miss Roberts. ' I can see you set yourself a high standard, and you work steadily in each subject. Considering that you are the youngest in the form—not yet fourteen—this is very good.'

All the girls stared at Pamela, who was sitting upright in her desk, red with pleasure. The twins looked at her curiously. They were nearly fifteen, and it seemed marvellous to them that a thirteen-year-old should be top of their form.

' She's very small even for thirteen,' thought Pat. ' And she's pale now that she's not red any more. She looks as if she worked too hard ! '

Pamela was not very attractive-looking. She wore big glasses, and her straight hair was tightly plaited down her back. She had a very earnest face, and paid the greatest attention to everything Miss Roberts said.

Miss Roberts had some more to say. She flipped at the marks list with her first finger and then looked firmly at Alison, Sadie, Doris and Carlotta.

' You are all bottom,' she said. ' Well, we know *some* one has to be bottom—but nobody needs to be quite so very low-down as all of you are. Sit up, Sadie ! Carlotta, there is no need to grin round the class like that. It isn't funny to get so few marks in any and every subject ! '

Carlotta stopped grinning round and scowled. She looked like a fiery little gypsy with her black curls, deep-brown eyes and creamy-brown skin. Not even her school uniform could make her look ordinary. She glared at Miss Roberts,

Miss Roberts took no notice of the scowl or the glare, but went calmly on. ' Doris, you have been in my form for four terms now, and I'm really tired of seeing you at the bottom still. You will have extra coaching this term, because you really mustn't stay in my form much longer.'

' Yes, Miss Roberts,' murmured poor Doris. The girls

glanced at her, trying to cheer her up. Doris was a real
dunce and knew it—and yet of all the girls in the school
she could be the very funniest, sending the class into
squeals of laughter by her imitations of mistresses and
other girls. Every one liked her, even the mistresses
who laboured so hard trying to teach her.

'Now you, Alison,' began Miss Roberts again, looking
at the twins' cousin with the intention of telling her that
she also could do better, 'now you, Alison . . .' Then
she stopped and looked at the girl carefully.

'Alison,' she said, 'there is something very strange
about you this morning. It seems to me that you have
forgotten to do your hair.''

'Oh no, Miss Roberts,' began Alison, eagerly. 'Sadie
showed me a new way. She said I had the kind of face
that . . .'

'Alison, you don't really mean to tell me that your hair
is done like that on *pur*pose!' said Miss Roberts, in
pretended horror. Alison subsided at once, and the girls
giggled. Alison really did look a little silly with her hair
all piled in floppy curls on top of her head. Miss Roberts
never could stand what she called 'frippery' in dress or
hair style.

'Much as I hate you to lose any part of my lesson,
Alison,' she said, 'I must ask you to go and do something
to your hair that will make you look a little less amazing.'

'I thought she'd be sent out to do her hair properly,'
whispered Janet to Pat. Miss Roberts's sharp ears
caught the whisper.

'No talking,' she said. 'We'll now get on with the
lesson. Open your maths books at page sixteen. Pat and
Isabel, bring your books up to my desk, please, and I
will try and explain to you what the class did last week
when you were away. The rest of you get on with what
you began yesterday.'

In a little while all was silence as the class applied

itself to its work. Alison slipped back into the room quietly, her cheeks flaming. Her hair was now taken down and brushed back properly, and she looked what she was, a fourteen-year-old schoolgirl. Sadie sent her a look of sympathy.

Prudence and Pamela bent their heads almost to their desks, so concentrated were they on their task. They sat next to each other. Prudence took a quick look at Pamela's book to see if her own sums showed the same answers. Janet nudged Hilary.

' Our pious little Prudence isn't above having a peep at Pam's work ! ' she whispered, opening her desk to hide the fact that she was speaking. Hilary nodded. She was about to open her own desk and make a remark, but Miss Roberts's eye caught hers and she decided not to. Miss Roberts didn't seem to be standing any nonsense that term ! She meant her class to do well, and to make a good showing when most of it went up into Miss Jenks's form the next term !

Pat and Isabel stood beside Miss Roberts struggling to understand what she was explaining. Their five weeks' holiday had made them rusty, and it was difficult to get back the habit of concentration again. But at last they understood and went back to their places to work. Miss Roberts got up to go round the class.

A suppressed giggle made her look round. Bobby Ellis had balanced a sheet of blotting-paper on the bent head of the unsuspecting Prudence. It sat there, moving slightly whenever Prudence turned her head a little to refer to her text-book. Then it floated gently to the ground, much to Prudence's surprise.

' I imagine that, as you find time to play about with blotting-paper, Roberta, you have also found time to do every one of the sums set,' said Miss Roberts in a cold sort of voice. Bobby said nothing. She hadn't done even half the sums.

' Well, if you haven't done all the sums and got them right too, by the time I get round to you, you will stay in at break and do them then,' said Miss Roberts. ' Prudence, pick up the blotting-paper and put it on my desk.'

' Miss Roberts, I didn't know anything about what Bobby was doing,' said Prudence, anxiously. ' I was quite lost in my work. I . . .'

' Quite so, Prudence,' said Miss Roberts. ' Now pick up the blotting-paper please and get lost again.'

Poor Bobby lost her time at break. There was no doubt about it—Miss Roberts was on the war-path that term !

' What did I tell you ? ' said Janet, when the morning ended at last, and the girls trooped out to wash for lunch. ' What a morning ! Alison sent out to do her hair again— most of us scolded—Bobby kept in for break—Janet ticked off for talking twice—Doris pulled up for dreaming in geography—Carlotta sent out of the room for answering back—and double the amount of prep we usually have ! Golly, this *is* going to be a term ! '

4   THE FIVE NEW GIRLS

IN a day or two the twins had settled down so well again that no one even remembered they had been late in coming back. They felt that it was a little unfair that the teachers so soon forgot this, for once or twice they were scolded for not knowing things that the rest of the class had been taught during the first week.

But the twins had good brains and soon caught up with the others. They had always loved the summer term at their old school, and they found that it was just as nice at St. Clare's. There was no lacrosse that term, of course, but instead there were tennis and swimming—and they were grand !

There were eight courts at St. Clare's, and Belinda Towers, who had charge of them, drew up a careful time-table so that every girl could have her turn at tennis practice. Miss Wilton, the sports mistress, was an excellent coach, and soon picked out the girls who would do well.

Margery Fenworthy, one of the old first-formers who had gone up into the second form, was brilliant at tennis, as she was at all sports. Miss Wilton was delighted with her.

' She's so strong,' she told Belinda, ' and she has a lovely style. Watch her serve, Belinda. See how she throws the ball up high, and gives it just the right smack when it comes down—and skims it over the top of the net. You know, I shouldn't be surprised if she wins the school championship this term, and beats all you top-formers ! '

' I don't mind if she does ! ' said Belinda, ' so long as she wins the matches against the other schools we play ! Oakdene and St. Christopher's are both running singles championships, you know, this term. Perhaps we can put Margery in for our player. She's better than I am.'

' Well, there's not much to choose between you,' said the sports mistress, ' except that Margery is immensely strong.'

The twins were quite good at tennis, and Miss Wilton was pleased with their style. ' Practise well and you may be in the tennis team for the first form,' she said. ' We shall be playing plenty of matches this term, so you'll have some fun if you get into the team.'

The twins flushed with pleasure, and made up their minds to practise every minute they could. They loved their school and were very anxious to do everything they could to bring it fame among other schools.

But Miss Wilton was not so pleased with their Cousin Alison. Alison did not like games. 'They make me get hot and messy,' she always complained. 'I hate running about, especially in the hot weather. My hair gets all wet at the back of my neck.'

'Alison, you make me feel sick,' said Bobby Ellis, who always said straight out what she was thinking. She was a bit like Janet that way, without Janet's hot temper. 'You're nothing but a little peacock, always hoping some one's going to admire you!'

'Alison got much better last term,' said Pat, trying to stick up for her cousin. 'She really did try to get on with lacrosse.'

'Well, Sadie says . . .' began Alison, quite forgetting what the girls thought about this refrain of hers. At once the girls nearby took up the chorus.

'Sadie says . . . Sadie says . . . Sadie says . . . What does Sadie say?' they chanted.

Alison turned away in a temper. She was usually quite a good-tempered girl, but she hated being teased, and she certainly was getting a lot of it that term. She flew off to find her precious Sadie. Sadie didn't care about games either. It was difficult to find out what she did care about, with the exception of clothes, hair, nails, complexion—and the cinema!

Sadie frankly didn't try at tennis or swimming. She hated the water. So did Alison. Alison couldn't bear going in. 'It's so icy-cold!' she complained, as she stood at the top of the steps leading down into the deliciously green water. She would stand there, shivering, until one of the girls gave her an exasperated push and sent her in with a gasp and a flop. Then she would come up, spluttering in fury, and glare round for the girl who had pushed her in. But Bobby or Janet or whoever it was would be well away at the top of the swimming-pool !

Only one of the new girls really took to tennis and swimming. That was Bobby Ellis. She was a good sport, and so daring that she even pushed Miss Wilton unexpectedly into the pool, a thing that no other girl would have dared to do. Nobody ever knew what Don't-Care-Bobby would do next. She really seemed to care for nothing and nobody, and went her own sweet way regardless of rules or punishments. She was good at tennis and a fast swimmer—but not one of the other new girls was any good at sports.

Prudence was no sport. She thought games were a waste of time, but only because she was no good at them. She fancied herself at clever conversation, and was always trying to get the other girls to argue about such things as ' Should women rule the world instead of men ? ' and ' Should girls be given exactly the same education as boys ? '

' Oh shut up ! ' Janet would say. ' Keep that sort of thing for the Debating Hour, for goodness' sake ! If you took a bit more interest in the jolly things of life, and *did* something instead of always talking and prating and airing your wonderful opinions, you'd get on better. I consider you're a silly little empty-head, for all your talk. Golly, you can't even play a simple game of cards ! '

' My father says cards lead to gambling,' said Prudence. Her father was a clergyman, and the girl had been brought up very strictly. ' My aunt, who married Sir Humphrey Bartlett . . .'

There was a groan at this. The girls were getting heartily sick of Prudence's grand relations, who were brought into the conversation whenever possible.

' Let me see,' said Bobby, pretending to be interested, ' was that the aunt who always had blue silk sheets on the beds ? Or was it the one who threw a fit because

the house-parlour-maid dared to give her a hot-water
bottle with a cover that didn't match the eiderdown ?
Or was it the one who kept table-napkins embroidered
with every letter in the alphabet so that no matter what
the names of her guests were, there was always a napkin
with the right initial ? '

Prudence flushed. She had once boasted about an
aunt who had blue silk sheets for her beds, but she hadn't
said anything about hot-water bottles or table napkins.
Those were clever make-ups on Bobby's part. She said
nothing.

' Well, go on, tell us ! ' said Bobby. ' We're all eager
to hear the latest Society News ! '

But Prudence had sense enough not to be drawn into
an argument with Bobby. Clever as she was at debating
things, she was no match for the quick-witted Bobby,
who got all the laughs whenever she argued with any
one.

Pamela Boardman was very earnest over her tennis and
swimming, but she was no good at them at all. 'You
see, I always had a governess before I came here,' she
explained to the girls, ' and my governess didn't play
games. Anyway, I was never interested in them. I
loved working at lessons.'

' All work and no play makes Jack a dull boy,' said
Pat. ' You're much too clever for thirteen ! I think it
would do you good to be bottom of the form for once,
and really enjoy yourself out in the open air ! You're
always stewing over a book.'

Carlotta had never played tennis before, and she was
quite wild at it. Miss Wilton said that she really thought
Carlotta imagined the tennis net to be about two miles
high, the way she hit the ball into the air, sky-high !

' Carlotta, when I was small, I played a game with my
brothers called " Chimney-pot tennis ",' she said solemnly
to the fiery little girl. ' We sent the ball up to the roof

and tried to get it down a chimney. Well, it seems to me you would be very good indeed at that game ! But as you are not playing with chimney-pots, I really would be very glad if you could have a look at the net over there, and see if you can get the ball anywhere near it when you serve. Now—throw it into the air—and hit it straight towards the net ! '

There would be a shriek of laughter from the watching girls as Carlotta hit wildly at the ball, and, as likely as not, sent it over the wall into the kitchen-garden !

Her swimming was much the same, though she liked the water and was quite at home in it. But, as Belinda complained, she swam just like a dog, splashing out with legs and arms just anyhow.

' You swim like my dog Binks,' said Kathleen. ' He sort of scrabbles along in the water, and so do you, Carlotta ! '

Sadie couldn't swim at all, and though she didn't mind the cold, as Alison did, she hated having to put her carefully-set hair under a tight bathing-cap, and complained that the water ruined her complexion. So, with the exception of Bobby Ellis, the first-formers voted the new girls a complete failure at sports.

' It's a pity our form have lost Margery Fenworthy," said Isabel, as she watched the straight-limbed girl swimming the whole length of the pool under water. ' She would win the championship for the school, and wouldn't we first-formers be proud ! '

May was a glorious month that year, warm and sunny. Swimming was in full swing, and daily tennis made the grass become worn at the service lines. A good many of the girls had school gardens, and these patches were soon full of growing seedlings of all kinds. Gardening was the one out-door thing that Pamela really seemed to like. She took a big patch and sowed many packets of seeds there She bought little plants too, gay double-daisies, velvet pansies and pretty polyanthus to make the borders of her patch gay.

There were nature-walks over the hills and through the woods. Sadie and Carlotta knew nothing about nature, it seemed, and made some curious mistakes. When Pat exclaimed at the amount of frogs in the pond, Sadie looked at them with interest.

'I got some early frog-spawn in the spring,' said Pat, 'and I got heaps of tadpoles from it. Most of them have turned into tiny little frogs now. They're sweet.'

'Do tadpoles turn into frogs, then?' said Sadie in the greatest surprise. The girls laughed at her. They couldn't imagine how it was that Sadie knew so little about the most ordinary things.

'Didn't you ever go to school before?' said Pat.

'Well, I lived mostly in hotels in America with my mother,' said Sadie. 'I had a sort of governess but she didn't know much! You see, most of the time my mother was fighting a law-case.'

'What's that?' asked Isabel.

'Well, when my father died he left a funny sort of will,' said Sadie. 'And it seemed as if all his money would go to his sisters. So Mother had to go to law about it, and it took years to settle. She won in the end—and I'm to have the money when I'm twenty-one. It's a proper fortune.'

'So you're an heiress?' said Prudence, admiringly. 'No wonder you have such nice clothes and things.'

It was the first time that Prudence had heard of Sadie's fortune. After that every one noticed that the girl hung around Sadie continually.

'See dear Prudence sucking up to the rich heiress?' said Janet, scornfully. 'She's made friends with Pamela so that she can pick her brains—and now she's making friends with Sadie because one day she'll be rich. Nasty little humbug!'

'That's a bit unkind,' said Pat. 'After all, Sadie's kind and generous, and we all like to be friends with her because of those things, not because she's well-off. And Pam's a nice little thing, though she's such a swotter. I'm not friends with her because I want to pick her brains but because there's something rather nice about her, in spite of her head always being inside a book.'

'Well, stick up for Prudence if you like,' said Janet. 'I think she's a humbug. I can't stick her goody-goody ways. Can you, Bobby ? '

Bobby agreed. There was no humbug about Bobby. You always knew where you were with her. She was warm, friendly and sincere for all her don't-care attitude to every one and everything.

'We're a mixed bunch this term,' said Pat to Isabel, as she gazed round her form one morning. 'A very mixed bunch. There'll be a few busts-up before we all shake down together ! '

5   BOBBY PLAYS A TRICK

AFTER two or three weeks the first form began to work quite well. The girls saw that Miss Roberts meant to have her way about the work, and they soon found that it was quicker to prepare work thoroughly, than to have it all to do again after the lesson because it was carelessly prepared beforehand.

Janet badly wanted to go up with the others the next term, so she worked hard. But Bobby Ellis, who had become her firm friend, could not work hard for more than a few days at a time. After that she became bored, and then the class had some fun. For when Bobby was

bored with work, she found relief in tricks and jokes.
Janet had always been marvellous at these, but Bobby
was ten times more ingenious!

Bobby always found the maths lesson far too long.
She hated maths and could never see the use of them.
'I wish I could make the lessons ten minutes shorter,'
she sighed, as she dressed one morning. 'Miss Roberts
said she was going to give us an oral test at the end of
maths today, and I know I shall be bottom. I can't
even think what seven times eight are!'

'Well, can't you think of some way of making the lesson
short?' said Janet. 'I don't like oral maths tests any
more than you do. If only we could put the clock on
when Miss Roberts isn't looking!'

'She's got eyes at the back of her head,' said Bobby.
'No good doing it when she's there. If only she'd go
out of the room for a minute. But she never does.'

'Can't you make her?' said Pat. 'You're always full
of ideas. Go on—I dare you to make her!'

Bobby always took on any 'dare'. She looked at Pat,
and grinned. 'Right!' she said. 'I'll bet you a stick
of toffee to a peppermint drop that Miss Roberts dis-
appears from our classroom during the maths lesson.'

All the girls began to feel excited. Bobby was such
fun. They knew she would do something unusual!

She did. She sat lost in thought at breakfast-time,
and forgot to have any marmalade with her toast.
Between breakfast and the first class, which was
geography, Bobby disappeared.

She went to the common room, which was empty, for
the girls were now tidying their cubicles and making
their beds. She got down her writing-pad and pen, and
in neat, mature writing, penned two lines.

'Kindly attend at the mistresses' common room in the
lesson after break.'

She added a squiggle at the bottom that looked like anybody's initials, popped the note into an envelope and printed Miss Roberts's name on it. Then she placed the note inside her writing-pad in readiness for when she meant to use it.

'Thought of a plan yet ?' asked Janet, when Bobby rejoined the girls upstairs. 'I've made your bed for you. What have you been doing ?'

'Wait and see,' said Bobby, with a grin.

Maths was the first lesson after break. The girls waited impatiently for it, wondering what was going to happen. At break they begged Bobby to tell them what she was going to do, but she wouldn't.

She slipped off to the common room whilst the others were out in the garden. She took the note she had written, and went into Miss Jenks's classroom, next to Miss Roberts. She laid the note on Miss Jenks's desk, and then, making sure that no one had seen her, she slipped out again and went into the garden.

'Miss Jenks will see the note and think it has been left in the wrong classroom by mistake,' grinned Bobby to herself. 'She'll send one of her girls in with it to Miss Roberts—and then maybe we'll see our Miss Roberts trotting off to the mistresses' common room. And if I don't move the hands of the clock on whilst she's gone, my name isn't Roberta Henrietta Ellis !'

All the girls trooped back when the school-bell rang. They went to their classrooms and waited for the mistresses to come and take the next lesson. Hilary stood at the door watching for Miss Roberts.

'Sssst ! Here she is !' warned Hilary. The girls stood up at once, and became silent. Miss Roberts came in and went to her desk.

'Sit,' she said, and the girls sat down with clatters and scrapes of their chairs.

' Now today,' said Miss Roberts, briskly, ' we will try
to do a *little* better than yesterday, when Pame a was the
only one who got even *one* sum right.   At the end of the
lesson there will be a ten minutes' oral test—and I warn
you, no one is to get less than half-marks, or there will be
trouble.   Alison, please sit up.   I don't like to see you
draped over your desk like that.   You are here to do
maths not to act like the Sleeping Beauty and go to
sleep for a hundred years ! '

' Oh, Miss Roberts, *must* we have an oral test on a hot
day like this ? ' said Alison, whose brains worked slowly
in the hot weather.   ' This hot sun does make me feel
so sleepy at the end of the morning.'

' Well, I shall wake you up thoroughly if you seem
sleepy in your oral test,' said Miss Roberts, grimly.
' Now—page twenty-seven, please.   Bobby, why do you
keep looking at the door ? '

Bobby had had no idea that her eyes were continually
on the door, waiting for it to open and a second-former
to appear.   She jumped.

' Er—was I looking at the door ? ' she said, at a loss
what to say, for once.

' You were,' said Miss Roberts.   ' Now for a change,
look at your book.   Begin work, every one ! '

Bobby looked at page twenty-seven, but she didn't see
the sums there.   She was wondering if Miss Jenks had
seen the note.   What a pity if she hadn't !   The whole
joke would be spoilt.

But Miss Jenks had.   She had not noticed it at first,
because she had put her books down on it.   Then she
had written something on the blackboard for the class to
do, and had gone round the form to make sure they all
understood what she had written.   It was not until she
sent Tessie to her desk to fetch a book that the note
was discovered.

Tessie lifted up the books—and the note was there

underneath. Tessie glanced at it and saw that Miss Roberts's name was printed on it.

'There's a note here on your desk for Miss Roberts, Miss Jenks,' she said. 'Do you suppose it was left here by mistake?'

'Bring it to me,' said Miss Jenks. Tessie took it to her. 'Yes—some one thought this was the first-form, I suppose,' said Miss Jenks. 'Take it straight in to Miss Roberts, Tessie—and come straight back.'

Tessie took the note and left the room. She knocked at the door of Miss Roberts's classroom. All was complete silence inside.

Bobby's heart jumped when she heard the knock. She looked up eagerly. 'Come in!' said Miss Roberts, impatiently. She always hated interruptions to her classwork. Tessie opened the door and came in.

'Excuse me, Miss Roberts,' she said, politely, 'but Miss Jenks told me to come and give you this.'

This was better than Bobby had hoped! Now it sounded as if Miss Jenks herself had sent the note. Miss Roberts wouldn't suspect a thing. Miss Roberts took the note, nodded to Tessie, and opened the envelope.

She read what was inside and frowned. It was a nuisance to have to leave her class in the middle of a difficult maths lesson. Well, she would slip along straightaway whilst the form was hard at work, and see why she was wanted.

She put the note back on her desk and stood up. 'Go on with your work, please,' she said. 'I shall be away a minute or two. No talking, of course. Finish what you are doing, and work hard.'

All the girls looked up, astonished, for they guessed that Bobby somehow had been the cause of Miss Roberts's disappearance—but how could she have made Miss Jenks send in a note to get her away? They gaped round at Bobby, who grinned back in delight.

' How did you do it, Bobby ? ' said Janet in a whisper, as soon as the door was shut.

' Bobby ! You didn't write that note, did you ? ' said Pat, amazed. Bobby nodded and leapt to her feet. She ran quietly to the mantelpiece and opened the glass covering of the big schoolroom clock. In a trice she had put the hands on more than ten minutes. She shut the glass with a click and returned to her place.

' You really are a monkey ! ' said Hilary, thrilled. Even Pamela was amused. Only Prudence looked disapproving.

' It seems rather a deceitful thing to do,' she murmured. Sadie gave her a push.

' Aw, don't be a ninny ! ' she said, in her American drawl. ' Can't you ever see a joke ? '

' I wonder what poor Miss Roberts is doing,' said Janet. ' What did you say in the note, Bobby ? How clever of you to leave it in the wrong classroom so that Tessie had to bring it in ! '

' Miss Roberts is probably waiting all alone in the mistresses' common room,' said Bobby, with her wide grin. ' I don't know how long she'll wait ! '

Miss Roberts was feeling very puzzled. She had hurried to the common room belonging to the Junior mistresses, and had found no one there. Thinking the others would come in a minute or two, she went to the window and waited. But still nobody came.

Miss Roberts tapped her foot impatiently on the floor. She hated leaving her class at any time. There were too many mischief-makers in it that term ! They couldn't safely be left for two minutes. What they would be up to now she couldn't think.

' I'll go and see if Miss Jenks knows what it's all about,' she thought. So she went to the second form, and was soon questioning a surprised Miss Jenks about the supposed meeting.

'I don't know anything about it,' said Miss Jenks.
'I just sent the note in by Tessie because it was left on
my desk for you by mistake. How funny, Miss Roberts!'

Miss Roberts, very much puzzled, went back to her
class. She took a quick look round, but every head
was bent and it seemed as if every girl was hard at
work.

'Too good to be true!' thought Miss Roberts dis-
believingly. 'Half the little monkeys have been playing
about, and the other half talking. It's impossible to
realize that when they are top-formers they will all be
thoroughly trustworthy, more dignified than the mistresses even, and so responsible that we could probably
trust the whole running of the school to them. Who
would have thought that Winifred James, our worthy
head-girl, was sent out of my class three times in one
morning for playing noughts and crosses with her best
friend?'

Miss Roberts was, for once, too engrossed in her thoughts
to look at the clock. She began to go round the class
to see what work had been done. When she came to the
last girl she stood up and gave an order.

'Time for the oral test. Shut your books please.'

Then she took a glance at the clock, and stared in
surprise. Why, it was the end of the lesson already!
How quickly the time had gone—but of course she had
had to waste some of it waiting about for nothing in
the common room.

'Good gracious, look at the time!' she said. 'We
can't have the oral test after all. Put away your books
quickly please. Mam'zelle will be here in a moment.'

With grins of delight, and secret nudges, the girls put
away their books quickly. Miss Roberts went out of the
room to the fourth form, where she was due to give a
maths lesson also. They were filled with surprise to see
her arrive so early!

'Oh Bobby, good for you! You've let us off that awful oral test!' said Alison. 'I do think you're a marvel!'

'Yes, you really are!' said Pat. 'It acted like clock-work. Wonderful!'

'Oh, it was nothing,' said Bobby, modestly, but secretly very thrilled at the admiration she was getting. Other girls loved to be praised for their work or their games—but Bobby revelled in admiration for her jokes and tricks!

Only Prudence again disapproved. 'Somehow it doesn't seem quite honest,' she said.

'Well, go and sneak about it to Miss Roberts then,' said Bobby at once. 'Little Miss Goody-Goody, aren't you? Where's your sense of fun?'

'What Prudence wants is a few jokes played on *her*,' said Janet. 'She's just too good to be true. Let's see if your wings are growing yet, Prudence!'

She pretended to feel down Prudence's thin back and the girl squirmed away angrily, for Janet's fingers were sharp. 'The budding angel,' said Janet. 'Tell me when you feel your wings sprouting, won't you?'

Miss Roberts was very much puzzled about the note and the fact that she was unexpectedly early for her next class. But this time she did not suspect a trick of any sort. She simply thought that some mistake had been made and dismissed it from her mind. She would never have thought of it again if Bobby and Janet, made bold by the success of the first trick, hadn't tried another of the same kind—far too soon!

6   JANET IN TROUBLE

THE girls were allowed to go down to the town together, either out to tea in a tea-shop, to the shops or to the cinema. No girl was allowed to go alone unless she was a top-former. The younger ones loved to slip off together. They went to buy sweets, hair-ribbons, or cakes, and if there was anything good on at the cinema, it was fun to go.

That week there was a fine film being shown about Clive of India, and as the first form were then doing the same period with Miss Lewis in the history lesson, they all made up their minds to see it.

Miss Lewis encouraged them. ' You should certainly go,' she said. ' It will make your history lesson come alive for you. I will give a special prize to the best criticism written of the film by any first- or second-former.'

It was more difficult for the first form to go that week than for the second form. The first form had every afternoon full, and four of its evenings were taken up by meetings of some sort or other.

' I shan't be able to go until Friday,' sighed Janet. ' I've got to clean out the art cupboard for Miss Walker tonight, when most of you others are going. Oh why did I offer to do it ? The kindness of my heart runs away with me ! '

' Well, it's not likely to run very far,' said Bobby. ' So cheer up ! '

Janet threw a rubber at Bobby. They were in the common room with the others, and there was a terrific noise going on. The wireless was on at one end of the room, some one had set the gramophone going at the other, and Sheila and Kathleen were arguing at the tops of their voices about something.

' NEED we have both the wireless AND the gramophone on together when nobody is listening to either ? ' pleaded Pamela's voice. ' I'm trying so hard to read and remember what I'm reading, and I simply can't.'

' Well, Pam, you shouldn't be working now,' said Pat, looking up from her knitting. ' You should slack off, like the rest of us. Why, you were saying history dates in your sleep last night, Sadie said ! '

' Bobby, book me a seat for Friday night,' said Janet, looking everywhere for her rubber. ' I shall have an awful rush, I know, unless I can get Miss Roberts to let me off prep that night.'

' She let *me* off,' said Hilary. ' I went last night, and Miss Roberts was an awful brick—let me off half an hour early so that I could see the picture.'

' Well, I'll ask her if she'll be a sport and let me off too,' said Janet. ' Oh blow, where *is* my rubber ? Why did I throw it at Bobby ? What a waste of a rubber ! '

The next day was Thursday, and that evening the rest of the first form went to the cinema, except Janet, who kept her promise and turned out the untidy art cupboard for Miss Walker.

' I'll ask Miss Roberts to let me off early to-morrow,' thought Janet, as she threw all sorts of peculiar things out of the cupboard on to the floor. ' Golly, what a collection of things the art classes get ! I don't believe this cupboard has been turned out for years ! '

The next day Janet was unlucky. She had to do the flowers for the classroom that week, and Miss Roberts discovered that there was very little water in the vases. She looked disapprovingly at Janet.

' No wonder our flowers look sorry for themselves this week, Janet,' she said, poking a finger into the nearest vase. ' This bowl is almost empty. I do think you should attend to your responsibilities better, even the little ones.'

Janet flushed. Usually she was good at remembering small things as well as big, but the flowers had just slipped her memory that day. She muttered an apology and went to get a jug of water.

She came into the classroom with it, and was just about to pour water into a vase on the window-sill when the school cat jumped in at the window.

Janet was startled. She jumped violently and jerked the jug of water. A stream flew into the air—and landed very neatly on the back of Prudence's head! It dripped down her neck at once and the girl gave a loud squeal. Miss Roberts looked up, annoyed.

'What's the matter, Prudence? Janet, what have you done?'

'Oh Miss Roberts! Janet has soaked me!' complained Prudence. 'She deliberately poured the water down my neck!'

'I didn't!' cried Janet. 'The cat sprang in through the window and made me jump, that's all.'

Miss Roberts eyed Janet coldly. She had seen too much of Janet's mischief to believe that it was entirely an accident.

'Prudence, go and dry yourself in the cloakroom,' she said. 'Janet, Prudence was engaged in writing out that list of geography facts for future reference. As she will not be able to finish it now, I would be glad if you would take her book and write the facts out for her during prep this evening.'

Janet stared in dismay, remembering that she had meant to ask for early leave. 'Miss Roberts, it really and truly was an accident,' she said. 'I'll write out what Prudence was doing, but may I do it in break, not in prep?'

'You will do it in prep,' said Miss Roberts. 'Now will you kindly finish playing about with that water and do a little work?'

Janet pursed up her lips and took the water out of the room. It looked as if she wouldn't be able to see the picture now. As she went to the cloakroom to put away the jug, she met Prudence, who had dried herself quickly, for she was not really very wet.

'Prudence! You know jolly well it was a complete accident,' said Janet, stopping her. 'I want to leave prep early tonight, to see "Clive of India". I shan't be able to unless you're decent and go and tell Miss Roberts you know it was an accident and ask her to let me off.'

'I shan't do anything of the sort,' said Prudence. 'You and Bobby are always playing silly tricks. I'm not going to get you out of trouble!'

She marched back to the classroom. Janet stared after her, angry and hurt. She stuck the jug back into the cupboard and slammed the door shut. Janet had a hot temper, and would willingly have poured a dozen jugs of icy-cold water all over Prudence at that moment!

When break came she told Bobby what had happened, and Bobby snorted in disgust. 'Prudence makes out she's so goody-goody,' she said, 'and yet she won't do a little thing like that. Now—let's see—is there any way of getting you off early to the pictures, Janet, in spite of everything?'

'No,' said Janet, dolefully. 'Miss Roberts is taking the first and second form together for prep tonight. If Miss Jenks was taking it I'd take a chance and slip out, hoping she wouldn't notice. But Miss Roberts will have her eye on me tonight.'

'I wonder—I just wonder—if I can't get Miss Roberts out of the room again,' said Bobby, her eyes beginning to gleam.

'Don't be an ass, Bobby,' said Janet, 'she can't be taken in twice that way—so soon after, too.'

'Well—what about doing it a bit differently?' said Bobby. 'Getting *you* called out, for instance?'

'Oooh,' said Janet, and her eyes danced. 'That *is* an idea! Yes—we might work it that way. But what about that beastly stuff I've got to write out for Prudence?'

'I'll do that for you,' said Bobby. 'I can make my writing like yours, in case Miss Roberts wants to see it.'

'All right,' said Janet. 'Well now—how are we going to work it?'

'I'll ask Miss Roberts if I can go and fetch a book from the library,' said Bobby. 'And when I come back I'll say "Please, Miss Roberts, Mam'zelle says can Janet go to her for some extra coaching?" And I bet Miss Roberts will let you go like a lamb—and you can slip off in time to see the whole of the picture.'

'It's a bit dangerous,' said Janet, 'but it's worth a try. Hope I shan't be caught.'

Don't-Care-Bobby grinned. 'Nothing venture, nothing have!' she said. 'Well, I'll do my best for you.'

So when the first and second form were all sitting quietly doing their prep that evening, Bobby put up her hand. 'Please, Miss Roberts, may I just slip along and get a book from the library?'

'Be quick, then,' said Miss Roberts, who was busy correcting books, and hardly looked up. Bobby grinned at Janet and slipped out of the room. She arrived back with a book under her arm and went to Miss Roberts's desk.

'Please, Miss Roberts, may Janet go to Mam'zelle now for a little extra coaching?' she said. Janet went red with excitement.

'Well,' said Miss Roberts, rather astonished, 'Mam'zelle didn't say anything to me about it when I saw her in the common room. I suppose she forgot. Yes, Janet— you had better go—and you can write out those geography facts later on this evening, when you are in the first form common room.'

'Thank you, Miss Roberts,' murmured Janet and scuttled out of the room like a rabbit. She rushed to the cloakroom, got her hat, flew out of the garden-door, went to the bicycle shed and was soon cycling down to the town as fast as she could go! How she hoped she would not meet any mistress or top-former who would see that she was alone!

She slipped into the cinema unseen and was soon lost in the picture, whilst the first form went on silently doing their prep for the next day. Only Prudence was suspicious, for she had seen the looks that passed between Janet and Bobby.

She was even more suspicious when she could not see Janet in the common room that night, after prep. 'Janet is having a very long lesson with Mam'zelle,' she said to Bobby.

'Really?' said Bobby. 'How nice for them both!'

Bobby had copied out the geography for Prudence trying to make her writing as like Janet's as possible. She laid the book down on Prudence's desk when the girl was out of the common room for a minute. Prudence found it there when she came back. At first she thought Janet had written out the pages and she looked round for her. But Janet was still not there. How strange!

Prudence looked closely at her book. She saw that the writing was not really Janet's, and she stared at Bobby, who was lying in a chair, unconcernedly reading, her feet swung over the arm.

'This isn't Janet's writing,' said Prudence to Bobby. Bobby took no notice but went on reading. 'BOBBY! I said this isn't Jane's writing,' said Prudence, annoyed.

'Did you really say so?' said Bobby. 'Well, say it again if you like. I don't know if any one is interested. I'm not.'

'I believe you and Janet made up a plot between you,' said Prudence, suddenly. 'I don't believe Mam'zelle wanted Janet at all—and I believe *you* wrote out these pages.'

'Shut up, I'm reading,' said Bobby. Prudence felt angry and spiteful. So Janet had managed to slip off to the cinema after all! Well, she would see that Miss Roberts knew it, anyway!

So the next morning, when Miss Roberts asked to see her geography book, to make sure that Janet had written out what she had been told, Prudence gave the game away. She went up to Miss Roberts's desk with her book and held it out. Miss Roberts gave a quick glance at it and nodded.

'All right!' she said, not noticing anything wrong with the writing.

'Bobby has written it out very nicely, hasn't she?' said Prudence, in a low, soft voice. Miss Roberts glanced sharply at the book and then at Prudence. She knew at once what the girl meant to tell her.

'You can go to your place,' she said to the girl, for she disliked sneaking. Prudence went, pleased that Miss Roberts had guessed what she meant.

Miss Roberts spoke to Mam'zelle when next she saw her. 'Did you by any chance give Janet Robins any extra coaching last night?' she asked. Mam'zelle lifted her eyebrows in astonishment.

'I was at the cinema,' she said. 'And so was Janet. I saw her! Why do you ask me such a question! I do not give coaching in the evenings.'

'Thank you,' said Miss Roberts, and beckoned to a passing girl.

'Go and find Janet Robins and ask her to come to me,' she said, grimly. The girl sped off and found Janet on the tennis-court.

'Wow!' said Janet when she got the message. 'Now

I'm for it.   The cat's out of the bag—but who let her
out ?   Bobby, say good-bye to me for ever—I've got to
face Miss Roberts in a rage—and I shan't come out
alive ! '

Bobby grinned.   ' Poor old Janet ! ' she said.   ' Good
luck to you.   I'll wait for you here, old thing.'

7   JANET, BOBBY—AND PRUDENCE

JANET went quickly to find Miss Roberts.   When there
was trouble brewing Janet faced up to it at once.   She
didn't run away from it, or make excuses.   She wasn't
looking forward to the interview with Miss Roberts, but
she thought the sooner it was over the better.

Miss Roberts was in the first-form classroom correcting
books.   She looked up as Janet came in.   Her face was
very cold and stern.

' Come over here, Janet,' she said.   Janet went to her
desk.   Miss Roberts finished correcting the book she had
before her and then put down her pencil.

' So you didn't go to Mam'zelle for extra coaching last
night ? ' she said.

' No, Miss Roberts, I didn't,' said Janet.   ' I went to
see " Clive of India " at the pictures.   Bobby had booked'
me a seat the night before.'

' And who wrote out Prudence's geography lists then ! '
asked Miss Roberts.

' Well, Miss Roberts, I didn't,' said Janet after a pause.
' I—I can't tell tales.'

' I don't want you to tell tales,' said Miss Roberts.
' There is nothing that I detest more.   I merely wanted to
make sure you hadn't done the lists yourself.'

'I suppose Prudence split on me?' said Janet, her good-tempered face suddenly flushing.

'Well, I'm not telling tales either,' said Miss Roberts, 'but it won't be difficult for your own common sense to tell you how I found out about your gross disobedience. Janet, I'm not going to have you behaving like this. You have plenty of character, you are plucky, just and kind, though you have too quick a temper and too rough a tongue sometimes—but you and Roberta have got to pull yourselves together and realize that I am NOT here to play tricks on, but to make you work and really learn something. Especially this term, which should be your last one with me. I really feel ashamed of you.'

Janet went red again. She hated being scolded, but she knew it was just that she should be. She looked Miss Roberts straight in the face.

'I'm sorry,' she said. 'I didn't feel it was fair having to miss going to the cinema when I really didn't mean to spill that water on Prudence. It was a pure accident. If I'd done it deliberately, then I wouldn't have minded being punished.'

'You will leave it to me to judge whether or not a punishment is just,' said Miss Roberts, coldly. 'Now, as you used a bit of trickery to go down to the town last night, I feel you are not to be trusted for some time. You will not go down again unless you come to me, say why you want to go, and get my permission. Even so, I shall not grant any for a week or two. You will also do what I told you to do yesterday and write out the geography facts yourself—in Prudence's book as I said.'

'Oh, need I do it in her book?' said Janet in dismay. 'After all, the geography is already written out there once. Prudence will grin like anything if I go and ask her for her book.'

'You've brought it on yourself,' said Miss Roberts. 'And just remember this, my dear Janet—that much as

I admire many things in your character, there is still
plenty of improvement to be made—especially in your
classwork. I feel very much inclined to go into the
matter of that note I had the other day, which resulted in
my leaving the maths class—it seems to me that that
episode and this have a certain likeness that makes me
feel very suspicious. Any more of that kind of thing
from either you or Roberta will be instantly punished.
Please tell Roberta this from me.'

'Yes, Miss Roberts,' said Janet, seeing from Miss
Roberts's face that the teacher was in no mood to be
generous or soft-hearted. Miss Roberts hated being
tricked, and usually prided herself on the fact that her
first-formers never *did* get the best of her. She was
annoyed to think that her class might be laughing up their
sleeves at her.

'You can go,' she said to Janet, and reached out for
another book to correct. Janet hesitated. She badly
wanted to get back into Miss Roberts's good books again,
but somehow she felt this was no time to try and make
amends. She must find a chance some other time, and
bear her punishment as gracefully as she could.

She left the room and went gloomily back to the tennis
court, where Bobby was anxiously awaiting her. Bobby
slipped her arm in Janet's.

'Was it very bad?' she asked, sympathetically.

'Beastly,' said Janet. 'I feel as small as that beetle
on the grass down there. I can't go down to the town
for a week or two, and after that I've got to go to Miss
Roberts and beg for permission whenever I want to go.
It's so humiliating. And oh, Bobby—I've got to write
out those hateful geography lists again—in Prudence's
book!'

'That's too bad,' said Bobby, feeling at once that
Prudence would crow over Janet in delight. 'How did
old Roberts find out about you?'

'There's only one way she could have,' said Janet, fiercely. 'That rotten Prudence must have split on me! I'll jolly well tell her what I think of her, that's all!'

The twins came up at that moment and heard with sympathy all that had happened to Janet. 'I heard that sneak of a Prudence say, "Bobby has written it out very nicely, hasn't she?" when she showed Miss Roberts one of her books this morning,' said Pat. 'I didn't know what she meant, of course. I just thought she was being nice about Bobby's writing. I didn't realize it was her horrid way of splitting on poor old Janet.'

'The beast!' said Bobby, her eyes flashing and her cheeks flaming. She was very fond of Janet. 'I'll pay her out all right! I'll make her squirm. The nasty little tell-tale. She always pretends to be so goody-goody too. I think she's a hypocrite. I'll go and get her beastly book for you, Jan. You shan't have to go and do that, anyway —and if she dares to say a single word to me in that soft sneering way she has, I'll slap her on the cheek.'

'No, Bobby, don't do that,' said Janet. 'It's never any good to do things like that. Leave that to our Carlotta!'

Every one grinned. Carlotta was a really fierce little monkey when she was in a temper, and had actually given Alison a hard slap the day before, because Alison had pointed out that Carlotta's two hair-ribbons did not match, were very dirty, and needed their frayed edges cutting. Carlotta had listened with a wild expression on her face, and had then given Alison a resounding slap, which had, of course, made Alison dissolve into tears.

'You find fault with me again, and I will give you *two* slaps!' threatened Carlotta.

'Carlotta, we don't slap each other in this country,' Hilary had said. 'Maybe you do in Spain—but you can't do it here; it just isn't done.'

Carlotta made a rude explosive sort of noise. 'Pah!

if I want to slap, I slap ! What right has this silly little
peacock to talk about my hair-ribbons ? See how she
cries, the baby ! She does not even slap me back ! '

Alison was not even thinking of such a thing. She was
very hurt and upset, especially when Sadie Greene gave
a laugh.

' My, Alison, you're just cat's-meat to that little
savage ! Cheer up. Don't you see she wanted to make
you howl ? '

The twins, Janet, and Bobby remembered this episode
as they stood on the tennis court listening to Bobby's
suggestion that she should treat Prudence in the same way
that Carlotta had treated Alison. They all knew that
such things as slapping and pinching were out of the
question ! But nevertheless each one of them would
dearly have loved to give Prudence a resounding smack !

' It's what she wants,' said Pat, with a sigh. ' However
—we'll see she's made to feel what a little beast she is,
somehow. She won't get away with this.'

' I'll go and get the geography book from her,' said
Bobby, and marched off. She sent to the common room,
thinking that Prudence might be there. She was like
Pam, always to be found indoors !

She was sitting doing a jigsaw puzzle. Bobby went up
to her. ' Where's your geography book ? ' she said. ' I
want it.'

' Oh, have you got to write something else in it ? ' said
Prudence, in her clear, soft voice. ' Poor Bobby ! Are
you going to do it again for Janet ? What will Miss
Roberts say ? '

' Look at me, you nasty little sneak ! ' said Bobby, in
such a peculiar, threatening voice that Prudence was
alarmed. She raised her eyes and looked at Bobby.
Bobby was white with rage, and her eyes glinted angrily.

' You're going to be sorry for this,' said Bobby, still in
the same peculiar voice, as if she was talking with her

teeth clenched. ' I hate sneaks worse than anything. If you dare to tell tales again, I'll make you very sorry.'

Prudence was frightened. Without a word she got up, went to her shelf and fetched her geography book. She gave it to Bobby with a trembling hand. Bobby snatched it from her and went out of the room.

' I say ! ' said a small voice from the corner of the room. ' I say ! Wasn't Bobby in a rage, Prudence ? Whatever have you done ? '

It was from Pam Boardman, curled up with a book as usual. She looked through her big glasses, her eyes very large.

' I've done nothing,' said Prudence. ' Nothing at all. I haven't sneaked or told any tales. But Bobby has got her knife into me because I think her tricks are a silly waste of time. Don't *you* think they are, Pam ? '

' Well, I'm not very fond of games or jokes or tricks,' said Pamela. ' I've always liked my work better. But some of Bobby's jokes and Janet's do make me laugh. Still, I agree with Miss Roberts—if most of the first form have got to go up next term, tricks and things are a silly waste of time.'

' You're such a sensible girl, Pam,' said Prudence, going over to her. ' And so brainy, I wish you'd be my friend. I like you and Sadie better than any one else in the form.'

Pam flushed with pleasure. She was a shy girl who found it very difficult to make friends, because she could not play games well, and found it impossible to think of funny things to say or do, as the others did. She did not see that Prudence wanted to make use of her.

' Of course I'll be friends,' she said, shyly.

' You've got such brains,' said Prudence, admiringly. ' I'd be so glad if you'd help me sometimes. I wish that Sadie would be friends with you too—it would do her good to think of something besides her hair and skin and nails. I like Sadie, don't you ? '

'Well, I'm a bit afraid of her,' said Pam, honestly.
'She's got such grand clothes, and she does look so lovely
sometimes, and she seems so very grown-up to me. I
always feel small and dowdy when she comes along. I
don't know whether I like her or not.'

Prudence tried to forget Bobby's unpleasant words to
her, but it was difficult. She wondered what had happened. Had Miss Roberts made Janet write out those
geography things all over again? What punishment
would she give the girl?

When her book was returned to her, Prudence looked
with curiosity inside the pages. Yes—there were the
geography lists neatly written for the second time—this
time in Janet's rather sprawly writing—and Miss Roberts
had ticked it.

'So she had to do it after all,' thought Prudence.
'Good! Serves her jolly well right. Now perhaps she
and Bobby will leave me alone for a bit, in case Miss
Roberts gets after them again!'

8　CARLOTTA IS SURPRISING

THE five new girls 'shook down' at St. Clare's each in
their different ways. Sadie Greene sailed through the
days, taking no notice of anything except the things she
was really interested in. Miss Roberts's cold remarks
passed right over her head. Mam'zelle made no impression on her at all. She thought her own thoughts, looked
after her appearance very carefully and took an interest
in Alison because the girl was really very pretty and
dainty.

Prudence and Pam settled down too, though Prudence

was careful not to come up against Bobby and Janet
more than she could help. Bobby settled in so well that
to the old first-formers it seemed as if she had belonged
to St. Clare's for years. Carlotta too settled down in some
sort of fashion, though she was a bit of a mystery to the
girls.

'She seems such a common little thing in most ways,'
said Pat, overhearing Carlotta talking to Pam in her
curious half-cockney, half-foreign voice. 'And she's so
untidy and hasn't any manners at all. Yet she's so
natural and truthful and outspoken that I can't help
liking her. I'm sure she'll come to blows with Mam'zelle
some day! They just can't bear each other!'

Mam'zelle was not having an easy time with the first
form that term. The girls who were to go up into the
second form were not up to the standard she wanted them
to be, and she was making them work very hard indeed,
which they didn't like at all. Pam was excellent at
French, though her accent was not too good. Sadie
Greene was hopeless. She didn't care and she wasn't
going to try! Prudence seemed to try her hardest but
didn't do very well. Bobby was another one who didn't
care—and as for Carlotta, she frankly detested poor
Mam'zelle and was as nearly rude to her as she dared to be.

So Mam'zelle had a bad time. 'Do you wonder we
called her " Mam'zelle Abominable " the first term we
were here?' said Pat to Bobby. 'She has called you
and your work " abominable " and " insupportable "
about twenty times this morning, Bobby! And as for
Carlotta, she has used up all the awful French names she
knows on her! But I must say Carlotta deserves them!
When she puts on that fierce scowl, and lets her curls drip
all over her face, and screws up her mouth till her lips are
white, she looks like a regular little gypsy.'

Carlotta was really rather a surprising person. Sometimes she gave the impression that she was really doing

her best to be good and to try hard—and then at other times it seemed as if she wasn't in the classroom at all! She was away somewhere else, dreaming of some other days, some other life. That would make Mam'zelle furious.

'Carlotta! What is there so interesting out of the window today?' Mam'zelle would inquire sarcastically. 'Ah—I see a cow in the distance? Is she so enthralling to you? Do you wait to hear her moo?'

'No,' Carlotta said, in a careless voice. 'I'm waiting to hear her bark, Mam'zelle.'

Then the class would chuckle and wait breathlessly for Mam'zelle's fury to descend on Carlotta's black head.

It was in gym that Carlotta was really surprising. Since Margery Fenworthy had gone up into the second form, there had been nobody really good at gym left in the first form. Carlotta had done the climbing and jumping and running more or less as the others had done, though with less effort and with a curious suppleness—until one day in the third week of the term.

The girl had been restless all the morning. The sun had shone in at the classroom window, and a steady wind had been blowing up the hill. Carlotta could not seem to keep still, and paid no attention at all to the lessons. Miss Roberts had really thought the girl must be ill, and seriously wondered if she should send her to Matron to have her temperature taken. Carlotta's eyes were bright, and her cheeks were flushed.

'Carlotta! What is the matter with you this morning?' said Miss Roberts. 'You haven't finished a single sum. What are you dreaming about?'

'Horses,' said Carlotta at once. 'My own horse, Terry. It's a day for galloping far away.'

'Well, I think differently,' said Miss Roberts. 'I think it's a day for turning your attention to some of the work you leave undone, Carlotta ! Pay attention to what I say ! '

Fortunately for Carlotta the bell went for break at that moment and the class was free to dismiss. After break it was gym. Carlotta worked off some of her restlessness in the playgrounds, but still had plenty left by the time the bell went for classes again.

Miss Wilton, the sports mistress, was gym mistress also. She had to call Carlotta to order several times because the girl would climb and jump out of her turn, or do more than she was told to do. Carlotta sulked, her eyes glowing angrily.

' It is such silly baby stuff we do ! ' she said.

' Don't be stupid,' said Miss Wilton. ' You do most advanced things considering you are the lowest form. I suppose you think you could do all kinds of amazing things that nobody else could possibly do, Carlotta.'

' Yes, of course I could,' said Carlotta. And to the astonishment of the entire class the dark-eyed girl suddenly threw herself over and over, and performed a series of the most graceful ' cart-wheels ' that could be imagined ! Round and round the gym she went, throwing herself over and over, first on her hands, then on her feet, as easily as any clown in a circus ! The girls gasped to see her.

Miss Wilton was most astonished. ' That will do, Carlotta,' she said. ' You are certainly extremely good at cart-wheels—better than any girl I have known.'

' Watch me climb the ropes as they should be climbed ! ' said Carlotta, rather beside herself now that she saw the plain admiration and amazement in the eyes of every one around. And before Miss Wilton could say yes or no, the little monkey had swung herself up a rope to the very top. Then she turned herself completely upside down there, and hung downwards by her knees, to Miss Wilton's complete horror.

' Carlotta ! Come down at once. What you are doing

"Watch me climb the ropes!" cried Carlotta

is extremely dangerous ! ' ordered Miss Wilton, terrified
that the girl would fall and break her neck. ' You are
just showing off. Come down at once ! '

Carlotta slid down like lightning, turned a double
somersault, went round the gym on hands and feet again
and then leapt lightly upright. Her eyes shone and her
cheeks were blazing. It was plain that she had enjoyed
it all thoroughly.

The girls gazed open-mouthed. They thought Carlotta
was marvellous, and every one of them wished that she
could do as Carlotta had done. Miss Wilton was just as
surprised as the girls. She stared at Carlotta and hardly
knew what to say.

' Shall I show you something else ? ' said Carlotta,
breathlessly. ' Shall I show you how I can walk upside
down ? Watch me ! '

' That's enough, Carlotta,' said Miss Wilton in a firm
voice. ' It's time the others did something ! You certainly are very supple and very clever—but I think
on the whole it would be best if you did the same
as the others, and didn't break out into these queer
performances.'

The gym class went on its usual way, but the girls could
hardly keep their eyes off Carlotta, hoping she would do
something else extraordinary. But the girl seemed to
sink into her dreams again, and scarcely looked at any
one else. After the class was over the girls pressed round
her.

' Carlotta ! Show us what you can do ! Walk on
your hands, upside-down.'

But Carlotta wasn't in the mood for anything more.
She pushed her way through the admiring girls, and suddenly looked rather depressed.

' I said I wouldn't—and I have,' she muttered to herself, and disappeared into the passage. The girls looked
at one another.

' Did you hear what she said ? ' said Pat. ' I wonder what she meant. Wasn't she marvellous ? '

It seemed to have done Carlotta good. She was much better in her next classes after her curious performance in the gym, quieter and happier. She lost her scowl and was not at all rude to Mam'zelle in French conversation.

The girls begged her to perform again when the gym was empty, but she wouldn't. ' No,' she said. ' No. Don't ask me to.'

' Carlotta, wherever did you learn all that ? ' asked Isabel, curiously. ' You did all those things just as well as any clown or acrobat in a circus ! The way you shinned up that rope ! We always thought Margery Fenworthy was marvellous—but you're far better ! '

' Perhaps Carlotta has relations who belong to a circus,' said Prudence, maliciously. She didn't like the admiration and attention suddenly given to the girl, and she was jealous. She thought Carlotta was common and she wanted to hurt her.

' Shut up, Prudence,' said Bobby. ' Sometimes you make me think how lovely it would be to spank you hard with a hair-brush.'

Prudence flushed angrily. The other girls grinned. They liked seeing Prudence taken down a peg or two.

' Come on to the tennis-court,' said Pat to Bobby, seeing that a quarrel was about to begin. ' We've got to practise our serving, Miss Wilton said. Let me serve twenty balls to you, and you serve back to me. Next month there are going to be matches against St. Christopher's and Oakdene, and I jolly well want to be in the team from the first form.'

' Well, I'll come and let you practise on *me*,' said Bobby, with a last glare at Prudence, ' but it's not a bit of good me hoping to be in any tennis team. Come on. Let's leave old Sour-Milk behind.'

How Prudence hated that name ! But whenever she

made one of her unkind remarks, some one was sure
to whisper ' Sour-Milk '. Prudence would look round
quickly, but every one would look most innocent, as if
they hadn't said a single word.

Prudence hated Bobby because she had begun the nick-
name, but she was afraid of her. She would dearly have
loved to give Bobby a clever, unkind name too—but she
couldn't think of one. And in any case Bobby was
' Bobby ' to the whole school. Even the mistresses pre-
sently ceased calling her Roberta, and gave her her
nick-name. Much to Prudence's anger, Bobby was one
of the most popular girls in the form !

9   PRUDENCE MAKES A DISCOVERY

TWO or three quite exciting things happened during the
next week or two, and all of them had to do with Carlotta.
The first happened at the swimming-pool. Carlotta was
no swimmer, but she adored diving and jumping. She
was excellent on the spring-board too, that jutted out over
the water.

Most of the girls could run lightly along the board and
dive off the end of it— but Carlotta could do far more than
that ! She could run along it, leap high into the air, turn
two or three somersaults and land in the water with her
body curled up into a ball—splash ! She could stand at
the end of the board, bounce herself up and down till the
board almost touched the water, and then with one last
enormous bounce send herself like a stone from a catapult
into the air, turning over and diving in beautifully as she
came down.

She jumped or dived from the topmost diving platform,

and she came down the water-chute in every possible
position, even standing, which was a quite impossible feat
for any other girl. Her swimming was always peculiar,
but for acrobatic feats in the water no one could possibly
beat Carlotta.

She didn't show off. She did all these things perfectly
naturally, and with the utmost enjoyment. Prudence,
who was a bad swimmer and disliked the water, never
joined in the general praise and admiration that the other
girls gave to Carlotta.

' She's just showing off,' Prudence said in a loud scornful
voice, as Carlotta did a beautiful somersault into the
water near her. Prudence herself was shivering at the
top of the steps, not yet having gone in. The water was
cold that morning, and courage was not Prudence's strong
point. Alison was beside her, also shivering.

' She's not showing off,' said Janet, who overheard
what Prudence said. ' It's just natural to her to do all
those things. You're jealous, my dear Prue! What
about going down another step and getting your knees
wet ? You've been shivering there for the last five
minutes.'

Prudence took no notice of Janet. Carlotta climbed
up to the topmost diving platform and did a graceful
swallow dive that made even Miss Wilton clap in
admiration.

' There she goes, showing off again,' said Prudence,
talking to Alison. ' Why people encourage her I can't
imagine. She's conceited enough as it is.'

' That's just the one thing Carlotta isn't,' said Bobby.
' Hold that horrid tongue of yours, Prudence. It's
difficult to believe you were brought up in a vicarage
when we hear you talk like that.'

' Well, it's quite plain our dear Carlotta was not brought
up in any vicarage,' said Prudence, spitefully. Carlotta
overheard this and grinned. She never seemed to mind

remarks of this sort, though it made the others angry
for her when Prudence said them.   Bobby pursed up her
mouth and looked at Prudence's white shivering back
with distaste.

'What about a dip, dear Prue?' she said suddenly,
and gave the girl a violent push.   Into the pool went the
surprised Prue with a loud squeal.   She came up angry
and spluttering.   She looked round for Bobby, but Bobby
had dived in immediately behind her and was now under
the water groping for Prudence's legs!

In half a second Prudence felt somebody getting tight
hold of the calf of her left leg and pulling her under the
water!   Down she went with another agonized squeal
and disappeared below the surface, gasping and spluttering.   She came up again, almost bursting for breath—
but no sooner had she got her wind again than once more
Bobby caught hold of her leg and pulled her under.

Prudence struggled away and made for the side of the
pool at once, calling to Miss Wilton.

'Miss Wilton, oh Miss Wilton, Bobby is almost drowning me!   Miss Wilton, call Bobby out!'

Miss Wilton looked round in surprise at the yells from
Prudence.   Bobby by this time had got to the other end
of the pool and was almost dying of laughter.

'What do you mean, saying that Bobby is drowning
you?' said Miss Wilton, impatiently.   'Bobby's right at
the other end of the pool.   Don't be an idiot, Prudence.
Pull yourself together and try to do a little swimming.
You seem to spend most of your time standing on the
steps like a scared three-year-old.'

There were a few titters from the girls nearby.   Prudence was so angry that she fell back into the water and
swallowed about two pints all at once.

'I'll pay you out for that!' she called to Bobby, but
Bobby merely waved her hand and grinned.

Perhaps you'll keep your tongue off Carlotta a bit if

you think you're going to have Bobby after you for it ! '
remarked Janet, who was nearby, enjoying the fun.

Prudence unburdened her mind to Pamela Boardman
as they walked back to the school building that afternoon.
' It's so bad for that common little Carlotta to have us all
staring at her open-mouthed, and thinking she's wonderful,' said Prudence.   ' I don't see why people like Carlotta
should be allowed to come to a good-class school like this,
do you, Pam ?   I mean, it's not fair on girls like us, is it,
who come of good families and have been well brought
up ?   Why, Carlotta might have a very bad influence on
us indeed.'

' Perhaps her parents think that *we* might have a
good influence on Carlotta ? ' suggested Pam, in her
soft voice. ' She *is* queer, I agree—but she's quite fun,
Prudence.'

' I don't think the things she does are really clever,'
said Prudence, spitefully. ' I don't think she's fun,
either. I think there's a decided mystery about our
Carlotta—and I'd dearly like to know what it is ! '

Pam was younger than Prudence, and although she
was a clever girl at her work, she was very easily influenced
by Prudence.   Soon she was agreeing to all that the older
girl said, and even when Prudence said things that were
plainly untrue and unkind about others, Pam listened to
her respectfully and nodded her head.

It was Pam and Prudence who discovered Carlotta
doing something extraordinary, not long after the episode
at the swimming-pool.   The two of them were going for
a nature walk together, taking with them their note-books
and their nature specimen cases.   They set off over the
hill and went across the fields that lay behind the school.
The country swept upwards again after a little, and big
fields lay behind high hedges.   It was a beautiful day
for a walk, and Pam, who seldom went out, was quite
enjoying herself.

Prudence would not have gone out at all for a walk if she hadn't seen Carlotta making off by herself. The girls were not allowed to go out alone, unless they were top-formers, and two or three times Prudence had suspected that Carlotta was disobeying the rules.

Today she had seen Carlotta slipping off through the school grounds to the little gate that was set in the garden wall a good way behind the school. Prudence had been in the dormitory, and her sharp eyes picked out the girl at once. ' I wonder what she does when she goes off alone,' thought Prudence, spitefully. ' Where does she go ? I bet she's got some common town friends that nobody knows anything about. I'd like to follow her and find out."

Prudence was cunning. She knew it would be no good to go to Pam Boardman and suggest spying on Carlotta because Pam, though having a great respect for Prudence, shied away from anything underhand. So Prudence ran downstairs and found Pam curled up as usual reading.

' Hallo, Pam ! ' she cried. ' Let's go out for a nature-walk ! The fields look lovely behind the school this afternoon. Do come with me. It will do you good.'

Pam was good-natured. She shut up her book and went to get her hat and notebook. The two girls set off. Down through the grounds they went, out of the gate and then across the field-paths. Prudence kept a sharp look-out for Carlotta, and soon caught sight of the figure in the school blazer, a good way off, going up the hill opposite.

' I wonder who that is,' she said carelessly to Pam. ' We'll keep her in sight and perhaps join up with her on our way home.'

' We can't do that,' said Pam. ' She's alone so it must be one of the top-formers. She wouldn't want to walk home with *us* ! '

'Oh, I forgot that,' said Prudence. 'Well, we may as well go the same way as she does. She probably knows the right paths.'

So the two girls kept Carlotta in sight. The girl made her way over the top of the hill and then down into the next valley. Here there was a big camp, for a circus had come to the next town. In a vast field many caravans and cages were arranged, and in the centre an enormous tent towered up.

'There must be a circus at Trenton,' said Prudence. 'But Carlotta can't be going to it, because the show won't be on now.'

'How do you know it's Carlotta?' said Pam, in surprise. 'It can't be! She's not allowed out by herself. However *can* you tell who it is so far away?'

Prudence was annoyed with herself. She hadn't meant to let Pam know she knew it was Carlotta. 'Oh, I've got wonderful eyesight,' she said. 'You have to wear glasses, so probably your eyes don't see as far as mine. But I'm pretty sure it's Carlotta. Isn't that just like her—slipping out and breaking the rules?'

'Yes, it is rather like her,' said Pam, who, however, could not help rather admiring the fiery little girl for her complete disregard of rules and regulations when she wanted to do something very badly. Carlotta always want straight for a thing, riding over objections and obstacles as if they were not there.

They followed Carlotta to the big field. They saw her speak to an untidy-haired, rough-looking groom. He smiled at Carlotta and nodded. The girl left him and went into the next field where there were some beautiful circus horses. In half a minute the girl had caught one, leapt on to its back and was galloping round the field, riding beautifully, although it was bareback.

Pam and Prudence stared in the utmost surprise. Whatever Prudence had imagined Carlotta might be going to do she certainly hadn't thought of this! She could hardly believe her eyes. The two girls watched Carlotta on the beautiful horse, which first galloped swiftly round the field, and then fell to a canter. The man she had spoken to came to watch her. He called out something to her and pointed to another horse. This was more the cart-horse type, broad-backed and staid.

Carlotta called something back to the man. She leapt off her horse and ran to the one he had pointed out to her. In a trice she was up on its back, calling to it. It began to run round the field.

And then Carlotta did something that made the two hidden girls gape even more! She stood up on the horse's back, and keeping her balance perfectly, made the horse trot round and round as if it were in a circus ring! Prudence's mouth shut in a straight line.

' I always thought there was something queer about Carlotta,' she said to Pam. ' Now we know what it is. I'm sure she's nothing but a jumped-up circus-girl. How *could* Miss Theobald have her here? It's wicked! Whatever will the others say? '

' Don't let's sneak, Prudence,' begged Pam, timidly. ' Please don't. This is Carlotta's secret, not ours. We'd better say nothing.'

' Well, we'll bide our time,' said Prudence, in a spiteful voice. ' We'll just bide our time. Come on—we'd better get back before she sees us watching.'

So the two girls made their way back to the school, mostly in silence. Prudence was gloating because she had discovered something so peculiar about Carlotta—and Pam was puzzled and worried, fearful that Prudence would give away Carlotta's secret, and drag her, Pam, into the unpleasantness too. They arrived back at school just in time for tea.

Pat and Isabel saw them going indoors and called to them in surprise. ' I say! You don't mean to say you two have actually been for a nature-walk! I thought neither of you could be dragged out of doors!'

'We had a *lovely* walk,' said Prudence, 'and we saw some very interesting things.'

'What have you brought back, Pam?' asked Hilary, seeing that Pam had her nature-specimen case slung over her shoulder.

Pam flushed. She had nothing, and neither had Prudence. It seemed as if the whole walk had been nothing but following Carlotta, spying on her, and then thinking about her all the way back. Prudence certainly hadn't spoken a word about nature, and Pam hadn't liked to ask her to stop when she saw anything that she herself was interested in.

Prudence saw that Pam was uncomfortable because they had brought nothing back for the nature-class. So she lied glibly.

'We've heaps of things,' she said. 'We'll keep them till after tea. We're hungry now—and there's the tea-bell.'

Prudence knew that no one would be interested enough to ask to see any nature-specimens after tea. She pushed Pam in the direction of the cloakroom, so that they might wash their hands.

Pam was silent as she washed. She was a truthful person herself, and it puzzled her when Prudence told fibs, for the girl was always condemning others who did wrong —and yet here she was lying quite cheerfully!

'Perhaps it was because she didn't want to say we'd seen Carlotta,' said Pam to herself. 'She was just shielding her.'

Carlotta arrived late for tea. She muttered an apology to Miss Roberts and sat down. She was red with running, and although she had brushed her unruly dark curls, she looked untidy and hot.

'Wherever have you been, Carlotta?' said Pat. 'I

looked all over the place for you this afternoon. It was
your turn to play tennis. Didn't you know ? '

' I forgot,' said Carlotta, taking a piece of bread and
butter. ' I went out for a walk.'

' Who with ? ' said Janet.

' By myself,' said Carlotta, honestly, lowering her voice
so that Miss Roberts could not hear. ' I know it's breaking the rules—but I couldn't help it. I wanted to be by
myself.'

' You'll get caught one of these days, you monkey,' said
Bobby. ' I break a good few of the rules myself at times
—but you seem to act as if there weren't any at all.
You be careful, Carlotta ! '

But Carlotta only grinned. She had a secret which she
meant to keep to herself. She didn't know that somebody else found it out !

10   AN UPROAR IN MAM'ZELLE'S CLASS!

THE next thing that happened was an uproar in Mam'-
zelle's French class. The term was getting on, and many
of the first-formers seemed to have made no progress in
French at all. The weather was very hot just then, and
most of the girls felt it and were disinclined to work hard.
Girls like Pam Boardman and Hilary Wentworth, both
of whom had brains, a steady outlook on their work, and
a determination to get on, worked just as well as ever—
but the twins slacked, and as for Sadie and Bobby, they
were the despair of all the teachers.

But it was Carlotta who roused Mam'zelle's anger the
most. When Carlotta disliked any one she did not hide
it. Neither did she hide her *liking* for any girl or teacher

—she would do anything for a person she liked. The twins, and Janet and Bobby, found her generous and kind, willing to do anything to help them. But she thoroughly disliked Alison, Sadie, Prudence, and one or two others.

Carlotta's idea of showing her dislike for any one was childish. She would make faces, turn her back, even slap. She would stamp her foot, call rude names, and often lapse into some foreign language, letting it flow out in an angry stream from her crimson lips. The girls rather enjoyed all this, though Hilary, as head of the form, often took the girl to task.

' Carlotta, you let yourself down when you act like this,' she said, after a scene in which Carlotta had called Alison and Sadie a string of extraordinary names. ' You let your parents down too. We are all more or less what our parents have made us, you know, and we want them to be proud of us. Don't let your people down.'

Carlotta turned away with a toss of her head. ' I don't let my parents down ! ' she said. ' They've let *me* down. I wouldn't stay here if I hadn't made a promise to some one. Do you suppose I would ever choose to be in a place where I had to see people like Alison and Sadie and Prudence every day ? Pah ! '

The girl almost spat in her rage. She was trembling, and Hilary hardly knew what else to say.

' We can't like every one,' she said at last. ' You *do* like some of us, Carlotta, and we like you. But can't you see that you only make things worse for yourself when you act like this ? When you live in a community together, you have to behave as the others do. I'm head of the form, and I just can't let you go around behaving like a four-year-old. After all, you are fifteen.'

Carlotta's rage vanished as suddenly as it had appeared. She genuinely liked the steady responsible Hilary. She put out her hand to her.

' I know you're right, Hilary,' she said.   ' But I haven't been brought up in the same way as you have—I haven't learnt the same things.   Don't dislike me because I'm different.'

' Idiot ! ' said Hilary, giving her a clap on the shoulder. ' We like you because you *are* so different.   You're a most exciting person to have in the form.   But don't play into the hands of people like Prudence, who will run to Miss Roberts if you bring out some of your rude names. If you really want to let off steam, let it off on people like me or Bobby, who won't mind ! '

' That's just it,' said Carlotta.   ' I *can't* go for you— you're too decent to me.   Hilary, I'll try to be calmer. I really will.   I'm getting on a bit better with Miss Roberts now—but Mam'zelle always drives me into a rage.   I'll have to be extra careful in her class.'

It was Bobby who really began the great uproar in Mam'zelle's class one morning.   Bobby was bored.   She hated French verbs, which had an irritating way of having different endings in their past tenses.   ' Just as if it was done on purpose to muddle us,' thought Bobby, with irritation.   ' And I never can remember when to use this stupid subjunctive.   Ugh ! '

Nearby Bobby was a vivarium, kept by the first-formers.   It was a big cage-like structure, with a glass front that could be slipped up and down.   In it lived a couple of large frogs and a clumsy toad.   With them lived six large snails.   The first-formers regarded these creatures with varying ideas.

Kathleen, who loved animals, was really attached to the frogs and toad, and vowed she could tell the difference between the six snails, which she had named after some of the dwarfs in the story of Snow-White.   The rest of the form could only recognize Dopey, who never seemed to move, and who had a white mark on the spiral of his shell.

The twins liked the frogs and toad, and Isabel often tickled the frog down his back with a straw because she liked to see him put his front foot round, with its funny little fingers, and scratch himself. Some of the class were merely interested in the creatures, the rest loathed them.

Sadie and Alison couldn't bear them, and Prudence shuddered every time she saw the frogs or toad move. Doris disliked them intensely too. Bobby neither liked nor disliked them, but she had no fear of the harmless creatures as Prudence and the others seemed to have, and she handled them fearlessly when their vivarium needed to be cleaned or re-arranged.

On this morning Bobby was bored. The French class seemed to have been going on for hours, and seemed likely to continue for hours too, though actually it was only a lesson lasting three-quarters of an hour. A movement in the vivarium caught the girl's eye.

One of the frogs had flicked out its tongue at a fly that had ventured in through the perforated zinc window at the back. Bobby took a quick look at Mam'zelle. She was writing French sentences on the blackboard, quite engrossed in her task. The girls were supposed to be reading a page of French, ready to translate it when she was ready.

Bobby nudged Janet. Janet looked up. 'Watch me!' whispered Bobby with a grin. Bobby slid the glass front of the vivarium to the back and put in her hand. She took one of the surprised frogs out and then shut the glass lid.

'Let's set him hopping off to Prudence!' whispered Bobby. 'It'll give her an awful fright!'

No one else had noticed Bobby's performance. Mam'zelle was irritable that morning, and the class were feverishly reading over their page of French, anxious not to annoy her more than they could help. Bobby reached over to set the frog on Prudence's desk.

But the poor creature leapt violently out of her hands on to the floor near Carlotta. The girl caught the movement and turned. She saw the frog on the floor, and Bobby nodding and pointing to show her that it was meant for the unsuspicious Prudence.

Carlotta grinned. She had been just as bored as Bobby in the French class, and the page of French had meant nothing to her at all. She hardly understood one word of it.

She picked up the frog and deposited it neatly on the edge of Prudence's desk. The girl sat next to her, so it was easy. Prudence looked up, saw the frog and gave such a scream that the whole class jumped in fright.

Mam'zelle dropped her chalk and the book she was holding, and turned round with an angry glare.

'PRUDENCE! What is this noise?'

The frog liked Prudence's desk. It hopped over her book and sat in the middle of it, staring with unwinking brown eyes at the horrified girl. She screamed loudly again and seemed quite unable to move. She was really terrified.

The frog took a leap into the air, and landed on Prudence's shoulder. It slipped down to her lap, and she leapt up in horror, shaking it off.

'Mam'zelle! It's the frog! Ugh, I can't bear it, I can't bear it! Oh, you beast, Carlotta! You took it out of the vivarium on purpose to give me a fright! How I hate you!' cried Prudence, quite beside herself with rage and fright.

Most of the class were laughing by now, for Prudence's horror was funny to watch. Mam'zelle began to lose her temper. The frog leapt once more and Prudence screamed again.

'Taisez-vous, Prudence!' cried Mam'zelle. 'Be silent.

A huge frog jumped on to Prue's desk

This class is a garden of bears and monkeys. I will not have it. It is *abominable* ! '

More giggles greeted this outburst. Prudence turned on Carlotta again and spoke to her with great malice in her voice.

' You hateful creature ! Nothing but a nasty little circus-girl with circus-girl ideas ! Oh you think I don't know things about you, but I do ! *I* saw you take the frog out of the vivarium to make him leap on me. I saw you ! '

' TAISEZ-VOUS, Prudence,' almost shouted Mam'zelle, rapping on her desk. ' Carlotta, leave the room. You will go straight to Miss Theobald and report what you have done. That such things should happen in my class ! It is not to be believed ! '

Carlotta did not hear a word Mam'zelle said. She had sprung up from her seat and was glaring at Prudence. Her eyes were flashing, and she looked very wild and very beautiful. Like a beautiful gypsy, Isabel thought.

She began to speak—but not one of the girls could understand a word, for Carlotta spoke in Spanish. The words came pouring out like a torrent, and Carlotta stamped her foot and shook her fist in Prudence's face. Prudence shrank back, afraid. Mam'zelle, furious at being entirely disregarded by Carlotta advanced on her with a heavy tread.

The whole class watched the scene, breathless. There had been one or two Big Rows, as they were called, in the first form at times, but nothing to equal this. Mam'-zelle took Carlotta firmly by the arm.

' *Vous êtes in-sup-por-table !* ' she said, separating the syllables of the word to make it even more emphatic. Carlotta shook off Mam'zelle's hand in a fury. She could not bear to be touched when she was in a rage. She turned on the astonished French mistress, and addressed her in a flow of violent Spanish, some of which Mam'zelle unfortunately understood. The mistress went pale with anger, and with difficulty prevented herself from giving Carlotta a box on the ears.

In the middle of this the door opened and Miss Roberts came in. It was time for the lesson to end, but every one had been far too engrossed in the scene to think of the time. Miss Roberts had been surprised to find the classroom door shut, as usually it was held open for her coming by one of the class. She was even more astonished to walk in and see Mam'zelle and Carlotta apparently about to have a free fight !

Mam'zelle recovered herself a little when she saw Miss Roberts. ' Ah, Miss Roberts ! ' she said, her voice quite weak with all the emotion she had felt during the last few minutes. ' You come in good time ! This class of yours is shocking—yes, most shocking and wicked. That girl Carlotta, she has defied me, she has called me names, she has—oh la, la, there is the frog again ! '

Every one had forgotten the frog—but it now made a most unexpected appearance again and leapt on to Mam'zelle's large foot. Mam'zelle had no liking for frogs. All insects and small creatures filled her with horror. She gave a squeal and stumbled backwards, falling heavily on to a chair.

Miss Roberts had taken everything in at a glance. Her face was extremely stern. She looked at Mam'zelle. She knew Mam'zelle's hot temper, and she felt that the best thing to do was to get the angry French mistress out of the class before making any inquiries herself.

" Mam'zelle, your next class is waiting for you,' she said in her clear cool tones. ' I will look into this matter for you and report to you at dinner-time. You had better go now and leave me to deal with everything.'

Mam'zelle could never bear to be late for any class. She got up at once and left the room, giving Carlotta one look of fury before she went. Miss Roberts nodded

to Hilary to shut the door and then went to her own desk.
There was a dead silence in the room, for there was not
a girl there who did not dread Miss Roberts when she
was in this kind of mood.

Carlotta was still standing, her hair rumpled over her
forehead, her fists clenched. Miss Roberts glanced at
her. She knew Carlotta's fiery nature by now, and felt
that it was of no use at all to attack her in that mood.
She spoke to her firmly and coldly.

'Carlotta, please go and do your hair. Wash your
inky hands too.'

The girl stared at her teacher, half-mutinous, but the
direct order calmed her and she obeyed it. She left the
room and there was a sigh of relief. Carlotta was exciting
—but this time she had been a little *too* exciting.

'Now please understand that I am not encouraging
any tale-bearing,' said Miss Roberts, looking round her
class with cold blue eyes, 'but I am going to insist on
finding out what this extraordinary scene is about.
Perhaps you, Hilary, as head of the class, can tell me.'

'Miss Roberts, let *me* tell you!' began Prudence, eager
to get her word in before any one else. 'Carlotta opened
the vivarium and took out the frog, and . . .'

'I don't want any information from you until I ask
for it, Prudence,' said Miss Roberts, in such a cutting
tone that the girl sank back into her seat, flushing.
'Now, Hilary—tell me as shortly as you can.'

'Well, apparently some one took a frog out of the
vivarium and put it on Prudence's desk,' said Hilary
reluctantly. Bobby got up, red in the face.

'Excuse me interrupting, Miss Roberts,' she said. '*I*
took the frog out.'

'It was that beast Carlotta who played the trick on
me!' exclaimed Prudence. 'You're shielding her.'

'Prudence, you'll leave the room if you speak again,'
said Miss Roberts. 'Go on, Bobby.'

' I was bored,' said Bobby, honestly. ' I took out the frog to make it jump on to Prudence for a bit of fun, because she's scared of frogs. But it leapt out of my hand on to the floor—and so I nodded to Carlotta to pick it up and put it on the desk—and she did. But I was the one to blame.'

Bobby sat down. ' Now you go on with this extra-ordinary tale, Hilary,' said Miss Roberts, wondering if her class could really be in its right senses that morning.

' Well, Miss Roberts, there isn't much else to tell except that Prudence got an awful fright and screamed and Mam'zelle was angry, and Prudence blamed it all on to Carlotta and said some pretty horrid things to her, and Carlotta flared up as she does—and when Mam'zelle ordered her from the room she wouldn't go—I really think she didn't even *hear* Mam'zelle ! Then Mam'zelle was furious because Carlotta didn't obey her and went over to her—and Carlotta turned on her and said something in Spanish that made Mam'zelle even more furious. And then *you* came in,' finished Hilary.

' And spoilt your fun, I suppose,' said Miss Roberts in the sarcastic voice that the class hated. ' A very entertaining French lesson, I must say. You appear to have begun it all, Bobby—Carlotta certainly had a hand in it—and the rest of the tale appears to be composed of bad tempers on the part of several people. I imagine that every one was simply delighted, and watched with bated breath. I'm disgusted and ashamed. Bobby, come to me at the end of the morning.'

' Yes, Miss Roberts,' said Bobby, dismally. Prudence looked round at Bobby with a pleased expression, delighted that the girl had a punishment coming to her. Miss Roberts caught sight of the look. She could not bear Prudence's meanness, nor her habit of tale-bearing and gloating over others' misfortunes. She snapped at her so suddenly that Prudence jumped.

'Prudence! You are not without blame, either! If you *can* make trouble for others, you invariably do. If you had not made such a stupid fuss none of this would have happened."

Prudence was deeply hurt. 'Oh, Miss Roberts!' she said, in an injured tone, 'that's not fair. Really I . . .'

'Since when have I allowed you to tell me what is fair and what is not?' inquired Miss Roberts. 'Hold your tongue and sit down. And while I think of it— your last essay was so bad that I cannot pass it. You will do it again this evening.'

Prudence flushed. She knew that Miss Roberts definitely meant to be unkind at that moment, and she felt that all the girls, except perhaps Pam, silently approved of Miss Roberts's sharp tongue, and were pleased at her 'ticking-off.' Her thoughts turned to Carlotta, and she brooded with bitterness over the fiery girl and what she had said. Miss Roberts had said nothing about punishing that beast Carlotta! Surely she wasn't going to let her go scot-free! Think of the things she had said to Mam'zelle! Carlotta was queer and bad —see how she broke the rules of the school and went off riding other people's horses!

The class was in a subdued mood for the rest of that morning. Bobby went to Miss Roberts and received such a scolding that she almost burst into tears—a thing that Bobby had not done for years! She also received a punishment that kept her busy for a whole week—a punishment consisting of writing out and learning all the things that Miss Roberts unaccountably appeared to think that Bobby didn't know. It is safe to say that at the end of that week Bobby knew a good deal more than at the beginning!

Carlotta appeared to receive no punishment at all, which caused Prudence much anger and annoyance. Actually, as Pat and Isabel knew, Carlotta had been sent to the head, Miss Theobald, and had come out of that dread drawing-room in tears, looking very subdued and unlike herself. She told no one what had passed there, and nobody dared to inquire.

Mam'zelle received a written apology from Bobby and from Carlotta—and, much to Prudence's anger, one from Prudence herself too! Miss Roberts had demanded it, and would not listen to any objections on Prudence's part. So the girl had not dared to disobey but had written out her apology too.

' I'll pay Carlotta out for this ! ' she thought. ' I'll go and find that man she was talking to—and ask him all about that horrid beast of a Carlotta ! I'm sure there's something funny about that.'

11   CARLOTTA'S SECRET

THE first chance that Prudence had of going for a walk over to the circus-camp was two days later. She sought out Pam and asked her to go with her.

' Oh, Prudence ! I did so badly want to finish reading this book,' said Pam, who was in the middle of a historical novel dealing with the class's period of history. It was quite a joke with the first form that Pam never read any book unless it had to do with some of the classwork.

' Pam, do come,' begged Prudence, slipping her hand under Pam's arm. Pam had had very little affection shown to her in her life and she was always easily moved by any gesture on Prudence's part. She got up at once, her short-sighted eyes beaming behind their big glasses. She put away her book and got her hat. The two girls set off, going the same way as before.

In half an hour's time they reached the camp. 'Why, we've come the same way that we came last week!' said Pam.

'Yes,' said Prudence, pretending to be astonished too. 'And look—the circus camp is still there—and those lovely horses are still in the field. Let's go down to the camp and see if we can see any elephants or exciting things like that.'

Pam wasn't at all sure that she wanted to find elephants, for she was nervous of animals, but she obediently followed Prudence. They went into the field, where the caravans and cages were arranged. No one took any notice of them.

After a while Prudence's sharp eyes found the untidy-haired man that she had seen Carlotta talking to. She went up to him.

'Does it matter us looking round the camp a bit?' she asked, with her sweetest smile.

'No, you go where you like, missy,' said the man.

'Are those the circus-horses in that field over there?' asked Prudence, pointing to the field where she had seen Carlotta riding.

'They are,' said the man, and he went on polishing the harness that lay across his knees.

'I wish we could ride them like Carlotta,' said Prudence, gazing at the horses with an innocent expression. The man looked at her sharply.

'Ay, she's a fine rider,' he said. 'Fine girl altogether, I say.'

'Have you known her long then?' said Prudence, still looking very innocent indeed.

'Since she was a baby,' said the man.

'She's had an awfully interesting life, hasn't she?' said Prudence, pretending that she knew far more than she did. 'I love to hear all her stories.'

Pam stared at Prudence open-mouthed. This was

news to her ! She wondered uncomfortably if Prudence
was telling one of her fibs—but why should she do that ?

' Oh, she's told you about her life, has she ? ' said the
man, looking rather surprised. ' I thought she wasn't . . .'

He stopped short. Prudence felt excited. She really
was discovering something now. She looked at the untidy
man, her eyes wide open with a most honest expression
in them. No one could beat Prudence at looking innocent
when she wasn't !

" Yes, I'm her best friend,' said Prudence. ' She told
me to come over here and look round the camp. She
said you wouldn't mind.'

Pam was now quite certain that Prudence was telling
dreadful untruths. In great discomfort the girl went off
to look at a nearby caravan. She felt that she could not
listen any more. She could not imagine what Prudence
was acting like this for. She had so little spite in her own
nature that it did not occur to her to think that Prudence
was trying to find out something that might damage
Carlotta.

Prudence was pleased to see Pam go off. Now she could
get on more quickly ! She felt certain somehow that
Carlotta really had been connected with circus life in some
way, so she took the plunge and asked the man the
question.

' I expect Carlotta loved circus-life, didn't she ? '

The man apparently saw nothing queer about the
question. He plainly thought that Carlotta had told
Prudence a great deal about herself. He nodded his
head.

' She oughtn't to have left it,' he said. ' My brother,
who was in the same show as Carlotta was, said it would
break her heart. That girl knew how to handle horses
better than a man. I was glad to let her have a gallop
when she came over here the other day. We move tomorrow—so you tell her when you get back that if she

wants another gallop, she'll have to come along pretty
early to-morrow morning, like she did two weeks ago.'

Prudence was almost trembling with excitement. She
had found out all she wanted to know. That nastly little
Carlotta was a circus-girl—a horrid, common, low-down
little circus-girl! How dare Miss Theobald accept a girl
like that for her school! Did she really expect girls like
Prudence, daughter of a good family, to mix with circus-
girls ?

She called Pam and the two set off to go back to the
school. Both were silent. Pam was still feeling very
uncomfortable about Prudence's untruths to the man in
the camp—and Prudence was thinking how clever she had
been. She did not realize that it was not real cleverness
—only shameful cunning.

She wondered how she could get the news round among
the girls. Should she drop a hint here and there ? If
she could get hold of that foolish Alison, she would soon
bleat it out everywhere ! She went to find Alison that
evening in the common room. The girl was sitting doing
a complicated jigsaw. She loved jigsaws, although she
was very bad at them, and usually ended in losing half
the pieces on the floor.

It was an interesting jigsaw. Four or five girls came
to see how Alison was getting on. Bobby picked up a
piece.

' Doesn't that go there ? ' she said, and tried it. Then
Hilary picked up another piece, and in trying to make it
fit, pushed the half-finished picture crooked.

' Oh ! ' cried Alison, exasperated. ' If there's one
thing I hate more than anything else it's having people
help me with a jigsaw puzzle. First it's Bobby, then it's
Hilary, then it's somebody else. I could finish it much
more quickly if only people didn't help me ! '

' I've never seen you finish a jigsaw puzzle yet, Alison,'
said Pat, teasingly.

'Why don't you do it properly?' said Doris, who however poor she was at lessons, was astonishingly quick at jigsaws. 'You always begin by putting little bits together here and there. What you should do is to begin with the outside pieces. You see, they've got a straight edge, and . . . ''

'I know all that,' said Alison, impatiently, 'but Sadie says . . .'

Immediately the chorus was taken up in the greatest delight by the girls around.

'Sadie says—oh Sadie says—Sadie, Sadie, Sadie SAYS!'

The girls at the back of the room took up the chorus too, and Sadie good-naturedly lifted her pretty head. 'Don't you mind them, Alison,' she said. But Alison did. She never could take teasing well. She muddled up her half-made jigsaw in peevishness, piled it into its box, dropped two or three pieces on the floor and went out of the room.

Prudence followed her, thinking she might drop a few words into Alison's ear. 'Alison!' she called. 'What a shame to tease you like that! Come out into the garden with me. It's a lovely evening.'

'No, thanks,' said Alison, half-rudely, for she did not like Prudence. 'I'm not in the mood to hear nasty things about half the girls in the form!'

Prudence flushed. It was true that she lost no chance of telling tales about the girls, trying to spread mischief among them—but she had not realized that the girls themselves knew it. It was plainly no use trying to get Alison to listen to tales about Carlotta.

'I'll have to think of some other way,' said Prudence to herself. But she did not have to think—for the whole thing came out that same evening far more quickly than Prudence had ever expected.

She went back into the common room. Carlotta was

there, laughing as she told some joke in her half-foreign voice, which was rather fascinating to listen to. The girls were grouped around her, and Prudence felt a sharp twinge of jealousy as she saw them.

Her face was so sour as she looked at Carlotta that Bobby laughed loudly. ' Here comes old Sour-Milk ! ' she said, and every one giggled.

' Sour-Milk ! ' said Carlotta. ' That is a very good name. Why have you gone sour, Prudence ? '

Prudence was suddenly full of spite. ' It's enough to make any one go sour when they have to live with a low-down circus-girl like you ! ' she said, her tone so full of hate that the girls glanced at her in astonishment. Carlotta laughed.

' I'd like to see *you* in a circus ! ' she said cheerfully. ' The tigers would like you for their dinner. And I don't believe any one would miss you.'

' Be careful, Carlotta,' said Prudence. ' I know all about you. All—about—you ! '

' How interesting ! ' said Carlotta, though her eyes began to gleam dangerously.

' Yes—very interesting,' said Prudence. ' The girls would soon despise you if they knew what I know. You wouldn't have any friends then. No one would want to know—a common little circus-girl ! '

' Shut up, Prudence,' said Bobby, afraid that Carlotta might lose her temper. ' Don't tell silly lies.'

' It's not silly lies,' said Prudence. ' It's the truth, the whole truth. There's a circus-camp over near Trenton, and I talked to a man there—and he told me Carlotta was a circus-girl, and knew how to handle horses, and was nothing but a common little girl from a circus belonging to his brother. And *we* have to put up with living with a girl like her ! '

There was a complete silence when Prudence had

finished.   Carlotta looked all round the girls with flashing eyes.   They stared at her.   Then Pat spoke.

'Carlotta—did you *really* live in a circus?'

Prudence watched every one, pleased with her bombshell.   Now Carlotta would see what decent, well-brought up girls would say to her.   She, Prudence, would have a fine revenge.   She waited impatiently for the downfall of the fiery little Carlotta.

At Pat's question Carlotta looked towards the twins. She nodded her head.   'Yes,' she said.   'I *was* a circus-girl.   And I loved it.'

The girls looked in amazement and delight at Carlotta. Her eyes were glowing and her cheeks were red.   They could all imagine her quite well riding in a circus-ring. They pressed round her eagerly.

'Carlotta!   How marvellous!'

'I say, Carlotta!   How simply wonderful!'

'Carlotta, you simply *must* tell us all about it!'

'I always knew there was something unusual about you.'

'Oh, Carlotta, to think you never told us!   Why didn't you, you wretch?'

'Well—I promised Miss Theobald I wouldn't,' said Carlotta.   'You see—it's a funny story really—my father married a circus-girl—and she ran away from him, taking me with her, when I was a baby.   She died soon after, and I was brought up by the circus-folk.   They were grand to me.'

She stopped, remembering many things.   'Go on,' said Kathleen, impatiently.   'Do go on!'

'Well—I loved horses, just as my mother did,' said Carlotta, 'so I naturally rode in the ring.   Well, not long ago, my father, who'd been trying to find me and my mother for years, suddenly discovered that mother was dead and I was in a circus.   Father is a rich man—and he made me leave the circus, and when he found how little education I'd had he thought he would send me to school to learn.'

' Oh, Carlotta—how awfully romantic ! ' said Alison. ' Just like a book. I always thought you looked unusual, Carlotta. But why are you so foreign ? '

' My mother was Spanish,' said Carlotta, ' and some of the folk in the circus were Spanish too, though many of them came from half Europe ! They were grand people. I wish I could go back to them. I don't fit in here. I don't belong. I don't think like you do. Our ideas are all different—and I'll never never learn.'

She looked so woe-begone that the girls wanted to comfort her.

' Don't you worry, Carlotta ! You'll soon fit in—better than ever now we know all about you. Why didn't Miss Theobald want us to know you'd been a circus-girl ? '

' Well, I suppose she thought maybe you might look down on me a bit ? ' said Carlotta. The girls snorted.

' Look down on you ! We're thrilled ! Carlotta, show us some of the things you can do ! '

' I promised Miss Theobald I wouldn't do any of my tricks,' said Carlotta, ' in case I gave the show away. I broke my promise the other day in the gym—but somehow I simply couldn't help it. I'd been thinking and dreaming of all the old circus-days—and of my darling beautiful horse, Terry—and I just went mad and did all those things in the gym. I can do much more than I showed you then ! '

' Carlotta ! Walk on your hands upside-down ! ' begged Bobby. ' Golly ! What fun you're going to be ! You're a fierce creature with your fly-away tempers and ready tongue—but you're natural and kind and we shall all like you even better now we understand the kind of life you've lived before. It's a wonder you've fitted in as well as you did. What a mercy you were honest about it—we

wouldn't have admired you nearly so much if you'd been
afraid to own up.'

'Afraid to own up—why, I'm proud of it!' said
Carlotta, with sparkling eyes.   'Why should I be ashamed
of knowing how to handle horses?   Why should I be
ashamed of living with simple people who have the
kindest hearts in the world?'

The girl threw herself lightly over and stood on her
hands.   Her skirt fell over her shoulders as she began
to walk solemnly round the room on her strong, supple
little hands.   The girls crowded round her, laughing and
admiring.

'My word—the second form will be jealous when they
hear about Carlotta!' said Bobby.

'They certainly will!' said Sadie, who was just as full
of astonishment and admiration as any one else.   It all
seemed most surprising and unreal.

Every one was pleased and thrilled—save for one girl.
That girl, of course, was Prudence.   She could not understand the attitude of the girls.   It was completely opposite
to what she had expected.   It was hard to believe.

Prudence stood in silence, listening to the squeals of
delight and admiration.   Her heart was very bitter
within her.   The bomb-shell she had thrown had certainly
exploded—but the only person it had harmed had been
the thrower!   Instead of making the girls despise Carlotta
and avoid her, she had only succeeded in making them
admire her and crowd round her in delight.   Now Carlotta
would show off even more—she would get more friends
than ever.   How *could* every one like a nasty common
little girl like that, who even, at times, dropped her
H's?

No one took any notice of Prudence.   For one thing
they were so excited about Carlotta—and for another
thing they despised her for her mean attempt to injure
another girl for something she couldn't help.   Bobby

elbowed her a little roughly, and Prudence almost burst into tears of rage and defeat.

She slipped out of the room. It was more than she could bear to see Carlotta walking on her hands, cheered on by the rest of the first-formers. The last words she heard were :

' Let's get the second-formers in ! Where are they ? In the gym ? Do let's go and tell them to come and see Carlotta ! She's marvellous ! '

' I meant my news to hurt her—and it's only brought her good luck and friendship,' thought Prudence, bitterly. ' Whatever shall I do about it ? '

12   BOBBY GETS A SHOCK

CARLOTTA was a very popular person after this up-heaval. Her complete honesty and frankness had disarmed every one, and to most of the girls she suddenly appeared as a most surprising and romantic person. Even the second-formers were thrilled, though as a rule they professed rather to turn up their noses at anything that happened in the first form. But Tessie, Queenie, and the rest of the second form, were just as persistent as the lower form in begging Carlotta to show off her circus tricks and accomplishments.

' It must have been a bit of a shock to that sneak of a Prudence to find that instead of looking down on our Carlotta we looked up to her and admired her instead ! ' said Pat. ' I bet dear darling Prudence thought we'd be shocked to the back teeth to hear she was a circus-girl. I vote we punish her by not taking a scrap of notice of her, and not listening to anything she says ! '

' I think we ought to do the same to Pam then,' said Bobby. ' Pam's Prudence's friend, you know, and she was with her when they spied on Carlotta. She's a silly little creature and thinks the world of Prudence. It will do her good to feel that we don't approve of Prudence's ways, and don't particularly want to be pleasant to Prudence's friends.'

' Well, I'm rather sorry for Pam,' said Isabel. ' She's a nervous little thing and awfully hard-working. Don't let's be too hard on her.'

Prudence didn't at all like the treatment meted out to her by the first-formers. The girl was very fond of the sound of her own voice, and it was most annoying to her to find that whenever she began to air her views about anything, all the girls around either suddenly disappeared, or else began to talk nonsense to one another at the tops of their voices.

Prudence would perhaps address herself to Hilary and say ' Hilary, what side are you taking in tonight's debate on " Should Women rule the world ? " I'm taking the side that they certainly should. After all, don't we . . .'

Then Hilary would suddenly address Janet in a very loud voice and say something perfectly ridiculous, such as ' I say, Janet, old thing, how many legs has a kitten ? '

And Janet, perfectly solemn, would answer in a loud voice ' Well, usually four. But you'd better count and see.'

Prudence would stare in astonishment, and then begin again. ' What I say is, if women ruled the world . . .'

Then Kathleen would chime in, cutting right across Prudence's rather affected little voice. ' Hilary, Janet ! Do you suppose a worm really grows into two worms when it's cut in half ? '

Then Bobby would cut in, rather cruelly. ' What about cutting dear Prudence in two, then we'll see ! '

And so it went on, nobody ever paying any attention to Prudence at all. Prudence was hurt and angry and went to Pam for comfort. She squeezed out a few tears and Pam tried to comfort her.

' Pam, you know quite well I wasn't spying on Carlotta.' wept Prudence. ' Can't you tell the girls I wasn't ? Do stick up for me. What's the good of being my friend if you don't ? '

And then poor Pam, trying her hardest to be loyal, would stick up for Prudence, although in her heart of hearts she no longer really trusted or liked her. But the thirteen-year-old girl was easily swayed, and any one in tears moved her heart.

So it came about that very soon the first-formers began to ignore poor Pam too, and laughed at her efforts to stick up for Prudence. Pam retired into her shell and felt very unhappy. She worried about the whole thing and turned to her work more than ever to help her to forget the many unpleasantnesses that seemed to be cropping up in those weeks.

Now that her secret was out, Carlotta was very happy. Hers was an honest nature, and she had not liked keeping everything to herself. Now the whole school knew what she was and eyed her with wonder, half-expecting her to do something extraordinary at any time. The twins took her under their wing, and they and Carlotta, Bobby and Janet were continually about together.

Carlotta had gone to Miss Theobald and had told her that every one now knew she had once been a circus-girl. ' But they don't seem to mind,' said Carlotta, looking straight at the Head Mistress with her fearless eyes. ' You thought they would, didn't you ? '

' No, Carlotta, I didn't think that most of them would mind at all,' said Miss Theobald. ' But I thought it might be easier for you to settle down if the girls did not regard you as anything out of the ordinary. Also your

father begged me to keep your " secret " as he called it.
Well—it's out now—and you must just show me that it
doesn't matter.   You are all your father has, you know—
so try and get used to the kind of life you will have to
lead with him later on.'

Carlotta sighed. She didn't want to lead any other
kind of life except the one she had always known—the
life of the circus-camp, always on the move, always
visiting new places, always making new friends. She left
Miss Theobald's drawing-room looking rather subdued.

After a while the excitement caused by the row in
Mam'zelle's class, and by Carlotta's secret died down a
little. This was partly because matches were looming
ahead—tennis and swimming-matches—and the school
was putting in a good deal of practice, hoping to win all
the matches against other schools.

The twins were practising hard, and Bobby was helping
them. Don't-Care Bobby would not do anything much
to help herself on, but never minded how much time she
gave to help any one else to become better at anything.
Janet and Hilary were both practising too, but were not
so good as the twins.

' You're getting a grand style at tennis, both of you,'
said Belinda Towers, approvingly, as she watched the
twins one afternoon. ' If you go on like this you'll be
chosen for the first form team against St. Christopher's !
Bobby, you're getting better too. Why don't you try a
bit harder and see if you can't be the reserve girl ? '

Two out of each form were chosen to play against two
girls from each form of the opposing school, and for each
two there was a reserve girl, in case one of the two fell
ill or could not play for any other reason. Bobby shook
her head when she heard Belinda say this.

' No, thanks ! ' she said. ' It makes tennis too much
like hard work if I have to practise up for reserve girl ! '

Belinda was not amused by this answer. She gave

Bobby a look that rather surprised her, because it held a certain amount of scorn in it.

'Oh, well,' said Belinda, 'of course we can't expect Don't-Care Bobby to care enough for the school, or to have enough pride in her form to do anything that might seem like hard work. Foolish of me to suggest it!'

She walked away and the three stared after her. 'What's bitten *her* this afternoon?' said Bobby, surprised. The twins looked at her uncomfortably.

'Well, Bobby, I suppose it must seem to the top girls that you do just what you like and don't bother about working or playing as hard as you might,' said Pat, at last. 'Mind you, I'm not blaming you, not one bit—I think you're grand as you are—but the top-formers have other ideas about things. You know how good and proper they get as they go up the school. Maybe one day *you*'ll be good and proper too—though I jolly well hope you won't!'

'Don't worry, I shan't,' said Bobby, shortly. She hadn't at all liked what Belinda had said. She wondered if she ought to put in a bit of hard practice at tennis herself, just to please Belinda. But she was obstinate and didn't, though she went on helping the twins all she could, standing at the other end of the court for a long time whilst they served ball after ball across the net, trying to improve their style.

Sadie, Alison, Pam, Prudence, and Carlotta made no pretence at all of trying to better their tennis. They either played because they had to, or because there wasn't anything better to do at the moment. Not one of the five, with the exception of Carlotta, visited the swimming-pool except on the days when it was compulsory to do so. These days came three times a week, and how Prudence and Sadie groaned when they had to go down to the pool and undress themselves, shivering, in the little wooden cubicles that ran alongside the water.

Carlotta was quite mad in the water, for although she could not swim well or fast, she performed all sorts of antics there, and her diving was lovely to watch. Miss Wilton hardly knew what to make of her.

'You'll never make a swimmer, Carlotta,' she said, 'but I shouldn't be surprised if you take all the prizes for your tricks! That was a lovely swallow-dive you did just now. But please don't come down the chute standing up any more. It's dangerous. And also, do try *not* to jump into the water from the top of the diving platform just when Prudence is underneath. You scare her terribly.'

'Oh, Miss Wilton, I wouldn't scare Prudence for worlds!' said Carlotta, in her queer little up-and-down voice, and a wicked look in her eyes. And the very next moment she ran along the marble floor, pretended to slip, and landed with an enormous splash in the water, right on top of the unfortunate Prudence! No one ever knew what Carlotta would do next.

The twins hoped against hope that they would be chosen to play against St. Christopher's. It would be such fun to play together. 'Won't Mummy be pleased if she hears we've both been chosen?' said Pat. 'I wish Bobby could be our reserve girl and come with us. But I bet Janet or Hilary will be chosen.'

The match was to be the following week, and three girls from each of the three lower forms were to go to St. Christopher's School for the matches against girls from similar forms there. Belinda promised to put up the names of the girls on the board the night before.

Before Belinda put up the names, she sent for Bobby. Bobby went to Belinda's study in surprise. The big girl was there, neatly writing out some sports lists.

'Hallo, Bobby,' she said, nodding her head towards a chair. 'Sit down for a minute. I've nearly finished.'

Bobby sat down and studied Belinda's clear-cut profile.

She liked Belinda very much, and knew how hard she worked at being sports captain. She wondered what Belinda was going to say to her.

The sports captain looked up and set down her pen. ' Look here, Bobby,' she said, ' I just want to know something. You're pretty good at tennis, and I'd half-thought of making you reserve girl for your form. But I want to know if you've been thinking about it too, and working for it.'

' No, I haven't,' said Bobby, going red. ' I told you that that would be too much like hard work, Belinda ! Anyway, reserve girls never play in the matches—they only watch—and I don't want to watch ! If I was going to do anything, I'd want to play, not watch ! '

' You're very disappointing,' said Belinda. ' You've got such good stuff in you, Bobby—but you won't seem to make the best of it. I believe if you'd practised as hard as the twins, I'd not have known who to choose for the two match-players ! You put yourself out to let Pat and Isabel practise all they like on you—but yet you won't try to make yourself good too. Don't-Care Bobby is a good name for you—but you won't get far if you don't begin to care about things.'

' I don't want to get far,' said Bobby, her obstinacy rising. ' I've told you, Belinda—I'd like to *play* in the match—but I'm not keen on watching—so choose Janet or Hilary for reserve girl. I don't care ! '

' Very well,' said Belinda, coldly. ' I shall choose one of the others. I was hoping you would be able to tell me you really had done a bit of hard practising on your own account—then I would certainly have chosen you for reserve girl—but seeing that you don't seem to care either way, I shall choose somebody else. You can go.'

Bobby went out of the room, red of cheek, and rather ashamed of herself. She was a queer mixture. She had plenty of brains, plenty of high spirits, plenty of kindliness

—but she seemed to have an incurable dislike of working hard at anything, and if any one tried to make her she became very obstinate and immovable. Belinda felt really impatient with her.

The sports captain made out the list of three girls chosen for the tennis match next day, and went to pin it on the notice-board. A crowd came round her immediately.

' Pat ! Isabel ! You're the two girls ! ' yelled Doris at the top of her voice. ' Who's reserve girl ? Take your fat head out of the way, Prudence ! '

The reserve girl was Janet. She was delighted. She turned to Bobby. ' I thought it would be *you*,' she said. ' You're much better than I am, really. I can't think why Belinda chose me instead of you, Bobby ! '

Bobby knew quite well, but she said nothing. She was cross because she couldn't help feeling ashamed of herself. ' I'm jolly glad it's you, old girl,' she said to Janet. ' Reserve girls never play—we all know that—but you'll have some fun, anyway !'

13   THREE TENNIS MATCHES— AND AN ACCIDENT

THE next day dawned warm and sunny—just right for a tennis match. There was a little breeze, but not enough to worry the players. The match was to start at three o'clock. The nine girls chosen—three from each of the three lower forms—were to go with Belinda and Miss Wilton in a small private bus that the school often used.

Pat and Isabel were in a great state of excitement. They had not played for their school before, and were proud and pleased

'Isn't it lovely that we're to play *together* ? ' said Pat joyfully. ' It would have been horrid if one of us had been chosen and not the other.'

Janet was almost as excited as they were, because although she was only reserve girl and hadn't a chance in a hundred of really playing, still it was great fun to go off in the bus to another school. She and the other two reserve girls would be able to sit with Belinda Towers and Miss Wilton and talk with them whilst the game was on.

' Good luck ! ' said every one, when the little bus drew up to the school door and the tennis players went to get in. ' Good luck ! Mind you win *all* the matches ! We'll give you three hearty cheers when you come back, if you do ! Good luck ! '

Bobby felt a little envious as she saw the happy faces of the twins and Janet smiling in the bus. She knew she herself might have been in that bus if she had really wanted to ! But nobody guessed her thoughts, for she shouted ' Good luck ! ' and waved as wildly as the rest.

It was fun to go driving through the countryside to St. Christopher's like that. The girls fingered the strings of their rackets and looked at them anxiously to make sure they were all tight and good. Their tennis shoes shone as white as snow. Their white frocks were spotless. They all hoped they would make a good showing in the matches against the opposing school.

They arrived at the school, and were met by the sports captain there, a tall graceful girl in white, and by the girls who were to play against them. They all went to the sports ground, chattering hard.

' Our courts badly want a little rain,' said a St. Christopher's girl. ' The service lines are getting very worn. We've hard courts as well as grass ones, but we thought we'd use the grass ones today because they are so much softer to the feet—and also there's more room

round our grass courts for the school to watch. We want
every one to see us giving you St. Clare girls a beating!
You beat us last year, so it's our turn this year!'

Margery Fenworthy was one of the second-formers
chosen, and she was eager to begin. She was wonderful
at all games, and had been practising hard in order to
perfect her tennis style. Her friend, Lucy Oriell, had
been chosen as her partner, and both girls were delighted.
Lucy was inclined to work far too hard, and Margery had
made her take as much recreation as possible—and now,
here was Lucy, her dark curls dancing round her face,
happy at having a whole afternoon away from her
scholarship work.

Jane Rickson and Winnie Hill were the third-formers
chosen. All six St. Clare players changed into their
tennis shoes and took off their cardigans.

'We thought, as you are nice and early, we would
play all three matches separately, instead of at the same
time,' said the St. Christopher's sports captain. 'The
third-formers could play first. Are you ready? Will
you toss for sides, please? Smooth or rough!'

Jane Rickson and Winnie Hill won the toss and chose
the side. The match was to be the best of three sets.
The players took their places. Jane was serving. She
threw the ball high into the air—and the match began!

It was really exciting to watch. The two sets of
partners were very evenly matched, and the games were
very close. Practically all of them ran up to deuce.
The first set was won by St. Clare's, seven–five. The
second one was won by St. Christopher's, six–four.

'And now for the third set!' said Pat, excitedly.
'Gosh, aren't Jane and Winnie playing well, Belinda?
Do you think they'll win?'

'I rather think they will,' said Belinda, smiling at
Pat's eager face. 'The other two seem to me to be
getting a little tired.'

Belinda was right. The St. Christopher girls were not now so fresh as the St. Clare two. All the same the last set was very close and very exciting, and went to five all. Then Janet won her serve straight off. Six-five !

' Play up, Jane and Winnie ! ' yelled the twins. ' Play UP ! '

And they played up ! They skipped about the court, they hit every ball, they smashed the gentle balls and killed the hard ones—and lo and behold, St. Clare's had won the first match, two sets to one !

' Match to St. Clare's, two sets to one,' called the umpire. ' Good game, everybody ! '

St. Christopher's cheered the winners. The girls shook hands across the net, and then went to drink long drinks of sweet lemonade with bits of ice bobbing at the top. How good it tasted !

' Golly, that was a good match,' panted Jane, stretching her long, tired body out over the grass. ' Look— there go the next lot. Play up, Margery. Play up, Lucy ! Belinda, I don't think there's any doubt about *this* match, do you ? I think Margery and Lucy will just wipe the floor with the St. Christopher girls.'

' I shall be very surprised indeed if our two don't win, I must say,' said Belinda. ' I'm jolly pleased *you* two managed to pull it off. There wasn't much in it, you know—but you and Winnie managed to keep a bit fresher. It was fine to see you skipping about like that in the last game. Well done ! '

There was never any doubt at all about the result of the second match. Lucy and Margery had it all their own way. The two girls opposing them were very good indeed—but Margery played a marvellous game. She and Lucy made perfect partners, never leaving any part of the court unprotected. Margery won all her serves outright.

'Golly, she's good,' said Belinda. '*Isn't* she good, Miss Wilton ? '

'Marvellous,' said the St. Clare's sports mistress. ' And how happy she looks too. Quite different from the sulky Margery we had to deal with last term ! '

The twins remembered what a sullen, bad-tempered girl Margery Fenworthy had been the term before, and then how her whole outlook had been changed when she had become a heroine in one night, through rescuing another girl in a fire at the San. Now here was that same Margery, winning honours for her school, as proud of St. Clare's as St. Clare's was proud of her !

The match was over in two sets. 'Match to St. Clare's,' called the umpire, 'won outright in two sets, six–one, six–love.'

'Now it's our turn ! ' said Pat to Isabel, in great excitement, as she watched the second-form girls shaking hands across the net. 'Come on, Isabel. We've just GOT to win ! '

'Play a steady game, twins,' said Belinda. 'You *ought* to win. You play almost as well together as Margery and Lucy. My word, how terribly proud St. Clare's would be of us if we went back to-night, having won all three matches ! We simply MUST ! '

The twins leapt to their feet, and ran on to the tennis court, rackets in hand. 'Call for sides ! ' cried the St. Clare girl, and twisted her racket.

'Rough ! ' called Pat, and 'rough' it was. Pat chose the side, and the four took up their places. Belinda was pleased to see how steady the twins were. They had practised continually together, and were almost as good partners to one another as Margery and Lucy.

They won the first three games, lost one and won another. And then a dreadful thing happened !

Pat was serving. The ball came back to the left-hand side of Isabel and swerved away unexpectedly. The girl

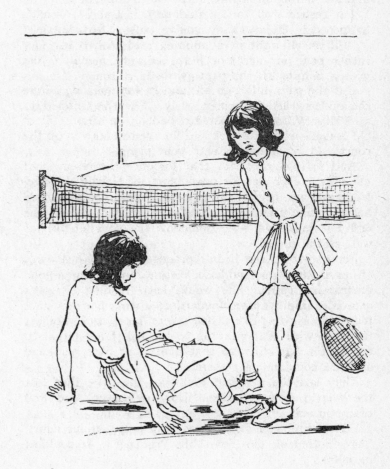

Isabel tried to get up but her ankle gave way

swung herself round to hit it, twisted her ankle and fell over, crashing quite heavily to the ground. She immediately tried to get up but her foot gave way beneath her and she fell again with a surprised cry of pain.

Pat rushed over to her anxiously. ' Isabel ! What's happened ? Oh, *don't* say you've twisted your ankle ! '

' I'll be all right in a minute,' said Isabel, her face rather pale, for her foot hurt her very much. ' Just wait a minute till the pain goes off.'

But the pain didn't go off, and it was not long before the ankle swelled up tremendously. ' You've strained it,' said Miss Wilton. ' Twisted it badly, I'm afraid. Poor old Isabel—what bad luck ! I'll have to take you off the court and get Janet to take your place.'

And so it came about that for once the reserve girl *did* play ! But alas for poor Janet—the sight of Isabel looking so woe-begone and pale quite upset her, and made her thoroughly nervous. She felt that at any costs she and Pat must win—but somehow she couldn't play as well as she hoped.

For one thing she hadn't practised a great deal with either of the twins, and hadn't learnt how to play a good partnership game. She would keep rushing to Pat's court, leaving her own unguarded, so that her opponent found it easy to place a ball where Janet could not get it. And when Pat went up to the net Janet forgot to run to the back-line, so that balls went over her head and she could not get them.

They lost the first set, four–six—and alas, they lost the second, four–six also. They were very sad and disappointed.

' Cheer up,' said Belinda, as they came off the court. ' You both look like Sour-Milk Prudence ! It couldn't be helped.'

' You'd have won if Isabel had been able to play with you,' said Janet to Pat. ' And I believe you'd have won if Bobby had been the reserve girl and not me. Bobby hasn't any nerves at all—she would just have stepped right into Isabel's place, and played magnificently. She always comes up to scratch when she has to. And she's practised with you so often that she knows your game better than I do. She'd have made a much better partner. Belinda, don't *you* think so ? '

' Well,' said Belinda, honestly, ' I agree that Bobby knows Pat's game better than you do—but all the same I'm not sure she'd have won the match.'

But Pat and Isabel, Janet and the others *were* sure ! They talked about it as they ate a good tea, and discussed it in the bus on the way home.

The St. Clare girls were delighted to hear that the third and second form had won their matches, and were sorry over poor Isabel's fall. Her ankle had now gone down a little, and was feeling very much better.

' It will be all right in a day or two,' said Matron, when she examined it. ' Bad luck, Isabel ! Just the wrong time to have a fall, in the middle of a most important match ! '

Isabel smiled wanly. She had been most bitterly disappointed about the whole thing, especially when she had seen Pat lose the match to the St. Clare girls. She poured out her disappointment to Bobby.

' Bobby, I believe Pat would have won if only Belinda had chosen *you* for reserve girl instead of Janet ! ' she said. ' Janet did her best—but she isn't as used to Pat's game as you are. Oh, why didn't Belinda choose *you* ? I do think that was a great mistake on her part. If you'd played in the match Pat and you would have won it, and then St. Clare's would have won all three ! '

Bobby listened in silence. She knew quite well why Belinda hadn't chosen her ! She had been silly and obstinate. She had let St. Clare's down ! She felt sure she wouldn't have been so nervous as Janet, and she *did* know Pat's style of game very well indeed.

She was so silent that Isabel was astonished. ' What's up, Bobby ? ' she said. ' You look awfully glum ? You don't mind as much as all that about the match being lost, do you ? '

' Yes, I do,' said Bobby. ' It wasn't Belinda's fault that Janet was chosen instead of me. Belinda did give me the chance—and I didn't take it. Don't blame Belinda. Blame me. You heard what Belinda said to me on the courts the other day—well I was sore and angry about it, and I just got all obstinate and thought I jolly well wouldn't do what she said and work hard at my tennis.'

' What a pity, Bobby,' said Isabel. ' You could have been reserve girl—and you weren't ! '

' Yes—Belinda sent for me last night,' said poor Bobby. ' I missed my chance—and the match was lost. I don't say I could have won it with Pat any more than Janet could—but I can't get rid of the horrid feeling that I might have—and then think how pleased every one would have been if we'd won all three matches. I thought I didn't care about anything, so long as I had a good time and did what I wanted to. But I find I do care after all ! '

She went off by herself, for once in a way looking unhappy. Poor Bobby ! She wasn't really as don't-carish as she pretended to be !

14   BOBBY AND THE SQUEAKING BISCUIT

THE term went on, passed the half-way mark, and slipped into full summer. It was wonderful weather and the girls thoroughly enjoyed everything—except having to work so hard with Miss Roberts and Mam'zelle !

' Bobby, can't you possibly think of something to stop Mam'zelle making us recite French verbs this morning ? ' said Pat, with a groan. ' I *have* learnt them—but they all slip out of my head this lovely summer weather. Just think of a little tiny trick to take Mam'zelle's attention off verbs for even five minutes.'

' You haven't played a trick on any one for at least a week ! ' said Isabel.

' Bobby's gone all serious,' laughed Janet.

Bobby smiled. She had certainly turned over a new leaf in some ways, for she had suddenly began to practise both her tennis and her swimming very hard indeed. She had swum under water for the whole length of the swimming-pool, and every one had clapped her. She had even tried diving, which as a rule she avoided because she so often dived in flat on her stomach, and hurt herself.

But although she was working hard at games, she still did as little as she possibly could in class. Miss Roberts looked grim sometimes, when she eyed Bobby. She knew quite well that the girl was not using her good brains to the utmost—but as neither sarcastic remarks nor punishments seemed to move Don't-Care Bobby to work harder, the teacher had almost given her up.

The girls around Bobby went on begging her to play some kind of joke on Mam'zelle to make the French class a little easier that day.

' Mam'zelle's in an awful temper this morning,' said Doris. ' The second form said she almost threw the blackboard chalk at Tessie because she sneezed seven times without stopping.'

The twins grinned. They knew Tessie's famous sneezes. It was quite an accomplishment of Tessie's—she had the ability to sneeze most realistically whenever she wanted to. She often used this gift to relieve the second form from boredom. All the teachers suspected that Tessie's sneezes were not at all necessary, but only Miss Jenks knew how to deal with them properly.

'Tessie! Another cold coming!' she would say. 'Go straight to Matron and ask her to give you a dose out of Bottle Number Three, please.'

Bottle No. 3 contained some very nasty-tasting medicine indeed. Tessie could never make up her mind whether it was a concoction specially made up for her, or really was medicine reserved for possible colds. So she used her sneezes rather sparingly in Miss Jenks's presence —but gave Mam'zelle the full benefit of them whenever she could.

This particular morning she had given seven very explosive sneezes, making Mam'zelle nearly jump out of her skin, and reducing the class to a state of helpless giggling. Mam'zelle had been very angry—and all the other classes expecting her to teach them that morning knew they would be in for a bad time.

'If you don't think of some trick or other to play, Mam'zelle will keep our noses to the grindstone every minute of the lesson,' groaned Doris. 'For goodness' sake think of something, Bobby.'

'I can't,' said Bobby, thinking hard. 'At least, I can't think of anything that Mam'zelle wouldn't know was a trick today. Oh—wait a minute though!'

The girls stared at Bobby expectantly. She turned to Janet. 'Where's that squeaking biscuit your brother sent you?' she asked.

Janet had a brother who was every bit as bad as Bobby

and Janet where tricks were concerned. He had sent
Janet a selection of jokes that week, and among them was
a very realistic biscuit, which, on being pressed between
finger and thumb, squeaked loudly, rather like a cat.
The girls had not thought that it was a very good trick.

'Rather babyish,' said Janet. 'Not a very good
selection this time!'

But now Bobby had thought of some way to use the
biscuit. Janet fished it out of her desk and gave it to
her.

'Here you are,' she said. 'What are you going to do
with it?'

Bobby pressed the biscuit slowly. It gave a pathetic
squeaking sound. 'Doesn't it sound like a kitten?' she
said with a grin. 'Now listen, everybody. The school
cat has kittens, as you know. Well, when Mam'zelle
comes into our classroom, she's going to find us talking
about a lost kitten. We'll be very disturbed about it.
And then, in the middle of the class, I press this biscuit—
and Mam'zelle will think the lost kitten is somewhere in
our room.'

Hilary chuckled. 'That's a good idea,' she said.
'And I know how we could improve on it too. I'll be
outside in the passage, crawling about on my hands and
knees, looking for the lost kitten, when Mam'zelle comes
along to our room. I can tell her what I'm looking
for.'

'Oooh yes,' said Pat, looking thrilled. Hilary was
very good at acting. 'Golly, we're going to have some
fun!'

'Well, what happens in class *after* I've squeaked the
biscuit will depend on all of you,' said Bobby. 'Look—
there's Prudence coming. Don't tell her a word about
it. You know what a sneak she is!'

The first form longed for the French lesson to come.
They winked at one another whenever they thought of it.

Miss Roberts caught one or two of the winks and pounced
on the winkers.

'What is the joke, Hilary?' she asked coldly.

'There isn't a joke, Miss Roberts,' answered Hilary,
opening her eyes wide as if astonished.

'Well, there had better *not* be,' said Miss Roberts.
'Go on with your geography map, please.'

Mam'zelle gave her French lesson after break. The
girls went to their room quickly when break was over,
giggling in delight. Prudence could not think why.
Pam was not in the secret either, but she did not notice
the chuckles of the girls. Pam was getting very much
wrapped up in her own thoughts these days.

Hilary was left outside. The twins popped their heads
out of the door and doubled themselves up with laughter
when they saw Hilary on hands and knees, looking under
a tall cupboard there, calling 'Kitty, kitty, kitty!'

'Sh! Here comes Mam'zelle!' suddenly cried Pat to
the class. She darted back to her seat, leaving Isabel
to hold the door for Mam'zelle. Hilary was still outside,
of course.

Mam'zelle came hurrying along on her big feet. Every
one always knew when Mam'zelle came, because she wore
big, flat-heeled shoes like a man's, and made a loud clip-
clap noise down the corridors.

Mam'zelle was most surprised to see Hilary crawling
about outside the classroom. She stopped and stared.

'Hilary, *ma petite! Que faites-vous?*' she cried.
'What are you doing there? Have you lost something?'

'Kitty, kitty, kitty!' called Hilary. 'Mam'zelle, you
haven't seen one of the school cat's kittens by any chance,
have you? I'm looking and looking for the poor little
lost thing.'

Mam'zelle looked up and down the passage. 'No, I
have seen no little cat,' she said. 'Hilary, you must

come to your class now.   It is good of you to seek for the tiny cat, but it is not to be found.'

'Oh, Mam'zelle, just let me look a little longer,' begged Hilary.   'It might be in this cupboard.   I thought I heard a sound.'

She opened the cupboard.   The girls in the classroom, hearing the sound of conversation outside, wondered how Hilary was getting on.   Isabel peeped out to see.

'Have you found the poor little kitten, Hilary?' she called.   'Oh, Mam'zelle, isn't it a shame?   It will be so frightened.'

Mam'zelle marched into the classroom and put her books down on her desk.   'The little cat will be found somewhere,' she said.   'Go to your places.   Hilary, for the last time I tell you to stop looking for the tiny cat and come to your French class.'

'Oh, Mam'zelle,' said Bobby, as Hilary came in and shut the door, 'do you think it has climbed up a chimney or something like that?   I once knew a cat that got up our chimney at home, and arrived on the top of a chimney-pot!'

'And Mam'zelle, *we* had a kitten once that . . .' began Doris, quick to follow up and waste a few more minutes of the class.   But Mam'zelle was not having any more fairy-tales about cats.   She rapped on her desk, and Doris stopped her tale.

'*Assez!*' said Mam'zelle, beginning to frown.   'That is quite enough, Hilary, *will* you sit down?   You surely do not imagine that the kitten is anywhere here?'

'Well, Mam'zelle, it *might* be,' said Hilary, looking all round.   'You know, my brother once had a cat that . . .'

'Any more tales about cats and the whole class will write me out two pages in French on the habits of the cat-family,' threatened Mam'zelle.   At this threat every one remained silent.   Mam'zelle had a horrid way of carrying out her curious threats.

' Get out your grammar books,' said Mam'zelle. ' Open at page eighty-seven. Today we will devote the whole time to irregular verbs. Doris, you will begin.'

Doris gave a groan. She stood up to recite the verbs she had learnt. Poor Doris ! No matter how much time she gave to her French preparation, every bit of it invariably went out of her head when she looked at Mam'zelle's expectant face. She began, in a halting voice.

' Doris, again you have not prepared your work properly,' said Mam'zelle, irritably. ' You will do it again. Pat, stand up. I hope you will give a better performance than Doris. You at least know how to roll your r's in the French way. R-r-r-r-r-r ! '

The class giggled. Mam'zelle always sounded exactly as if she were growling like a dog when she rolled her r-r-r-r's in her throat. Mam'zelle rapped on her desk.

' Silence ! Pat, begin.'

But before Pat could begin, Bobby pressed the trick-biscuit slowly and carefully between finger and thumb. A piteous squeak sounded somewhere in the room. Every one looked up.

' The kitten ! ' said Pat, stopping her recital of verbs. ' The kitten ! '

Even Mam'zelle listened. The squeak had been so very much like a kitten in trouble. Bobby waited until Pat had begun her verbs again, and then she once more pressed the biscuit.

' EEEeeeeeeeee ! ' squeaked the biscuit, exactly like a cat. Pat stopped again and looked all round the room. Mam'zelle was puzzled.

Where *is* the poor little creature ? ' said Kathleen. ' Oh, Mam'zelle—where can it be ? '

' Mam'zelle, I'm pretty certain it must be up the chimney,' said Hilary, jumping up as if she was going to see.

' *Asseyez-vous*, Hilary ! ' rapped out Mam'zelle. ' You have looked enough for the little cat. Pat, continue.'

Pat began again, Bobby let her recite her verbs until she made a mistake—and then, before Mam'zelle could pounce on her mistake, Bobby pressed the biscuit once more.

A loud wail interrupted the recital of verbs. A babel of voices arose.

' Mam'zelle, the cat must be in the room ! '

' Mam'zelle, do let's look for the poor little thing.'

' Mam'zelle, perhaps it's HURT ! '

Bobby made the biscuit wail again. Mam'zelle rapped on her desk in despair.

' Sit still, please. I will see if the little cat is up the chimney.'

She left her desk and went to the fireplace. She bent down and tried to look up the chimney. Bobby pressed the biscuit softly and made a very small mew come. Mam'zelle half-thought it came from up the chimney-place. She got a ruler and felt about there.

A shower of soot came down, and Mam'zelle jumped back, her hand covered with soot. The class began to giggle.

' Mam'zelle, perhaps the cat's in the cupboard,' suggested Janet. ' Do let me look. I'm sure it's there.'

Mam'zelle was glad to leave the chimney. She gazed in dismay at her sooty hand.

' Hilary, open the cupboard,' she said at last. Hilary leapt to open it. Of course there was no animal there at all, but Hilary rummaged violently over the shelves, sending books and handwork material on the floor.

' Hilary ! Is it necessary to do this ! ' cried Mam'zelle, beginning to lose her temper again. ' I begin to disbelieve in this cat. But I warn you, if it is a trick, I will punish you all with a terrible punishment. I go now to wash my hands. You will all learn the verbs on page eighty-

Mam'zelle jumped back as a shower of soot fell at her feet

eight while I am gone.   You will not talk.   You are bad
children.'

Mam'zelle disappeared out of the room, holding her
sooty hand before her.   When the door shut, a gale of
laughter burst out.   Bobby squeaked the biscuit for all
she was worth.   Prudence stared in surprise at it.   As no
one had let her into the secret, she really had believed in
the tale of the lost kitten.   She looked at Bobby with
a sour face.   So Bobby had once more got away with
a trick.   How Prudence wished she could give her away
to Mam'zelle !

'Well, wasn't that fine ? ' said Bobby, putting the
biscuit into her pocket.   'Half the lesson gone, and
hardly any one has had to say their verbs.   Good old
biscuit !   You can tell your brother it was a success,
Janet ! '

When Mam'zelle came back she was in one of her black
tempers.   She had felt sure, as she washed her hands,
that there had been some trick about the lost kitten, but
she could not for the life of her imagine what it was.
She washed her hands grimly and stalked back to the first
form, determined to get her own back somehow.

She chose Prudence to say her verbs next.   Prudence
stood up.   She was bad at French, and she faltered over
her verbs, trying in vain to get them right.

'Prrrrrudence!   You are even more stupid than
Dorrrris ! ' cried Mam'zelle, rolling her r's in her fiercest
manner.   'Ah, this first-form !   You have learnt nothing
this term !   NOTHING, I say.   Ahhhhhh !   Tomorrow I
will give you a test.   A test to see what you have learnt.
Prudence, do not stare at me like a duck that is dying !
You and Doris are bad girls.   You will not work for me.
If you do not get more than half-marks tomorrow I
shall go and complain to Miss Theobald.   Ah, this first
form ! '

The girls listened in horror.   A French test !   Of all the things they hated, a French test was the worst. The girls always felt certain that Mam'zelle chose questions that hardly anyone could possibly answer !

Prudence sat down, hating Mam'zelle. She knew she would do badly in the test. She had cribbed most of her written work from Pam—but in a test she would have to rely on her own knowledge—unless she could copy Pam's answers.

The girl sat and brooded. If it hadn't been for Bobby's trick, Mam'zelle wouldn't have lost her temper and suggested a beastly, horrible test ! How Prudence wished she could find some way to get out of it. If only she could—or better still, if only she could know what the test questions were to be, so that she might look up the answers first !

15   PRUDENCE IS A CHEAT

THE more Prudence thought about the French test, the angrier she felt with Bobby. ' I suppose she thinks those silly tricks of hers are clever ! ' thought Prudence to herself. ' And now look what they've led to—a horrible French test that I know I shall fail hopelessly in. Then I shall get into a frightful row and perhaps be sent down to Miss Theobald ! '

She went to find Pam to talk to her about it. She felt sure Pam would be in the library, hunting for some learned book or other to read. On the way there she passed the open door of the Mistresses' common room. Prudence glanced in.

Mam'zelle was there alone. She was writing out what looked like a list of questions. Prudence felt certain they were the questions for the test. How she longed to have a look at them!

She stood at the door uncertainly, trying to think of some excuse to go in. Mam'zelle saw her shadow there and glanced up.

'Ah, Prudence!' she said, in rather a fierce voice. 'Ah! Tomorrow you will have this French test, yes? I will show you first-formers what hard work really means!'

Prudence made up her mind quickly. She would go into the common room, and tell Mam'zelle about the trick —and perhaps she would be able to get a peep at the questions on Mam'zelle's desk! So in she went, looking the picture of wide-eyed innocence and goodness.

'Mam'zelle! I'm awfully sorry we played about so much in your class,' she began. 'It was all that silly trick, you know—the squeaking biscuit.'

Mam'zelle stared at Prudence as if the girl had suddenly gone mad.

'The squeaking biscuit?' said Mam'zelle, in the greatest astonishment. 'What is this nonsense you are saying?'

'Mam'zelle, it isn't nonsense,' said Prudence. 'You see, Bobby had a trick biscuit that squeaked like a cat when it was pressed . . .'

Prudence was doing her best to get a look at the French questions as she spoke. Apparently Mam'zelle had finished making them out. There were about twelve questions. Prudence managed to read the first one.

Mam'zelle listened to what Prudence was saying, and at once knew two things—the true explanation of the lost kitten—and that Prudence was what the English girls called 'sneaking'. Mam'zelle had been in England a long time and had learnt to regard sneaking with dislike, although when she had first arrived she had listened to tale-bearers and thought nothing of it. But through

long years of being with English mistresses she had come
to the conclusion that they were right about 'sneaks'.
On no account must they be encouraged.

So Mam'zelle's face suddenly changed, and became
hard and cold as Prudence went on speaking.

'And Bobby thought it would be a good idea if we
wasted some of your lesson by pretending that a kitten
was lost . . .' she went on. Then she stopped as she saw
Mam'zelle's face.

'Prudence, you are a nasty little girl,' said Mam'zelle.
Yes—a very nasty little girl. I do not like you. It
may seem surprising to you—but I would rather have a
silly trick played on me than listen to some one who sneaks
about it I Go away at once. I do not like you at all.'

Prudence felt her face flame red. She was angry and
hurt—and she hadn't been able to read more than one
test question after all I Mam'zelle took up the paper and
slipped it inside her desk, taking no more notice of
Prudence. The girl went out of the room, ready to burst
into angry tears.

'Well, I know *where* the questions are, anyway,' she
thought, fiercely. 'I've a good mind to slip out of bed
at night and have a look at them. Nobody would know.
And I'd have a good chan. of being top, then, and
giving every one a surprise I I'd love to see their faces
if I got top marks I '

The more she thought about it, the more determined
she became. 'I *will* get those questions somehow I ' she
decided. 'I don't care what happens—I will I '

She wondered if Mam'zelle would punish Bobby for the
trick she had played, but to her surprise not a word was
said about it that day, though Mam'zelle took prep and
even had Bobby up to her desk to explain something to
her.

'I wonder she doesn't send Bobby to Miss Theobald,'
thought the girl, spitefully.

Mam'zelle's sense of humour had come to her rescue after Prudence had left the common room that morning. She had felt angry with Bobby first of all—and then when she thought of herself poking up the chimney to find a kitten that wasn't there, she had begun to laugh. That was one very good thing about Mam'zelle—she really did have a sense of humour, and when she thought something was funny, she could laugh at it whole-heartedly and forget her annoyance. So her anger against the first-formers melted away—though she was determined to give them the test, all the same.

She could not, however, resist giving Bobby a little shock. When the girl came up to her desk at prep Mam'zelle made a remark that caused Bobby to feel most uncomfortable.

' Do you like biscuits, Bobby ? ' she asked, her large brown eyes looking at Bobby through their glasses.

' Er—er—yes, Mam'zelle,' said Bobby, wondering what was coming next.

' I thought so,' said Mam'zelle, and then turned to Bobby's French book. Bobby did not dare to ask her what she meant, but she felt certain that Mam'zelle had found out about her trick. Who could have told her ? Prudence, of course ! Nasty little sneak ! Bobby waited for Mam'zelle to say something more, and it was with great relief that she found Mam'zelle speaking about her French mistakes.

' Now you may go to your place,' said Mam'zelle. She gave Bobby a sharp look. ' You may like to know that I do not like biscuits as much as you do, *ma chère* Bobby ! '

' No, Mam'zelle—er, I mean, yes, Mam'zelle,' said poor Bobby, and escaped to her seat as quickly as she could. ' If Mam'zelle *does* know what I did and isn't going to punish me, it's jolly decent of her,' thought the girl. ' I'll work really hard in her classes if she's as decent as all that ! '

That night, when all the girls in her dormitory were asleep, Prudence sat up in bed. She listened to the steady breathing of the sleepers around her, and then slipped out of bed. It was very warm, and she did not put on her dressing-gown or slippers. She crept out of the room in her bare feet and went down the stairs to the mistresses' common room. It was in complete darkness. Prudence had brought a torch with her, and she switched it on to see where Mam'zelle's desk was. Good—there it was, just in front of her.

' Now I can just go all through the test questions, and look up the answers ! ' thought Prudence, gleefully. ' It's lucky nobody waked up and saw me leaving the dormitory.'

But somebody *had* seen her leaving the dormitory !

That somebody was Carlotta, who always slept very lightly indeed, waking at the least sound. She had heard the click of the door being opened, and had sat up at once. She dimly saw a figure vanishing through the doorway, and wondered who it was. Perhaps it was some one from the next dormitory. She decided to go and see. Sometimes a girl from another dormitory was dared to slip into some one else's room at night and play some kind of joke.

Carlotta slipped out of bed. She went to the dormitory where Bobby, Pam, Doris, and others slept. She popped her head inside. All was quiet—but one girl was awake. It was Bobby. She saw the door opening, and the dim light from the passage came into the room, showing up the figure at the door.

' Who's there ? ' whispered Bobby.

' Me,' said Carlotta. ' I saw somebody slipping out of our dormitory and I thought it might be some one from yours, playing a joke.'

' Well, we're all here,' said Bobby, looking down the

line of beds. ' Are you sure it wasn't somebody out of your *own* room ? '

' Never thought of that,' whispered back Carlotta. ' I'll go and see.' She went and found that Prudence's bed was empty. She slipped back again to Bobby and went to her bed.

' Prudence is gone,' she whispered. ' What do you think she's doing ? I bet she's up to some mischief, don't you ? '

' Well, let's go and see,' said Bobby, and slid quietly out of bed. Together the two made their way down the passage, and then down the stairs. They stood and listened at the bottom, wondering where Prudence was.

' There's a light coming from the mistresses' common room,' whispered Carlotta. ' Perhaps she is in there. What *can* she be doing ? '

' I'm not sure I quite like spying like this,' said Bobby, a little uncomfortably. But Carlotta had no doubts of that sort. She went quietly on bare feet to the half-open door of the common room. She looked in—and there she saw Prudence carefully reading the list of French test questions, a French grammar book beside her. She was looking up the answers one by one.

Both girls knew at once what she was doing. Bobby had very strict ideas of honour and she was really horrified and shocked. Carlotta was not shocked, because she had seen many odd things in her life—also she knew Prudence well and was not at all surprised to find her cheating in such an outrageous way.

Bobby went into the room at once, and Prudence was so startled that she dropped the grammar book on the floor. She stared at Bobby and Carlotta with horror.

' What are you doing ? ' said Bobby, so angry that she forgot to whisper. ' Cheating ? '

' No, I'm not,' said Prudence, making up her mind to brazen it out. ' I just came to look something up in the

French grammar book, ready for the test tomorrow. So there ! '

Carlotta darted to the desk and picked up the list of questions. ' See, Bobby,' she cried. ' She *is* cheating ! Here are the test questions.'

Bobby looked at Prudence with the utmost scorn. ' What a hypocrite you are, Prudence ! ' she said. ' You go about pretending to be so good and religious and proper—and yet you sneak and cheat whenever you get a chance. You look down on Carlotta because she was a circus-girl—but I tell you, *we* look down on *you* because you are all the things people hate worse than any other in school, or in life—you are cunning, deceitful, untruthful —and an out-an-out cheat ! '

These were terrible things to hear. Prudence burst out sobbing, and put her head down on the desk. A pile of books upset and fell with thuds to the floor. Nobody noticed the noise they made, for all three girls were too wrapped up in what was happening.

It so happened that Miss Theobald's bedroom was just below the mistresses' common room. She heard the succession of thuds and wondered what the noise could be. She thought she heard the sound of voices too. She switched on her light and looked at her watch. It was a quarter-past two ! Whoever could be up at that time of night ?

Miss Theobald put on her dressing-gown, tied the girdle firmly round her waist, put on her slippers, and left the room. She went upstairs to the corridor that led to the mistresses' common room. She arrived at the door just in time to hear the end of Bobby's scornful speech. She paused in the greatest astonishment. Whatever could be happening ?

16 MISS THEOBALD DEALS WITH THREE GIRLS

'GIRLS,' said Miss Theobald, in her clear low voice. 'Girls! What are you doing here?'

There was a petrified silence as all three girls saw the Head Mistress standing at the door. A cold chill came over Prudence's heart, and Bobby had the shock of her life. Only Carlotta seemed undisturbed.

'Well?' said Miss Theobald, going into the room, and shutting the door. 'I really think some explanation of this scene is needed. Roberta, surely you can explain?'

'Yes, I can,' blurted out Bobby. 'Surely you can guess what Carlotta and I discovered Prudence doing, Miss Theobald?'

'She is cheating,' said Carlotta, in her little foreign-sounding voice. 'She is looking at the French test questions and finding the answers, Miss Theobald, so that she will be top tomorrow. But it is nothing surprising. Prudence is like that.'

Prudence broke out into loud sobbing again.

'I wasn't, I wasn't,' she wailed. 'Carlotta only says that because I found out she was nothing but a circus-girl. I hate her! I hate Bobby too—but Carlotta is the worst of the lot, always showing off and bragging about her circus-life.'

Carlotta laughed. 'I am glad you hate me, Prudence,' she said. 'I would not care to be liked by you! You are worse than any one I have ever met in circus-camps. Much worse!'

'Be quiet, Carlotta,' said Miss Theobald. She was very worried. This was a dreadful thing to happen. 'Go back to bed, all of you. I will deal with this in the morning. Is Prudence in the same dormitory as you two?'

' No, she's in mine, but not in Bobby's,' said Carlotta.

' Well—go back, all of you,' said Miss Theobald. ' If I hear another sound tonight, I shall treat the matter even more seriously tomorrow.'

She watched the three girls go back to their dormitories, and then went to her own room, wondering how to deal with things in the best way. Had she done right in letting Carlotta, the little circus-girl, come to St. Clare's ? She might have known that the secret wouldn't be kept ! And now there was Prudence Arnold to deal with—Miss Theobald could not like the girl any more than any one else did. And Roberta—what should she say to her ? She had had bad reports of her work from every one !

The three girls went back to their beds. Carlotta fell asleep again at once. She rarely worried about anything and she did not feel any cause to be upset. Bobby lay and thought for a long time. She disliked and despised Prudence—but she did not want the girl to get into serious trouble because of her.

Prudence was the most upset of the three. It was a very serious matter to be caught cheating. She had always set herself up to be such a model—so honest and straight and had always condemned underhand, mean, or silly tricks. Now every one would know she was not what she seemed. And it was all because of that hateful interfering Bobby and Carlotta. She felt a great surge of bitterness against Carlotta, who had so calmly told Miss Theobald what the two girls had found her doing. Prudence did not realize that practically every girl had seen through her silly pretences and had set her down as a smug hypocrite and sneak.

Next day the three girls were called into Miss Theobald's room one by one. First Carlotta, who told Miss Theobald again, quite calmly and straightforwardly, what they had found Prudence doing, and also added a few remarks of her own about Prudence.

'She looks down on me because I was a circus-girl,' said Carlotta, 'but Miss Theobald, no circus would keep a person like Prudence for more than a week. I think she is a dangerous girl.'

Miss Theobald said nothing to this but in her heart she agreed with Carlotta. Prudence was dangerous. She would do no good to St. Clare's, and privately Miss Theobald doubted if St. Clare's would do much good for Prudence. She prided herself on the knowledge that it was very few girls indeed that St. Clare's would not benefit— but it seemed to her as if Prudence was one of those few. She was the only child of doting, indulging parents, who believed that Prudence was all she seemed. Poor Prudence ! What a pity her father and mother hadn't been sensible with her, and punished her when she did wrong, instead of getting upset and begging her to do better !

Miss Theobald had Bobby in next. Bobby did not want to say much about Prudence, and she was surprised to find that Miss Theobald looked at her coldly, and did not give her even a small smile when she came in.

'It is an unpleasant thing to find any one in the act of cheating,' said Miss Theobald, looking straight at Bobby. 'I expect you hate the idea of cheating almost worse than anything else, Roberta.'

'Yes, Miss Theobald,' said Bobby, who was an honest and truthful girl, in spite of all the tricks she played. 'I think cheating is horrible. I'd just hate myself if I cheated like Prudence.'

Then Miss Theobald said a surprising thing. 'It is odd to me, Roberta,' she said, 'that you, who seem to have such strict ideas about cheating, should be such a cheat yourself.'

Bobby stared at Miss Theobald as if she couldn't believe her ears. 'What did you say, Miss Theobald ?' she asked at last, 'I think I didn't hear it correctly.'

'Yes, you did, Roberta,' said Miss Theobald. 'I said

that it was odd that *you* should be a cheat, when you hold such strict ideas about cheating.'

'I'm not a cheat,' said Bobby, her cheeks crimson, and her eyes beginning to sparkle with anger and surprise. 'I've never cheated in my life.'

'I don't know about *all* your life,' said the Head Mistress, 'but I do know about the last two months of it, Roberta. Why have your parents sent you here? To have a good time and nothing but a good time? Why are they paying high fees for you? In order to let you slack and play tricks the whole time? You *are* cheating, Roberta—yes, cheating badly. You are cheating your parents, who are willing to pay for you to learn what we can teach you here—and you won't learn. You are cheating the school, for you have good brains and could do well for St. Clare's—but you won't try. And last of all you are cheating yourself—depriving yourself of all the benefits that hard work, well done, can bring you, and you are weakening your character instead of making it strong and fine, because you will not accept duty and responsibility. You just want to go your own way, do as little work as you can, and make yourself popular by being amusing and thinking out ingenious jokes and tricks to entertain your form. I think, in your own way, you are just as much a cheat as Prudence is.'

Bobby's face went white. No one had ever said anything like this to her before. She had always been popular with girls and teachers alike—but here was the Head Mistress pointing out cold and horrid truths that Bobby had never even thought of before. It was dreadful.

The girl sat quite still and said nothing at all. 'You had better go now, Roberta,' said Miss Theobald. 'I would like you to think over what I have said and see if your sense of honesty is as high as you think it to be—if it is you will admit to yourself that I am right, and perhaps I shall then get good reports of you.'

Bobby stood up, still white. She mumbled something to Miss Theobald and went out of the room as if she was in a dream. She had had a real shock. It had never before occurred to Bobby that it was possible to cheat in many more ways than the ordinary one.

Prudence was the last of the three called before the Head Mistress. She was likely to be the most difficult to deal with. Miss Theobald decided that plain speaking was the best. Prudence must know exactly how she stood—and make her own choice.

The girl came in, looking rather frightened. She tried to look Miss Theobald straight in the eyes but could not. The Head told her to sit down, and then looked just as coldly at her as she had looked at Bobby.

'Please, Miss Theobald,' began Prudence, who always believed in getting a word in first, ' please don't think the worst of me.'

'Well, I *do* think the worst of you,' said the Head Mistress at once. ' The very worst. And unfortunately I know it to be true. Prudence, I know the character of every girl in this school. It is my business to know it. I may not know what type of brain you have, I may not know exactly where you stand in class, or what your gifts and capabilities are, without referring to your form-mistress—but at any rate I know your characters—the good and bad in you, the possibilities in your nature, your tendencies, your faults, your virtues. These I know very well. And therefore I know all too clearly, Prudence, what you really are.'

Prudence burst into tears. She often found this useful when people were what she called ' being unkind ' to her. The tears had no effect at all on Miss Theobald. She stared at Prudence all the more coldly.

' Cry if you wish,' she said, ' but I would think more of you if you faced up to me and listened with a little courage. I need not tell you what you are, Prudence.

I need not show you the dishonesty, deceitfulness and spite in your own nature. You are clever enough to know them yourself—and alas, cunning enough to use them, and to hide them too. St. Clare's, Prudence, has nothing to offer a girl like you—unless you have enough courage to face up to yourself, and try to tear out the unpleasant failings that are spoiling and weakening what character you have. I do not want to keep you at St. Clare's unless you can do this. Think it over and face things out honestly with yourself. I give you to the end of the term to make up your mind. Otherwise, Prudence, I will not keep you here.'

This was actually the only kind of treatment that Prudence really understood. She stared in horror at Miss Theobald.

' But—but—what would my father and mother say ? ' she half-whispered.

'That rests with you,' said the Head. 'Now go, please. I am busy this morning, and have already wasted too much time on you and the others.'

Prudence went out of the room, as shocked and horrified as poor Bobby had been a few minutes earlier. She had to get her books and go to her form for a lesson, but she heard practically nothing of what Miss Lewis, the history teacher, was saying. Bobby heard very little too. Both girls were busy with their own thoughts.

After school that morning, Bobby disappeared. Pat and Isabel saw her running off in the direction of the tennis court.

' Doesn't she look white ? ' said Pat. ' I wonder if anything's up ? '

' Let's go and see,' said Isabel. So they went to find Bobby. She was nowhere on the courts—but Pat caught sight of the white blouse and navy skirt in a little copse of trees by the courts. She ran up to see if Bobby was there.

' Bobby, what's up ? ' she cried, for it was quite plain

to see that Bobby was in trouble. Her usually merry face, with its sparkling eyes, was white and drawn.

' Go away, please,' said Bobby, in a tight sort of voice. ' I want to think. I—I—I've been accused of cheating —and—I've got to think about it.'

' *You !* You, accused of cheating ! ' cried Pat, in angry amazement. ' What rot ! Who dared to do that ? You tell me, and I'll go and tell them what I think of them.'

' It was Miss Theobald,' said Bobby, lifting her troubled face and looking at the twins.

' Miss *Theobald* ! ' said the twins, in the greatest astonishment. ' But why ? How awful of her ! We'll go and tell her she's wrong.'

' Well—she's not wrong,' said Bobby. ' I see she's right. She said I was a cheat because I let my parents pay high fees for me to learn what St. Clare's could teach —and I wasted my time and wouldn't work—and that was cheating, because I've got good brains. She said I was cheating my parents—and the school—and myself too. It was—simply awful.'

The twins stared uncomfortably at Bobby. They couldn't think of a word to say. Bobby motioned to them to go away.

' Go away, please,' she said. ' I've got to think this out. I simply must. It's—it's somehow very important. I do play the fool a lot—but I'm not such an idiot as not to see that I've come to a sort of—sort of—cross-roads in my life. I've got to choose which way I'll go. And I've got to choose by myself. So leave me alone for a bit, will you ? '

' Of course, Bobby,' said Pat, understanding. She and Isabel ran off, admiring Bobby for her ability to face herself, and make up her own mind what she was going to do.

And there was no doubt as to what Bobby was going to

do. Her tremendous sense of honesty and fairness made her see at once that Miss Theobald was perfectly right. She had been given good brains, and she was wasting them. That was cheating. She had good parents who wanted her to go to a fine school and learn from good teachers. She was cheating them too. And perhaps worst of all she was cheating herself, and growing into a weaker and poorer character than she needed to be—and the world wanted fine, strong characters, able to help others on—not poor, weak, don't-care people who themselves needed to be helped all the time.

'I badly want to be the sort of person who can lead others, and guide them,' thought Bobby, pulling at the grass, as she sat thinking. 'I want others to lean on me—not me on them. Well—I've had my fun. Now I'll work. I'll just show Miss Roberts what I really can do when I make up my mind. I've already shown Belinda and Miss Wilton what I can do at sports when I try. I'll go straight to Miss Theobald and tell her now. I—I don't feel as if I like her very much now—she had such cold, angry eyes when she looked at me. But I'd better go and tell her—I'll get it off my chest and make a fresh start.'

Poor Bobby felt nervous as she ran back to the school. Miss Theobald had given her a real shock, and she dreaded seeing her again, and felt half-frightened as she thought of looking into the Head Mistress's scornful eyes. But Bobby had courage, and she was soon knocking at Miss Theobald's door.

'Come in,' said a calm voice, and Bobby went in. She went straight to the Head Mistress's desk.

'Miss Theobald,' she said, 'I've come to say I know you were right. I *have* been cheating—and I didn't realize it. But—I'm not going to cheat any more. Please believe me. I really do mean what I say, and you can trust me to—to do my very best from today.'

Bobby said this bravely, looking straight at Miss Theobald as she spoke.   Her voice trembled a little, but she said her little speech right to the end.

Miss Theobald smiled her rare, sweet smile, and her eyes became warm and admiring.   ' My dear child,' she said, and her voice was warm too, ' my dear child, I knew quite well that you would make this decision, and that you would soon come to tell me.   I am proud of you—and I am going to be even more proud of you in the future.   You are honest enough by nature to be able to see and judge your own self clearly—and that is a great thing.   Never lose that honesty, Bobby—always be honest with yourself, know your own motives for what they are, good or bad, make your own decisions firmly and justly—and you will be a fine, strong character, of some real use in this muddled world of ours ! '

' I'll try, Miss Theobald,' said Bobby, happily, so glad to see the warmth and friendliness in the Head's face that she felt she could work twelve hours a day if necessary ! How could she have thought she didn't like Miss Theobald ?   How *could* she ?

' She's one of the finest people I've ever met,' thought the girl, as she left the room with a light step.   ' No wonder she's head of a great school like St. Clare's !   We are jolly lucky to have her.'

Miss Theobald was happy too.   Bobby had pleased her beyond measure.   It was good to feel that she had been successful in handling an obstinate character like Bobby's —now she might hope that the girl would have a splendid influence on the others, instead of the opposite.

' If I could only hope that Prudence would have the same kind of courage as Bobby ! ' thought the head. ' But Prudence, I'm afraid, is not brave enough to face up to herself.   That's her only chance—but I don't believe she will take it ! '

WHILST Bobby was thinking out things for herself, and making her big decision, Prudence was also brooding over all that Miss Theobald had said.   Mixed up with her brooding was a hatred of Carlotta, who seemed to be at the bottom of Prudence's troubles.   Prudence could not see that it was her own jealousy of the girl that caused her troubles, filling her with ideas of spite and revenge. No one can ever see things clearly when jealousy or envy cast a fog over the mind.

Prudence felt that she had to get right with Miss Theobald.   The girl could never bear to feel that any one was despising her.   But she had not got Bobby's courage —she dared not face the head again.   Also, in her heart of hearts she was afraid that Miss Theobald would see that her repentance was not real—that it was only to make things more comfortable !

So Prudence wrote a note, and slipped it on Miss Theobald's desk, when she knew she was not in her room. The head found it there and opened it.   She read it and sighed.   She did not believe one word of the letter.

' Dear Miss Theobald,' Prudence had written, ' I have thought over what you said to me, and I do assure you I am sorry and ashamed, and I will do my best in future to turn over a new leaf and have a good influence on others.'

' Little humbug ! ' thought Miss Theobald, sadly.   ' I suppose she really believes she *is* going to turn over a new leaf.   Well—we shall see ! '

Pat and Isabel were glad to see that Bobby looked happier that evening.   She smiled at them, and her old merry twinkle came back.

' I'm all right again,' she said.   ' But from now on

I'm going to play fair—I'm going to use my brains and work. No more squeaking biscuits for *me* ! '

The twins and Janet looked sorry. ' Oh,' said Pat in disappointment, ' Bobby—you don't mean to say you're going to go all prim and proper like that awful Prudence —never make another joke or play another trick ? '

' Golly ! ' said Janet, ' I couldn't bear that, Bobby. For pity's sake, tell us you're going to be the same jolly old Bobby—the Don't-Care Bobby we all like so much ! '

Bobby laughed and slipped her arm through Janet's. ' Don't worry,' she said. ' I *am* going to play the game now and work hard—but I shan't go all prim and proper. I couldn't. I shall be playing tricks all right—but I don't particularly want to be Don't-Care Bobby any more. I *do* care now, you see ! '

Bobby kept her word to Miss Theobald, of course. She worked hard and steadily in class, and was surprised to find how well her mind worked when she really set it to something—and she was even more surprised to find how enjoyable good work was !

' I should never be able to slave at my lessons like you do though, Pam,' she said, looking at the thirteen-year-old girl hunched over a book. ' You're looking awfully pale lately. I'm sure you read too much.'

Pam *was* pale—and not only pale but unhappy-looking too. She was terribly sorry now that she had made firm friends with Prudence, because she was beginning to dislike her heartily, but was not strong enough to tell her so. So she found refuge in her lessons, and was working twice as hard as any one else. She smiled a pale smile at Bobby, and envied her. Bobby didn't mind saying anything that came into her mind, and was as strong as Pam was weak. How Pam wished she could have made friends with Bobby instead of with Prudence !

Prudence was feeling rather pleased with herself. Miss Theobald had not said anything about her letter and the

girl felt sure it had made a good impression on the Head.
For some reason Mam'zelle had not given the French
test after all, so the class had heaved a sigh of relief—
especially Prudence, who felt certain that Carlotta would
blurt out that she, Prudence, had seen the questions
before.

'Things are going better,' thought Prudence. 'If only
that beastly Carlotta could get into a row! She just
flaunts about as if she were a princess and not a common
little circus-girl! I wonder if she visits any of her low-
down friends any more? I saw her going off early
yesterday morning before breakfast.'

It was true that Carlotta did go off each morning—but
not to visit any circus-friend. She had discovered that
some lovely hunting-horses were kept in a field not far
off, and the girl was visiting them regularly. Sometimes
she rode one or other bareback, if there was nobody
about. The girl was quite mad about horses, and never
lost a chance of going near them if she could.

Nobody knew this. Prudence knew Carlotta was
slipping off, but told no one else, for she had found that
none of the girls encouraged her confidences at all. She
determined to keep a watch herself.

She and Pam went off one afternoon together, Pam
not at all pleased about it, but not daring to say no.
Prudence had seen Carlotta going off—but somehow or
other she missed following her, and the two girls stopped
in a little lane, whilst Prudence tried to think where
Carlotta had gone.

A man came riding by on a bicycle. He was not a
pleasant-looking fellow, for he was very dark, and his
eyes were set very close together. He got off his bicycle
when he came up to the girls, and spoke to them. His
voice sounded rather foreign, and had a slow American
drawl with it. Prudence felt absolutely certain that he
had come to see Carlotta.

'Excuse me, missy,' said the man, taking off his cap, politely. 'Am I anywhere near St. Clare's school?'

'Well—about a mile away,' said Prudence. 'Why? Do you want to see some one there?'

'I should like to,' said the man. 'It's very important indeed. I suppose you couldn't take a message for me?'

Prudence's heart beat fast. What trouble she could get Carlotta into now! What would Miss Theobald say if she knew Carlotta was slipping out to see awful people like this?'

'Of course I could take a message for you,' she said.

The man took a letter from his pocket and handed it to Prudence. 'Don't you tell a single soul,' he said. 'It's very very important. I'll be here at eleven o'clock tonight without fail.'

'All right,' said Prudence. 'I'll see to it for you.'

'You're a brick,' said the man. 'You're dandy! I'll give you a fine present, see if I don't!'

Some one else came down the lane at that moment, and the man jumped on his bicycle and rode away, saluting the two girls as he went. Pam shivered a little.

'Prudence! I don't like him! I don't think you ought to have spoken to him. You know it's a rule we never speak to strangers. You're not going to get Carlotta into trouble are you?'

'Oh be quiet!' said Prudence, impatiently. She pushed the letter into her pocket without looking at it. 'Aren't I *doing* something for Carlotta, silly? Aren't I taking a message to her from a friend? What awful friends she has, too!'

Pam was worried. Her head ached, and she felt miserable. She wished she had never, never become friendly with Prudence. Her mind turned once again to her work—she could only forget things if she worked.

She hadn't been sleeping well at night, and her work was becoming difficult to do which made her worry all the more.

'Now listen to me, Pam,' said Prudence. 'You and I are going to go out to-night at half-past ten and come here. We are going to hide behind the hedge, and hear what goes on between our dear Carlotta and her circus-friend. If she is planning any more escapades, we can report them.'

Pam stared at her friend in distress. 'I can't do that,' she said. 'I can't.'

'You've got to,' said Prudence, and she stared at Pam out of her pale blue eyes. Pam felt too tired and weak to argue. She simply nodded her head miserably and turned back to go home. The girls walked back in silence, Prudence thinking with delight that now she had Carlotta at her mercy!

As soon as they got back to school Hilary hailed Prudence. 'Prudence! You know quite well it's your turn to brush up all the tennis-balls and get them clean this week. You haven't done it once, you lazy creature. You jolly well do it now, or you'll be sorry.'

'I've just got to take a message to somebody,' said Prudence. 'I won't be a minute.'

'You just let somebody else take the message,' said Hilary, annoyed. 'I know your little ways, Prudence— you'll *just* do this and you'll *just* do that—and the little jobs you ought to do aren't done!'

'*I'll* take the letter, Prudence,' said Pam, wearily. She felt that she could not stand arguments a minute more. Prudence handed her the letter with a sulky face. Pam went off to find Carlotta. She was in the common room with the others. Pam went up to her and gave her the letter.

'This is for you,' she said. Carlotta took the note, and, without looking at the envelope, tore it open. She read the first line or two in evident amazement. Then she looked at the envelope.

' Why, it isn't for me,' she said, looking round for Pam, who, however, had gone. ' It's for Sadie. I suppose Pam didn't see her name on the envelope. How odd ! Where's Sadie, Alison ? "

' Doing her hair,' said Alison. There was a shout of laughter at this. When Sadie was missed she was always either Doing Her Hair, Doing Her Nails or Doing Her Face. Carlotta grinned and went to find her.

' Hie, Sadie,' she said, ' here's a note for you. Sorry I opened it by mistake, but that little idiot of a Pam gave it to me instead of you. I haven't read it.'

' Who's it from ? How did Pam get it ? ' asked Sadie curiously, taking the note.

' Don't know,' said Carlotta, and went. Sadie opened the envelope and took out the letter inside. She read it and her face changed. She sat down on the bed, and thought hard. She read the letter again.

DEAR MISS SADIE,

Do you remember your old maid, Hannah ? Well, I'm over here and I'd like to see you. I don't like to come to the school. Can you come down to the lane by the farm and see me for a few minutes ? I'll be there at eleven o'clock to-night.

HANNAH.

Sadie had been very fond of Hannah, who had been her own and her mother's personal maid for some years. She was astonished that Hannah should be in England, for she had thought she was in America. Why did she want to see her ? Had anything happened ? Sadie wondered whether to tell Alison or not—and then she decided not to. Alison was a nice girl and a pretty one, but she was a feather-head. She might go and bleat it out to somebody !

Sadie tucked the note into her pocket and went downstairs. 'Hallo!' said Alison. 'I was wondering whenever you were coming down. It's nearly supper-time.'

Sadie was rather silent at supper-time. She felt puzzled and a little worried. She thought she would ask Pam where she had got the note from—but Pam was not at supper.

'She's got a frightful headache and Miss Roberts sent her to Matron,' said Janet. 'She's got a temperature.'

Prudence was quite pleased to think she would not have Pam with her that night after all. She was getting a little tired of pretending to Pam that everything she was doing was for Carlotta's good. She looked at Carlotta to see if the girl showed any signs of receiving the letter. Carlotta saw her glancing her way and made one of her peculiarly rude faces. Prudence looked down her nose in disgust and turned away. Carlotta grinned. She didn't care a ha'-penny for Prudence and delighted in shocking her.

18   AN EXCITING NIGHT

THAT evening Sadie lay awake until the clock struck a quarter to eleven. It was still fairly light, but every one in the dormitory was asleep. Sadie got up quietly and dressed. No one heard her. She slipped out of the dormitory and down the stairs. In a few moments she was out of the garden-door and in the school grounds. Behind her slipped a dark little shadow—Prudence! Prudence thought that she was following Carlotta, of course. She had no idea it was Sadie. Prudence had got up at a quarter-past ten, and had slipped out of the dormitory next to Sadie's, afraid that if she waited any later, Carlotta might get away before she had a chance of keeping up with her. She had felt so certain that it was Carlotta the letter had been for—she had never even looked at the envelope to see what name was written there!

Now, at about a quarter-past eleven, Alison awoke suddenly with a sore throat. She cleared it and swallowed. It felt most unpleasant. She knew that Sadie had some lozenges and she decided to wake her and ask for them. So the girl slipped out of bed and went to Sadie's cubicle.

She put out her hand to shake Sadie—and to her great astonishment found that she was not there! Her bed was empty! Her clothes had gone—so she had dressed. Alison sat down on the bed in surprise. She was hurt. Why hadn't Sadie told her she was going somewhere? But where in the world could she have gone? There couldn't be a midnight feast or anything like that—because it was obvious that every one was in bed—unless the other dormitory was holding a feast and had asked Sadie.

'Well, Sadie might at least have told me, even if I wasn't asked,' thought Alison, aggrieved. 'I'll go and peep in at the twins' dormitory and see if there's anything going on there.'

So she slipped into the next dormitory—but every one's bed seemed filled—with the exception of one. How odd. Alison stood thinking—and then she heard a whisper. It was Pat.

'Who's that? What are you doing?'

'Oh Pat—are you awake?' said Alison in a low voice, going to Pat's bed. 'I say—Sadie's gone. She's dressed —and her bed is empty. I don't know why, Pat, but I feel worried about it. Sadie didn't seem herself this evening—she was all quiet and sort of worried. I noticed it.'

Pat sat up. She was puzzled. Sadie didn't usually do anything out of the ordinary at all. 'Wherever can she have gone?' she said.

'There's one bed empty in your dorm, too,' said Alison. 'Whose is it?'

'Golly—it's Prudence's,' said Pat, in astonishment. 'Don't tell me those two are somewhere together! I thought Sadie detested Prudence.'

'She does,' said Alison, more puzzled than ever. A movement in the next bed made them look round. Carlotta's voice came to them, low and guarded.

'What *are* you two doing? You'll wake every one up! Anything up?'

'Carlotta—it's so funny—both Sadie and Prudence are gone from their beds,' said Pat. Carlotta sat up at once. She remembered the note she had given to Sadie.

'I wonder if it's anything to do with the note that Pam gave to me instead of to Sadie,' she said.

'What note?' asked Alison. Carlotta told her, and Pat and Alison listened in surprise.

'Somehow I think there's something a bit queer about this,' said Carlotta. 'I do really.'

'So do I,' said Alison, uncomfortably. 'I'm awfully fond of Sadie. You don't think—you don't think, do you—that's she being kidnapped—or anything. She said once that she nearly had been, over in America. She's awfully rich, you know. Her mother sent her over here because she was afraid she might be kidnapped again in America. She told me that.'

Carlotta could more readily believe this than the more stolid Pat. She got out of bed.

'I think the first thing we'd better do is to ask Pam where she got that note,' said Carlotta.

'She's in the san.,' said Pat.

'Well, we'll go there then,' said Carlotta. 'Let's wake Isabel. Hurry!'

It was not long before the twins, Alison and Carlotta were creeping across the school grounds to the building called the san. This was the sanatorium, where any girl who was ill was kept in bed. The door was locked, but a downstairs window was open. Carlotta got in quietly. She could climb like a cat!

'Stay here,' she whispered to the others. 'We don't want to wake Matron. I'll find Pam and ask her what we want to know.'

She made her way through the dark little room and up the stairs to where a dim light was burning in a bedroom. Here Pam lay, wide awake, trying to cool her burning forehead with a wet handkerchief. She was amazed and frightened when she saw Carlotta creeping into the room.

'Sh!' whispered Carlotta. 'It's only me, Carlotta! Pam—where did you get that note from—the one you gave me?'

'Prudence and I met a funny-looking man down the lane by the farm this afternoon,' said Pam. 'He said he wanted to send a message to some one. So Prudence took the note and meant to give it to you. But I had to give it to you instead. The man wanted you to meet him there at eleven o'clock to-night—or to meet somebody there. Why? What's happened?'

'The note wasn't for me—it was for Sadie,' said Carlotta, feeling puzzled. 'Did the man *say* it was for me?'

'Well, now I come to think of it, no names were mentioned at all,' said Pam, frowning as she tried to remember the conversation. 'But somehow Prudence seemed to think we were talking about you.'

'She would!' said Carlotta, grimly. 'I know where she is too! She thought that the man was one of my

low-down circus-friends, as she calls them—and she
wanted to get me down there—and she would spy on me
and report me. I know Prudence! But as it happens,
the note *wasn't* for me—and I've a feeling that there's
some dirty work going on round poor Sadie. She's gone
down to the lane by the farm—and I bet Prudence has
gone there too—to spy.'

'Yes, she has,' said Pam, feeling frightened and
miserable. Tears ran down her cheeks. 'Oh, Carlotta—
I'm supposed to be Prudence's friend—but I do so dislike
her. It's making me ill. I'm really afraid of her.'

'Don't you worry,' said Carlotta, comfortingly, and she
patted Pam's hot hand. 'We'll deal with Miss Sour-
Milk Prudence after this. She'll get herself into serious
trouble if she's not careful.'

The girl slipped away and went back to the others who
were waiting impatiently by the open window. She told
them in a few words all she had learnt.

'Had we better wake Miss Theobald?' said Pat,
troubled.

'No—we'll see what's happening first. It mayn't be
anything much,' said Carlotta. 'Come on down to the
lane by the farm.'

The four girls took bicycles and cycled away in the
dark. The summer twilight was just enough for them
to see their way. Half-way to the farm they met a
sobbing figure running up towards them. It was
Prudence!

'Prudence! What's the matter? What's happening?'
cried Pat, in alarm.

'Oh Pat! Is it you? Oh Pat! Something dreadful
has happened!' sobbed Prudence. 'Sadie has been
kidnapped! She has, she has! I thought I was following
Carlotta when I went out this evening just before eleven—
but it was Sadie after all—and when she got near the
farm, two men came up and took hold of her. And they

dragged her to a hidden car and put her in. I was hiding behind the hedge.'

'Did you hear them say anything?' demanded Carlotta.

'Yes—they said something about a place called Jalebury,' wept Prudence. 'Where is it?'

'Jalebury!' said Carlotta, in astonishment. 'I know where Jalebury is. Why, that's where the circus-camp went to! Are you sure you heard them say they were taking Sadie there, Prudence?'

Prudence was quite sure. Carlotta jumped on her bicycle. 'I'm just going to cycle to the telephone kiosk down the lane,' she called. 'The kidnappers will get a shock when they get to Jalebury!'

She rode to the kiosk, jumped off her bicycle, disappeared into the little telephone box, and looked up a number there. In a minute or two her excited voice filled the kiosk as she poured out her story to some one, and asked for their help.

In about five minutes she was back with the others. 'I telephoned the circus-camp,' she said. 'They'll be on the watch for the car. They'll stop it and surround it— and if they don't rescue Sadie, I'll eat my hat!'

'Oh, Carlotta—you really are marvellous!' said Pat. 'But wouldn't it have been better to call the police?'

'I never thought of that,' said Carlotta. 'You see— in circus-life we don't somehow call in the police. Now— I'm off to join in the fun! I know my way to Jalebury. But I'm not going by bike!'

'How are you going then?' asked Pat.

'On horseback!' said Carlotta. 'I shall borrow one of the hunters I've ridden on in the early morning. They are quite near here—and any of them will come to me if I call to them. I'm going to be in at the fun!'

The girl disappeared into a field. The twins, Alison, and Prudence stared after her in the starlight. Carlotta

was such a surprising person. She went straight for
what she wanted, and nothing could stop her. In a few
minutes they heard the sound of galloping hoofs—and
that was the last they saw of Carlotta that night !

19   CARLOTTA TO THE RESCUE!

CARLOTTA knew the countryside around very well.
She took the horse across fields and hills, her sense of
direction telling her exactly where to go. She thought
hard all the time, and smiled grimly when Prudence came
into her mind.

'She's gone just too far this time !' she thought, as
she galloped on through the night, the horse responding
marvellously to the girl's sure hands. 'I do hope I get
to Jalebury in time to see the fun.'

She didn't get there in time ! But when she reached
the little town after some time, she saw lights in the big
field where the camp was, and galloped swiftly to it.
She put the horse to jump the fence that ran round the
field and it rose high in the air.

A voice hailed her. 'Who's that ? '

'Oh, Jim—it's me, Carlotta !' she cried. 'Has anything happened ? Did you get my message ? '

'We did,' said the man, coming up to take the panting
horse. 'And we've got the girl for you. Mighty pretty,
isn't she ? '

'Very,' said Carlotta, with a laugh. 'And if I know
anything about Sadie, she wanted to borrow a comb and
do her hair, or powder her nose, as soon as you rescued
her ! Tell me what happened."

Well, as soon as we got your message we dragged a

caravan out of the field and set it across the road there—
see, where it runs down into the town,' said the man,
pointing in the starlight to where a road, not much wider
than a big lane, ran between high hedges. 'Nobody was
about, and not a car came by—till suddenly one appeared,
racing along. We guessed it must be the one we wanted.'

'Oh—if only I'd been there!' groaned Carlotta. 'Go
on. What happened?'

'Well, when the car saw the caravan by the light of
its head-lamps, it stopped, of course,' said Jim. 'We
pretended that our caravan had got stuck, and we were
pulling and heaving at it like anything. One of the men
in the car jumped out to see what was up—and he called
to the other man to come and help us so that we could
shift the caravan out of his way. So I slipped off to the
car, and there, in the back, all tied up like a chicken,
with a handkerchief round her mouth, was your friend.
I got her out in half a tick, of course, and bundled her
behind a hedge.'

'Quick work!' said Carlotta, enjoying the tale
thoroughly.

'Very quick,' agreed the man. 'Well, then I went
back to the others, tipped them the wink, and we moved
the caravan away in a jiffy, leaving the road clear. The
two men went back to the car, hopped in, never looked
behind at all to see if the girl was there—and drove off
in the night without her!'

Carlotta began to laugh. It struck her as very funny
indeed to think of the two kidnappers being so easily
tricked and racing away in the night with an empty
car!

'Whatever will they think when they take a look
behind and see Sadie is gone?' she said. 'You did
awfully well, Jim. Now we don't need to call in the police
or have a fuss made or anything. I can just take Sadie
back to the school and nobody needs to know anything

about it. I'm sure Miss Theobald wouldn't want the papers to splash head-lines all about the kidnapping of Miss Sadie Greene ! '

'Come along and have a word with her,' said Jim. Carlotta went along with him, leading the horse by a lock of its thick mane. She came to a large caravan and went up the steps. Inside was Sadie, combing out her ruffled hair by the light of an oil-lamp. A woman was sitting watching her. Nobody appeared to think that anything extraordinary had happened. It seemed as if rescuing kidnapped girls was quite an ordinary thing to happen in the middle of the night ! Not even Sadie was excited— but then, she seldom was !

'Hallo, Sadie,' said Carlotta. 'Doing Your Hair, as usual ! '

'Carlotta ! ' said Sadie, in surprise. 'How did *you* get here ? I was an awful idiot, I got kidnapped again. That note you opened by mistake was supposed to be from an old maid of ours that I was very fond of—and I went out to see her—and two men caught me. And then somebody bundled me out and rescued me—but I haven't quite got the hang of things yet. And my hair got frightfully untidy, so I'm just putting it right.'

Carlotta grinned. 'If you fell out of an aeroplane you'd wonder if your hair was getting windblown ! ' she said. She told Sadie all that had happened, and how Prudence had followed her, thinking she was after Carlotta.

'Gracious ! ' said Sadie. 'What a night. I suppose we'd better go back to St. Clare's, hadn't we ? '

'Well, I think we had,' said Carlotta. 'You see, Sadie, I guess Miss Theobald won't want this story known all over the country—and I know the circus-people won't want the police called in. They never do. So I think we'd better just go quietly back to school, and hush it all up. I've got a horse outside—a hunter I took from

a field. Do you think you could manage to ride it with
me ? '

'I'm sure I couldn't,' said Sadie, promptly.

'Oh well—you'll have to try, said Carlotta impatiently.
'You can put your arms round my waist and hang on
to me. Come on !'

The two girls went to find the horse. Jim had it
outside the caravan. Carlotta jumped up and spoke to
Jim.

'Thanks for doing all you did,' she said. 'I won't
forget it. Hold your tongue about everything, won't
you ? '

'You bet !' said Jim. 'It's all in the day's work.
Come and see us again, Carlotta. I always say and I
always shall say you're wasted at school—you ought
to be in a circus like you've always been—handling
horses. You're a marvel with them.'

'Ah well,' said Carlotta, 'things don't always happen
as we want them to. Sadie, what are you doing ? Surely
you can jump up behind me ? '

'I can't,' said Sadie. 'The horse seems so enormous.'

Jim gave her a heave and the surprised girl found herself
sitting behind Carlotta. She clung to her with all her
might. The horse set off at a gallop. Carlotta put him
to jump the fence. Up he went with the two girls on
his back and came down lightly the other side. Sadie
squealed with fright. She had nearly fallen off.

'Let me off, oh let me off !' she shouted. 'Carlotta,
LET ME OFF !'

But Carlotta didn't. She galloped on through the
starlit night, poor Sadie bumping up and down, up and
down behind her.

'Oh !' gasped Sadie, 'tell the horse not to bump me
so, Carlotta ! Carlotta, do you hear ? '

'It's you that are bumping the horse !' said Carlotta,

Sadie and Carlotta galloped back to school

with a squeal of laughter. 'Hang on, Sadie! Hang on!'

But it was too much for Sadie. When they had gone about half-way back, she suddenly loosened her hold on Carlotta, and slid right off the horse. She fell to the ground with a bump and gave a yell. Carlotta stopped the horse at once.

'Sadie! Are you hurt? Why did you do that?'

'I'm awfully bruised,' came Sadie's voice from the ground. 'Carlotta, I will NOT ride that bumpy horse another step. I'd rather walk.'

'How tiresome you are!' said Carlotta, springing lightly to the ground. She pulled Sadie up and soon made sure that the girl was not really hurt. 'It will take us ages to get back. We shall have to walk all the way and I must lead the horse. We shan't get back till daylight!'

'I wonder what the others are thinking,' said Sadie, limping along beside Carlotta. 'I bet they're wondering and wondering what's happened!'

The others had worried and wondered till they were tired! They had all gone back to school, and had awakened the rest of the twins' dormitory. The girls had sat and discussed the night's happenings, wondering whether to go and tell Miss Theobald or not. Hilary at last decided that they really must. Carlotta and Sadie had not come back, and Prudence was almost in hysterics. She really was frightened out of her life to think of the trouble that she had caused through being such a mischief maker.

'Look—there's the dawn coming,' said Pat, looking to the east, where a pale silvery light was spreading. 'In another half-hour the sun will be up. For goodness' sake —let's tell Miss Theobald now. We can't wait for Carlotta any longer.'

So Pat and Isabel went down to awaken Miss Theobald,

and the Head listened in growing alarm to their curious
tale. She had just reached out to take the telephone
receiver in order to get into touch with the police when
Pat gave a cry.

' Look! Look, Miss Theobald! There's Carlotta
coming back—and she's got Sadie with her! Oh—good
old Carlotta! '

Sure enough, there was Carlotta coming up the school
grounds, with Sadie limping beside her. They had
returned the hunter to its field and had come wearily up
the school grounds just as the sun was rising. They had
had a long way to walk and were very tired indeed.

Miss Theobald had them in her room in a trice, quite
bewildered with the strange tale she had heard. She
made the tired girls hot cocoa and gave them biscuits to
eat. Then, to Carlotta's immense disgust she took the
sleepy girls across to the san., woke up Matron, and bade
her put the girls to bed in peace and quietness and keep
them there.

' But Miss Theobald,' began Carlotta. Not a scrap of
notice was taken of her, however, and it was not long
before both she and Sadie were tucked up in comfortable
beds and were sound asleep!

' If I had let them go back to their dormitory they
would have talked until the dressing-bell,' said Miss
Theobald. ' Now go back to your beds too, you others,
and we will sort things out in the morning. Really, I
feel I must be dreaming all this! '

But it was no dream, and in the morning, as Miss
Theobald had said, things had to be ' sorted out '.

It was decided that the matter must certainly be reported
to the police, but kept as quiet as possible. Carlotta had
the excitement of being interviewed by admiring police-
men—and Prudence had the ordeal of being closely
questioned too. She was frightened out of her life at it
all. She had been able to lie and get away with so many

unpleasant things before in her life—but there was no getting away with this.

'I want to go home,' she sobbed to Miss Theobald. 'I feel ill. Let me go home.'

'No,' said Miss Theobald. 'You want to run away from the troubles you have caused, Prudence. You are going to remain here and face them, however unpleasant things may be for you. Unless you want me to tell your parents everything, you will stay here and face things out. I hope this will be a lesson to you. I am not going to keep you at St. Clare's after this term, of course. You will never be liked by any of the girls now. But you are going to learn a very bitter lesson for the rest of this term—and I hope, Prudence, you will derive some good from it. You need a punishment to make you learn what you have to learn.'

Sadie's mother had to be told about the attempted kidnapping and she arrived at St. Clare's in a great state two weeks before the end of the term. She wanted to take Sadie away at once, but Miss Theobald persuaded her not to.

'You may be sure that such a thing will not be allowed to happen again now,' she said. 'If you wish, of course, you must take her away at the end of the term. Maybe you will want to take her back to America with you. Sadie is too grown up for St. Clare's, Mrs. Greene. If you *could* leave her for a term or two, so that she might shake down a little and try to become more of a schoolgirl, I should be delighted to have her. But maybe you don't want her to be an ordinary school-girl!'

Miss Theobald was right. Mrs. Greene was like Alison, a feather-head! She had no brains at all, and her only interests in life were her clothes and entertaining others—and her precious pretty daughter, Sadie! She looked round at the girls of St. Clare's, some with pig-tails, some with short hair, some freckled, some plain, some pretty.

' Well,' she said, ' don't you get sore at me for saying
it, Miss Theobald—but I don't feel I want Sadie to be
like these girls ! My Sadie's pretty, and she's cute too.
I wouldn't call any of these girls cute. Would you ? '

' No, I wouldn't,' said Miss Theobald, smiling. ' We
don't teach them to be " cute " Mrs. Greene. We teach
them to be independent, responsible, kind and intelligent,
but we don't teach them to be " cute ".'

' Well—I guess I'll leave Sadie here for the rest of the
term, anyway,' said Mrs. Greene, after a pause. ' I'll
stay at the hotel down in the town and keep an eye on
her. She seems fond of that pretty little thing called
Alison. I'll let her stay on just for the rest of the term.
Then I'll take her off to America again—and maybe
Alison would like to come along too. She's about the
cutest girl here.'

Miss Theobald made a private note in her mind to tell
Alison's mother not to let her go with Sadie to America.
She was not pleased with Alison that term. The girl had
much better stuff in her than she had shown the last two
or three months, and Miss Theobald did not want her to
be completely spoilt.

So it came about that both Sadie and Prudence stayed
on for the rest of the term and did not leave. Sadie
was pleased—but Prudence was angry and unhappy. It
was terribly difficult to face so many hostile girls every
minute of the day. For the first time in her life she was
really getting a punishment she deserved.

AND now the term drew swiftly to an end.   There were tennis matches, swimming matches and the Sports. There were, alas, exams. too !   The days were very full, and every one had plenty to do from morning to night. The girls were very happy—all but Prudence, and nobody, not even Pam, felt sorry for the little humbug.   No one knew she was leaving, and Prudence did not say a word about it.

Pam had been ill for a week or two—and Miss Theobald had come to the conclusion that her illness was due to over-work and unhappiness.   Carlotta had told her about Pam's friendship with Prudence and how unhappy she had become about it.

' Now, Carlotta, you can do something for me,' said Miss Theobald.   ' You can make friends with Pam, please, and see that Prudence does not try to get her under her thumb again.   Pam is a good little thing, too advanced for her age—and it seems to me it will do her good to slack a little, instead of working so hard.   Take her under your wing, Carlotta, and make her laugh a bit ! '

Carlotta was surprised at this request, but rather proud. She had a great admiration for the sensible and wise Head Mistress, and the two understood each other very well.   So, when Pam came out of the san. looking rather white and worn, and afraid that Prudence would attach herself to her once again, Pam had a pleasant surprise. Carlotta always seemed to be there !   Carlotta pushed Prudence off, and asked Pam to go for walks with her instead, and got her to help her with her prep.   Pam soon felt much happier, and her small face glowed whenever Carlotta came up.

' It's been a funny term, hasn't it ? ' said Miss Roberts

to Mam'zelle. 'First of all I thought the new girls were
never going to settle down and work—and I gave up
Bobby in despair.'

'Ah, that Bobby!' said Mam'zelle, lifting her hands
as she remembered all Bobby's tricks. 'That Bobby!
But now she has turned over a new stalk—no, what is it
you say—a new leaf—and she works and she works!'

'Yes—something has certainly happened to Bobby,'
said Miss Roberts. 'She's using her brains—and she's
got good ones too. I'm pleased with her. I'm going
easy with little Pam Boardman though—she's inclined to
work too hard.'

Mam'zelle smiled. 'Ah yes—but now that she has
Carlotta for a friend, she does not work so hard. Always
we have to hold Pam back or she would over-work
herself—she does not play enough. But Carlotta will
help her to do that. It is odd, that friendship.'

'I shouldn't be surprised if the Head had something
to do with it,' said Miss Roberts. 'She's a very
remarkable woman, you know. She knows the girls
inside-out.'

'Well—I hear that both Prudence and Sadie are
leaving,' said Mam'zelle. 'That is good. Ah, that
Prrrrrrrudence! How I detest her!'

'She has a lot of lessons to learn in life,' said Miss
Roberts, seriously. 'She has been taught a very big one
here, and has learnt for the first time to see herself as
she really is—and for two or three weeks she has to
undergo the ordeal of knowing that others see her as she
is, too. Ah, well—I don't know how she will turn out.
She's a problem—and I'm glad I haven't got to solve it!'

'Sadie will not be missed either,' said Mam'zelle.
'Except by silly little Alison. She has had her head
turned properly by that American girl. Ah, how cross
they have both made me this term!'

Miss Roberts laughed. 'Yes—you've been in some

fine tempers this term, Mam'zelle,' she said. 'But never mind—the term will soon be at an end—then summer holidays—and no tiresome girls to teach!'

'And when September comes, we shall both be saying, "Ah, how nice it will be to see those tiresome girls again!"' laughed Mam'zelle.

The girls were sorry that the summer term was coming to an end. Margery Fenworthy won the tennis championship for the school, and also the swimming matches. Carlotta won the diving. Bobby put up a record for the first form in swimming under water and was loudly cheered and clapped. Nobody was more surprised than she was!

'You deserve it, Bobby,' said Belinda, clapping her on the back. 'My word, how you've improved in tennis and swimming. I'm proud of you, Don't-Care Bobby!'

Bobby felt happy. Her work had improved as much as her sports, and she had felt a new self-respect and content. Janet worked well too, now that Bobby was working, and the twins followed suit.

'You'll be able to go up into the second form next term, and do me credit,' said Miss Roberts, as she gave out the exam. marks. 'Bobby, you are top in geography! Simply marvellous! Pam, you have done very well indeed. You O'Sullivan twins have managed to tie for second place in most things—that's very good. Hilary, you are top of the form, as you should be! Prudence, Doris, Alison and Sadie are, I regret to say, settling down near the bottom as usual. The great surprise is Carlotta who has done far better than I expected! I think, Pam, that your help has done a good deal towards putting Carlotta into a higher place than I expected.'

Pam glowed with pleasure. Carlotta looked surprised and amused. Miss Roberts went on with her remarks, picking out each girl and commenting shrewdly on their term's work and exam. results. Most of the first-form girls, with the exception of Pam, who was too young, were to go up into the second form the next term.

'That's good,' said Janet, afterwards. 'We shall all keep together now—and the two we like least, Sadie and Prudence, won't be here. I overheard by accident something Mam'zelle said in her loud voice to Miss Roberts. Well—I must say it's good news that Prudence won't be back.'

'Won't she really?' said Janet. 'Well, I vote if that's so, we're a bit nicer to her then. She's looking pretty miserable lately.'

So for the last two or three days of term the girls relaxed their hostile attitude towards Prudence and the girl regained some of her confidence and happiness. She had begun to learn her lesson, though, and made no attempt to boast or to lie, as she always used to do. Poor Prudence—she was her own worst enemy, and always would be.

The last day came, and the usual wild rush of packing and saying good-bye. Margery Fenworthy proudly packed the beautiful racket she had won for her tennis prize. Bobby just as proudly packed her swimming-under-water prize—a lovely new bathing-costume. All the girls were happy and excited.

'It's a shame I can't come to America with you,' said Alison, to Sadie, half-tearful at the thought of saying good-bye to her friend. 'I can't think why Mother won't let me. Don't forget me, Sadie, will you?'

'Of course not,' said Sadie, quite meaning what she said—but the girl was incapable of remembering any one for long! Her real interest in life was in herself and in her looks—her friends would never last with her! But Alison did not know this and squeezed Sadie's arm tightly. She knew she would miss her terribly.

The last minutes came. Good-byes were shouted as the school coach came up to the door for the first batch of girls. Mam'zelle screamed as some one dropped a suit-case on her toes.

'Pat ! Que vous êtes. . . .' she began. And a whole chorus of girls finished her sentence for her . . .

'ABOMINABLE ! ' There was a shriek of laughter as they tried to get away from Mam'zelle's large hands, dealing out friendly slaps all the way round.

'Good-bye, Miss Roberts,' said the twins. 'Good-bye, Miss Roberts,' said Bobby. 'Good-bye, Miss Roberts,' said all the other first-formers one by one.

'Good-bye, girls,' said Miss Roberts. 'Well—you won't stand in awe of me any more next term ! You'll all be second-formers, very important indeed—and I'll be left behind with the first form ! Dear me—to think how you all grow up ! '

'They'll long to be back with you, Miss Roberts ! ' laughed Miss Jenks, who was nearby. 'My goodness, they don't know what a dragon they are coming to, next term. How I'll make them work ! What terrible punishments I shall have in store for them ! How I shall see through all their tricks ! '

The girls laughed. They liked Miss Jenks, and were looking forward to going up into her class. It would be fun. A new class and a new teacher—yes, they really would have fun !

The first-formers got into the coach that was waiting for them. Alison heaved herself up, and her hat went crooked and then fell off. The girls stared at her hair.

'Alison ! You've done your hair all funny again ! ' cried Pat. 'Piled it all on top as if you were twenty-one or something. You *do* look a freak ! Honestly you do.'

Alison went red. She put her hat on again and turned defiantly to the twins.

'Well, Sadie says . . .' she began. And at once, in the greatest delight the whole coachful of girls took up

the chorus they knew so well, and chanted it all the way
down to the station.

'Sadie says—Sadie says—what does Sadie *say*?   Sadie
says—oh Sadie says—what does Sadie *say*!'

And there we will leave them, first-formers for the last
time, singing on their way home for the holidays.   What
will happen to them when they are important second-
formers?   Ah—that is another story altogether!